THE CHRISTMAS CRADLE

As he hugged her from behind, Ben prayed for words that would lift Miriam's spirits. She had so much on her mind, with a baby coming and a big decision to make about running her business—not to mention the two kids who'd landed on their doorstep about to have a baby of their own. Ben held her gently, inhaling the clean scent he'd always found so appealing, so Miriam.

She turned in his arms. When she rested her head on his shoulder, Ben savored the closeness of this moment as the baby shifted inside her. He glanced at the two baskets on the table and got an idea. "Sit down and finish that glass of water, honey-girl. I've got a present for ya."

More Seasons of the Heart books
by Charlotte Hubbard

The CHRISTMAS CRADLE

Charlotte Hubbard

ZEBRA BOOKS
KENSINGTON PUBLISHING CORP.
http://www.kensingtonbooks.com

ZEBRA BOOKS are published by

Kensington Publishing Corp.
119 West 40th Street
New York, NY 10018

All Kensington titles, imprints, and distributed lines are available at special quantity discounts for bulk purchases for sales promotion, premiums, fund-raising, educational, or institutional use.

Special book excerpts or customized printings can also be created to fit specific needs. For details, write or phone the office of the Kensington Sales Manager: Attn.: Sales Department. Kensington Publishing Corp., 119 West 40th Street, New York, NY 10018. Phone: 1-800-221-2647.

Zebra and the Z logo Reg. U.S. Pat. & TM Off.

First Printing: October 2015
ISBN-13: 978-1-4201-3311-0
ISBN-10: 1-4201-3311-X

eISBN-13: 978-1-4201-3312-7
eISBN-10: 1-4201-3312-8

10 9 8 7 6 5 4 3 2 1

Printed in the United States of America

Chapter One

Ben Hooley sprayed lemon furniture polish on a rag and wiped his fingerprints from the wooden cradle he'd just completed. His pulse thrummed steadily as he gazed at his work, a Christmas gift for his dear wife Miriam, who was round and rosy-cheeked as they anticipated the birth of their first child. For weeks he'd been crafting and sanding and staining this special cradle in his spare time, so the wood would be smooth and glossy—as beautiful as the love he'd shared with Miriam for nearly a year. He'd welded a hummingbird in pewter to adorn the headboard because she loved to watch those amazing little birds flit from flower to flower in her summertime garden.

As the snow and wind howled around his cozy smithy on this November night, however, Ben's conflicting thoughts were anything but warm and sunny. His dilemma felt as sharp and pointed as the hummingbird's beak, and he couldn't seem to resolve the conflict that weighed heavily on his mind.

How could he uphold the tenets of the Old Order if he allowed his pregnant wife to continue working outside their home? The bishop of Willow Ridge, Tom Hostetler, had been gently reminding Ben that it was a husband's job to keep his wife at home, caring for her family—just as it was Ben's duty as a preacher to insist that Miriam follow the ways of their Plain faith.

But how could he convince Miriam to leave her beloved Sweet Seasons Café without crushing her spirit? Feeding people fulfilled her personal mission— gave her a way to reach out to folks, just as Jesus had preached that His disciples should feed His sheep. Ben could simply order her to stay home, but he didn't have it in him to remove the smile from her lovely face. Miriam was *everything* to him—and that, too, posed a problem, because his love for God was supposed to be his first priority.

Ben put away his tools, craving the company of his wife as he pondered this important issue. He asked God for guidance, for the right words to win Miriam's compliance—

A beam of headlights pulled him from his deep thoughts. Ben was amazed to see how much snow had clung to his window since he'd come to the smithy after supper, and the longer the lights shone into his shop, the more concerned he became. He slipped into his coat and hat, wondering why anyone would be traveling in a snowstorm so late in the evening. He pushed hard against the door, sweeping three or four inches of fresh snow aside with it as he stepped out into the nasty weather.

The bay mare hitched to the buggy in front of his shop hung her head tiredly as the white snow collected on her back. Ben had walked only a few yards before he heard two loud voices coming from the rig. He sensed a conflict far greater than his own as a young woman raised desperate questions while her driver lashed out in frustrated exhaustion. He had no desire to get involved in this couple's argument—yearned to rejoin Miriam in their cozy kitchen—but he couldn't leave two stranded travelers to fend for themselves on such a dangerous night.

Magdalena Esh wrapped the worn blanket more snugly around her shoulders, groaning from exhaustion. Fat, icy flakes were pelting the buggy, threatening to overwhelm the windshield wipers. She was so tired of riding—so stiff from clutching the bulge of her unborn child—she wanted to scream.

"Why have we pulled over, Josiah?" she demanded. "This *can't* be Higher Ground. There's supposed to be a big stone sign out by the road, and—"

"We took a wrong turn," the young man beside her snapped. He yanked on the lines to halt the horse. "You haven't stopped whining since we left this morning. I can't think straight—can't *see* a blasted thing because of this snowstorm—and your yammering is driving me nuts!"

Lena sat taller despite her aching back. "I suppose it's also my fault that Dolly threw a shoe and that your cell phone wasn't charged before we left?"

"If you want to take the blame for those problems, be my guest." Josiah glared at her, his dark eyes narrowing beneath the brim of his black hat. "I should never have told you I had a new job in Higher Ground. Should've just—"

"Taken off without me?" Lena finished hotly. "What

a lovely thing to say, just a month before *your* baby's to be born! You liked me well enough when we were—"

"You didn't exactly push me away, Lena!" he countered. "Now shut up! There's a light in that building, so I'm going inside to see—"

A sharp rapping on the side of the buggy made them both suck in their breath. Through the fogged window Lena could make out the shape of a man's head. She hoped by some far-flung miracle it would be the Hiram Knepp who'd hired Josiah rather than someone bent on taking advantage of their desperate situation.

Why did you ever think Josiah Witmer would look after you? Your parents warned you to forget about him and join the church, but you didn't listen.

The baby shifted restlessly, kicking her insides. Lena knew she'd start crying again if she didn't get out of this rig soon.

Josiah opened the buggy door, letting in a gust of snowy air as the man's face became visible. Lena was relieved that his broad-brimmed hat and beard were signs he was Plain.

"How can I help ya?" he asked earnestly. "It's not fit weather for man nor beast, and it's gettin' too dark to be out on these snowy roads."

"We've veered off our route," Josiah replied. "Where might I get my horse a new shoe, and maybe find a place to stay the night?"

The man's face lit up. "You're not as lost as ya thought. I'm a farrier and this is my smithy," he replied, gesturing toward the building behind him. "Pull your rig over here. Let's get you kids in out of the cold."

"*Denki*," Josiah murmured. "Show me where to park, all right?"

The man grasped the harness to guide Dolly closer to the smithy. As the buggy lurched forward, Josiah closed the door with a tired sigh.

"What if he turns us away when he realizes we're not married?" Lena asked with a hitch in her voice. "What if we're not even *close* to Higher Ground and—"

"We'll deal with it, okay?" he muttered. "If I'd known you were the type to worry over every little thing, I'd never have—"

"You're calling this baby a *little* thing?" Lena countered. "When are you going to figure out that this little *person* will need food and clothes and—"

The buggy halted, and once again a rapping on the window silenced them. Josiah flashed her a warning scowl before opening the door. Lena thought he might leave her to clamber out of the rig by herself—being short and eight months along made even the simplest maneuvering more difficult these days—so when Josiah offered his hand, Lena grabbed it before he could change his mind.

As they followed the man into the smithy, Lena was immediately grateful for the fire in the forge. She shook the snow from her old blanket, sensing their host was assessing her and Josiah. He removed his hat and offered his hand.

"Ben Hooley," he said. "You've made it to Willow Ridge, but you intended to be somewhere else, I take it?"

"*Jah*, we're going to the new colony at Higher Ground," Josiah replied as he grasped Ben's sturdy hand. "I'm Josiah Witmer, and Hiram Knepp's hired me to cook in his new supper club. This is Lena Esh. We're mighty glad we found you because I don't think either of us can take much more of that rig and the road today."

"It's gotten dangerous out," Ben agreed. His hazel eyes had widened while Josiah was talking, and he seemed to be considering his reply carefully.

He noticed we have different last names, so he might not let us stay. Lena pressed her lips together to keep from crying. *It's been one disaster after another these past eight months.*

"It's awful late to shoe your mare," Ben remarked. "How about if I stable her here for the night? I've got a place for ya to stay, and my wife'll fix ya some supper, *but*—"

Lena held her breath when the man's face stiffened.

"You'll have to stop fightin'," he stated firmly. "My Miriam is also expectin' a child soon and I won't have our home turned into a battleground. If I see her gettin' upset because of your raised voices, you'll be on your way. Understand?"

Lena's face went hot. Had she and Josiah been squabbling so loudly that their words had carried outside the buggy? It seemed they were constantly pushing each other's buttons—although it hadn't been that way before she'd told Josiah she was pregnant.

Lena closed her eyes, exhausted. "I'm so tired of fighting," she murmured, pressing her hand into the small of her back. "I'll hold my tongue if *you* will, Josiah."

Josiah's eyebrows rose in resentment, but then he exhaled wearily. "All right, we'll call a truce."

"Glad to hear it. You'll feel better for speakin' more kindly to each other," Ben said with a nod. "I'll tend your horse and be back in a few."

Lena watched their host head back outside into the

flying snow. The walls of Ben Hooley's shop were lined with tools hung on pegs and cabinets that were cleared of all extraneous items—a place for everything and everything in its place. On a worktable near the forge she spotted a cradle that glimmered in the firelight.

"Oh, Josiah, look," she murmured. Like the old-fashioned cradles often passed down from generation to generation, this one sat on a table or the floor rather than on tall legs. Lena ran her finger along its glossy wooden sides, in awe of the headboard's intricate metalwork. A pewter hummingbird sipped from a morning glory bloom, with vines and tinier blooms flowing along the headboard's curved edges. "Do you suppose Ben made this?"

"For his upcoming baby, most likely," Josiah replied as he, too, admired the piece. With one finger, he made the cradle rock on the worktable—and then he backed away as though the hummingbird had stabbed him with its long, pointed beak.

See how spooked he is about this baby? Lena thought ruefully. No doubt Ben Hooley was devoted to his wife and eagerly awaiting their child. How she yearned for that kind of love—a rock-solid relationship that she feared Josiah Witmer wasn't ready to give her. Her mother had begged her to return home rather than leaving with this good-looking, impetuous young man. Her *dat* had told her not to bother coming home if she took up with such a no-account, restless dreamer. If their Missouri adventure went wrong, Lena couldn't return to Bloomfield, Iowa. She'd have to face the consequences of loving a man who wouldn't commit himself to her and their baby.

Lena swallowed the lump in her throat. *Lord, every time I come to You I'm begging, but please, please get me through this ordeal. Help me raise this child right,* she prayed. *Even if I have to do it alone.*

While Miriam watched the young couple at her table devour scrambled eggs and fried potatoes as though they hadn't eaten in days, her heart went out to them. They looked painfully young to be roaming the roads on a snowy November night. The set of Josiah's jaw and Lena's pink-rimmed eyes suggested that their journey had been bumpier than Mother Nature alone was making it, and that the path ahead of them wouldn't smooth out any time soon.

"So you're on your way to Higher Ground?" Miriam asked carefully. She broke a few more eggs into the cast-iron skillet.

"*Jah*, I saw an ad in *The Budget* inviting new residents, so I called the phone number. Now a fellow there wants me to cook in his supper club," the young man answered. His hat had flattened his dark, wavy hair, and his brown eyes met hers with a sense of confidence that bordered on cockiness. "When he heard about my catering business—roasting whole hogs and grilling ribs and briskets for parties—he told me I'd be in charge of the kitchen at his new place."

Miriam's eyebrows rose. It was unusual for a Plain man to do so much cooking—but it was the mention of a supper club in Higher Ground that piqued her curiosity. She noticed how Ben's expression was tightening, so she proceeded cautiously. "Who would this fella be? I've not heard anyone speak of a supper club—but then, I've not been to Higher Ground, either."

Lena's eyes widened. "Are we that far off course?"

She glanced fearfully at Josiah. "I—I thought you knew where we were headed—"

"And I do!" he blurted out testily. He inhaled deeply to quell his impatience when Ben flashed him a warning glance. "His name's Hiram Knepp. He's offered me a nice salary and a place to stay while I get his restaurant going."

Miriam noticed immediately that Josiah's reply seemed to be only about himself, which might explain the way Lena's china blue eyes widened in her pale face. She didn't appear to be out of her teens, a mere child about to have a baby in what seemed to be an iffy situation. And if Hiram Knepp, the excommunicated bishop of Willow Ridge, had made such glowing promises to lure Josiah to the new settlement . . .

"Hiram must've heard *gut* things about your way with food," Ben spoke up from his seat at the end of the table. "But have ya met him yet? Have ya seen this supper club he told ya about?"

Josiah's eyes flashed. "I talked to him on the phone. His offer would put me way ahead of where I'd be in Bloomfield, working out of my house."

Miriam shared Ben's concerned gaze, stirring the eggs in the skillet. Surely if Hiram had hired Josiah, there really was a supper club—whatever *that* was— for the young man to cook in. But she had an uneasy feeling about this whole situation.

"I can see you're eager to start to work—and anybody would be excited about bein' in charge of a new place," Ben added quickly. "But I'd be real careful, dealin' with Hiram Knepp. He used to be our bishop here in Willow Ridge, but when we learned of his underhanded dealings, we banned him from our church. Told him not to come back to town."

Lena sucked in her breath. "What did he do that was so awful? I've never heard of a church district banning their bishop."

"You sure we're talking about the same fellow?" Josiah challenged. "Lots of Plain folks have the same names, after all."

"Oh, there's only *one* like this Hiram Knepp," Miriam murmured. She sprinkled the eggs with salt and pepper. "Findin' a car in his barn, and learnin' that he'd made a crooked deal to acquire land for Higher Ground was just scratchin' the surface, I'm afraid."

"*Jah,* Hiram paints a pretty picture when he talks." Ben gazed first at Josiah and then at Lena, his face tight with concern. "I'm not tellin' ya what to do, understand. But ya might want to stay here in Willow Ridge and check out the situation in Higher Ground before ya commit to anything."

"You can stay with us for as long as ya need to," Miriam insisted. She carried the skillet to the table and poured the scrambled eggs into the serving bowl. "We've got a *dawdi haus* on this level you could stay in, Lena, and Josiah, you can bunk in one of the guest rooms upstairs."

"It'd be a shame if you'd come all this way only to find out Hiram's supper club isn't even built yet," Ben added. "Might be a long time before you'd have any money comin' in. And with a baby on the way—"

"It's a done deal. Knepp says I'll be drawing pay as soon as I show up," Josiah stated impatiently. He spooned more scrambled eggs onto his plate and smeared jelly on another slice of toast. "I appreciate the way you're looking after us, but once the roads are clear, I'll be heading to Higher Ground."

Lena's fork clattered to her plate. She wrapped her

arms around her bulging middle, hanging her head. "*Jah*, there's no going back," she murmured. "My folks and Aunt Clara warned me—told me this situation sounded awfully chancy—"

"You could've stayed in Iowa," Josiah muttered.

"—but I wanted the baby to be with its father," Lena continued sadly. "So Dat told me not to come home. 'I've made my bed, so I'm to lie in it,' he said."

Miriam set the skillet down and gently grasped Lena's shaking shoulders. "A nice warm bed is exactly what ya need right now, too," she murmured. "You've both had a hard day. Things'll look clearer to ya after a night's rest."

A sob escaped the girl. "I—I didn't mean to cause you so much trouble."

"Oh, honey-bug, you're no trouble at all," Miriam insisted as she massaged Lena's back. "We'd be doin' ya both wrong if we didn't give ya a place to stay on such a snowy night."

"And we want ya to know that things might not be the way they seem, far as what's happenin' in Higher Ground," Ben insisted. "God might've had His reasons for slowin' ya down, bringing ya to Willow Ridge instead. I'll shoe your horse first thing tomorrow, and then ya can decide for yourselves, all right?"

Josiah cleared his throat as though he intended to challenge Ben's opinion, but then he shrugged. "Sure, why not? We're at your mercy until my horse is fit to travel, ain't so?"

Miriam met her husband's gaze over the top of Lena's head. She and Ben were no strangers to such an attitude, after helping Ben's two younger brothers establish a milling business over the past year while convincing them to join the church and accept adult responsibilities. Luke and Ira were now both engaged and following paths of faith, however, so there was hope and help for Josiah—if he would accept it.

"How about if I get ya settled in the *dawdi haus?*" Miriam asked Lena. "Ben can show Josiah his room upstairs—"

"And I'll bring in Lena's suitcase," Ben insisted, "because neither of you girls should be totin' anything heavier than those precious lives you're carryin'. I'll be back in a few."

"But I feel bad about accepting your hospitality without repaying you," Lena protested. "After the way you've fed us and taken us in, it's only right to give you some money or help out somehow."

"Tell ya what," Miriam suggested as she watched the weary girl rise from her chair. "If either of ya wants to help in the Sweet Seasons tomorrow, that'll be fine. That's my café across the road, and I'll be bakin' in the wee hours while you two should be gettin' your rest. You're welcome to eat your breakfast there while ya figure out what ya want to do next."

"*Denki* so much," Lena murmured as she and Miriam entered the hallway at the back of the house. "Sleeping late sounds heavenly."

Miriam opened the door to the small apartment she and Ben would share when they were too old to climb the stairs anymore. As she closed the curtains in the sitting room and the bedroom, she glanced out the windows into a cold, crisp night. Only a few snowflakes drifted in the air now. In the glow of the moon, the snow-covered hills and rooftops took on a make-believe quality—but the couple she and Ben had welcomed into their home were dealing with more reality than they seemed to be aware of.

"Not meanin' to be a busybody," Miriam murmured as she put fresh towels in the bathroom, "but if you and Josiah aren't married—"

"*Jah*, you got that right," the girl said with a sigh.

"—then ya want to be sure you've got a place to stay and folks nearby who can help ya when your wee one's born," Miriam continued earnestly. "If Josiah seems set on cookin' in Higher Ground—even if ya get the feelin' that's not a *gut* idea—you can stay with us, Lena. All right?"

Lena landed heavily on the edge of the double bed. "Miriam, you don't have to—I'm sticking with Josiah, even if it seems we're at odds," she insisted. "He'll come around once the baby's born. He's angry now because we lost our way in the snowstorm."

Miriam smiled. She knew all about young girls falling head over heels in love and not seeing their men's flaws. "How old are ya, Lena?"

"Eighteen. Josiah's twenty-one, though," she added quickly. "And he really is a wonderful-*gut* cook, when it comes to roasting hogs and grilling all kinds of meat. He'll make a go of it at the supper club. Really he will."

Miriam wished she could believe that Hiram's job offer was the solid opportunity this young couple needed it to be. This late in the evening, however, it was best to keep her doubts to herself.

"My daughter Rebecca stayed here for a while," Miriam murmured as she glanced around to see if anything else needed doing. "She was raised in an English family—a long story—but now she's livin' in the apartment above Ben's smithy and helpin' at the Sweet Seasons and the Willow Ridge clinic while she runs her computer design business." Miriam smiled at the thought of her three dear girls, grown and living purposeful lives now. "My daughter Rhoda just married the nurse fella who runs the clinic, and my other girl, Rachel, lives across the road with her husband and their new baby. If Ben and I aren't around, any of those girls'll be happy to help ya."

"This is so nice of you," Lena murmured. "More than I deserve."

Miriam grasped the young woman's shoulders, gazing into her pale blue eyes. "Don't ya be thinkin' that way, child," she insisted. "God's lookin' after ya because ya *do* deserve a *gut* life for yourself and your wee one. If ya settle for less, I'll be mighty disappointed in ya."

Lena's eye's widened, but then she smiled tiredly. "I'll keep that in mind, Miriam. He steered us toward you and Ben tonight, after all."

Satisfied with that response, Miriam turned toward the door. "I don't want to see ya until you've gotten a *gut* night's rest, hear me?"

"Loud and clear. *Denki* ever so much for not casting me out like—well, never mind," the girl murmured. "I'm grateful."

Miriam closed the *dawdi haus* door, shaking her head. She had a feeling Lena's parents and her aunt Clara had reached the end of their ropes, dealing with an unwed pregnancy and the brash young man who'd caused it. While Amish parents often sent their unmarried pregnant daughters to stay with relatives in another town, Miriam had never understood how mothers could turn their backs on young girls at the neediest time of their lives. Then again, it was the man of the house who made the rules about this situation, so Lena's mother might've been bound by his decision.

But Lena was now dependent upon a young fellow who seemed unaware of her impending responsibilities, or of how a few reckless moments of passion had cost Lena her family's support. She must be feeling terribly desperate and alone, facing the birth of her baby among folks she didn't know.

Show me what we can do for these young people, Lord. You know how I can't bear to watch Your lost lambs suffer.

Chapter Two

Very early Saturday morning Ben entered the Sweet Seasons kitchen and went immediately to the oven, where Miriam was pulling out a large pan of cinnamon rolls. "Are ya supposed to be liftin' this much weight?" he asked as he took the pan from her. "Yesterday Andy reminded me—again—that ya need to find help if you're gonna keep workin'. And it would be better if ya weren't workin'," he added emphatically.

As he set the hot pan on a cooling rack, Miriam sighed. "I'm not helpless, Ben," she insisted. "What would I do with myself if I weren't in this kitchen? It's another month and a half until the baby comes—and it's not like I haven't given birth before."

Although Old Order wives weren't to work outside the home, Miriam's dedication to her café was one of the reasons he loved her, so Ben spoke more gently. "I'm lookin' after ya, followin' Andy's orders," he replied. He kissed her, caressing the bulge of her sweet belly where their baby was kicking. "Plant your backside on that stool. What else can I do for ya?"

"For starters, you can tell me what you're doin' here

so early of a Saturday morning, Mr. Hooley," she teased. She perched on the tall stool beside the counter to mix the powdered sugar in her big glass measuring cup with milk. As she drizzled the white frosting over the hot rolls, Ben's stomach rumbled so loudly they both laughed.

"I came to see if my woman would feed me something before I shoe Josiah's mare," Ben said, following every hypnotic swirl of the frosting as it soaked into the warm rolls.

"*Puh.* You didn't sleep any better than I did last night for thinkin' about those kids."

Ben smiled. His wife of ten months had figured him out long ago, so it was useless to refute her. "It's that supper club that's got me wonderin'," he muttered. "Considerin' how Higher Ground's not nearly as big as Willow Ridge—and it has a diner already—how do ya suppose a second restaurant'll survive?"

"And what on earth is a supper club?" Miriam eased one of the fresh rolls from the corner of the pan. "It sounds like a place that might have members, so only certain folks would be goin' there to eat. But what do *I* know?"

When she'd laid the fresh cinnamon roll on a piece of paper towel and placed it in front of him, Ben kissed her loudly on the cheek. "Well, girlie, ya know how to make the best food a fella ever sank his teeth into, and ya make my heart dance. What else matters, really?"

The roses bloomed in Miriam's face. "Oh, Ben, ya say the sweetest things."

"Just statin' the facts," he replied as he uncoiled the outer layer of the roll. "I love ya more than I ever thought possible, honey-girl. Share this with me, will ya? We don't want ya gettin' puny from workin' so hard."

When he held the first bite in front of her mouth, Miriam let her lips linger on his fingers. "Puny," she echoed as she patted her girth. "The only time I've been this huge is when I was carryin' the triplets."

Ben tucked in the brown hair that had loosened beneath Miriam's *kapp*, loving the strands of silver that glimmered there. "*Denki* for havin' my baby," he whispered. "I'm so excited and—and scared about raisin' a wee one. Especially since ya thought ya weren't able to conceive."

Miriam's eyebrow arched. "Scared? You, Ben?"

He savored the warm pastry's cinnamon sweetness while he thought of a reply. "What if I'm no *gut* at bein' a *dat*? What if—"

"You, Ben Hooley, will be a father other fellas could take lessons from," Miriam insisted. "Fellas like Josiah, for starters. Now *his* child I worry about. And what'll become of Lena if Josiah goes his own way without marryin' her?" she asked in a rising voice. "She's only eighteen, and with her family sendin' her away—"

Ben grasped Miriam's shoulders. "Don't let those young folks drag ya down into their muck, honey-bunch. Our church district excommunicated Hiram so we'd be finished with his deceit," he reminded her. "How do we know he's not figurin' to suck us all in again with his harebrained supper club idea?"

Her mouth formed an O and no sound came out. Miriam looked so pretty, with her fuller face and rosy cheeks, Ben wished they didn't have to think about the man who'd supposedly hired Josiah.

"I suppose that's a far-fetched idea, considerin' how Hiram couldn't have known Josiah would be waylaid in Willow Ridge," he admitted. "But let's don't forget about him. We can't guess what he has in mind for Josiah's cookin', and I suspect he doesn't know anything about Lena or the baby."

"Oh, let's hope Hiram won't get ideas about *her*," Miriam rasped. "Now that Delilah's left him, he'll be huntin' for more female company." She sighed deeply. "We really do need to look out for those kids, Ben. They have no idea—but there I go, gettin' involved, doin' exactly what ya just told me not to."

"Can't fault ya for havin' their best interests at heart." Ben closed his eyes over another bite of the warm, gooey roll. "Let's stick together far as how we're gonna help Lena and Josiah, all right?"

"*Jah.* United we stand, and divided we might fall into that muck ya mentioned." Miriam slid off her stool. "I've got biscuits and chocolate bread to bake before Naomi and the girls get here. Then I'll have plenty of helpers makin' sure I don't overdo it," she added with a playful smile.

"You're tellin' me to get on with my work so you can do yours," Ben teased. "I'll check in later—and I'll let Bishop Tom and the other fellas know Josiah's lookin' for steady work. I love ya, Miriam."

"Love ya right back, Bennie-bug," she whispered. "What would I do without ya?"

As Ben headed toward the smithy next door, he was thankful he didn't have to do without his beautiful, compassionate wife, either. Nobody was more kind-hearted than his Miriam—which was why he had to protect her. She was more vulnerable to her emotions these days, more likely to say and do things before she thought them through. She believed she was fully capable of handling this birth, just as she'd done when her triplets were born twenty-two years ago.

But Miriam was over forty now—and a grandmother,

as well. She had a lot of wonderful, motherly concerns these days as her daughter Rachel cared for little Amelia, and Ben was determined that she would bear his child without getting caught in Hiram Knepp's web of lies and deceit again.

When he passed the workbench, Ben rocked the wooden cradle he'd made, imagining the sweet child who would soon sleep in it. Such dreams he had for this baby, such hopes and aspirations as Christmas and Miriam's due date grew near.

All is calm, all is bright.

As Ben hammered the glowing-hot horseshoe for Josiah's mare, he hummed the beloved carol those words had come from. His life was so much more blessed than he could possibly have imagined last year at this time when, as a newcomer to Willow Ridge, he'd first met Miriam. No two ways about it, she'd transformed his life, his faith. She was nothing short of a miracle worker.

Lena's going to drag you down. You've got to move on—without her.

Josiah sat in the back corner of the Sweet Seasons, devouring the plateful of food he'd gotten from the steam table. He'd heard Miriam and Ben stirring at an insanely early hour, so he'd arrived at six when the café had opened. Through the window of Ben's smithy, he'd seen the forge fire glowing. With any luck, Dolly would have her new shoe and he could roll out of town before Lena showed up—which would save a lot of explaining on his part and crying on hers. Lord, but he was tired of her crying!

But what if the Hooleys have told you the truth? What if

you get to Higher Ground and there's no sign of a supper club? Should you get the whole story from Knepp or keep on driving?

His older sister Savilla had suggested that he look around Higher Ground before he committed to living in Missouri, but Josiah had seen Knepp's offer as his ticket out of a dicey situation with Lena. Never had he figured that a quick coupling in the hayloft would have such consequences—but he hadn't exactly been thinking when Lena's kisses had taken him over the edge all those months ago. He hadn't planned to bring Lena to Missouri, either, yet he couldn't resist seeing her one last time—and once again he'd fallen for Lena's expressive eyes and her persuasive voice when she'd insisted on coming with him. So here they were.

Josiah stopped eating in such a hurry so he could really taste his slice of chocolate bread. It was moist and spicy-sweet and fabulous, loaded with apple and walnut chunks and chocolate chips. The breakfast casserole was a savory blend of sausage, bread, onions, and melting cheese, and the fried apples tickled his tongue with cinnamon rather than being overloaded with butter and sugar. The happy chatter of Miriam and the two Brenneman gals in the kitchen suggested a love for their work—and for each other—that he suddenly envied.

"Want me to top off your coffee?"

"How about another round at the breakfast buffet? It's one price for all ya can eat."

Josiah came out of his musings to look at the two young women standing beside his table. Their smiling faces were identical, yet one was dressed Plain and the other wore jeans and a plaid flannel shirt. "I—sorry,

I don't mean to stare," he stammered, "but you two could be sisters."

"We are!" the one in the deep green cape dress proclaimed. "I'm Rhoda—"

"And I'm Rebecca," the waitress in jeans joined in as she slung her arm around Rhoda's shoulders. "We're Miriam's girls—"

"And with our sister Rachel, we make triplets!" her look-alike clarified.

"I was washed down the river when I was a toddler and raised by the English couple who rescued me," Rebecca explained, "while my two sisters grew up here in Willow Ridge. You must be Lena's man."

Lena's man. Josiah didn't want to discuss that label, so he kept to his original subject. "That's an incredible story about you three sisters—and this is incredibly *gut* food, too. I'm almost finished, though," he added, waving away Rebecca's coffee carafe. "As soon as Ben's got my mare shod, I'm hitting the road."

Rebecca glanced around at the handful of other fellows who'd come in to eat. "Mamma mentioned your offer from Hiram," she murmured near his ear. "I did a Google search for Higher Ground, but I've found nothing about a supper club. Be really careful, Josiah," she insisted. "Hiram Knepp's brought on so much trouble around here that—well, I hope he's not telling pretty tales to lure you to his new colony."

"*Jah*, he's caused us all more problems—Mamma especially—than we care to recall," Rhoda added with a shake of her head. "You and Lena would be better off stayin' in Willow Ridge—not that we're tellin' ya what to do," she added quickly.

Josiah's pulse pounded. He had no idea what a Google search was, but if English Rebecca and Amish

Rhoda were giving him such dire warnings about Knepp . . .

Josiah sighed. He'd traveled a long way with high hopes, so he didn't want to write off that supper club job without checking it out. And if he sat here too long, Lena would find him before he could start down the road. He pulled a ten-dollar bill from his wallet as he stood up. "I appreciate your advice. I'll keep it in mind while I check out what Hiram told me."

Josiah strode across the dining area without meeting any of the other customers' curious gazes. He grabbed his coat and hat, making the bell above the door jingle as he stepped outside. It wasn't yet six thirty—still dark—but he itched to settle this supper club situation so he could decide what to do if all the warnings he'd heard appeared to be true.

"*Denki* for seeing to Dolly so early this morning," he said as he entered Ben's smithy. "What do I owe you for her shoe?"

Ben gave the mare's hind foot a couple of final strokes with his rasp. He released her leg and straightened to his full height. "Not a thing. I wanted ya to be safe on the roads, so Dolly's got a full set of new shoes."

Josiah's jaw dropped. "But I've got the money," he protested as he reached for his wallet.

"The things that matter aren't about money," the farrier replied as he grasped Josiah's wrist. For a few moments only the crackling of the forge fire interrupted Ben's hazel-eyed gaze. "I'm doin' this as much for Lena and your baby as I am for you, young man. Miriam and I want all of ya to be healthy. Happy."

Why do you care what happens to us? Josiah almost blurted out. He had a feeling this muscular, sandy-haired farrier had guessed that he planned to leave

Lena behind—but how could that be? Josiah braced himself for a sermon he figured would come on like a train, yet Ben began to put away his tools.

Of course he cares, Josiah realized. *If you abandon Lena, they'll be taking care of her until the baby's born. And after that, too.*

He let out the breath he'd been holding. "I'm driving over to Higher Ground. I'll be back after I get a feel for things there," he said, hoping his smile covered his original intentions. "If Lena goes along and decides Knepp's ideas won't work out, I'll never hear the end of it. Worries over every little thing, that girl."

Ben's lips flickered. "Women get touchy when they're in the family way."

"I stand a chance of coming up with a better idea if she's not riding along, getting upset," Josiah explained further. "Her crying drives me straight up the wall."

One of Ben's eyebrows rose. "Women also get *scared* when they're carryin'. Can't say as I blame them," he remarked. "I've found it's best to kiss Miriam and say 'yes, dear' a lot when she's in a mood, knowin' it'll pass. She does the same for me."

Josiah almost wished Ben had lit into him with a lecture, because his show of patience and kindness was setting an example he didn't think he could follow with Lena. When it came to mothering skills and maturity, Magdalena Esh would never measure up to Miriam Hooley—

And where do you fall on the maturity scale?

Josiah smiled at Ben despite feeling as though he were wading in the river and might be swept away by an undertow of guilt at any moment. "*Denki* again for looking after me and my horse. I'll be back in a while."

"Turn right onto the blacktop. The first road on your right'll eventually take ya past Morning Star," Ben said. "You'll see the Higher Ground sign a little ways beyond that."

"Ah. That explains the turn I missed in the snow last night."

Ben's smile was warm and sincere. "I'll be waitin' to hear your account of Hiram's new town. Never been there myself."

Josiah led his mare outside toward his buggy, again puzzled by how the Hooleys seemed intent upon avoiding Higher Ground. Wouldn't curiosity coax these folks to take a Sunday drive over that way, to see the colony their former bishop had established? The illustrated ads in *The Budget* made Higher Ground sound like a new Eden, a paradise for Plain folks—although he'd never seen mention of whether Knepp's new homes and business district were intended for Old Order Amish, New Order Mennonites, or sects that fell somewhere in between.

He hitched up the buggy and stroked his mare's neck. "Well, let's go see for ourselves, Dolly. Things are bound to look better in the light of day."

Chapter Three

Lena gazed forlornly out the Hooleys' picture window, watching Josiah drive off without her. The warm, comfortable bed had enveloped her, and she hadn't wakened until nearly seven o'clock. Josiah had left her alone in this big house to eat breakfast without him.

And now he's gone forever. No sense in figuring it any other way.

Embracing her baby, Lena hung her head. Why had her mother not told her what could happen when a boy knew a girl in the biblical sense? It seemed to be all her fault that a baby had resulted—and that her sin had separated her from her family. Before the baby had become obvious, her parents had shipped her off to Aunt Clara's, and her *mamm*'s sister had all but forbidden her to be seen in public. When Josiah had succumbed to her pleas and brought her to Missouri with him on the spur of the moment, Lena had jumped at the chance for a fresh start. But now he obviously regretted his decision.

"Let's get some breakfast, punkin," she murmured.

"If it weren't for you, I'd have no reason to make it from one day to the next."

Lena slipped into her coat and bonnet and started across the road toward the Sweet Seasons. She squinted in the sunshine of a bright, crisp morning that glistened with fresh snow. The ice-coated branches of the trees sparkled like diamonds. As she approached Miriam's café, aromas of frying bacon, hot coffee, and baking bread teased at her. A tinkling bell above the door welcomed her into a cozy little café she liked immediately. Most of the customers were Plain and male at this hour, which surprised her. Did none of these men have wives?

A young woman dressed in jeans and a flannel shirt strode toward her. "You must be Lena, and I'm Miriam's Rebecca," she said as she gestured toward a table for two. "Sit with me! I'm ready for coffee and a sticky bun."

Sit with me. It was the invitation Lena's lonely heart longed for. Her pulse sped up as she took a seat at the table Rebecca had indicated.

Miriam poked her head through the kitchen door, smiling. "Fill a plate at the buffet table, or ya can order off the menu," she encouraged. "Get whatever ya want, Lena. It's *gut* to see ya lookin' more rested."

Lena returned Miriam's smile, her spirits lifting. The tables and chairs were sturdy, made in a rustic split-log design, and denim curtains were tied back at each window. Some of the fellows looked at her but then continued chatting with their friends, while a young waitress in a green cape dress circulated among them with a coffee carafe. When she saw Lena, she hurried over.

"I'm Rhoda Leitner," she said as she filled Lena's

mug with steaming coffee. "We met your Josiah earlier this morning. He'll have an interesting report when he gets back from Higher Ground. Cream?"

"*Jah*, please." Lena warned herself not to fall for the way Miriam's daughter assumed Josiah would return— or that he was hers. She couldn't help smiling, however, when Rebecca came to the table with two huge sticky buns and a red-haired woman whose plaid Plain-style dress suggested she was a Mennonite.

"Lena, this is Nora Landwehr. She runs the Simple Gifts shop in the big barn up the road," Rebecca said. "Nora's engaged to that gorgeous guy who can't keep his eyes off her—Luke Hooley. He's Ben's younger brother, and he runs the mill that sits on the river."

"It's so nice to meet you, Lena," Nora said as she pulled a chair up to their table. She had a sparkle in her hazel eyes as she leaned closer. "We've not told Miriam yet, but I'm having a baby shower at my place next Friday evening. I sure hope you'll come. It'll be a great way to meet the ladies around here—and a lot of them are close to your age, too."

"But keep this under your *kapp*," Rebecca insisted in a whisper. "If anybody deserves a surprise party, it's Mamma."

"You've got that right," Nora agreed with a grin that lit up her freckled face. "Willow Ridge would be just another ho-hum little town if it weren't for Miriam's nudging us all toward our dreams. She's everybody's other mother!"

"I—I'd love to come," Lena replied. For the first time in weeks she felt a genuine smile on her face. "Awfully nice of you to ask, considering you don't even know me."

"*Yet*," Nora insisted, grasping Lena's wrist. "Trust me,

if these people welcomed *me* back, they're the best folks you could ever hope to meet." She turned and wiggled her fingers at a handsome fellow across the room. "Better get back to Luke. This is the only time we'll see each other until we close our shops this evening."

Lena cut into her sticky bun, watching Nora chat with everyone as she returned to her table. "How could anyone not want such a happy, thoughtful woman in Willow Ridge?"

Rebecca smiled, attacking her own pastry with her fork. "Nora had to leave town when she was sixteen and pregnant—and *then* she left the baby on her brother and sister-in-law's front porch for them to raise while she lived with an English husband, whom she divorced last year," she explained in a gossipy rush. "*Then* she bought Hiram Knepp's place—the priciest house in town—and came back to reunite with her daughter and her parents, after being away for sixteen years."

Lena's fork stopped in front of her open mouth. "Oh, my."

"Uh-huh. But she's reconciled with her daughter and her family," Rebecca went on. "Now she and Millie are engaged to Ben's two younger brothers. Top that!"

Lena giggled. "I don't think I can."

"See what I'm saying? No matter how badly you've messed up your life," Rebecca insisted, "you can consider yourself forgiven here. Mamma believes Jesus wipes our slates clean, and nobody—not even Nora's strict old preacher of a dad—can hold a grudge in this town. So relax. You're in."

Rebecca's earnest words sounded too good to be true, yet Lena clung to the hope they gave her. "Wow," she murmured.

"Picture me with spiky black hair, black fingernails, a lot of metal and piercings—and an attitude to match," Rebecca continued with a nod. "That's how I looked when I showed up here, after my English mom died and I'd found out she and Dad weren't my birth parents. I wanted nothing to do with Miriam and her Old Order faith, but I was her long-lost daughter and she refused to let me go. You can't tell that woman *no*, so you might as well accept the love she's offering."

This wasn't Sunday, yet Rebecca's words moved Lena more than any sermon. Jesus's love suddenly felt *real*—something present-day folks could rely upon instead of just a story from centuries ago. It was the same unconditional love Lena had felt when she and Josiah had been eating the supper Miriam had cooked last night. Miriam and Ben had known they weren't married—and probably weren't suited to be—yet she'd sensed no judgment or disgust. She and Josiah had received love instead of lectures.

"This all feels too *gut* to be true," Lena murmured as she took another bite of the delicious sticky bun.

Rebecca chuckled. "I know exactly how you feel. I figured Miriam for a goody-goody when I first met her," she went on. "But my mother is the most genuine person I know—a doer instead of a talker. Mamma saw through my hard-core attitude and appearance to the lonely, confused young woman I was inside."

Lena nodded, hanging on Rebecca's every word. What would it be like to have a mother who loved you as completely—as fiercely—as Miriam had loved her lost daughter?

"I hate to think about what might've become of me had she not welcomed me back," Rebecca went on. "She was a widow then, getting the Sweet Seasons going while she was planning my sister Rachel's wedding. Hiram Knepp was harassing her, insisting she needed to marry him, so we were all glad when Ben Hooley showed up from Lancaster County. It was love at first sight for them."

Lena sensed Rebecca, like the Hooleys, was advising her to steer clear of this Hiram character. And she longed to believe that a true, romantic love like the one Ben and Miriam shared would someday be hers.

"Here's an egg and some bacon to get your day off to a *gut* start," Miriam said as she interrupted Lena's wool-gathering. "And since ya offered to help, I've got some veggies that need scrubbin' for the lunch menu—but not until you've cleaned your plate."

"*Denki* so much," Lena replied gratefully. "You and your girls are taking such *gut* care of me, I don't know how to act!"

When Lena went into the kitchen, she immediately sensed an industrious cheerfulness. Miriam's partner, Naomi Brenneman, stood at the stove combining cooked hamburger and onions with a mixture of tomatoes and beans to make a chili that already smelled heavenly. Naomi's teenage daughter, Hannah, was slicing pies at the back counter to replenish the glass bakery case.

"If ya could scrub these spuds," Miriam said, pointing toward a large bag of russets, "we'll have loaded baked potatoes on the lunch menu."

Lena sat on a small chair beside a dishpan of warm water, a stiff-bristled brush, and a vegetable peeler. She set to work, chatting with Rhoda and Rebecca as well as the two Brennemans. Her thoughts wandered briefly back to Bloomfield. If she were there, she'd be cooking or cleaning alongside her tight-lipped aunt—

An outcast from your own home.

Lena blinked. It was a harsh thought, but it was true. She felt happier here among these busy women than she'd been in months. She scrubbed the large potatoes with renewed energy, knowing her efforts were appreciated. What a difference that made!

Josiah spotted the stone slab with HIGHER GROUND carved in large letters and slowed Dolly's pace. Although the sign reminded him of fancy gravestones he'd seen in English cemeteries, it made an impressive statement.

As his mare drew him slowly into town, they passed a bank, a diner, and a few other shops—built of brick and all in a row, rather than situated on the owners' properties—with a concrete sidewalk in front of them. "They've got power poles for electricity, so this can't be an Amish colony. What do you think of that, Dolly?" Josiah murmured.

His horse tossed her head as they passed parked cars as well as horse-drawn buggies tied to hitching rails. Outside the white schoolhouse, kids were playing tag in their coats, hats, and bonnets. Josiah sensed a progressive optimism in the people on the street and as he gazed up the snow-covered hillside at the new houses built in rows. The plots of ground were much smaller than the usual acreage a Plain family owned, yet it made sense: men who didn't farm for a living didn't need a lot of land. Instinct told him that the large house perched on the top of the hill belonged to Hiram Knepp—but he didn't drive up there to introduce himself.

Instead, Josiah hitched Dolly to the post at the bank building and strolled to the diner. It seemed like a good idea to order something and observe how the place was run. After a Mennonite waitress in a polka-dot dress brought his cherry pie and coffee, Josiah studied the red vinyl booths and the black-and-white checkerboard floor. A jukebox filled the place with the twang of country music and the waitresses walked in time to the catchy beat—something he'd never seen in a Plain town.

Josiah sighed. His coffee was lukewarm and his sister put a lot more cherries in her pie. He left a five-dollar bill and went outside again.

Over the phone, Hiram had raved about how his supper club would have uniformed waiters serving upscale food on tables draped in white tablecloths with linen napkins, but Josiah knew better than to compare Hiram's new place to this diner—or to the community halls and park pavilions where he and Savilla usually catered.

His pulse thrummed as he thought about bringing his cookers to Higher Ground, where everything looked brand new and well organized. One of the houses had a FOR RENT sign in the window, and he knew Lena and Savilla would be excited about living so close to where they could do their shopping. No one could say he wasn't taking good care of Lena if he moved her into such a place and began working for Hiram Knepp.

That evening, however, as Josiah ate supper with Ben, Miriam, and Rebecca, Lena shot him down before he'd even finished describing Higher Ground.

"I'm staying in Willow Ridge," she informed him. "From everything these folks have told me about Hiram Knepp, he's trouble—and I don't need any more trouble in my life."

Josiah's face went hot. "How can you decide that

without even going there?" he demanded. "Higher Ground's a progressive town—and I found a brand-new house that's for rent. You're expecting me to give you and the baby a home, yet now that I have an opportunity to provide for you, you're refusing to—"

"What did the supper club look like?" Miriam interrupted with a curious smile. "How does it compare to the Sweet Seasons, as far as how many folks it'll seat?"

"Did it match what Hiram told ya over the phone?" Ben asked. "Sounds like a great place for ya to cook, if it measures up to what ya were expectin'."

Josiah exhaled impatiently. At least the Hooleys were asking pertinent questions instead of blowing him off. "I had pie and coffee at the diner—which was bigger than your place, Miriam, but the pie wasn't wonderful," he replied. "The supper club must be in the planning stages. I didn't see any new construction, or any buildings where a restaurant would be."

Ben stroked his light brown beard. "These snowy November days aren't the best time for pourin' concrete foundations, so—"

"See there?" Lena blurted out. "I can't believe Hiram Knepp will pay you while his building goes up. The more I hear, the more I question his intentions."

Josiah didn't want to admit he'd had the same reservations as he'd driven back from Higher Ground, even though he'd been impressed by everything he'd observed. "I bet if I call him, he'll explain everything. Maybe I didn't see the entire town, so—"

"So you're going to be stubborn because you always have to be *right*." Lena's blue eyes widened with impending tears, even as her tone challenged him. "And how do you think you'll manage a restaurant without

Savilla? She made all your side dishes and kept your books!"

He couldn't endure another of Lena's crying spells, so Josiah focused on the chili and corn bread Miriam had brought home from her lunch shift. The meat and beans weren't quite as spicy as he preferred them, but the moist corn bread filled his mouth with a wonderful sweet-salty combination.

"Savilla's your sister, *jah*?" Ben asked. He took some celery from the relish plate and passed it to Josiah. "I'm not doubtin' your decision, understand, but if you're here and Savilla's in Bloomfield, can she make a go of caterin' without your grilled meats? What sort of income does she have now?"

Josiah sighed. How did this man pinpoint potential problems that he himself hadn't had a glimmer about?

"What if you stayed in Willow Ridge and cooked a supper shift at the Sweet Seasons?" Rebecca blurted out. "With Andy—our local nurse—telling Mamma to get more help, and no place around here that serves an evening meal, you could rake in some serious cash."

Josiah gazed across the table. Rebecca, too, had a gift for seeing problems and finding solutions, but that didn't mean he'd go along with her ideas. For all he knew, this family had a hidden agenda for keeping him in Willow Ridge—reasons as underhanded as they claimed Hiram Knepp's were.

"Plenty of folks say they'd eat supper there," Rebecca continued in a rush, "but we don't have the staff to manage another shift. What with Rachel having her baby a couple of months ago and Rhoda getting married—and Mamma's child due at Christmastime," she added in a rising voice, "you'd be the answer to a lot of prayers, Josiah."

"That idea had occurred to me, too," Miriam admitted with a girlish grin.

"You could fetch your equipment and bring Savilla back to cook with you," Lena chimed in. "You'd be *set*, Josiah!"

Josiah's head began spinning. It did seem more feasible to cook in an established café, yet he yearned for the excitement of building up Hiram's new restaurant from its beginning. And he didn't like it that the Hooleys, Rebecca, and Lena believed they'd just decided his future for him.

"Let's not put the cart before the horse," Ben warned as he looked at the women. "After all, we don't even know if Josiah can cook. We've not eaten his food—nor read any references from folks who have."

Josiah frowned. Why didn't Ben trust him?

"And I'd want you and Miriam to write up a business agreement, about the rent you'll pay for usin' her kitchen and utilities," Ben said to Josiah. "You'll have to hire some folks to help serve and clean up, too, because the gals who work for Miriam are already pullin' a full load."

"I'd help for as long as I could," Lena insisted. She gazed at Josiah with wide blue eyes. "You can do this! Doesn't it feel like the hand of God's been leading you here?"

"I need to think about this—a lot," Josiah added as he rose abruptly from the table.

He couldn't get out of the house fast enough. And he didn't like it one bit that the ladies assumed he'd go along with their ideas—nor did he appreciate Ben's requirements for a business agreement. Hiram Knepp had hired him sight unseen, without so much as a handshake, which was usually all most Plain folks required.

And since when has Lena found religion? Where was God when she got pregnant? Where was He when my parents drowned? Is it any wonder that I doubt God led us to Willow Ridge?

Josiah inhaled the frosty night air to settle his conflicting thoughts. He detested other people telling him what to do. He'd made his own decisions since he'd gotten out of school several years ago, and his life had gone just fine—until Lena had teased him beyond his control.

Don't listen to these people. What do they know?

Josiah entered the barn, where the earthy scents of manure and horse feed soothed him. While Ben had done very well for himself in Willow Ridge—his beautiful new home and barn were evidence of his business sense—Josiah didn't appreciate him being such a naysayer. Why didn't Hooley believe he could cook? Who would make up a story about catering? The proof was in the pork chops—and the brisket and baked beans and other food he and Savilla dished up.

As he climbed the ladder to drop a few bales of hay from the loft, Josiah's temper rose and his thoughts spun faster. What if Miriam expected him to audition—to work during her day shift and prove himself? It was one thing for the neighbor ladies to cook at the Sweet Seasons, but it was another thing altogether if they thought he would peel potatoes and wash dishes and—

"No women's work for *me*, thank you very much!" Josiah hollered. "I'll do this my way!" The echo of his voice in the high ceiling gave him a sense of release and satisfaction as the horses glanced up from their stalls.

"Sounds like something I would've said at your age."

Josiah winced. Just inside the barn, Ben stood with his arms crossed, smiling. "My attitude cost me several years of productive life, considerin' how I didn't settle down with Miriam until I turned thirty-five," he went on. "But *jah*, I left home to run my business *my* way."

Josiah stood stock-still, bracing for a sermon. Ben was a preacher, after all.

"That's why you'll not partner with my wife until the details are in writing, Josiah," Ben went on. "You're too much like I was—like my brothers Luke and Ira, too. Reckless. Fearless. *Careless*," he insisted. Then he shrugged. "But since you're not gonna follow anybody else's rules, I don't have to worry about ya messin' up Miriam's business, do I?"

Josiah's lips twitched. He felt really stupid, but that was no reason to back down or act as though he was sorry. "Nope."

"I'm glad we understand each other," Ben replied. "*Denki* for doin' my horse chores. It's *gut*, solid men's work."

Josiah nipped his lip. Where did he stand with Hooley, really? He and Savilla shared the cooking and cleanup without separating the tasks according to gender—he made a pretty fair batch of biscuits in a pinch, and his sister could change a rig wheel. She was a crack shot when they went deer hunting, too.

Josiah climbed down to the barn floor and filled a bucket with water. When he'd topped off the troughs for Ben's animals and fed them, he tended Dolly. Then he stood before Ben, figuring he'd better clarify his living arrangements. "If you figure me for a bad apple—too irresponsible—I can be on the road as soon as I throw my clothes in my duffel."

Ben's face fell like a sad old hound dog's. "And break Lena's heart?" he asked quietly. "I'm hopin' it won't come to that, son. But that's your choice, too."

Josiah let out an exasperated sigh. "I've broken Lena's heart countless times—not because I've done her wrong but because she gets upset at every little thing," he protested. "Now that you folks have taken her in, maybe I should make myself scarce. We'll get on everybody's nerves if I hang around haggling about where I should cook. I've made a perfectly fine living in Bloomfield, after all."

Ben held Josiah's gaze for a few moments beyond his comfort zone. "I suppose you'll leave after Lena goes to bed, without sayin' anything to her."

"I'll be sparing everybody one of her crying jags."

"*Jah*, and it'll save ya the trouble of ownin' up to your actions, ain't so?" Ben fired back. "It'll leave the rest of us to clean up your mess. I suspect you've had a lot of practice at that."

"At least I'm *gut* at *something*," Josiah retorted.

He'd crossed the line with that remark, but he'd heard enough of Ben's opinions. He did have a successful catering business in Bloomfield, and Savilla would assist him without giving him any flack. He could live a simple life again, free from Lena's yammering about the baby, and he wouldn't have to sign papers for Miriam or wonder if Hiram Knepp had lured him into a shady deal.

"I believe you're probably *gut* at a lot of things," Ben said after a few more tense moments. "If you're gone in the morning, I won't be surprised—but I hope you'll stick around and prove yourself, Josiah. We need young fellas with spunk and fresh ideas in Willow Ridge."

Josiah left the barn. His breath blew around his face in wisps as he strode down the road that ran between the Hooley place and the Sweet Seasons. He passed Zook's Market, a quilt shop, a small clinic, a cabinetry shop, and a dairy. As he followed the curve in the road, he saw a sign pointing toward an auction barn. He eventually walked past a herd of wooly sheep and a huge barn that housed the Simple Gifts shop, next door to the Mill at Willow Ridge, a gristmill with a waterwheel, situated on the river.

So many thriving businesses. Surely a supper shift at Miriam's café would be more successful than the catering he did by grilling at gatherings—and a lot easier than hauling his cookers around, too, especially in the winter. He passed homes with pale smoke rising from their chimneys, their windows aglow with lantern light. No one's house looked as new as the ones in Higher Ground, yet Josiah sensed that the folks in Willow Ridge had everything they needed. They were happy here.

Why not talk to Miriam about a partnership? Josiah wondered as he returned to where he'd started walking half an hour earlier. The lamp was burning in Rebecca's apartment above Ben's smithy. If he knocked now, he could ask her about the café's business before her lights went out.

But then the apartment went dark.

Josiah sighed. He should probably move on. Cooking at the Sweet Seasons would mean getting involved with the Hooleys and the Brennemans, and he was used to being his own man. A lone wolf didn't run well with a pack.

He saw that Ben and Miriam's house was dark, too. They'd probably been asleep for a while, and so had Lena.

Ten minutes later Josiah had hitched Dolly to his rig and was rolling down the dark road without a backward glance. He'd be back in Bloomfield by midnight.

Chapter Four

"Don't know how to tell ya this, so I'll say it straight out," Miriam murmured as Lena entered the kitchen. "Josiah's clothes are gone."

Lena nipped her lip. She gazed out the back window, toward the barn where his rig had been parked.

"Ben told me he and Josiah had words last night. He's guessin' your fella's either gone to Higher Ground or back to Bloomfield."

Considering how Josiah usually reacted to criticism, this came as no surprise. As Lena assessed how she felt about his leaving, however, her eyes remained dry. She hugged her unborn baby. "Josiah's gotten *gut* at *gut*-bye. He's like a bee, flitting from flower to flower. Doesn't like to be tied down."

"I'm sorry you're feelin' his stinger again," Miriam remarked. "But you've got a place to stay as long as ya need one. You and the baby will be just fine, and you'll eventually figure out what God's got in mind for ya. He always has a plan."

"I'm counting on that," Lena said with a sigh. "It seems every time I make my own plans, someone changes them for me. What can I do to help you, Miriam?"

The lines around Miriam's chocolate brown eyes crinkled. "We don't have church today, so Ben and I figure to read a bit and spend a quiet morning. Rebecca, Rhoda, Andy, and his kids'll be here for dinner, along with Rachel, Micah, and their new baby—and Ben's brothers'll join us, too, along with Nora and her daughter, Millie. Our whole family will be together, except for Ben's two aunts bein' in Cedar Creek for the weekend."

Lena smiled sadly, missing her family back home. "I feel honored that you're including me—"

"Don't get down on yourself just because Josiah's judgment took a turn for the worse." Miriam came over to grasp Lena's shoulders. "Everybody hits bottom now and again. It's how we bounce back that determines how high—and how far—we'll go once we're headed in the right direction."

A smile eased over Lena's face, which was a huge improvement over the way she usually fell apart when Josiah left her. "Keep reminding me of that. These past couple of days with you folks has already improved my outlook."

"Glad to hear it." Miriam opened the cabinet where she kept the dishes. "Wonder if Rebecca's joinin' us for breakfast? She never says so, knowin' I'd like her to be in church, but I suspect she catches up on her Web site design business on Sundays." She chuckled as though this secret about her English daughter tickled her. "What with helpin' Andy Leitner at his clinic and waitin' tables during the breakfast shift, I don't know how that girl keeps up with her computer work. She's brought us a lot of new business by designin' Web sites for the café and the Schrocks' quilt shop, and now the mill and Nora's consignment store, too."

Lena's eyebrows rose as she set the table. "Your bishop's agreeable to online advertising? Josiah and Savilla would be in big trouble if the church leaders in Bloomfield found out they had a Web site."

"Oh, we couldn't be online without Rebecca bein' English," Miriam replied. "And because Willow Ridge is just a wee spot in the road, Bishop Tom knows our shops wouldn't support us without tourists findin' us. Tom put his foot down, though, when we discovered that Hiram Knepp had a fancy Web site with his full-face picture on it."

"Oh, my. He should've known better."

"Ya got that right," Miriam agreed as she took a pan of baked oatmeal from the oven. "He had a big business breedin' and trainin' Belgians—in the barn where Nora's Simple Gifts shop is. That photograph was the first in a string of forbidden things we found out about Hiram when he was our bishop. Sad story. And a nasty breakup of his family, as well."

Once again Lena felt uneasy about Higher Ground, and she hoped Josiah had headed back to Bloomfield. It would be just like him to hire on with Hiram, however, if only because these well-intentioned folks had told him not to.

Maybe he's not ready to be a father. Josiah has a contrary attitude about everything that's important.

Lena kept this startling thought to herself. If her baby's father was going to run the other way for the rest of his life, she should indeed consider staying with the Hooleys rather than doggedly standing by Josiah. The midwife in Bloomfield had said the baby would come in less than two months, so she needed to have her plan in place.

When they'd put the baked oatmeal and a bowl of fried apples on the table, Miriam called Ben. The three of them bowed their heads for a moment of silent thanks.

"We're gettin' in some quiet time before the others arrive," Ben said as he spooned up some baked oatmeal. "Once Andy Leitner's kids get here with Rhoda—"

"Taylor and Brett, from Andy's first marriage," Miriam clarified.

"—and Rachel's new baby starts fussin', it'll get noisier than we're used to," he finished with a chuckle.

"*Puh!* You'll grab little Amelia at the first sign of a whimper," Miriam teased. She smiled brightly at Lena. "Amelia's our first grandbaby, born just a couple of months ago. And with Andy joinin' the Old Order and marryin' my Rhoda in September, we've got his kids in the family now, too. It's been an exciting autumn."

"Not many brides have their wedding interrupted by the birthin' of a baby," Ben recounted with a chuckle. "Rachel was Rhoda's side-sitter, and she'd gone past her due date. What with Andy bein' the groom *and* the local nurse, Bishop Tom halted the vows so Andy could take Rachel upstairs when her contractions got the best of her."

"The wedding was in that big white house down the lane behind the Sweet Seasons. That's where my girls grew up, and where Rachel and Micah live now," Miriam explained. "We ladies decided to serve the wedding dinner—over in the Brennemans' shop—so the guests wouldn't be listenin' to Rachel cry out with her birthin' pains. By the time the second shift of guests had eaten their meal, Amelia had been born, and everybody returned to the house so Rhoda and Andy could take their vows. We got a new son-in-law and a new grandbaby on the same day!"

Lena hugged her unborn child, touched by the love on the Hooleys' faces—and amazed at yet another unusual situation in their family. It was rare for an English person—and a divorced one—to be accepted into the Amish faith. "I wish my baby was going to have a family like yours," she blurted out.

"Oh, Lena, I can't imagine your *mamm* and *dat* will stay mad once they've got a grandchild," Miriam insisted as she reached for Lena's hand.

Lena sighed. Maybe she should explain how things had been at home, before the rest of Miriam and Ben's family arrived. Her feelings about her parents were so upsetting, so jumbled up. "My *mamm* didn't tell me a thing about how babies happen," she began tentatively, "so when she figured out why I was throwing up, she got really mad at me—and at Josiah. I was hardly even showing when my folks sent me to stay with my *maidel* aunt Clara up in Keota."

"That's the way it often goes," Miriam remarked. "So were ya figurin' to give the baby up for adoption?"

Lena smiled ruefully. "That's the way my parents had it planned. But I just *can't* give this baby away, Miriam! I *know* it's a boy, and he's such a part of me that—"

"*Jah*, I understand about that," Miriam murmured sympathetically.

"—I can't stand to think about anybody else raising him, even though my circumstances aren't the best," Lena finished in a rush. "Sometimes Josiah's with me on that, and then he gets scared—like he is now."

"I think you've hit the nail on the head," Ben said

with a nod. "No matter what Josiah says, though, I suspect he's in this for the long haul. Otherwise he wouldn't have brought you to Missouri."

Lena's breath escaped in a rush. "Truth be told, he came to Aunt Clara's to visit me one last time before he took the job in Higher Ground, and when she caught us chatting in her basement, she called my parents—said she was setting me out. Mamm wanted me to stay with them rather than leaving with Josiah, but Dat told me not to come home if I went with him. I—I got really upset and begged Josiah not to leave me alone. So here we are."

Lena waited for the Hooleys' expressions to register their disgust and disapproval. During the next few moments of silence, however, she saw compassion on their faces rather than any sign that they, too, wanted to be rid of her.

"What about Josiah's family? Would they help ya?" Ben asked as he passed her the biscuits.

"They died in a buggy wreck. Josiah and Savilla were at their grandparents' house that day—not even in school yet—so that's who raised them."

"*Ach*, what a nasty way to go," Miriam murmured. "And what a shock to those poor children."

"That might explain why Josiah's afraid to get too attached to ya," Ben remarked pensively. "Maybe he believes the folks he loves will get snatched away like his parents did."

Lena blinked. Ben's perspective on Josiah's personality made a lot of sense. "Their *dawdi* died years ago, and their *mammi* passed last winter, so he and his sister stayed on the farm to run their catering business," she explained. "Josiah was so excited when he saw the ad for the Higher Ground colony—he refuses to listen to anything negative about Hiram Knepp. But I'm glad you've told us the truth."

"We couldn't let ya go to Higher Ground with such high hopes, knowin' how Hiram's led so many folks astray with his lies," Ben explained. "He tried to force Miriam to marry him—"

"And he thought he could buy the Sweet Seasons building on the sly, so he could take my café away from me," Miriam chimed in with a shake of her head. "Nora and Luke sent him packin' a couple of months ago when he was playin' one against the other with his lies, too. Ya can't believe anything he says."

Once again Lena felt grateful to be staying with such generous people. When she bit into her biscuit, it was surprisingly light and puffy, with a sweet crunchiness of sunflower seeds and raisins. "This is tasty! I've never eaten a biscuit with *stuff* in it."

Miriam chuckled. "Every now and again I try new recipes. These are angel biscuits, made with yeast and—"

The back door burst open and two apple-cheeked children rushed inside. "Mammi and Dawdi!" the girl cried as she hugged Ben and Miriam.

"We're eating breakfast with you because the grown-ups are sleeping in," her little brother exclaimed.

"And we just happen to have something tasty for you kids," Ben said as he squeezed them playfully. "This is our new friend, Lena Esh. Lena, these wild monkeys belong to Rhoda and Andy—the newlyweds," he added with a smile. "Taylor is ten and Brett's eight."

"Almost nine," the boy piped up. "You're gonna have a baby!"

"I am," Lena replied, wondering what path this conversation might take. The kids still sounded English, yet they appeared comfortable wearing Plain clothing. They seemed in awe of her condition, rather than inclined to ask embarrassing questions.

"Aunt Rachel's baby is so cute," Taylor said as she hung up their coats. "We've told Mamm and Dat we want a baby brother or sister for Christmas, but I doubt it'll happen that fast."

"I suspect you're right about that," Miriam said as she steered them toward chairs near Ben. "Besides baked oatmeal and biscuits, I've got bread for toast—"

"Toast with peanut butter and jelly, please," Taylor said.

"And a banana," Brett added as he clambered into his chair.

"Monkey food for monkeys," Ben teased.

Miriam glanced at the giggling kids as she sliced some bread. "God's waitin' to hear from ya before ya eat, remember."

The two children bowed their heads, assuming an angelic air that Lena found charming. As she listened to their talk about changing from public school to Teacher Alberta's Plain schoolroom, she got another glimpse of Willow Ridge from a newcomer's viewpoint.

By the time they were cleaning up the breakfast dishes, Nora had arrived with her fiancé Luke, her daughter Millie, and Luke's younger brother Ira. Millie, who was Lena's age and redheaded like her mother, was engaged to Ira. Ben played checkers with Brett in the front room while he discussed his younger brothers' week at their gristmill, making specialty flours and selling fresh eggs, as well as goat cheese their aunts made and butter from Bishop Tom Hostetler's dairy.

Nora and Millie had brought a big macaroni and goat cheese casserole as their dinner contribution.

Soon Miriam's daughter Rachel came in with a pan of apple pie bars, followed by her blond husband Micah, who carried baby Amelia in a basket.

"Oh, here's our new girl!" Miriam cooed. She took the basket while Rachel and Micah removed their coats. As though drawn by a magnet, Ben left his checkers game to greet his new granddaughter, and the kids crowded around her, too.

What a picture it made, with three generations smiling at tiny Amelia, nestled in Ben's arms. Lena hoped with all her heart that someday her family would welcome her baby with such love. Soon after Rhoda and Andy arrived with Andy's mother, Betty, the women began setting the table for dinner. Rebecca breezed in through the back door, joining the kitchen chatter as though she were a young Plain woman instead of a Web site designer. The delectable aroma of Rhoda's oven-fried chicken mingled with the fragrance of Nora's mac and cheese and the home-canned green beans Miriam was heating on the stove.

Lena felt a pang of homesickness. Aunt Clara hadn't cooked much, so the loaded table—and all the folks who were taking seats around it—carried her back to happier times and Sunday dinners her extended family had shared at home.

"Is Josiah in Higher Ground checking out the supper club?" Rhoda asked after they'd given thanks. "I'm anxious to hear about it."

Lena took two crisp chicken tenderloins and passed the platter to Rebecca. "I hope he's headed back to Bloomfield instead of signing on with Hiram," she replied. "He didn't see a building for a new restaurant while he was in Higher Ground."

Rebecca shook her head doubtfully. "I was hoping Josiah would cook a supper shift at Mamma's place."

"He and I have chatted about that," Ben remarked, smiling at Lena from the head of the table. "I'd like to see him take on that challenge, too. It would be *gut* for a lot of us."

"This could be a way to relieve Miriam of working so many hours, too," Andy Leitner put in. He was a nice-looking fellow with deep brown eyes who hadn't let his medical training stand in the way of becoming Amish.

"What kind of cooking does Josiah do?" Millie asked. She smiled at Lena from across the table. "I've never heard of a Plain fellow being a cook."

Lena felt the gazes of all fifteen people around the table, sensing they were sincerely interested in Josiah's grilling rather than skeptical of it. "He makes the best pulled pork you've ever eaten. Roasts whole hogs, too, but he's also *gut* with chicken and ribs. I hope he'll convince his sister Savilla to return to Willow Ridge with him because she makes the side dishes. They're quite a team."

"Now that sounds like *gut* eating!" Ira said.

"And nobody else in this area offers that sort of meal," Luke remarked. "Folks who stick to something they do really well—like Miriam baking and Nora bringing so many different crafts into her shop—can make *gut* money at it here. Customers pay more than I ever figured on for the specialty grains and cage-free eggs we sell at the mill."

"And everyone's shop attracts customers who visit everyone else's," Nora chimed in, "Once folks get to Willow Ridge, they spend most of a day shopping in our stores."

Lena nodded, her hopes rising. In Bloomfield, Josiah and Savilla had to travel to the events they catered. Cooking in one place, where their customers came to them, would save them a lot of road time and effort.

Across the table, Millie lit up like a lamp. "What if we asked Josiah to cook your wedding feast, Mamma?" she asked excitedly. "It would be something different from the traditional chicken roast."

"That sounds awesome!" Ira replied. "You broke the mold by joining the Mennonites, so why not serve a different sort of dinner?"

Nora's eyes widened. "*I'm* no cook," she teased, "so I was depending on Miriam and the usual helpers to handle the meal. But if Josiah grilled, those ladies wouldn't have to work so hard."

"That might help Josiah decide whether he wants to set up his business here, too," Ben pointed out. "He and Savilla would meet everybody for miles around—and if the guests leave a lot of food, they'll know our folks don't like his cooking before he commits."

"Do you suppose Josiah and his sister could do that on such short notice?" Luke asked.

"We're getting hitched a week from this Thursday," Nora explained. "But that should give Henry Zook at the market plenty of time to get the meat ordered, along with the other food they would need."

The baby began kicking inside Lena, picking up on her excitement. "I'll call his cell and ask him. Maybe if Josiah knew he had a special event to cater, he'd warm up to the idea of settling here."

"We'll pay him whatever he wants to charge," Luke insisted as he grinned at Nora. "The more I think about this idea, the more I like it."

"So ya won't want me to do *anything* for your wedding?"

The room got quiet as everyone took in Miriam's plaintive expression. Lena thought the poor woman might cry because she wasn't needed for the wedding preparations.

Rhoda grabbed her mother's hand. "Nobody makes a wedding cake like you do, Mamma," she said with a knowing smile at Nora.

"And the neighbor ladies are planning a pie frolic, so there will be lots of other desserts, too," Rachel remarked.

Lena chuckled. "You make a *gut* point because I don't think Savilla's ever made a wedding cake."

"That settles it," Nora proclaimed. "I'm glad you spoke up, Miriam, because the cake you baked for Rhoda and Andy's wedding was fabulous."

Miriam shrugged modestly. "I love makin' them," she admitted, "and I'm happy that so many young folks are hitchin' up and settlin' down here. But we haven't heard Josiah's answer."

Once again everyone gazed at Lena with a sense of expectation that lifted her spirits. "I'll call him right now."

"Our phone shanty's behind the Sweet Seasons—and take your time with Josiah," Miriam added. "I think he'll be mighty glad to hear from ya."

When Lena stepped outside, gray clouds hung low over the horizon, hinting at snow, yet she felt like a little girl who held a handful of colorful balloons. From the Hooleys' lane she gazed at snow-blanketed fields dotted with dairy cows, sheep, and horses. Red barns added color to the otherwise snowy scene, and she yearned to call Willow Ridge her new home.

After Lena crossed the snow-packed blacktop and eased into the phone shanty, she stared at the phone. How could she convince Josiah to accept the opportunity Nora and the Hooleys were offering him? Although his cell was always in his pocket, Lena suspected he wouldn't answer when he saw where this call was coming from. She tapped in Josiah's number. His voice mail prompted her to leave a message.

"Josiah, you won't believe it!" she began. "Nora's asked you to cater her and Luke's wedding a week from Thursday. Everybody wants to try your food—wants you and Savilla to set up your business here. Wouldn't working at the Sweet Seasons be easier than hauling your cookers everywhere?" she added.

If she made this sound like a command performance, however, Josiah would turn a deaf ear. Lena closed her eyes, praying for the right words. "Why not give it a shot?" she murmured earnestly. "If this event doesn't go the way you want—or if you and Savilla have a better idea for your catering business—it's okay. You have to do this your way or it won't work. I—I love you, Josiah. And I miss you something awful."

Lena hung up, fearing she'd sounded desperate—and hoping Josiah didn't think she was using this wedding to lure him back to her.

"This is bigger than you and me and the baby, Josiah," she whispered as she hugged their unborn child. "It's about taking your place in another part of God's world, where you'll do well—if you'll only believe that."

Josiah didn't call her back, so Lena left the phone shanty. There was nothing to do but wait.

Chapter Five

Josiah waited for the incoming call to end and the voice mail number to appear on his cell phone screen. If it was Lena, he wasn't sure he could resist the sound of her voice. It had been a knee-jerk reaction to abandon her the moment he heard her neediness and saw the disappointment in her blue eyes, and he regretted that. Maybe if he'd had a *dat* to show him how to be the man of a family . . . maybe if Dat and his *mamm* hadn't been killed in that rig wreck, snatched away without any rhyme or reason, he wouldn't be so afraid to love Lena. If he lost her, too . . .

Josiah finally tapped his phone screen and listened as Lena's voice rose with excitement, telling him of a Willow Ridge wedding dinner before easing into that husky murmur that did crazy things to him.

I love you, Josiah. And I miss you something awful.

Why had Lena stuck with him so long, believing he could make something of himself? Josiah tucked his cell into his pocket. She'd probably used the Hooleys' phone, which meant Ben or Miriam might hear his message if he called her back. So he didn't.

"What was that all about?" Savilla demanded. She stood at the stove, warming a can of soup for their Sunday dinner. Her purple dress was faded and her face seemed pale beneath the black hair that was tucked under her *kapp*. "For a moment you lost that hangdog look you've had lately. Must've been Lena, huh?"

Josiah's lips twitched. How did women figure out what he was caught up in—and how he should respond—before *he* knew? "You and I have been asked to cater a wedding dinner next week," he replied. "I'm guessing we could use the kitchen of that café I told you about—"

"We've worked in worse places."

"—and the whole town would probably come out for it," Josiah continued in the most nonchalant tone he could muster. "We could run our business from there, too, once everybody gets a taste of our food. Miriam's all for it, but Ben wants the details in writing. I just don't know about that."

Savilla planted a fist on her hip. "Fine and dandy, but what'll we do with this farm and the animals? What'll we say to the neighbors? And what'll you tell that Knepp fellow?" she demanded. "Lots of questions have been hanging fire since you saw his ad, and I've not heard any answers!"

"You know, I've had *enough* of people telling me what to do," Josiah retorted.

"Then make up your mind," his sister shot back. "You suddenly have some new opportunities, and until you commit to one of them, Lena and I are left hanging. I don't like feeling so betwixt and between, Josiah."

"So marry Floyd Stoltzfus and your troubles will be

over," he blurted out, regretting his words even before they rang in the high-ceilinged kitchen.

As Savilla faced the stove again, her crestfallen expression made Josiah want to kick himself. Why did he smart off to everyone lately, wounding the two young women who loved and depended on him? Floyd had wanted to court Savilla for months, but why would his beautiful sister hitch up with a widower who was ten years her senior and had four rambunctious kids? Stoltzfus ran a sawmill and had all the personality of the sawdust that clung to his shaggy hair.

"That was a low blow. Sorry," Josiah mumbled.

The color rose in Savilla's cheeks. "Join the church and marry Lena and *your* troubles will be over," she shot back. "Or at least your soul—and your baby—will have a future. If marrying Floyd would make you take charge of your life, Josiah, I'd do it in a heartbeat."

Josiah went to the counter to slice some bread. He couldn't expect Savilla to keep this old place running by herself, and he really didn't want her to marry Floyd. "Okay, so let's cater that wedding next week," he suggested. "If our food's a hit, we can sign on with Miriam to do a supper shift in her café."

"And if her husband tells us to move on? What then?"

"Maybe by then Knepp's supper club will be built."

"And what'll we do about this farm?" Savilla repeated. "Considering the consequences of your snap decisions has never been your strong point, little brother."

Josiah winced, knowing she was right. But if he put their property up for sale, who would buy it? The dingy paint in the kitchen was a minor detail compared to the deteriorating boards in the barn and the leaning pasture fences. He'd been too busy cooking the past few years to remedy the many problems of this poor old place.

"Let's say we could sell the farm," Josiah began cautiously. "Then we could probably afford a house in Willow Ridge. Meanwhile, the Hooleys have offered Lena their *dawdi haus*, and they were letting me stay in a spare bedroom—"

"Buying a house in a new town is a big step," Savilla interrupted. "If the farm sells and then we can't support ourselves in Willow Ridge—along with Lena and the baby—what'll we do? If we stay here, at least we won't have to worry about keeping a roof over our heads."

Why did new opportunities present so many problems? Savilla was making valid points, however, and she wouldn't let him pretend he had no responsibility for creating a new life—and for the mother of his child. Savilla and Lena expected him to be the man of this family, so why couldn't he step up and do right by them?

"All right, here's the deal," Josiah stated, hoping to be done with this push and pull of conflicting feelings. "We'll cook for that wedding. If Willow Ridge and the people there don't appeal to you, we'll come back to Bloomfield and keep on catering."

Savilla ladled soup into two bowls, considering her response. "We'll have a lot more work than we've been used to, serving supper five or six nights a week," she mused aloud. "You and I can't do that by ourselves, and Lena will have a baby to care for, so she won't be helping us."

Josiah considered the folks he'd observed while

he'd eaten breakfast in the Sweet Seasons. "With Miriam having a baby at Christmastime, and one of her waitress daughters getting married a while back, we might have to scout the wedding crowd for help," he replied as he set the bread on the table. "And I have a feeling that because Miriam wants a supper shift to succeed, she'll help us find the folks we need. She's a woman who makes *gut* things happen, you know?"

A tentative smile warmed Savilla's dark eyes. "I'd like to meet this Miriam," she murmured. "I miss being with our *mammi*. She always believed that if she asked God for something, she would receive His answer in due time."

"She was a strong woman, our grandmother. Miriam's a lot like her," Josiah murmured, reaching for his sister's hand. "You're strong, too, Savilla. I don't know what I'd do if you ever gave up on me."

"Don't you forget that," she teased. "Who knows? Maybe I'll meet a nice guy in Willow Ridge and get hitched. You'd better take care of Lena, or someday you'll be all by your lonesome."

Was that a sparkle in his sister's eyes? A whisper of hope for her future? None of the eligible fellows around Bloomfield suited her so maybe a fresh start in Missouri was a better idea than he'd originally figured on.

It was worth the effort of cooking up a wedding feast to find out.

Ben shifted one of the two wrought-iron trellises he'd made for the Simple Gifts shop, following Nora's directions.

"Shift it a hair to the left," she said from behind him. "Perfect! These will probably be gone by the end of the week, considering how fast your other pieces have sold."

Ben gazed at the amazing amount of merchandise Plain crafters had consigned to Nora's store. Walnut bedroom sets, hand-tooled saddles, and wooden rocking horses sold soon after they were tagged. Magnificent quilts and hand-sewn banners hung from the loft railing. Even on this dreary Monday afternoon, ladies eagerly fingered embroidered linens and pottery— customers he'd seen eating lunch at the Sweet Seasons earlier.

"I'm glad your place is doing so well," he remarked. "And these orders for trellises and garden gates keep me busy when nobody's bringing their horses in to be shod."

"I never dreamed I'd attract so much business so fast," the redheaded shopkeeper confessed as she accompanied him to the door. "The store's only been open two months, and every day I'm calling my crafters with special orders or asking them to replenish their stock."

"And to think ya might not've come back to Willow Ridge," Ben teased as he slung an arm around her shoulders. "I'm glad you'll be my sister-in-law, Nora. Luke might've wandered like a lost sheep for the rest of his life had ya not come along to straighten him out!"

As they laughed together, Ben put on his hat and coat. He opened the door to leave, and then gazed toward the county road that ran between his home and the café. "Are my eyes playin' tricks on me or is that horse pullin' a wagonload of grills?"

Nora peered around his shoulder and then clapped him on the back. "Looks like Luke and I will have quite a wedding feast! I hope this all works out," she added pensively. "Lena and Josiah are so young, and they have no idea what they've set themselves up for by, um, accident."

"No child happens by accident," Ben reminded her. "God's got a plan for Lena's baby, just like he did for your Millie."

"You're right," Nora replied with a grateful smile. "Don't let on, but at the surprise shower I'm having for Miriam, we'll be making diapers and baby things for Lena, too. You two have given them rooms and a chance to succeed. Now the rest of us need to step up."

"The harder part will be gettin' Josiah to accept what we want to give him," Ben pointed out. "I'd best see where he wants to put those cookers. See ya."

Ben jogged down the snow-packed road, waving a hand above his head. He was pleased to see a young woman on the wagon seat beside Josiah. It was too bad the kid had shown up without returning Lena's call because she'd been on pins and needles ever since she'd called him.

That's the way some fellas behave until the right woman teaches them a better way. Ben laughed—at himself, mostly, for being much like Josiah at one time.

"Josiah! It's *gut* to see you and all this gear," Ben called out as he caught up to the wagon. "And I'm not includin' *you* as part of the gear, Savilla. I'm real happy to meet ya."

When the young woman with the coal black hair and snapping eyes smiled, Ben knew the local bachelors would be glad she'd come, as well. "After what Josiah's told me about you and your wife, I can't wait to cater this wedding, Ben," she said as he helped her to the ground. "Our food's not fancy, but folks scrape our pans clean when we cook at community events."

"I'm gettin' hungry just thinkin' about it." Ben focused on Josiah then, and on his wagonload of equipment. "What sort of a place do ya need for your cookers?"

"Some of them use propane and I burn charcoal and wood chips in the others," Josiah replied. "In the winter they have to be out of the wind or it's impossible to maintain the temperature for cooking whole hogs."

"We brought our steam table, too," Savilla said. "I wasn't sure what you might already have for serving the food."

"It'll be *gut* to have another one besides Miriam's." Ben pointed to a long building that sat across a field behind his smithy. "Nora and Luke are havin' their dinner in the Brennemans' cabinetry shop because it holds more folks than anyplace else for weddings and funerals and such."

"We'll need to speak with Nora about the menu and get our food ordered," Savilla said. She turned slowly, taking in the surrounding houses and Bishop Tom's Holsteins, as well as Miriam's orchard and the sheep at the Kanagy place. "What a homey town this is. And the buildings are in better condition than several we saw between here and Iowa."

Ben smiled at her observation. "We take pride in our home places, and in our new businesses, too. Plain communities where folks depend mostly on farmin' are strugglin' these days."

"And some Plain folks—like us—aren't cut out to be crop farmers." Savilla looked at him with sparkling coffee-brown eyes. "How's Lena? I'm grateful to you and your wife for giving her and Josiah a place to stay."

"Last I saw of them, she and my Miriam were cro-chetin' baby things," Ben said, gesturing toward his home across the road. "We've got room for you, as well, Savilla. Let's head over there and get out of this cold wind. Miriam and Lena will be happy to see the two of ya."

As they crossed the county blacktop, Ben felt much better about the possibility of a supper shift in the Sweet Seasons. Savilla Witmer impressed him as an astute young woman who probably kept the books for their catering business—and kept her brother focused on his cooking. He also sensed that Josiah's attitude had improved since he'd left on Saturday night. If they could take over in the café's kitchen, maybe Miriam would finally be willing to stay at home. . . .

"It would be a *gut* idea to either call Hiram Knepp or drop him a line to tell him you're not gonna cook in Higher Ground—at least not for a while," Ben added, to leave Josiah's options open. "If he gets word you're caterin' the wedding next week—and then if ya decide to stay on—he'll be mighty perturbed."

"I suspect Mr. Knepp will be unhappy anyway, considering that Josiah had agreed to be in Higher Ground by now," Savilla remarked with a rise of her eyebrow. "If you don't *tell* him you've changed your mind, Josiah, you've gone back on your word and lied to him."

"Higher Ground's not that far away," Ben pointed out, "and we know first-hand about the trouble Hiram causes when folks cross him. If I were you, son, I'd get squared away with him sooner rather than later."

"*Jah, jah,* I get that," Josiah replied impatiently. "I'll take care of it as soon as we're settled."

Ben sensed Josiah had once again turned a deaf ear toward him, so he hoped the kid would listen to his sister. The last thing they needed was a brushup with Hiram at Luke and Nora's wedding—or while the Witmers stayed with him and Miriam.

As he entered his home, however, Ben set aside his concerns. Miriam's creamed chicken and biscuits smelled heavenly. She and Lena looked happy and relaxed, as though they'd been enjoying each other's company. *A lot of* gut *things can come from these young people stayin' with us, Lord,* he thought as he removed his coat. *Please let it be so.*

Chapter Six

Miriam smiled as she looked into the Sweet Seasons dining room on Thursday morning. Savilla Witmer had insisted on helping in the café as payment for her bed and board. Along with Rhoda and Rebecca, she was seating customers, pouring coffee, and calling orders into the kitchen as though the three of them had worked together for a long time. She was quick about bussing the tables, too.

"Our crew's lookin' sharp this morning," Naomi murmured as she came to stand beside Miriam. "Everything's goin' like clockwork—and my youngest son's takin' in the new scenery, too, I see."

Miriam chuckled. Her partner handled the menu orders and kept the steam table stocked so Miriam could concentrate on baking the breads, pastries, and pies. "*Jah,* your Aaron and Matthias Wagler both seem real perky this morning. It's nice that Savilla's as capable as she is pretty."

"Let's hope she and her brother stay in Willow Ridge, so she'll know how the café runs when Rhoda quits workin' to have kids," Naomi remarked. "My Hannah's better in the kitchen—"

"And even if Lena and Josiah were married, it wouldn't be proper for her to be out amongst the customers in her condition," Miriam added.

Naomi leaned out to assess the breakfast buffet, where Bishop Tom and retired preacher Gabe Glick were loading their plates. "I'd better refill the creamed chicken pan and have Lena make more waffles. Our new breakfast dish is a big hit."

When the timer dinged, Miriam opened the oven door. Her loaves of chocolate apple bread had risen into nut-crusted humps, and their cinnamon-cocoa fragrance would make the whole café smell luscious. Customers snapped up the goodies in the bakery case a lot faster when the aromas of her breads greeted them at the door.

"Miriam, let me help you!" Savilla insisted as she grabbed some pot holders. "My word, how do you carry six loaves of hot bread at one time?"

Miriam shrugged as the young woman grasped the rack's other side. "I've baked my bread in big batches ever since we opened the Sweet Seasons," she explained. "Makes more sense to have the pans in one rack than to handle pan after pan after pan. *Denki* for helpin'."

After she and Savilla had removed the six-loaf rack of apricot banana bread from the oven, Savilla inhaled deeply. "These smell terrific," she murmured. "And Bishop Tom wants me to pass along his compliments on the chicken and waffles, too. He's on his second plateful."

Miriam laughed, watching Lena remove steaming waffles from the two irons. "It's the butter and milk from his cows, along with the chickens and eggs from our deacon, Reuben Riehl, that makes everything we serve extra-special *gut*. Send my compliments right back to the bishop, will ya?"

Savilla's laughter rang in the kitchen. "The city English we serve at our barbecues love knowing their food is locally grown. Never mind that we Amish have been growing what we eat for centuries."

"Here's creamed chicken for the buffet table," Naomi said from the stove.

"I'm making these waffles as fast as I can," Lena added as she closed the lids on her waffle irons. "Those guys are putting away a lot of food this morning."

"And they're not gonna starve any time soon, so don't get in a dither about bein' a little behind," Miriam said as Savilla carried the creamed chicken to the steam table.

Lena focused on the waffle irons' red monitor lights. Hannah began filling individual teapots with hot water to serve the residents of a nearby senior center, who'd come for their weekly breakfast outing. Miriam mixed powdered sugar, almond flavoring, and milk in a large glass measuring cup to drizzle over the fruit breads, pleased that her kitchen was running so smoothly. As she loosened the loaves from their pans, however, both Lena and Hannah cried out.

"*Ach*, I didn't mean to bump—"

"Watch out for this boiling—"

"*Oh*—oohh!"

Lena's waffles and Hannah's hot water flew all over the center of the kitchen as the girls grabbed each other. Stainless-steel pots clattered to the floor and rolled around.

"Everybody all right?" Miriam asked as she fetched the mop.

"We're fine, but we've made a big mess!" Hannah exclaimed.

"And now I've ruined the waffles, and it'll be a long time before—before—" Lena burst into tears and turned away, her shoulders shuddering.

Stepping carefully, Miriam mopped the puddles while Naomi scooped up the soggy waffles with a dust-pan. Savilla hurried back into the kitchen and relieved Miriam of her mop.

"Bless her heart, Lena's always been one to cry when something goes wrong," she murmured.

"I've noticed that, *jah*." Miriam crossed the damp floor to where Hannah was trying her best to console Lena. The two girls clasped hands as though they'd had quite a fright.

"Honey-bug, if I had a dollar for every time I spilled something, I'd be the richest gal in Willow Ridge," Miriam murmured to the sobbing blonde. "It's okay, really it is."

"But I didn't want to—I didn't mean to—"

"Of course ya didn't, but ya know what?" Miriam asked as she slung her arm around Lena's shuddering shoulders. "The floor's gettin' mopped. And the little goats Bishop Tom's wife keeps will think those waffles are a special treat. So all we've lost is some time and batter."

As Lena kept blubbering, Miriam sensed the girl's hormones were in high gear. "Why not take a break over home?" she suggested gently.

"I got upset over every little thing while I was carryin' each one of my four kids," Naomi joined in. "The best part about that is that it'll soon be behind ya, dearie."

"But—but how will I work here in the kitchen after my baby's born?" Lena wailed. "I'll have to feed him and change him and—" When the back door opened and Ben stepped inside, she hastily mopped her eyes with her apron. "I want to do my fair share, but I don't see how I can."

Miriam knew Lena's reservations were right on target, for she'd need some recovery time after she gave birth, and every new mother discovered worries that hadn't occurred to her before she held her first-born. "After I've had my wee one, maybe you can keep the babies in the morning while I bake, and then I'll tend them in the afternoon if ya want to help Josiah and Savilla with their cookin'," Miriam said. "Will ya think about that?"

Lena nodded dolefully. She smiled forlornly at Ben as she slipped into her coat and bonnet. When she stepped outside, everyone in the kitchen breathed easier.

Ben set aside his insulated coffee mug to hold the bucket so Naomi could scoop the last of the watery waffles into it. "Is Lena gonna be okay walkin' home?"

"She'll be more embarrassed if ya offer to go with her," Miriam replied. "She's feelin' frazzled today. We're *gut* to go now, thanks to these ladies helpin' so quick."

"More waffles comin' right up!" Hannah said as she returned from taking the hot tea to the dining room.

"And to what do we owe your kitchen visit, Bennie-bug? Time for a coffee break?" Miriam teased. He wasn't wearing his coat because he'd come over from the smithy, where his forge kept him warm. "There might be a sample in it for ya if ya talk to me while I drizzle frosting on this warm bread."

Ben smiled, but as he followed her to the back counter his expression turned serious. "I'm not so sure Lena should care for both babies," he murmured as Miriam removed the warm loaves from the pans. "If droppin' waffles upsets her, what'll she be like when two wee ones are cryin' and she's there by herself? She might not spring back real quick after givin' birth either, so helpin' Josiah and Savilla might be a long shot—and for all we know, the Witmers might move on to Higher Ground. And Lena might go with them."

Miriam kept drizzling the frosting over the tops of her warm loaves as she listened. "We'll cross that bridge when we come to it," she murmured. She glanced behind her to be sure the other ladies were out of earshot. "If it makes ya feel better, Rachel has offered to tend our baby when I come back to work, as she'll be home with Amelia anyway."

Ben cleared his throat. White frosting had run down a loaf of chocolate bread to puddle on the countertop, but he ignored the temptation to scoop it up with his fingertip. "What makes ya so sure you'll be able to separate yourself from your child? Once it's born, I'm guessin' you'll let Naomi run this place while ya take on your motherin' duties."

Miriam's mouth clamped shut. Although Ben's words were spoken gently, they had an unmistakable undercurrent. "Are ya sayin' these things as an excited new *dat*—or as Preacher Ben upholdin' the Old Order, tellin' me to stay home after the baby's born?" She gazed directly into her husband's hazel eyes. "Or maybe ya think I should already be at home. Is that it?"

Ben's lips flickered, but he didn't look away. "Bishop Tom's been askin' me about that—mostly because he's concerned about your welfare, and the child's. But *jah*, you're a preacher's wife, Miriam, and there's already been some murmurin' about ya runnin' this café, defyin' Old Order ways," he replied matter-of-factly. "And me, I'm wonderin' how you'll maintain a regular feedin' schedule, and what you'll do if the wee one's sick, or—well, ya sure can't be changin' dirty diapers in this kitchen. Have ya even thought about such things? *I* sure have."

Miriam suddenly needed to sit on the stool she kept close at hand. She'd known all along that their church leaders would expect her to take time off—or quit working altogether—after the baby was born. She sensed Bishop Tom was allowing her to work because she remained in the kitchen rather than carrying out orders or refilling coffee mugs, as she'd done before she married Ben at the first of the year. Amish wives were to remain modest and not show their pregnant bodies in public.

But Tom and the others have all enjoyed eatin' here these past several months—and where would they go if we closed up? Surely they know I run the Sweet Seasons more because I love feedin' people than for the money. I—I've worked so hard to build up this business. The café has seen me through some tough times.

Was she overstepping her boundaries, thinking she could continue to work? Had she ignored her responsibilities as a wife and mother? Was Ben expressing his disappointment in her because she loved running her café even as she yearned to hold his child and raise it with him?

Are You *disappointed in me, God? Have I been thinkin' like a crazy woman, forgettin' how You'd have me live this life You've blessed me with?*

The clatter of dishes and the chatter from the dining

room brought Miriam out of her uncomfortable musings. She released the breath she'd been holding. "I'll pray on it," she whispered.

But she had a feeling she'd gone far too long assuming that God—and Ben—were happy with the choices she'd been making. Miriam focused on getting the drizzle just right over the tops of two more loaves of chocolate apple bread.

"Didn't mean to hurt your feelings, Miriam."

"I know. Ya don't have a mean—or untruthful— bone in your body, Ben." She blinked back tears, determined not to let this thought-provoking conversation get the best of her. "Here—ya might as well have the first taste before I put this out for lunch."

When Miriam sliced off the end of a dark chocolate loaf and handed it to her husband, his boyish smile returned. "Guess I wouldn't get so many samples if ya weren't here bakin' every day," he admitted.

"Ya said a mouthful there." It lifted her spirits when her husband bit into the warm bread and closed his eyes with pleasure. "I'll think about what ya said, Ben."

"I know ya will, honey-bug," he murmured. "Ya understand when to follow your own notions and when to change them. That's just one more thing I love about ya."

Miriam couldn't resist kissing off a drop of frosting that had lodged in Ben's sandy-brown beard. Even when her husband acted older and sterner than she was, she counted her blessings. Before Ben had come into her life a year ago, she'd been lonelier than she cared to recall. He kissed her full on the lips before refilling his mug at the coffeemaker. Nodding at Naomi and Hannah, he returned to his smithy.

Miriam inhaled deeply to settle her thoughts. She

felt caught up in a tug-of-war, longing to continue with her business yet eager to hold a newborn for the first time in twenty-two years. Before her Jesse had died—before she'd opened the Sweet Seasons to make ends meet—she wouldn't even have *considered* working outside her home.

Is this what a taste of independence has done to me, Lord? Have I wandered from the path You'd have me follow? I want to believe You brought me to this place in my life for a gut reason . . .

"Miriam! You're just the woman I want to see!" a cheerful, familiar voice called out.

When Miriam looked up, she couldn't help smiling. Nora was wearing a cape dress made of a paisley pattern in shades of pink, green, purple, and orange that brightened the entire kitchen. "How's our bride-to-be?" she asked.

"Never better." Nora's freckled face lit up. "I'm having a hen party at my place Saturday night for the gals who're helping at the wedding—so you're all invited!" she gushed, opening her arms to include everyone in the kitchen. "Savilla, I want you and Lena to come, too. What a party we're going to have after the wedding, thanks to you and Josiah—so we'll celebrate before the wedding, as well!"

Miriam felt her clouds of gloom dissipating. "What a fine idea, Nora. I could use some fun and frolic."

"Oh, we'll frolic all right," Nora replied lightly.

Was that a wink the redhead gave Naomi and Hannah? And did their smiles seem just a little bit secretive?

Miriam didn't ask. It was blessing enough to return to her usual good mood after her talk with Ben had caught her off guard. *There's a time to mourn and a time to dance,* she reminded herself as she finished frosting her bread.

The baby within her shifted as Nora chatted about the menu she and the Witmers had chosen for her wedding dinner. To Miriam, it was a sign that life went on despite a few rocks in the road. She decided to rejoice and be glad for that.

When the Sweet Season's back door slammed and he heard Lena bawling, Josiah focused on pounding nails. The enclosure he was building would provide a windbreak for his cookers: It attached to the café and quilt shop building on one end and to Ben's smithy on the other, and the single wooden wall would be easy to dismantle if he went on to Higher Ground.

He was keeping his options open, by not hinting to Hiram Knepp about a change of plans until after Luke and Nora's wedding dinner. No matter what Savilla thought, he hadn't really set a date for starting work at the supper club. He'd discussed several ideas during that phone call with Knepp, but as far as Josiah was concerned, nothing had been nailed down.

When Lena's wailing got louder, he turned to look at her. Despite her advanced pregnancy, she appeared small and fragile. Framed by her black bonnet, her face looked very pale as she wiped her eyes on the sleeve of her coat.

"Trouble in the kitchen?" he ventured cautiously. "I thought you and the ladies were getting along."

Lena blew her nose loudly. "The kitchen's fine now that everyone's cleaned up the big mess I made," she whimpered. "The problem is *me*. I feel so fat and clumsy, so lost and alone that I—I don't belong anywhere anymore. I just want to go *home!*"

Josiah's eyebrows rose. Some of Lena's problems were in her head—or so it seemed to him—and most of them went beyond his ability to fix them. "Sorry, girl, but I can't take you," he murmured. "I'm not even sure where home is right now. I'm riding this wave of change, seeing where I land when it drops me off."

"I'm not asking you to take me back to Bloomfield," Lena countered testily. "My folks wouldn't allow me into their house anyway. But—but—"

Josiah sighed as she burst into tears again. He'd grown tired of the drama Lena created, yet he slung a sympathetic arm around her. "My room's above yours, and I heard you shifting a lot in bed last night," he remarked. "Are you not getting enough sleep?"

"Could *you* sleep with somebody rolling and kicking inside you?" she retorted. "No matter how I position myself, my back hurts. My legs ache from standing on hard floors and—"

"Sounds like it's time for a nap."

"*Nap?*" Lena shot back. She sighed loudly. "That's what Miriam said, too, but I feel like I'd be slacking—" When the door clicked, she buried her head against Josiah's chest. "Phooey. Now Ben's out here."

Josiah glanced over his shoulder, waving at Hooley. "We're taking a little time out," he explained. "Got my wall built, though. Thanks for the lumber."

"Looks real *gut*, too," the farrier replied as he studied the wooden enclosure. He smiled knowingly. "I'll leave you two to settle things."

When Ben had gone inside his smithy, Josiah eased

away from Lena. "What if I walk you across the road
and we have some cocoa before I unload my cookers?"
he murmured. "Maybe we could snuggle while nobody
else is there."

When Lena's blue eyes lit up, Josiah's insides tightened. He craved physical contact, yet he was wary of
making her think this was a forever kind of situation.
He just didn't know if he could navigate all the changes
that were coming at him—wasn't sure he could be
the *dat* she wanted for her baby, even though he was
supposed to act responsible. If his own father had
lived, maybe he'd be stronger, more confident when it
came to loving—but such wishes wouldn't get Lena
through her crying spell.

As Josiah steered Lena across the road, he noticed
that her waddle was more pronounced, and that she
held the small of her back with both hands. Her protruding belly led the way across the blacktop, and by
the time they had topped the Hooleys' lane, she was
short of breath.

Lena perked up, however, as she made two mugs of
cocoa. While they sat together on the couch in the
front room, Josiah wondered if he'd ever be able to
afford a home like this one, and if he would ever make
anything of himself. As they sipped the warm cocoa,
he listened to Lena prattling about her morning in
Miriam's kitchen. He enjoyed the feel of her warm
body as he held her and she rested her head against
his chest.

Within minutes, Lena was asleep.

Josiah set her empty mug on the end table. He let
the peace of the moment wash over him, awed by the
way the baby in Lena's belly shifted against him. When
she was sound asleep, he eased away from her and

placed a pillow beneath her head. Struck by her fragile beauty, Josiah kissed her cheek. He gently tucked an afghan around her and left the house, careful not to let the wind snatch the door from his hand.

Now what? It'll take a lot more than cocoa and a nap to solve Lena's problems—and yours.

To keep from stewing over how he could support himself, his sister, Lena, and a helpless newborn, he unloaded his grilling equipment. Hefting the weight of his icy-cold barrel cookers and grills made Josiah work quickly, without distracting thoughts. Soon the tools of his trade—most of them rusty and blackened with burned grease—were lined up along the new wall like old friends.

Josiah allowed himself to believe the wedding feast would be a huge success, after which he and Savilla would become welcome new residents in Willow Ridge. Whistling under his breath, he strode toward the blue-roofed Zook's Market down the road to finalize his menu order. Because Luke Hooley had advanced the cash to cover the wedding feast, Preacher Henry had been pleased to provide the beef, pork, and chickens Josiah would grill—food that would give wedding guests something to talk about for months to come.

That was his plan, anyway. Serving up success one tasty plateful at a time.

Chapter Seven

Lena huffed up Nora's long driveway Saturday evening, wondering if she would ever again be able to draw full, deep breaths. Miriam walked alongside her without any apparent discomfort despite her age. In fact, her companion's face lit up with girlish glee as they approached the largest, fanciest house in town.

"What a treat to be comin' here," Miriam exclaimed as they stepped onto the big front porch. "I've known Nora since she was a wee girl, ya see—and when her *dat* banished her for gettin' in the family way, I felt awful bad for her. Couldn't believe bright, responsible Nora would get herself into such a predicament, much less dump her baby off at her brother's place," she added in a lower voice. "But God was leadin' her all along—even though she didn't realize it when the bishop in Morning Star took advantage of her fear and innocence."

Lena's eyes widened. She'd heard Nora's situation had been similar to her own, yet the story had a different spin when a church leader came into the picture.

If Nora had reunited with her family and turned her life around, maybe there was hope for her and Josiah's baby.

"Come on in—it's open!" a female voice called out.

When they stepped inside, a loud chorus of "Surprise! Surprise!" made Miriam stop in her tracks. Her mouth dropped open. A roomful of smiling faces greeted them, and from the crowd Lena picked out Rebecca, Rhoda, Naomi, Hannah, Rachel—and even Savilla!

"What's goin' on here?" Miriam asked in a tight voice. A big banner that said WELCOME, BABIES! was hanging across the kitchen entryway, and Lena noticed a long table in the front room where women sat cutting lengths of fabric.

Nora hurried over to them, wearing a mischievous grin. "Okay, I fibbed a little when I called this a party for my wedding helpers," she said as she grabbed their hands. "It *is* a party, but it's a shower for you two! We've been sewing diapers and gowns and onesies, figuring you've neither one had much of a chance to do that."

Lena's hand fluttered to her mouth as she spotted the stack of diapers already folded at the end of the table. Aunt Clara hadn't had a lot of money to spare—not that she'd been inclined to spend any on Lena's baby—so Lena had worried about having basic necessities before the baby arrived. "Oh, I never expected anybody to go to such trouble—and for *me*," she gasped.

"This is the way we do it in Willow Ridge," Miriam said, "so we'd better just let everybody spoil us, Lena. There's no stoppin' these gals when they decide to have a frolic for somebody."

"You've done more than your share of helpin' other

folks, Miriam," Naomi piped up from one of the sewing machines.

"For sure and for certain," a young dark-haired woman joined in. She looked up from the diaper she was cutting. "The surprise birthday party you threw when I turned eighteen was—well, you almost had to pick me up off the floor. And I'm forever grateful."

"Lena, this is Annie Mae Wagler," Miriam said. "She and Adam married this past summer. They live down the hill, and along with Annie Mae's sister, Nellie—"

The younger girl on the other side of Annie Mae waved at Lena.

"—they're takin' care of their four younger siblings," Miriam continued. She gazed purposefully at Lena, lowering her voice. "Annie Mae and her sibs are Hiram Knepp's kids. It's a long story, about how she and Nellie refused to go to Higher Ground with their *dat.*"

The back of Lena's neck prickled. Here was another example of how out-of-kilter Hiram's relationships seemed to be.

"But all's well that ends well," Nora insisted cheerfully. "Come to the kitchen! We've got warm cider and all sorts of goodies."

Lena didn't realize how hungry she was until she saw the refreshments that covered the kitchen table. She put chunks of bread on a plate and covered them with warm cheese sauce, then spooned up some fruity salad sweetened with cherry pie filling and whipped topping.

"What's on the menu for your wedding dinner, Nora?" somebody called out. "I've heard it's not the typical chicken roast and creamed celery."

"Do tell, Savilla," someone else insisted. "I see there's

a whole lineup of grills and barrel cookers behind Miriam's café."

Lena sat on the couch beside Hannah, eager to hear about the wedding meal. Josiah and his sister hadn't said much about what Luke and Nora had decided upon.

Nora laughed. "We Mennonites like to do things a little differently," she teased. "The ceremony's at the church in Morning Star next Thursday morning— and I hope you'll all come," she added. "The dinner's at the Brennemans' furniture shop. With most of Luke's and my families living right here in Willow Ridge, we're not anticipating hundreds of out-of-town guests."

"Josiah was tickled that Luke wanted him to roast a whole hog," Savilla continued with a grin. "He'll also be grilling chicken quarters and slow-cooking beef briskets."

"Wow, that'll be quite a feed!" Nora's daughter Millie exclaimed. "And what're you cooking for side dishes, Savilla? It's so cool that you and your brother run this catering business together."

Lena's heart fluttered. All the women around the big front room were nodding, eager to hear the dinner details as they kept sewing.

"Nora chose spaghetti pie—which is a twist on mac and cheese—along with zucchini and carrot casserole, potato loaf, pickled eggs and relishes, baked beans, slaw, and some fruit salads," Savilla replied. "Several of you are making pies for us, and Miriam is the queen of wedding cakes in this area," she added with a big grin. "I'm thankful for that, because my cake frosting tends to look like a five-year-old smeared it on."

Friendly laughter filled the room. As Lena finished her refreshments, she realized how happy she felt despite the fact that she only knew a handful of these women. Maybe the good food had settled her nerves—or perhaps she was coming to believe that Willow Ridge was a town where neighbor helped neighbor, and where the women came together to support one another. She glanced at Hannah, who was seated beside her. "I suppose you've known all along that Nora's party was to be a frolic," she murmured.

Hannah laughed. "It wasn't easy keeping such a secret from Miriam while we were working this week," she replied, "and then Nora decided to include you, too."

Lena sighed, looking out over the roomful of women, several of whom were near her age. "I feel odd that gals I don't know are sewing baby things for me," she murmured.

"Let's fix that right now." Hannah grabbed Lena's hand and stood up. "We'll start at the far end of the room, and by the time you leave, you'll have a passel of new friends."

Lena's heart pounded. She stood up as gracefully as her baby bulk allowed and followed Hannah to the crowded worktable. "I've met Millie," she said as Nora's redheaded daughter smiled at her, "and this little pixie is Rhoda's Taylor."

"Lena, hi!" the girl exclaimed. "Mary's showing me how to hand stitch, and it's fun!"

"That would be Mary Schrock," Hannah clarified as the gray-haired woman next to Taylor smiled at them. "She and Eva and Priscilla run the quilting shop next to Miriam's café, and they provided the fabric for the diapers and gowns."

"Oh, what a gift you've given me," Lena blurted out

as she reached for the three women's hands. "I have no idea how I'll repay all these favors."

"Love your baby," Mary replied as the two women beside her nodded their agreement. "It's the gift that keeps on giving, the love we get from our *mamms*."

Lena blinked, determined not to cry—or to wonder if her own mother's love had lessened because of her unwed pregnancy. When Hannah led her further along the table, Lena noticed that the pile of diapers had gotten noticeably higher, and then she realized that the dark-haired young woman Miriam had identified as Hiram's daughter was pregnant, as well.

"Annie Mae Wagler and Nellie live next door," Hannah was saying. "We're all excited because Annie Mae's expecting, too."

"It's nice to see so many gals my own age," Lena remarked as Annie Mae gripped her hand. "Come time to have a frolic for your baby, I'll be stitching up diapers for *you!*"

The young woman's face bloomed with a smile as she adjusted her rimless glasses. "I'll appreciate that because today Nurse Andy told me I'm going to have twins!"

"Oh, my! You'll need twice as much of everything," Hannah gushed as she hugged Annie Mae's shoulders.

"Twice the patience and stamina, especially," Nellie remarked. "If Annie Mae's twins are anything like our little brothers, Josh and Joey, it'll be a full-time job just keeping the roof on the house."

"Let's hope your babies are girls rather than boys," a young woman at the end of the table teased.

"That's Katie Zook," Hannah said as she continued her introductions. "Her family runs the market—and that gal talking to Miriam is Katie's *mamm*, Lydia. Beside

Lydia is Nora's *mamm*, Wilma Glick, who lives in the little house just south of Miriam and Ben. Do you see anybody else you've not met? A few gals couldn't come tonight, but you'll meet them at Nora and Luke's wedding."

Lena sighed. "I'll try to recall everybody's name, but it seems that as the baby expands my memory contracts."

As everyone laughed with her, Lena felt better than she had since she'd left Bloomfield. She sensed that the women in this room would value her friendship and give her the advice she needed to raise her baby. By the time she'd eaten a piece of wonderfully moist apple cake and sipped a cup of warm cider, the diaper makers were clearing the scraps from their worktable. As Lydia Zook and Wilma Glick folded the little gowns and onesies, Nora was setting two large wrapped packages on the long table.

"Time for you guests of honor to open your gifts now," Nora announced.

Lena's mouth dropped. "But you've already made so many—"

"Now what'd ya go and do that for?" Miriam protested as she gaped at the packages. "It's not like this is my first baby."

"*Jah*, but how many bottles and bibs do you have at your place?" Mary Schrock teased. "The last babies you had are here amongst us, and one of them has a baby of her own!"

Lena chuckled. She sensed it was a rare occasion when Miriam's friends could take her by surprise.

"You go first, missy," Miriam said, gesturing toward the bundle with Lena's name on it.

Lena's heart overflowed with gratitude. When she

popped the wrapping paper's seam, Lena let out a gasp. "It's a carrier basket! And it's full of *stuff!*"

Miriam then ripped the paper from her package, an identical basket for taking a newborn places. "Stuff indeed!" she said. "My word, here's a diaper pail and ointment for rashy bottoms—"

"And baby shampoo and powder, and wee little socks!" Lena chimed in as she held up the items from her basket.

Miriam giggled as she grabbed a fleecy stuffed lamb and a crocheted pig. "Why do I suspect you made these, Mary Schrock?"

The lady who owned the quilting shop shrugged. "Maybe because I still like to play with toys?"

Once again laughter rose around her, and Lena's heart swelled. When she and Miriam had thanked everyone, Nora offered the three of them a ride home in her van. A warm feeling wrapped around Lena like a cuddly afghan as they rode the short distance to the Hooleys' home with Savilla.

"We'll get Ben and Josiah to carry all these gifts inside," Miriam said as Nora pulled up into the lane. "And once again, Nora, we thank ya from the bottom of our hearts. That was mighty nice of ya to have everybody over when you're busy gettin' ready for your wedding."

"You have no idea how much this evening meant to me," Lena murmured.

"I had a great time, too," Savilla said. "It was a chance to get acquainted with the women who live here."

Nora beamed at them as she shut off the engine. "That's what I was hoping for. One of the things I missed most when I was living English were the frolics Plain women have," she said. "It's even more fun to hostess one than it is to attend, so I'll have more of them. It feels good to fill my house with laughter and friends!"

Isn't that a wonderful thought? Lena mused as she entered Miriam's kitchen. *Someday I want to fill my house with laughter and friends, too!*

Chapter Eight

For Ben, carrying a loaded baby basket in each hand was the easiest part of the evening. The three women's bright eyes told him they'd had a wonderful time at Nora's, and he hated to spoil their buoyant mood. A few things needed to be said, however, because Lena would soon realize something was amiss.

"It seems Josiah has left again," he began with a rueful smile. "His horse and wagon are gone—but some of his clothes are still here."

Lena's smile withered. "I wanted to show him the nice baby things we got," she murmured. "I figured he'd feel better about the wee one coming, now that we've got the basic necessities."

"And why would he leave without saying something?" Savilla pondered aloud. "I thought we were ready to start preparations for the wedding buffet— which I will *not* cater by myself," she added emphatically.

"Maybe he's gone to speak with Hiram," Miriam remarked.

"Or maybe he wanted more cooking utensils from

your house in Iowa," Lena said as they hung up their coats.

Ben listened to them making reasonable excuses for Josiah's behavior. Truth be told, he found the kid's second disappearance in a week a sign that he'd leave again in the future—probably when Lena or Savilla needed him most. "Lena, have ya thought about what comes next for you and the baby if ya don't marry Josiah?" he asked gently.

"It's not like he's *asked* me," the girl blurted out. "Everybody assumes we'll marry, but I wonder if that'll happen." She sighed loudly. "I've been crazy in love with Josiah since we were kids, but maybe that's the crazy part. Maybe we were too young to know any better and I need to move on without him."

"Josiah's never had feelings for anybody but you, Lena," Savilla insisted. "But he has a lot of growing up to do."

"Could be he's in Bloomfield, speakin' with your parents," Miriam said. "Now that he's cookin' for Luke and Nora's wedding, I want to believe he's lookin' toward the future—for you and for his caterin' business, as well."

Ben sensed his wife was trying to keep Lena from getting upset. She'd offered him a useful thread of conversation, however. "Josiah might be tellin' your folks where the three of ya have landed," he suggested. "Could be he's—"

"Emory and Dorcas Esh have nothing to say to Josiah," Lena declared wearily. "They warned me time and again that he wasn't dependable, and—much as I hate to say it—maybe they're right. It's late. I'm going to bed."

When Savilla had followed Lena back into the *dawdi haus*, Ben shook his head. "Wish I saw a solution to the fix that girl's in. I hated to rain on her parade when she was lookin' so happy."

"At least we know her parents' names now," Miriam pointed out. "I'll ask Rebecca to look up Emory Esh's phone number on her computer. I can't imagine how worried her *mamm* must be—and I can't believe Dorcas is as hard-hearted as Lena's lettin' on, either."

Ben smiled. "Lena's folks watched that boy grow up, so they probably had him pegged as a drifter early on. That's why I want you to write out a business agreement, if he and his sister take on a shift in your café."

Miriam went to the sink and ran a glass of cold water. "*Jah*, that makes a lot of sense. Especially when he didn't even tell Savilla he was leavin', right before their big caterin' date."

As he hugged her from behind, Ben prayed for words that would lift Miriam's spirits. She had so much on her mind, with a baby coming and a big decision to make about running her business—not to mention the two kids who'd landed on their doorstep about to have a baby of their own. Ben held her gently, inhaling the clean scent he'd always found so appealing, so Miriam.

She turned in his arms. When she rested her head on his shoulder, Ben savored the closeness of this moment as the baby shifted inside her. He glanced at the two baskets on the table and got an idea. "Sit down and finish that glass of water, honey-girl. I've got a present for ya."

When her eyes sparkled with curiosity, Ben was grateful that inspiration had struck. His pulse thrummed as he grabbed his coat and jogged out to the barn. The scents of horses and manure greeted him as he hurried between the buggies and the animals in their stalls. He took the cradle he'd made from its hiding spot in the empty back stall, brushing away the clean hay. Miriam deserved a gift every day, so why wait for Christmas? Giving her presents and watching her excitement when she received them had become a special joy in his life.

Ben loped across the snowy yard with the cradle in his arms. He wrapped his coat around it so Miriam would have a few moments of anticipation. She was sitting at the table, watching him as he came inside. Ben stood in the doorway, breathing deeply. He hadn't thought about what he'd say, and he wanted to make this a special moment.

"I—I made this for ya, honey-bug," he murmured. "I want ya to have it now, rather than waitin' for Christmas."

Miriam's bright eyes followed his every move as he approached with his gift concealed in his coat. "It's not wigglin', so it must not be a foal or a calf."

"You're right." Ben set his bundle on the table in front of her. "And as ya can see, I took special pains to wrap it for ya."

Miriam's laughter made his heart dance. When her finger found a wooden rocker and the bulky bundle began to move, her face lit up. "Oh, Bennie," she exclaimed as she yanked his coat away, "ya made the baby a cradle! And what a cradle it is, too! Such glossy wood and—and a hummingbird on the top of it!"

Miriam stood up to run her hands over the wood Ben had sanded and stained so many times to get it perfectly smooth and flawless. Tears came to her eyes as her fingertips traced the outline of the hummingbird poised in front of a morning glory, which he'd fashioned from pewter at his forge. At this precious moment, Ben knew that every painstaking hour he'd spent getting the bird, the blossom, and the curving vines just right had been worth his effort.

"I'm glad ya like it, Miriam," he murmured. "I figured a lot of folks would be givin' ya baby things but that this would be something—"

"Only you could give me," she whispered. "A gift from your hands and your heart. Bennie, I love ya so much I can't put it into words."

When Miriam embraced him, he felt the deepest sweetness—feelings he'd never known were possible before he'd married this woman on New Year's Day. "Have we ever really needed words?" he murmured against her ear. "From the moment I met ya, I knew you'd understand me like nobody else ever had. That's why I can never do enough to show ya how much I love ya."

"*Denki* from the bottom of my ever-lovin' heart." She squeezed him tighter and kissed the side of his face. "This baby we've made has the best *dat* in the world."

Ben closed his eyes as his soul overflowed with gladness. Not all that long ago he'd been wandering the countryside in his farrier wagon, a man without roots or a purpose. Miriam had changed that—had made him the man he was now. "I'm so blessed to have you," he murmured.

"You're a blessing," she insisted. Miriam gazed into his eyes. "I've been thinkin' on what ya said, about me lettin' go of the Sweet Seasons to be a wife and a mother. I'll work it out, but I'm not quite there yet."

"I know you'll do what's best for all of us."

Miriam nodded, once again running a finger over the wooden cradle. "I'm ready to call it a day. We've got to get up and around for church in the morning."

"I'll be upstairs in a bit."

Who can find a virtuous woman? for her price is far above rubies. As Ben watched Miriam start up the stairway, he savored the passage of Scripture that came to mind whenever he thought of her. *The heart of her husband doth safely trust in her. She will do him good, and not evil, all the days of her life.*

"*Denki,* Lord," he murmured, for sometimes it just seemed right to pray aloud. "I couldn't have found Miriam without Your help."

Lena's attention wandered on Sunday morning. Bishop Vernon Gingerich was preaching, and his sermon about stewardship and giving back to the Lord in this season of thanksgiving seemed pointless. Hadn't she already sacrificed everything to be with Josiah? Her back ached something awful and her eyes stung from crying all night. She just wanted to curl up somewhere quiet and sleep.

"You okay, Lena?" Savilla whispered.

Was it a sin to say she was all right when *nothing* felt right? "Exhausted," she murmured. At least that part was true.

"Let's head back to the house after church instead of staying for the common meal. I'm in no mood for chitchat today."

Once again Lena wondered where Josiah had gone and why he hadn't told his sister. Why would he have left Willow Ridge when it was nearly dark? The drive to Bloomfield took hours, and the roads weren't the best even in full daylight. Or, if he'd gone to Higher Ground, why hadn't he returned? These questions had pestered Lena all night, and she was very tired of Josiah's disappearing acts.

"As we enter into God's gates with thanksgiving and into His courts with praise," Bishop Vernon paraphrased a favorite psalm, "let's take our neighbor along with us. Let's be sure none are left behind, or left out of God's bounty because we've not seen to their needs. We're His hands and feet on this earth, a direct extension of His love for all mankind, and we're to share what the *gut* Lord has blessed us with." He gazed at the roomful of people with blue eyes that sparkled above his full white beard. "Let's practice what we preach—what we believe—as we prepare to celebrate Thanksgiving with our families next week."

Unable to sit on the hard wooden pew any longer, Lena rose as the congregation prepared to sing the final hymn. After sidling past the other young women's knees, Lena headed toward the bathroom in the side hallway. Her head was pounding and she was so hungry she couldn't see straight as she entered the bathroom—

"Sorry!" Lena blurted out. The door had been ajar, but a young woman was preparing to change her baby. "I'll wait outside—"

"If you'd hold Emmanuel while I get out a diaper and the ointment, I'd be grateful," she said. "He's been fussy with tummy troubles, so I thought he'd feel better if I cleaned him up. I'm Mary Kauffman, by the way."

"I—I'm Lena Esh," she replied as she gingerly accepted Mary's pudgy son.

"Ah, the new gal living with the Hooleys," Mary replied with a smile. "I stayed home from Nora's yesterday tending this sick boy. It's *gut* to meet you, Lena. How're you doing?"

As a distinctive odor drifted out of Emmanuel's pants, Lena turned her head to breathe fresher air. "Hanging on for another month until this baby's born," she murmured. It was hard to talk while she was holding her breath and trying to keep the boy in her arms from squirming loose. He screwed up his face and started crying.

How am I supposed to quiet him when I don't dare squeeze him any tighter—don't want to breathe—

"Here we go, Emmanuel," Mary said as she reached for him.

The small bathroom rang with the boy's cries. Lena wanted to bolt—except she needed to watch someone change a baby's diaper. Her sisters had moved away when they'd married, so as the youngest child, she'd spent little time around babies.

As Mary fastened the changing table's strap around her son, he wailed louder. Lena looked on helplessly, watching Mary unpin the sides of a cloth diaper like the ones she'd received at the frolic. When Mary lifted the soiled diaper out from under her son, however, the stench made Lena pivot to vomit violently into the toilet. Sweat bathed her forehead as she clutched her bulging belly.

"I'm so sorry," Mary murmured. "I probably should've kept him home, but—"

Lena pressed the flush lever and rushed into the hall. Her head was reeling as she made her way into the mudroom off the back of the kitchen. She took deep, gulping breaths of the cooler air, willing herself not to vomit again. As she looked out the windows at the overcast morning, her thoughts seemed as bleak as the gray sky.

What if the smell of my baby's dirty diapers makes me throw up? What if I jab him with the pins or—I'm going to be the poorest excuse for a mother there ever was, and now everyone will know it because Mary will tell them.

Lena hung her head, wondering if she'd ever run out of tears. When people heard how she'd made Emmanuel cry, they would know how ill-prepared she was to be a mother, and she'd be humiliated yet again.

"Hey there, Lena. Let's head back to Miriam's. I've told her we're leaving so she won't worry about you."

Lena turned to smile weakly. "I'm glad you're here, Savilla. I just got really sick when Mary Kauffman was changing her baby, and I'm not sure I could make it back to the house by myself."

Josiah's sister grimaced. "Diapers can get pretty nasty, they tell me. I don't know much about that, and I'm not sure I want to find out!"

As they found their coats from among the other black wraps piled in the back bedroom, Lena was glad the embroidered initials inside the collars served as identification. Why couldn't everything in life be so simple and clear-cut? It was a comfort to hear Savilla admit she wasn't eager for motherhood, yet this confession rubbed salt into Lena's emotional wounds. Savilla still had a choice about having children, while Lena had given that up—with so many other things—the moment she'd surrendered to Josiah.

As they walked along the snow-packed road, fat

white flakes began to whirl around them. Lena lowered her head, waddling as fast as she could to keep up with Savilla.

Might as well get used to the uphill climb. Your life's going to feel this way for a long, long while.

Chapter Nine

Josiah halted his mare on the crest of the last hill overlooking Willow Ridge. With a fresh coating of snow, the homes, shops, and farm buildings reminded him of the miniature towns model railroad enthusiasts constructed to show off their train sets. A few ice floes drifted in the river near the mill's water wheel and honking geese flew overhead. Wisps of smoke rose from the chimneys, while the bishop's Holsteins and Dan Kanagy's sheep milled around bales of hay near their barns.

It felt like a panoramic view of *contentment*—and now this little burg would be his home! He couldn't wait to share his news with Savilla and Lena. The Hooleys would be impressed to hear that he'd made so much progress in only a few days, taking steps that made his future secure.

"Geddap, Dolly. Let's get on into town."

Josiah figured his sister and Lena would be working at the café, so he would find something for lunch in Miriam's home kitchen. He wanted to share his news with only his sister, the Hooleys, and Lena, rather than have everyone in the Sweet Seasons eavesdropping while they piled their plates at the buffet.

It was going to be a great day—the first in a new lifetime of great days. He just knew it!

Josiah drove past Leah Kanagy's garden plots and then in front of Matthias Wagler's roadside harness shop. The Simple Gifts parking lot was nearly full—which was unheard of in most small towns on a Tuesday afternoon. Willow Ridge was so much more *alive* than most Plain communities; he'd be a fool not to settle there.

When he'd unhitched the wagon behind Ben's barn and tended to Dolly, Josiah headed for the house. He was whistling as he grabbed the doorknob. A shower and clean clothes would feel good after all the packing and hefting he'd—

"Savilla! What're you and Lena doing here?" he blurted out.

His sister stopped stirring the pot on the stove. "I could ask you the same question," she retorted. "I thought you'd backed out of cooking for the wedding—"

"So I'm helping her," Lena added in a similarly irritated tone. "Nurse Andy says my due date's so close that I shouldn't be working in the Sweet Seasons. But you wouldn't know that because you took off again!"

"Without bothering to tell anybody!" Savilla chimed in, her voice rising. "Henry Zook's keeping your meat in the market's cooler, but again, you wouldn't know that. What's with you, anyway?"

Josiah scowled. He felt like keeping his good news for people who deserved to hear it—people who would praise him for making the decisions that needed to be made. "I've been taking care of business," he replied tersely. "Since I'm the man of the family—"

"Could've fooled me," Savilla muttered. She stirred the sauce in her pot so fast that some of it hissed when it landed near the gas flame.

"Suit yourself," Josiah muttered. "If you don't want to hear what a *gut* price I got for selling the farm, then—"

"You *what?*" His wide-eyed sister looked ready to throw her metal spoon at him. "Why on God's earth would you do that without asking me? That's my home, too."

"And what about waiting to see how the wedding dinner goes?" Lena demanded. "What happens if you decide Missouri's not the right place to set up your business?"

"Savilla, we discussed the possibility of selling the farm on Thanksgiving—remember?" Josiah bit back the words he wanted to hurl at both glaring young women. "Where'd you think the money for more catering events would come from until we've got a steady income?" he demanded. "I'm not living under Ben Hooley's roof any longer than I have to. Everybody's been telling me to man up, so I have! And all I'm getting in return is your static! I don't need this."

Josiah stepped outside, giving the door a satisfying slam. With Savilla and Lena's remarks replaying in his head, he strode across the county highway. Did his sister really think he'd backed out of the biggest opportunity they'd landed in years? Did she want to rely on the Hooleys' goodwill forever? With Miriam's kid due in December and Lena's coming sooner, there would be two babies bawling and two nervous, sleepless mothers—

Never mind what they think—they'll soon see that you're right. Meanwhile, you're going to wow this town with the best barbeque anybody's ever tasted.

Josiah walked behind the café, into the enclosure he'd built. He threw open the two big barrel cookers where he would roast the whole hogs. As he arranged the firewood and added the kindling and charcoal that would maintain the needed heat, it felt good to work off his frustration by hefting logs and big bags of briquettes.

He figured the time it would take the fire to get hot enough and added about twelve hours for cooking. For convenience and safe handling, it was best to have the meat sauced and in roasting pans the day before an event, so his timing was perfect. And when the aroma of the grilling meats circulated around town, folks were sure to get curious—and hungry. Their anticipation would play into the success of the wedding feast.

"Ah, so it's you bangin' around out here," Ben said as he emerged from his smithy. "Thought I'd better check to be sure nobody was fiddlin' with your cookers."

Josiah almost shot back a remark, but he caught himself. "*Denki* for looking after my stuff," he replied. "After I fire up these barrel cookers, I'll fetch the meat from the market. I've got a lot of cooking to do, but I'm excited! This'll be a wedding dinner like nobody around here's ever tasted!"

"I can't wait to try it," Ben replied. "Your sister's got the house smellin' so *gut*, I've wanted to sneak samples of what she's stashed in the Sweet Seasons fridges."

Josiah nodded, checking his mental list. "I need to be sure Miriam's got room for the pans of finished meat—or I can store them at Zook's," he remarked as he considered his options. "I, uh, suspect I ruffled some feathers by leaving for Bloomfield the other day—and I just got Savilla and Lena riled up by telling them I've sold the farm."

Ben's startled expression told Josiah that he'd probably leaped before he'd looked—again. "That must've felt mighty sudden to your sister and—"

"The man who bought it has been renting our cropland for years, and he offered me a great price," Josiah insisted. "He didn't expect me to fix up the house or the barn, either, which saved me a lot of effort and money. I—I really appreciate you and Miriam keeping the three of us, but it's time I paid our way," he explained earnestly. "When the sale's final, I'll be looking for a house somewhere near here, so if you hear of anyplace, let me know, all right?"

"*Jah*, I'll do that." Ben gazed steadily at Josiah. "I understand where you're comin' from, son, and I hope all the details fall into place like they're supposed to. I hope the reception ya get from folks at Thursday's wedding justifies your quick decision to settle here, too."

Josiah detected an undercurrent of warning in Ben's words—a hint that he might've sold the farm prematurely. *So you have to succeed in Willow Ridge. No second-guessing. No chance to change what you've done.*

"Does this mean you'll want to start up a supper shift at Miriam's place?"

Josiah saw no reason to hedge. "*Jah*, I do. I think a lot of folks in this area will be real glad for a place to eat in the evening."

"Let's figure on drawin' up your agreement with Miriam tonight after supper, then," Ben suggested. "That way ya can set up your menu and start servin' whenever you're ready."

"Fair enough." Josiah waved as Ben went back inside his smithy. He lit the fires in his two barrel cookers and then knocked on the café's back door. When Miriam motioned him inside, her expression showed her mixed emotions—she was pleased to see him, yet wary.

Josiah paused in the doorway, watching Hannah and Naomi Brenneman plate an order at the stove while Rebecca and Rhoda refilled coffee and chatted with customers in the dining room. He'd be hard-pressed to match the efficiency of the Sweet Seasons' breakfast and lunch shifts—mostly because the cooks and waitresses never exchanged cross words or glared at each other. Why were he and Savilla—and he and Lena—so often at odds?

"Glad to see ya, Josiah," Miriam said as she returned to her work area. She dipped flour from a fifty-pound sack into a big bowl and began to cut lard into it. "Do the girls know you're back?"

"Yeah—and I've once again cranked their handles in the wrong direction," Josiah replied with a sigh. "I can't believe Savilla thought I'd ducked out of catering the wedding. Her reaction to my selling our farm in Bloomfield was something to behold, too."

Miriam sucked in her breath. "Ever thought about givin' her and Lena some *warning* before ya do stuff like that? How would ya feel if Savilla up and left—and after the fact told ya she'd married somebody and wouldn't be cookin' with ya anymore?"

Josiah scowled. "She'd never do that! She refuses to date the old guy down the road who's tried to court her."

Miriam stopped mixing her piecrust. "Ya just don't get it, do ya? If Savilla decided her chances were better with that old guy than with you—if she just *took off*— what would ya do, Josiah?" she demanded.

He blinked. If Savilla quit—for whatever reason—he couldn't continue catering on the scale he'd become accustomed to. And running a supper shift without her would be impossible. But he suspected that wasn't really the point Miriam was trying to make.

"Okay, so she's reminded me that I have this habit of doing my own thing without consulting her," Josiah admitted. To switch to a more comfortable subject, he gestured toward the big lumps beneath wet tea towels on the countertop. "What's all this? Piecrust?"

"A bunch of us gals are havin' a frolic here after we close this afternoon," she explained. "We'll bake Nora and Luke's pies today, and I'll make the wedding cake tomorrow."

Once again Josiah was impressed by the level of cooperation among folks in Willow Ridge—and by the way Miriam always contributed time and ingredients. "Now tell me straight out. Will it be a problem to store my cooked meat in your fridges?" he asked. "I'll have two whole hogs cooked by tomorrow around this time, and I'll need some workspace to bone them—and to prep the chickens and briskets."

"Plenty of room to go around. We're cartin' the pies to the Brennemans' shop in the morning," Miriam replied. "I'll be decoratin' the cake in this corner, so that leaves the whole counter over there for ya. I want to see how ya do those pigs," she added with a grin. Then she raised a purposeful eyebrow. "Hug your sister for speakin' on your behalf. We've already cleared out a whole fridge for your meat."

Suddenly overcome by Miriam's good-hearted

generosity, Josiah stooped to hug her. "*Denki* for—well, for lookin' after me," he said, surprised at how tight his voice sounded.

"Well, now," Miriam murmured, patting his wrist with her floury hand. "This is kinda nice comin' from you, Josiah."

The tension eased out of his shoulders as he allowed Miriam's warmth to soak into his soul. "I miss my grandmother. She and our grandfather raised Savilla and me after our parents drowned in a flood," he said. "I've probably rushed into a few rash decisions that Mammi would've made me think harder about."

"That's how it works when somebody ya love passes on," Miriam murmured. "Would that be the flood of 1993 you're speakin' of?"

He nodded. "I was just a little kid. Can hardly recall my parents' faces."

Miriam's grip tightened on his wrist. "I'm sorry that happened to ya, Josiah. My toddler Rebecca was washed away from me in that flood," she recalled in a faraway voice. "But nineteen years later she came back to me, after I'd figured she was dead. It's my favorite miracle—and you'll have your share of them, too, if ya believe ya will."

Josiah desperately wanted to buy into Miriam's talk of miracles. He realized then that Naomi, Hannah, the two waitresses—and the end of the lunch shift—had kept on going while he'd been temporarily lost in Miriam's cozy strength. He straightened to his full height, wondering if anyone had thought it odd for him to be hugging her.

So what? It's not a sin to open up to someone—and it's nobody else's business anyway.

Miriam smiled up at him and began working the lard into her flour with her pastry cutter again. "Still thinkin' to cook here in the evenings?"

"*Jah*, I really, really want that to work out," he replied. "Ben says we can write up an agreement tonight, so I can start sooner rather than later."

"I like the sound of that. We'll make it happen, Josiah."

Josiah suddenly felt as though he could accomplish anything he set out to do. With Miriam standing up for him, who could possibly be against him? "*Jah*, we will," he stated. "I'll head over to Zook's and get those hogs ready for the cookers."

"Give Preacher Henry my best, and Lydia, too. *Gut* folks, the Zooks."

As Josiah strode down the road, he felt like a better man. Miriam was committed to his success now, so he had no one but himself to blame if his dinner shift failed.

Miriam straightened her back as she sat on her stool Wednesday afternoon, weary from being on her feet for the previous afternoon's pie frolic. She was glad she'd baked and frozen the layers of Nora's wedding cake and the sheet cakes last week, so all she had to do was decorate them. A tapping on the back door alerted her to a visitor.

"Come on in, Tom!" she called out.

Bishop Tom Hostetler's smile crinkled the skin around his eyes as he entered the Sweet Seasons kitchen. "There's a whole lotta cookin' goin' on," he quipped, removing his hat. "Willow Ridge has never smelled so *gut*, what with the aroma of Josiah's meats in the air. And this must be the cake for the wedding?"

"*Jah*, and the pies are all made, so this is the last thing I'm responsible for," Miriam replied. "It'll be nice to enjoy the wedding without havin' to help serve."

"I'm kinda glad I don't have to officiate, so I can enjoy the whole day, as well," Tom remarked. "We've had a lot of weddings lately—a real positive sign for the future of our little town. Not to mention a lot of babies."

Miriam kept her spatula moving over the buttercream frosting so the cake's main layer would have a perfectly smooth finish. She had a pretty good idea what Bishop Tom wanted to discuss next.

Help me to remember humility, Lord, and to obey this fine bishop Ya chose for us. Ya know how I tend to do what I want rather than askin' for Your opinion.

"How're ya feelin' these days, Miriam? Ya look a little tired, and that concerns me," Tom said gently.

"I can tell ya that carryin' a baby at forty-one is different from doin' it at twenty—even though I had triplets that time around," Miriam replied with a chuckle. She looked him in the eye. "I suppose you've come to tell me I shouldn't be workin'—that I should've hung up my pots and pans when I married Ben. I know the *Ordnung* says I should be a wife and a mother now instead of runnin' a restaurant."

Tom looked relieved that she'd broached this difficult subject herself. "My feelings are as mixed as yours, Miriam," he admitted. "When ya opened this place after Jesse died, we all thought it was right for ya to bring in some income because the Lord helps those who help themselves. I should've talked ya into quittin' earlier, but you and I go back a long ways. Truth be told, I don't know how I would've kept myself fed and together after Lettie left me if ya hadn't opened the Sweet Seasons."

Miriam chuckled as she piped a border around the cake's bottom layer. "Our single fellas have been the mainstay of my business," she agreed. "And a lot of them who've married are still comin' here for breakfast even though they've got wives to cook for them."

"We value the time we spend with one another while we eat here," the bishop replied pensively. "Breakin' bread together builds a strong connection—a tie that binds. You've started our days off right, Miriam, and nobody wants to give that up. But there comes a time for change. A time to reassess our priorities."

Miriam's heart thudded. She began frosting the top layer of Nora's cake so the familiar movements would keep her emotions in check. If she quit cooking, what would she do with herself for the two months before the baby came? Would Naomi be able to keep the place going? *That* was a priority because Naomi's husband Ezra was in a wheelchair, no longer able to earn a living.

"When I was a first-time bride," she mused aloud, "I never dreamed I'd outlive my husband and then hitch up with another fella after my girls were grown. I believed I wasn't able to conceive any more kids, too, so Ben's baby is an unexpected gift from God."

"Marryin' Nazareth has changed my life, as well," the bishop said with a sweet smile. "After Lettie ran off with that English fella, I figured I was doomed to be alone for the rest of my life. God's been extra-special *gut* to you and me, Miriam."

"Ya took on another load when ya became our bishop, too." She refilled her pastry bag to pipe the border around the cake's top layer. "I'm sorry my workin' has put ya in a tough spot, Tom. I suspect the men in the district are askin' why ya haven't flat-out sent me home."

"They're selfish, like me. And while I think folks will support Josiah and his sister's supper shift," Tom continued earnestly, "the Sweet Seasons won't be the same without *you*, Miriam. We all want ya to do the right thing by our faith, but we're spoiled enough to wish ya didn't have to."

Miriam's pulse pounded in triple time. Did she dare push for an end date closer to when the baby was due? Or was Tom hoping she'd quit now?

She completed the scalloped border and took a deep breath. "Do ya want me to stay home after tomorrow's wedding, Tom? Or maybe startin' next week? I'd do that in a heartbeat if Naomi could find more kitchen help. She came into this business with me to support her family—"

"Ezra's disability is the reason the preachers have allowed her to cook with ya," he agreed. "We felt the benefits of bendin' the rules about married women workin' outweighed the risks of displeasin' God. And maybe we've all acted mighty presumptuous, assumin' our decisions have been right in His eyes."

Miriam rested her pastry tube on the countertop. "Ya said a mouthful there, Tom," she murmured. "I'll do the right thing, then. I'll tell Naomi I won't be comin' back next week, and God will take it from there."

She closed her eyes, not ready to face the finality of that statement. "I appreciate your patience with me,

Tom," Miriam whispered. "Ya could've ordered me to kneel before the members and confess that I've been sinnin' by continuin' to work. You're a *gut* friend."

Tom chuckled, his eyes sparkling with relief. "The way I see it, we're *gut* friends who've been bad together, but we're makin' it right. *Denki* for understandin' why this has been difficult for me, Miriam. I think God'll forgive my lenience quicker because you're puttin' in a *gut* word for both our souls."

"*Jah*, I'll soon have plenty of time for prayin'."

A heavy stillness pressed in around her. Miriam closed her eyes and sat absolutely still.

She'd done it. She'd told the bishop she'd be a stay-at-home wife starting next Monday, no matter what the consequences might be for the Sweet Seasons and her best friend. Eventually her faith would kick in and she would believe she'd done exactly what God wanted her to do, but Miriam had to squeeze her eyes tight to keep from crying. Tom put his hand on her shoulder, allowing her a moment to compose herself.

The back door creaked and Josiah stuck his head inside. "I'll be proppin' this door open while I carry in the cooked pigs," he announced.

Miriam shared a smile with Tom. "Do what ya need to do, Josiah," she called out. "I'll stay out of your way."

"Let me know how I can help," Tom offered.

Josiah entered and quickly covered the other counter-top with a plastic sheet. "*Denki*, Bishop, but I've been handling these hot, heavy beasts for a long while. I've got it covered."

I've got it covered.

Miriam told herself that was exactly how God saw her situation with the Sweet Seasons. It would take her a while to adjust to not being in charge—but then, she'd been silly to believe the café's success was her own doing. It was God who'd helped her business prosper. And it was high time she gave Him credit and praise for that.

Chapter Ten

As Josiah refilled the metal pans with pulled pork, ribs, and sliced brisket at the wedding feast, he felt absolutely ecstatic. He was amazed at how many tables had been set up in the Brennemans' shop, and at how many folks had filed through the serving line. Savilla was putting her last pan of spaghetti pie into the steam table, so he motioned to Adam and Matthias Wagler, who were helping them move food from the Sweet Seasons ovens.

"Better fetch us more chicken and pulled pork, along with potato loaf and spaghetti pie," he told the brothers.

"Bring more baked beans and fried apples while you're at it," Savilla chimed in. "These folks are really loading their plates!"

Matthias smiled and held Savilla's gaze. "This is quite a feast you're putting on," he said. "I'm glad I can see the end of the line, because then I'll get my chance to taste everything—and I hope you'll sit with me, Savilla."

As the Wagler brothers grabbed the handles on their high-sided wagons, Josiah suspected Matthias was flirting with his sister—just as the other unattached fellows had been giving her the eye as they went through the serving line. Maybe Miriam's question about what he'd do if his sister got hitched wasn't so far-fetched.

He glanced behind him, where Lena and Miriam sat cutting pies. Other ladies moved around the huge room, refilling water glasses and bread baskets. Their service was seamless, a sign that these gals had worked together for years. Up on the *eck* —the raised corner table where the wedding party sat—Nora and Luke beamed at each other as they ate.

Josiah sighed. The newlyweds seemed so in love, so close, even though they'd only been married for a couple of hours. He wondered if he and Lena could spend even ten minutes together without squabbling. Were they really so different from other couples, or did those folks hold their harsh words until no one else was around to hear them? Was their tendency toward confrontation a sign that he and Lena shouldn't marry— or did *he* cause their turmoil? Miriam's words about doing everything his way were making Josiah think in ways he hadn't before.

"I've been hungry ever since you fired up your cookers a couple of days ago," a broad-shouldered fellow remarked as he reached across the steam table to shake Josiah's hand. "Dan Kanagy, and this is my wife Leah—Miriam's sister," he added. "We live down the lane behind here, where the sheep are pastured."

"And if this is the sort of food you'd be serving during a supper shift," Leah said as she grabbed a grilled chicken quarter with tongs, "you're already a huge hit!"

"That's what we like to hear," Josiah replied, grinning

at his sister. "Savilla and I have catered for a few years now, so we make a pretty *gut* team."

As Dan and Leah moved through the line, Josiah noticed that a black-haired man with a close-clipped beard, piercing eyes, and a commanding presence had taken a plate. The stranger stood for a moment, assessing the various pans of food on the buffet line. His face eased into a debonair smile as he leaned closer to speak to Savilla. "Do I understand correctly that you are in charge of these fabulous side dishes while Josiah grills the meat?" he asked in a melodious voice.

Savilla returned his smile and then gestured for Adam and Matthias to pull their loaded wagons into the space behind her. "*Jah*, we stick with what folks seem to like best. Nothing fancy, just *gut* food."

When the man's focus shifted to him, Josiah got a prickly feeling in his stomach. The charm that had oozed while this fellow spoke to his sister was hardening into an expression of extreme ill will.

"Hiram Knepp," Matthias muttered. "What brings *you* to this party?"

"If you figure to bother Annie Mae and the rest of our family, ya better get on out of here," Adam said sternly.

In a flash, Josiah realized he'd made a couple of huge mistakes: hooking up with Knepp in the first place and then not contacting him as Ben had recommended. He also knew he was about to start paying for his lack of judgment right this moment. Was it his imagination or had the whole dining area—where a couple hundred people were eating—gone totally silent?

"My business doesn't concern you, Wagler," Hiram replied in a clipped tone. "I have an agreement with

Josiah Witmer, who signed on to cook for me in Higher
Ground. It seems he's made himself right at home in
Willow Ridge instead, and I demand an explanation."

Savilla's face had gone pale, but she found her voice
before Josiah did. "The way I understand it, Mr. Knepp,
my brother merely talked with you over the phone.
So—"

"We stopped in Willow Ridge because we got lost in
a snowstorm." Lena spoke up behind Josiah. She came
to stand beside him, glaring up at Knepp. "And since
then, we've been told that things in Higher Ground
aren't the way you made them out to be."

"This wedding party's not the time or place to be
bringin' up such business and you know it, Hiram."
Ben, who'd been chatting with folks at a nearby table,
stepped up beside Savilla, crossing his arms as he
scowled at Knepp. "We've told ya not to return here, so
you'd best move along."

Hiram's smile turned menacing. "And I've told *you*
that I'll go wherever I please, Hooley," he shot back. He
sneered at Josiah. "Cat got your tongue, Witmer? I'm
hearing from everyone except you—excuses that have
nothing to do with your agreement to cook at my
supper club."

"Where *is* this so-called supper club?" Bishop Tom
demanded. He was wiping barbeque sauce from his
face with a napkin, looking stern and stiff—quite
unlike the patient, easygoing bishop of Willow Ridge
Josiah had seen previously. "Josiah and I have both
driven through Higher Ground and we've seen no
evidence of such a place. Folks hereabouts have warned
him it's a hoax—"

"You're out of line, Hostetler." Knepp's voice was
rising with the color in his face. "When I see this spread

the Witmers have put on, I'm inclined to call my lawyer to—well, *Miriam*," he exclaimed in a theatrical voice. "Here you are, just *bursting* with a child you swore to me you couldn't conceive! Why do I suspect you snatched Josiah away to cook in your restaurant because you'll soon be indisposed? You're going straight to hell for lying—"

"And you've got a date with the sheriff, Hiram," Luke Hooley announced as he, too, approached the steam table. He held up his cell phone. "Remember when you were harassing Nora in her shop and I told you I had the law on speed dial? Sheriff Banks and Officer McClatchey are on their way."

"We didn't invite you in the first place," Nora said as she stalked up beside Hiram to glare at him. "Nobody here believes a word you say anymore, so why would we let Josiah and his sister fall into your trap?"

Josiah couldn't believe the way people were approaching the buffet table to stand in support of him, scowling at their former bishop as though they'd rather lynch him than listen to him. He heard a siren approaching and caught the flash of red and blue lights through the window. Within moments, a portly fellow wearing a brown uniform and a sheriff's star came inside, followed by a younger, fitter lawman. Their no-nonsense expressions told Josiah they were well acquainted with the man who'd been stirring up such a hornet's nest.

"Got a call that you've been disturbing the peace again, Knepp," the sheriff said as he came to stand beside Hiram.

The younger fellow, whose badge flashed McCLATCHEY, went immediately to Hiram's other side and snapped a handcuff around his wrist.

"You're violating my rights!" Hiram cried as he tried to jerk free. "I have the right to be present at a public gathering—the right to an attorney—"

"We'll add resisting arrest and contempt of court to the original charge," the sheriff said as he held Hiram's other arm so McClatchey could finish cuffing him. "You didn't show up for your last two meetings with your parole officer, so you were in trouble long before Luke informed us of your whereabouts. Let's go, Knepp."

Josiah's eyes widened with each of the charges the sheriff reeled off. During his phone interview, he'd had no idea Hiram was in hot water with the law or even inclined to cause trouble. Guided by the sheriff's beefy hand around his upper arm, Knepp went toward the door—but then he turned.

"Witmer, I'm not finished with you," he announced. "We had a business agreement and you're going to uphold your end of it. I'll see you in court if I have to."

"Move along," Officer McClatchey said as he turned Knepp toward the exit again. Everyone watched through the windows as the sheriff escorted his charge to the police car. Then Officer McClatchey came inside again. "Sorry you folks had to put up with such a disturbance—and congratulations, Luke and Nora. Can't say I've ever had to come to a wedding under such unfortunate circumstances."

"Please come eat with us," Nora replied. "We've got all this fabulous food—and you won't want to miss the wedding cake Miriam made."

"I'd be happy to have a piece soon as I file this report," the lawman said with a grin.

Bishop Tom stepped forward, looking relieved but curious. "I'm not up on legal lingo, so I've gotta ask ya," he said earnestly. "What's a parole officer? And what'd Sheriff Banks mean when he was talkin' about contempt of court? Sounds serious."

Officer McClatchey sighed regretfully. "You remember how Hiram had a young gal living with him in Higher Ground? Well, she left him," he explained.

"That would be Delilah," Adam Wagler murmured. "Sounds like she got smart."

"When Hiram found her and tried to make her come back, a neighbor called us about a domestic disturbance at his place," the lawman went on. "He served some jail time, and meanwhile, Delilah filed a restraining order—which means Hiram was legally forbidden to speak with her or to be around her."

"My word," Miriam murmured. "Sounds like he's toppled over the edge."

Officer McClatchey nodded. "Once Knepp got out of jail he was to report to his parole officer every week," he explained. "Twice now he hasn't shown up, and Delilah's recently informed us that he's made some threatening phone calls. So that means he's in contempt of court because he refused to abide by the rules the judge set. It's complicated."

"It's a cryin' shame our former bishop's sunk so low," Ben remarked. "Josiah, I'm even more grateful that God convinced ya to stay here with us rather than goin' on to Higher Ground. It's a real cesspool Hiram's swimmin' in."

Josiah's head was spinning with all the startling information he'd heard. "I—I am *so sorry*," he blurted out as he looked at Ben and then Miriam. "You warned me about Knepp—told me to get out of the deal we'd made—and now I've brought all this trouble to Willow Ridge. And I've ruined your wedding feast,

Luke and Nora. I can't possibly charge you for this meal when it's my fault that Hiram came and—"

"Oh, no," Luke insisted as he slung an arm around Josiah's shoulders. "It's nobody's fault that Hiram does what he does, and if anybody thinks we've got him under control, he's delusional. You and Savilla have cooked up a wedding feast way beyond my expectations—"

"And who else can say the cops arrested somebody at their wedding party?" Nora piped up with a grin. "It's a day we'll never forget!"

As everyone around them chuckled, Josiah couldn't believe how forgiving and understanding these people were—how they'd all come to his defense the moment they saw Knepp. "It's been our pleasure to cook for your party," he told the bride and groom.

"And we're grateful to everyone for making us so welcome here," Savilla said as she gazed around at the crowd. "Willow Ridge is a wonderful town."

"And I'm thankful for the baby gifts," Lena spoke up in a quivering voice. "You've all been wonderful-*gut* to me—especially you, Miriam and Ben. I—I was ready to clobber Knepp when he got so nasty about you having a baby."

"Stand in line, Lena," Matthias Wagler said. "I think we should get back to celebrating Luke and Nora's wedding, but we're all sadder and wiser because of what we've learned today."

The guests nodded, returning to their places. Josiah began removing foil-covered pans from the wagons, and within minutes the buffet had been replenished. Adam and Annie Mae filled their plates and Miriam and Ben got their meals, as well. When Lena handed him a plate, Josiah realized how hungry he was.

"You two go ahead. I'll tend the table until you're done," Savilla offered as she stirred the baked beans and fried apples. Then she took hold of his wrist, lowering her voice. "I'll save my I-told-you-so lecture for later, little brother. I thought you'd informed Hiram we wouldn't be cooking for him."

"And I deserve whatever you dish up for being too stupid to listen to Ben and Miriam," he said ruefully. "What a mess I've made. What a mess Knepp's made."

"At least we didn't get sucked into his lies," Lena insisted as she filled her plate. "The snowstorm that rerouted us to Willow Ridge was a gift from God as far as I'm concerned."

Josiah heaped his plate with pulled pork, brisket, and the side dishes his sister had made, grateful they'd all escaped a dicey situation in Higher Ground. *I've not paid much attention to You or my faith,* he prayed quickly, *but You pulled my butt out of the fire today, Lord, and I promise to listen more closely to what You'd have me do from here on out.*

It felt good to sit down at the table where Lena and Miriam had finished cutting the pies. He noticed that Matthias and Savilla were filling plates, remaining at the serving table as they got better acquainted—and that seemed like a good sign.

Josiah closed his eyes over spicy-sweet baked beans and a mouthful of tender pork. The guests' praise for the wedding food reassured him that their new supper shift would have a profitable following, and he was satisfied with the business agreement he and Miriam had written up. But it would be a long time before he stopped replaying the scene Hiram had caused, and before he could dismiss Knepp's threats about going to court.

Witmer, I'm not finished with you.

Josiah heaved a tired, worried sigh. Even with the sheriff and Officer McClatchey watching out for him, he sensed he hadn't seen the last of Hiram Knepp.

Chapter Eleven

After Nora and Luke had cut their tiered wedding cake, Miriam, Lena, and a few other ladies began to plate cake for the guests. Nora had decided to serve the cake right after dinner rather than later in the day, as newlyweds traditionally did. This suited Miriam because she was feeling heavy and tired—maybe because she needed to speak with Naomi about her decision not to work at the Sweet Seasons anymore.

How should she break the news to her business partner, her cook, her best friend? As she sliced the large bottom layer of the beautiful white cake she'd made, Miriam searched for the right words and the right time. When all the guests were visiting and Lena had gone to sit with Josiah and Savilla, she smiled at Naomi. "How about us two stayin' right here in this corner to chat?" she suggested. "I've got something to say, and it's not for just anybody to hear."

Naomi's brown eyes widened. She picked up two plates of cake and handed one to Miriam before scooting her chair over so they sat side by side. "I hope ya haven't had a bad report from Andy about the baby," she murmured.

"No, no, nothin' like that." Miriam pressed her fork through the layer of moist cake and frosting but didn't eat the bite she'd cut. "Ben and Tom are sayin' I've overstepped by workin' at the café, especially with the baby comin'. So Saturday'll be my last day," she murmured. "I hate springin' it on ya this way, but—"

"Oh, dearie, I've been waitin' for this shoe to drop ever since ya married Ben," Naomi said with a chuckle. "When we closed up for a couple of weeks between last Christmas and your New Year's Day wedding, I figured ya wouldn't come back to work after that."

Miriam let out the breath she'd been holding. Why had she lain awake the past two nights, fearing Naomi would fuss or feel overwhelmed?

"I'm mighty glad ya did come back to work, though," her partner added as she squeezed Miriam's hand. "Won't be the same without ya there, Miriam. It'll be a challenge to find enough help with the bakin' and servin', though, because *three* people won't be able to fill your shoes."

"I'm relieved that you're takin' this so well." Miriam laughed nervously. "Should've known you'd be prepared for this situation."

Naomi blinked quickly, busying herself with a bite of cake before she spoke again. "Like everybody else, I knew ya should be stayin' home, but I was hangin' on to every day we could work together."

"*Jah*, we've had some wonderful-*gut* times in that kitchen, ain't so? Cooked up a lot of laughter along with our food." Miriam closed her eyes over her first bite of cake, which tasted even moister and sweeter now that she'd said what needed saying.

"And think what all's happened since we opened the Sweet Seasons," Naomi continued in a nostalgic tone. "Your Rebecca returned to ya, and your Rachel married my Micah and they've had wee Amelia—and Rhoda's made a family with Andy and his kids. Me, I've sorta stayed the same," she reflected as she cut another bite of cake. "I've been grateful for the money comin' in—not to mention havin' a place to spend cheerful mornings with you on days when Ezra was grumpy."

Miriam smiled tenderly. Naomi didn't let on to most folks about her husband's moodiness since a construction accident had confined him to a wheelchair. "I feel bad about leavin' ya shorthanded. I figure Rhoda will soon have a baby, and with Rebecca workin' at the clinic and designin' Web sites, she's only part-time at best."

"We can't expect our kids to stay the same forever, or to live their lives so they're convenient for *us*," Naomi mused. "And you—why, you've got a whole new life ahead of ya! I'm so happy you're able to have Ben's baby. You two are such *gut*, solid partners. Examples for us all."

"*Denki* for seein' things this way," Miriam replied. She gazed around the large, noisy room, crowded with people she knew and loved. "Maybe Nellie Knepp would work for ya. Or Katie Zook."

"Oh, I think Lydia wants to keep Katie helpin' at the market. The younger Zook boys sometimes make more work than they get done."

As they laughed together, Miriam realized she would miss talk like this even more than the baking she loved to do. Spending her days at home would feel *very* different from what she'd become accustomed to. "Let's don't say anything about Saturday bein' my last day," she suggested. "I don't want folks makin' a big deal of it—or lettin' on like the place'll close down without me there."

"My lips're sealed," Naomi murmured. "What with us closin' for Thanksgiving next Thursday and Friday, next week'll be short anyway. Might give Rebecca a chance to advertise for somebody."

"*Gut* idea. Rebecca's a whiz at that sort of thing," Miriam replied. "At least Hiram won't be comin' to pester anybody—for a while, anyway. I won't miss all the drama he stirs up every time he shows his face."

"Can you believe that snake, raisin' such a ruckus here at Nora and Luke's wedding?" Naomi muttered. "I thought we'd seen the worst of it when he whacked off Annie Mae's hair last spring, but it seems there's no limit to his wickedness."

Nodding, Miriam took another bite of her cake. She would miss her chats with Naomi. The two of them had shared opinions and wisdom and inside jokes for so long that they could finish each other's sentences. When Monday morning came, she knew she'd be wide awake, ready to begin her baking at three o'clock— and wondering what to do with the day that stretched ahead of her. She'd done some of her best thinking and praying during those quiet hours alone, kneading and shaping dough as she put her life in order.

It'll all work out, Lord. But You might have to remind me about that for a while.

After the wedding festivities, Ben walked Miriam home. She was moving slower, sighing tiredly, so after he helped her out of her coat, he placed his hands on her shoulders. "Honey-girl, I'm not naggin', but I'd feel a lot better if ya didn't work at the Sweet Seasons anymore."

Miriam laughed ruefully. "Ya get your wish, Ben. Saturday's my last day," she said. "It's the right thing to do, but I'm not sure how I feel about it. Naomi took it better than I figured."

Ben hugged her tenderly. "*Denki* for decidin' that, Miriam. I doubt the talk I've gotta have with Josiah will be as easy. When Hiram showed up, I was ready to tell that kid he was *out* as far as cookin' that supper shift goes. It's time somebody gave Josiah the what-for about some things that have bothered me all along," he insisted. "Bear with me, all right?"

Miriam considered this idea. "He couldn't have known Hiram would come today," she said in Josiah's defense. "And who could've guessed what the police said—"

"That's not the point," Ben said gently. "Josiah's gonna get an earful, and I wanted ya to be prepared."

Miriam nodded. "I'll heat some cider and then put my feet up. I hope Lena won't feel she has to help clean up the mess from the dinner."

Ben watched her amble toward the stove, noting how her side-to-side gait was getting more pronounced. He went to the picture window in the front room, where he saw the wedding guests hitching up their buggies to get on the road home. His parents and other family members from Lancaster County were staying either with Luke and Nora or with his aunts, Nazareth and Jerusalem, at Tom's place, and that suited Ben fine. It gave his Pennsylvania family more time with Nora, Bishop Tom, and Bishop Vernon Gingerich, the newer members of the family—and it gave him a chance to speak his mind without spoiling the occasion.

It was after seven before the Witmers and Lena returned to the house. Ben was pleased to hear Josiah and Savilla telling Miriam that they'd washed all the utensils and pans and put them away.

"I was amazed at how many folks we fed today, and at how they raved about the food," Lena said. She settled on the couch with Miriam and picked up her crochet bag. "Everyone's excited about the new evening hours for the Sweet Seasons, too."

Ben prayed for the words that would accomplish his difficult purpose. "I think we need to reconsider that situation," he stated. As Savilla joined them in the front room, Ben gestured for Josiah to sit down in one of the upholstered chairs.

"I'm mighty disappointed that ya didn't contact Hiram earlier," Ben continued after the Witmers were settled. "Now that he's found you and Savilla and Lena—and he believes Miriam kept ya from goin' to Higher Ground—he's got lots of ammunition," Ben began sternly. "As ya heard, Hiram didn't like it one bit that ya backed out on him. Nobody would've. And now Miriam's smack in the middle of this new hornet's nest."

"I said I was sorry about that," Josiah protested. "I had no idea Knepp would find out we were cooking for—" He stopped talking when he saw Ben picking up the sheet of notebook paper on which he and Miriam had written their business agreement.

"But I *told* ya he'd cause trouble," Ben insisted, "and ya either didn't believe me or ya chose to ignore my advice. So I need to see some compensation to Miriam for the trouble you've caused her."

Ben ripped the sheet of paper down the middle, doubled it, and then tore it again. Josiah, Savilla, and Lena became silent and wide-eyed, while Miriam remained focused on what she was crocheting. Her tense expression told Ben she was listening closely, however.

"Wh—what do you mean, *compensation?*" Josiah asked. "Until the money comes through from selling the farm in Bloomfield, I don't have any cash."

"Money's not the issue here. A sense that you're takin' responsibility is what I'm after," Ben replied. He stood in front of Josiah with his arms crossed. "I think workin' in the Sweet Seasons for the next couple of weeks would be a *gut* thing for everyone involved."

Josiah's jaw dropped. "Without pay? But how am I supposed to—"

Ben kept looking the kid in the eye. He didn't appreciate the stubborn, rebellious expression on Josiah's face. "It's not like you'll be buyin' the food ya serve. And you've been livin' here with us, so your expenses haven't been real high."

"I think that's a fair offer," Savilla stated. The rise of one eyebrow suggested that she'd also been ready to call her brother out about not contacting Hiram. "Consider it an internship—a chance to see if running a restaurant is really your cup of tea—and mine," she added. "It'll be different from cooking mostly on the weekends and taking only the jobs that appeal to you."

Josiah glared at his sister. "Why does everybody think I'm incapable of managing an evening shift—"

"Because you've not done it before," Ben insisted. "And also because of the way ya opened the door for Hiram to lash out at Miriam. He believes she kept ya from workin' for him because ya didn't tell him any different, Josiah," he continued urgently. "Ya heard

how he spoke to her—saw how he was eyeballin'
Savilla, too, and figurin' out where Lena fits into this
picture. He targets women, so we don't dare let
down our guard now."

"It was like Hiram changed personalities without
batting an eye," Savilla murmured. She shuddered,
hugging herself. "One minute he was sweet-talking me
and in the next breath he was hurling threats and ac-
cusations at you, Josiah. I'm *really* glad we're not going
to Higher Ground. Hiram Knepp is bad news."

"Fine then. Just *fine!*" Josiah snapped as he rose
from his chair to pace. "Ben's torn up my business
agreement and now my sister's slamming me, too. Anybody else care to take a shot?"

Miriam glanced up from her handiwork, frowning.
"What I'm seein' and hearin' tells me you'd be out the
door the minute something didn't go your way, young
man. If ya can't harness that bad attitude, it'll be like
havin' an untamed horse in my kitchen." Her voice remained deceptively calm, but she was clearly losing her
patience. "I've worked too hard buildin' up my business
to have ya upsettin' the routine or my customers—or
Naomi. You're a fine cook, but it takes more than that
to keep a café goin'."

Ben was pleased that Miriam had spoken this way,
and that she fully grasped the risk Josiah represented.

Josiah stopped pacing to stand in front of the couch.
"How about you, Lena?" he demanded. "Are you going
to take a turn now?"

Lena, who'd followed this escalating conversation
with wide blue eyes, burst into tears. Before Ben could
respond, Miriam grabbed the girl's hand.

"Because ya asked, there *is* another matter that needs
tendin'," Miriam said in a tone Ben had never heard

her use. "Lena and your baby deserve a decision about your place in their lives. Ya can't waffle on this, Josiah. You're either in or you're out."

Josiah opened his mouth but closed it before he made another rash remark.

Ben stood firm, watching the emotions play on the kid's face. Neither Miriam nor Savilla said a word. Lena stopped crying to focus on Josiah as though her life depended on his reply—because it did. The clock ticked away several tense, uncomfortable moments.

Josiah stood motionless, caught between the proverbial rock and the hard place where he would either find faith and courage or lose them. Ben sensed the kid would later come to see this discussion as the crossroad that had determined which path his life would take, so he let Josiah stew. Silence was a potent form of communication. Pain was a powerful teacher.

"Do you expect an answer right now?" Josiah finally rasped.

"You've had eight months to figure it out," Miriam pointed out. "Everybody in this room needs to know your answer, and needs to know you're gonna stand by it."

Ben's heart swelled. Miriam had stopped defending Josiah and wasn't letting him wiggle out of this situation. Just as a man consciously hung his hat on a peg and then took it off again, the young fellow in their midst would either follow the rules of their faith and do right by Lena or he'd forever be an outsider.

Josiah cleared his throat nervously. "Do you want me to leave?" he asked, looking from Miriam to Ben. "I don't know where else to go—"

"Maybe Ira would let ya share his apartment above the mill," Ben suggested.

Josiah frowned. "You've already planned this out. You want to get rid of me."

"Nope, it's just an option," Ben replied with a shrug. "Luke's movin' to Nora's place, so Ira's got an empty bedroom. Maybe you'd be more comfortable there, without the rest of us gawkin' at ya, waitin' for your answer."

"We're not castin' ya out—yet," Miriam confirmed. "Whatever you're thinkin' about your relationship with Lena, I want ya at the café tomorrow morning so we can talk about orderin' food and supplies and such. If you're not there by five, when Naomi and Hannah start cookin', I'll figure you're not gonna partner with us."

"I'll be there," Savilla stated as she rose from her chair. "Josiah's sold the farm, so Willow Ridge is my home now. No matter what my brother decides, my future's at the Sweet Seasons, so I'm *in*." She held out her hand to Lena. "Shall we get some rest, sweetie? We've had a busy day."

As the two young women went down the hallway toward the *dawdi haus*, Ben smiled to himself. Savilla had grit. She wasn't whining about the way her brother had so drastically changed her life, and she wasn't afraid to forge ahead. He was pleased that such a capable young woman wanted to work at the Sweet Seasons because it would make Miriam's exit easier.

Josiah sighed. "I'll go ask Ira about bunking with him for a while. *Denki* for giving me alternatives instead of just kicking me out."

"You're welcome," Ben replied. As Josiah fetched his coat in the kitchen, Ben slipped onto the couch beside Miriam. They kept quiet until they heard the back door close. "Bootin' Josiah out of our house could give him a quick excuse for leavin' altogether," he remarked. "It would be easier on us, maybe, but it wouldn't do him a bit of *gut.*"

"Maybe he'll open up to Ira—get some things off his chest," Miriam murmured as she snuggled against him. "Your brother's traveled the same road Josiah's on. I suspect Ira won't put up with much whinin' or complainin', either."

"He might even charge Josiah some rent, which wouldn't be a bad thing," Ben said with a chuckle. He wrapped his arms around Miriam to savor the comforting warmth of her body . . . the shifting of the baby against his side. "Whatever happens, God'll see to it. For now, it's just you and me, honey-girl, after a wonderful day celebratin' Luke and Nora's marriage—and eatin' some mighty fine food."

"*Jah*, the Witmers put on quite a feast," Miriam agreed. "Let's hope Josiah gets his act together so there'll be more where that came from."

Chapter Twelve

As the bell above the Sweet Seasons door jangled behind the last departing lunch customers on Saturday, Miriam sighed heavily. She stood at the serving window, gazing at the sturdy furniture the Brenneman brothers had built for her, the blue denim curtains she'd sewn for the café's opening, and the white board where Rhoda wrote the daily specials. Aromas of Josiah's brisket and ribs came into the kitchen as he carried the pans from the steam table into the kitchen. Rhoda, Rebecca, and Savilla chatted as they wiped down the tables. It had been a bittersweet day of keeping her emotions to herself, but at this moment Miriam felt as empty as the bakery case beside the cash register.

Naomi came to stand next to her. "Ya gonna be all right, dearie?" she murmured beneath the clattering of Josiah's metal pans. "If it makes ya feel any better, Savilla is top-notch help—and her brother'll come around, I believe. It was a *gut* idea for him to start cookin' his meats for the lunch shift."

"*Jah*, that's truly his talent," Miriam replied softly.

"Savilla's a natural-born organizer, so I suspect they'll do fine in the evenings without your supervisin'. I'll probably write out another business agreement in a couple of weeks."

Naomi smiled, grasping Miriam's hand. "It'll all work out. And I don't want to hear about how you're mopin' around at home or frettin' over how we're doin' without ya, understand me?" she insisted. "I can well imagine how *different* you're gonna feel, though. I don't know what I'd do with myself if I had to stay at home. Cookin' here keeps me goin' from one day to the next."

"I know all about that." Miriam turned her head so Naomi wouldn't see her blinking back tears. "Stayin' home's the right thing to do. But I can't think I'll be doin' anything that *matters*—leastways not until the baby's born."

"Get some rest while ya can. You've forgotten how a wee one'll take up a lot of the time ya used to spend sleepin'." Naomi slung an arm around Miriam's shoulders and leaned closer. "Why not slip out before the kids see ya gettin' teary-eyed?" she whispered. "After ya go, I'll give them a pep talk about how I expect things to keep runnin' smooth now that I'm to be in charge."

Miriam swiped at her eyes. "*Gut* idea. I don't want anybody hoverin' or quizzin' me. You *are* the boss now, Naomi—and you're the best friend ever, too."

Miriam got her wraps and quickly let herself out the back door. She stood beside the phone shanty, inhaling the frosty air to fortify herself—along with the luscious aromas that lingered around Josiah's cookers, which lined the windbreak wall between her building and Ben's smithy. When had she ever felt so fidgety? So unsure of what to do next?

As Miriam gazed past the white house where she and Jesse had raised their girls and beyond Bishop Tom's rolling pastures, however, a resonant voice filled her thoughts. *I will lift up mine eyes unto the hills, from whence cometh my help. My help cometh from the Lord, which made heaven and earth.*

Miriam stood taller. She felt as though Vernon Gingerich had somehow sensed her desperation and had shared Psalm 121 to comfort her. The passage had brought her peace on many occasions, especially after Jesse had passed, and as she recalled more of the familiar words she began to feel better. *The Lord shall preserve thy going out and thy coming in from this time forth, and even for evermore.*

"And why have I forgotten that?" she murmured. Maybe she was a lot wearier than she'd allowed herself to believe—or this was a wake-up call to realign herself with God's plan. It wasn't as though the Lord or His Son had forsaken her, after all. She was merely crossing the road to spend her days in the wonderful home Ben had built for her—not entering unfamiliar territory or the valley of the shadow of death.

I sure do pick silly things to get agitated about.

When Miriam felt frosty little lines on her face where her tears had frozen, she chuckled at herself. She had a few loose ends to tie up before she walked away from the café, so she sat down on the wooden chair in the phone shanty. She removed her bonnet and dialed the number for Zook's Market.

"*Jah*, it's Miriam," she said when the store's message machine beeped. "I'm stayin' home from here on out, so I won't be bakin' any more pies for your store. Naomi'll be callin' with an order real soon, I expect—

and *denki* for that wonderful-*gut* beef and pork ya furnished for Josiah's grillin'. Don't be strangers!"

In the next several minutes she contacted the places around mid-Missouri where she'd provided baked goods. With each call it became easier to explain why she would no longer be cooking commercially. By the time she hung up and put on her black bonnet again, Miriam felt stronger. Ready to move forward.

Even so, as she paused at the top of her lane to look at the Sweet Seasons, Miriam knew it wouldn't be easy to see her café from the picture window without wishing she could be there. How many loaves of bread and pies had she made in that kitchen before anyone else in Willow Ridge was even awake? How many dozens of cinnamon rolls and cookies? How many folks had eaten at her tables, nourishing themselves so they could go on about their work?

Well done, good and faithful servant. Enter thou into the joy of thy Lord.

Miriam blinked. Once again it seemed that Vernon had shared eloquent, uplifting passages from the Scriptures just for her. She smiled up at the sun, which appeared subdued in the hazy winter sky—yet it was shining faithfully.

You should do no less, she reminded herself. Then she stepped through the back door of her home, into the kitchen Ben had built for her, to begin a new phase of the life God had blessed her with.

As Lena finished setting the table on Monday night, she suspected Josiah knew things he wasn't telling. He was staring out the picture window in the front room, raking his dark, wavy hair back from his face. Had

Hiram Knepp confronted him again? Had his day gone so badly that he'd decided not to cook at the Sweet Seasons anymore?

"Come to supper," Miriam called as she and Savilla carried food to the table.

Ben rose from the couch, setting aside his copy of *The Budget.* He clapped Josiah on the back as they approached the table. "How's it goin', workin' amongst all those hens?" he asked good-naturedly. "I've heard several fellas sayin' how much they enjoy your grilled pork steaks and ribs."

"Far as I know, it's going all right," Josiah replied cautiously. "Naomi seems glad to have me there—but it's only been four days."

When they'd bowed their heads for the silent prayer, Lena peered at Josiah between her half-closed eyelids. His Adam's apple bobbed as he swallowed repeatedly, as though words were stuck in his throat.

"I heard from the banker in Bloomfield today," he said as Ben passed the bowl of macaroni and cheese. "The paperwork's in order, so the guy who bought the farm takes possession of it next week. After we finish at the café tomorrow, I'm heading up there to sign all the papers."

Savilla's fork clattered to the table. "Who's going to pack all the stuff in that house?" she demanded. "What'll we do with the furniture, and Mammi's things, and—and all those jars of food in the cellar?"

"The neighbors said they'd be glad to help—I asked them last time I was home," Josiah responded tersely. "You don't seem to think so, but I do plan ahead sometimes."

Lena's heart ached for Savilla. Clearing out that big old house would be a daunting job. Stacks of old magazines and catalogs were piled in the corners, and she suspected that their *dawdi*'s clothing and tools were still around, as well.

"So you told our friends about this before you told *me*?" Savilla blurted out. "That's where I grew up, too, you know! Maybe I'd like to go through Mammi's things—our parents' things—and save a few to remember them by!"

"And I'm thinkin' your brother would like ya to do that, too," Miriam said as she rose from her chair. She slipped her arm around Savilla's shoulders, gazing purposefully at Josiah. "After all, you've both been busy at the café, so if your brother got that call from the bank fella today, he's not had a lot of time to tell ya about it, Savilla."

Josiah smiled gratefully at Miriam as he reached across the table for his sister's hand. "Miriam's got it right," he murmured. "I wasn't leaving you out of this, Savilla. I *want* you to go—and our friends all want to see you, too. They'll help us whenever I ask them to come over."

"I'll go, too," Lena insisted. "I couldn't carry furniture, but I could pack boxes or—"

"It's gettin' awfully close to your due date for ya to be liftin' things, or even ridin' that far in a rig," Ben reminded her gently. "But *I'd* be happy to go along, Josiah, and I know fellas who have trailers and Belgians for haulin' your furniture back to Willow Ridge, if ya need them. Not tryin' to intrude, understand."

Lena sat back. Ben was right about her staying off the roads and close to the clinic. Once again she was amazed at his generosity—his willingness to set aside his own work to help them, especially considering the fact that Josiah had caused the Hooleys so much trouble.

Savilla let out a long sigh. "I guess the idea that I'll never be going back home is finally setting in," she murmured. "I didn't mean to lash out at you, little brother."

Josiah chuckled. He was more than six feet tall, and with his broad shoulders and sturdy build, he dwarfed his sister, so *little* had always been a joke between them. Lena watched their faces relax. Along with a stubborn streak, the Witmers shared coal-black hair and dazzling blue eyes. Lena often found herself hoping the baby would have their striking features, dreaming of a little boy with Josiah's handsome face and the winsome grin she wished she saw more often.

That grin lit up his eyes as he gazed at Lena. "Thanks for offering to help, but I'd feel better if you stayed here where folks can look after you, Lena. You'd probably pick up heavier things than you should if you were packing because you're always trying to be helpful. Okay?"

Lena's heart fluttered and the baby kicked inside her. It seemed Josiah cared about her welfare, after all. "I'll stay put, then."

"Glad to hear it," Miriam affirmed. "What with a houseful of folks comin' for Thanksgiving in a couple of days, I'll be glad for your help with the cookin'—and I'm sorry you and Josiah will miss that day with us, Savilla," she added kindly. "I can imagine how fast the thoughts are spinnin' in your heads, considerin' what all needs to be done at your home place."

Miriam sat down again and supper continued on a happier note. Lena savored the ham loaf and the creamy mac and cheese she'd helped prepare. She was

secretly relieved that she wouldn't be returning to
Bloomfield for the flurry of packing and cleaning out
at the Witmer place. It tired her just thinking about
how much work needed to be done there in a short
time. Then a different issue occurred to her. "Once
you empty out your *mammi*'s house, where will you put
all that stuff?"

Josiah glanced at Ben. "I have no idea," he admitted.
"We've not been in Willow Ridge long enough to look
for a place. Do you know where we can store what we
bring—or where to rent a house near here?"

Ben chewed his mouthful of food. "Can't think of
any place right off—"

"But if Rebecca looks on her computer, she might
steer ya toward some rentals," Miriam chimed in.
"There's one of those store-it-yourself places in New
Haven, too. Wouldn't cost much to keep your boxes
and furniture in one of those units until ya find a
house."

Find a house. As the others continued the conversation, Lena imagined a neatly kept home with trees and
a garden, an outbuilding for the horses and rigs . . .
rooms where a family could grow and a baby's laughter
would lift their hearts. Was she naïve, dreaming of such
a place? Would Josiah ask her to live there with him, as
his wife and the mother of his child?

When she glanced up, Josiah met her gaze. In that
moment, as his eyes took on a dreamy, faraway look,
Lena could believe his thoughts were in step with hers.

*I won't go hungry or homeless after the wee one's born,
Lord,* she prayed gratefully. *But if You could arrange it—
if You could help him understand—I'd really like to spend my
life with Josiah. We push each other's buttons, but he's the
right man for me.*

Chapter Thirteen

As Miriam gazed down the length of her crowded extended kitchen table on Thanksgiving, she had many blessings to be grateful for. She spooned some stuffing onto her plate, smiling at Ben. "When ya built this home, how'd ya know we'd be needin' such a big kitchen and a table with so many leaves?" she asked. "Twenty people we've got here today, and they all fit in this one room."

Ben held her gaze for a lovely moment. "From the first, I knew your mission was to feed people, honey-girl," he replied beneath the chatter going on around them. "I'm happy I could help ya make that happen. Glad our family and extended family have blessed us with their presence today."

Miriam nodded. Except for Rachel, who was eating dinner with the Brennemans this noon, and Ben's Aunt Jerusalem, who was celebrating with Vernon's family in Cedar Creek, all of her girls and the Hooleys were here. She smiled as she watched newlywed Nora chatting with her daughter Millie Glick, and she was pleased that Gabe and Wilma, Atlee, Lizzie, and little Ella Glick had come, too, so Wilma didn't have to cook. Ben's Aunt Nazareth and Bishop Tom sat at the far end of the table with Rhoda, Andy, and their kids—as well as Andy's mother, Betty. All of these folks had come through times of trial to find new lives this past year, and Miriam felt honored to have been part of their journeys.

Beside Miriam, Lena was tucking away a plateful of corn casserole, turkey that Josiah had roasted before he left, mashed potatoes and gravy—and she was taking a second helping of cranberry sauce. "Sure do appreciate your helpin' me make all this food," Miriam told her. "Your glazed carrots are a big hit! Rhoda's kids love them, so that bowl's nearly empty."

"Mamm always fixed those for our Thanksgiving dinners," she replied wistfully. "I can't help but wonder who might be at home eating dinner right now—"

"Why not call them?" Miriam encouraged her. "I'm sure your *mamm* would be glad to hear your voice, even if ya just leave a message."

Lena sighed. "When I was leaving with Josiah, Dat made it clear I wasn't to bother them anymore," she replied. "But if it's all right with you, I might call Josiah this afternoon. I bet he and Savilla are way too busy packing to enjoy a nice meal today."

"Fine idea. Give them our best," Miriam said. It bothered her that Lena's family had cast her out so coldly—although Nora had lived through that same situation when she'd been carrying Millie. As Miriam watched the two redheads laughing together, mother and daughter, she asked the Lord for a similar reconciliation in Lena's family. God already knew whether their relationship would heal, but it never hurt to request His special attention when a baby was involved.

"I'm proud of ya, Lena," Miriam insisted as she passed the crescent rolls. "You're handlin' this situation better than I would've at your age. Keep on believin' your life'll work out for the best and that's what'll happen."

When Lena focused on her dinner again, Miriam noticed how her arm remained wrapped around her unborn child—and how a grimace flickered across Lena's face. As a blue-eyed blonde, Lena often looked pale, but today she appeared very fragile. Lost in her own little world.

Feed my lambs.

Miriam gripped her forkful of corn casserole. Once again that voice that resembled Vernon's had spoken to her. The words came from a story about Jesus telling Simon Peter that caring for those around him was the earthly work he'd been commissioned to do.

Feed my lambs. Feed my sheep.

As Miriam contemplated what these words might mean to her, her crowded kitchen rang with conversation and laughter while the people she loved most were stuffing themselves silly with too much food. So why was she being reminded to feed Jesus's sheep?

These words were your mission statement when ya opened the café with Naomi. Miriam blinked. She'd begun baking full-time because she believed that feeding people was a special talent God had blessed her with. Yet last week, He'd told her to leave her restaurant and live according to the *Ordnung,* and to take up a different life purpose.

We are His people and the sheep of His pasture. Enter into His gates with thanksgiving and into His courts with praise. And feed my sheep.

Miriam let the words of Psalm 100 seep into her

soul. Why was she so focused on this still, small voice while nineteen other people conversed in her kitchen? Although no one else seemed to notice, she felt as if a special messenger had taken her aside.

When she glanced at Lena again, Miriam felt a jolt of understanding. Lena and Josiah were vulnerable lambs who'd lost their way. And even though Savilla was more mature, she was leaving the only home she'd ever known, boxing up memories of her grandparents and the parents who'd died when she was so young. It was no mistake that Josiah and Lena had gotten lost in a snowstorm and had found their way to her door because the Lord never left anything to chance. He worked out His purpose even during the least notable moments, whether or not His sheep listened or obeyed His commands.

As this concept sank in, Miriam accepted it. Sometimes God made it rain for forty days and nights, and sometimes He whispered hints into His followers' ears. There was no mistaking His message now, however. If He intended for Miriam to shepherd the young sheep He'd herded into her life, wasn't that more worthwhile—much more important—than running a café? Considering that Lena's baby might be born any day now, Miriam knew she had no time to waste.

As her own unborn child shifted in her swollen belly, Miriam was filled with gratitude. She emerged from her soul searching to participate in Thanksgiving dinner again, knowing why it was so important to remain at home. Three precious lambs—and a new baby— would depend upon her love for the next several weeks.

When Ben caught her eye, Miriam smiled. *I love you, Bennie-bug,* she mouthed.

Her husband reached beneath the table to caress

her protruding belly. *I'm so glad I'm yours,* he replied silently. His beard rippled with a smile that made his hazel eyes shine. *You and me—and baby makes three.*

Miriam felt her face turning pink. God had guided this fine younger man to her doorstep a year ago— and who could have foreseen the wondrous love they had shared ever since?

God saw it coming! What further proof do ya need of His will for your life?

Miriam pressed her hand on top of Ben's and held it against their shifting baby. She knew her time at the Sweet Seasons had been well spent, just as she now believed a more important purpose awaited her.

And she was finally ready to accept it.

As Josiah opened the box of delivery pizza, he was so tired he almost didn't care that the turkey he'd roasted Tuesday morning wasn't on his own table. Almost.

"Good thing the pizza place isn't closed today," Savilla said as she took a steaming slice. "With all these boxes piled around us, we won't be fixing any more food in this kitchen. That's kind of sad."

"Miriam's kitchen is full of people right now and her table's loaded with all sorts of great food," Josiah murmured. He didn't have the heart to mention how much cheerier the Hooley kitchen was, either, because the house they'd grown up in had faded into a shabby state of disrepair. "It's a little late to ask, but do you think we've done the right thing? I never dreamed it would take so much work to clear this place out."

Savilla's weary shrug told him she was feeling as wistful—and worn out—as he was.

For a moment, Josiah flashed back to Thanksgiving dinners of his childhood, when this house had rung with the stories and laughter of aunts, uncles, and their grandparents. It made him very sad that except for Savilla, everyone in his family had either moved or passed away. It bothered him, as well, that he couldn't remember what his *mamm* and *dat* looked like, and couldn't recall their voices.

He studied his sister's face, trusting Mammi's remarks about how Savilla was the image of their mother. "I'm sorry I've overturned your life, sis," he murmured. "I've made a lot of major decisions lately without considering your feelings."

Savilla's blue eyes widened. "Is this the voice of reason and responsibility I'm hearing?" she asked softly. "Or are you so exhausted you're out of your head?"

Josiah laughed and grabbed another slice of pizza. "I can't *ever* recall being this sore and worn out," he admitted. "But when our helpers come tomorrow, we'll be a lot readier for them to load the wagons. That was a *gut* idea you had, getting us a Dumpster."

Savilla smiled glumly. "Most of the stuff in the house is worn out or broken. Not worth packing."

"*Jah*, Mammi used everything until it fell apart. Growing up, I never felt we were poor—but I was also clueless about how short the money got after Dawdi had to stop working."

"She was an expert at making a little go a long way," Savilla agreed. Her dust-smudged face flickered with a smile. "I think she'd be pleased that we've found a town where there's more opportunity to support ourselves with our catering."

"*Denki* for saying that. Our lives went on the same

way for so many years," Josiah remarked as he reached for more pizza, "and then *bang!* Everything changed at once."

"We've done some scrambling lately, *jah*. But we've landed on our feet," Savilla insisted. "Long as we stick together—"

A guitar riff played in Josiah's shirt pocket and he grabbed his cell phone. "It's a call from Willow Ridge—"

"Answer it! They wouldn't be calling unless it was important."

Was Lena having her baby? Josiah's mouth went dry as he pressed the button on his phone. What with having to clean out the house so quickly, he'd not responded to Miriam's challenge about being *in* or *out* of Lena's life. Once again, his priorities hadn't been in order, had they? *"Jah*, hullo?"

"Josiah! We've finished dinner and I wanted to hear how you're doing," Lena said. "Even with a houseful of people, it's not the same without you here."

Josiah's eyes closed. Lena sounded fine, thank goodness. He pictured her sitting in the phone shanty behind the café as he savored the sweetness of her voice, her words. "Savilla and I are taking a pizza break. I can only imagine all the wonderful-*gut* food you and Miriam cooked up for Thanksgiving dinner."

"I don't know how she does it," Lena replied in a breathy voice. "We had the table extended out so far that twenty people were gathered around it! And your turkey was fabulous, Josiah. Everybody said to tell you so."

When Savilla scooted her chair back to leave him to his conversation, Josiah motioned for her to stay put. He envied Lena—not just because she'd enjoyed a traditional Thanksgiving dinner but because everyone in Miriam's kitchen *cared* about her. "Roasting that turkey was a small favor, considering how much the Hooleys have done for us," he said wistfully. "Savilla and I have made a lot of progress, but we have a long way to go."

Lena's soft sigh tickled his ear. "I bet that's a tougher job than you thought. You're both saying good-bye to your lifelong home."

A pang of realization sliced through him. Lena had immediately recognized the emotional consequences of selling his family's farm, and it struck Josiah that because of him—because they'd made a baby without being married—Lena had lost her lifelong home, as well. Why had it taken him so long to figure out what his sister and his girlfriend had known all along?

"You've got that right," Josiah murmured. "Most of the furnishings and Mammi's belongings aren't worth bringing to Willow Ridge, and they're too worn out to donate to the thrift stores. That's a sad thing to say about the stuff she loved."

Lena got so quiet that Josiah checked to see if their call had cut out. "Um, does that mean you and Savilla won't be finding a house in Willow Ridge?" she finally asked.

Josiah heard anxiety in her remark and didn't know what to say. Had Lena set her heart on living with him and Savilla instead of staying with the Hooleys? She seemed so comfortable there. *Why can't you get it through your head that she wants to be with you—to be a family and have a home?*

"We'll be moving into a place as soon as we find one," Josiah murmured. "I hate to bother Ben and Miriam any longer than we have to." His conscience prodded him to reassure Lena that she would have a place in their home, too, but he didn't want to start a discussion about marriage over the phone. So he changed the subject. "How are you feeling, Lena? I bet you've been on your feet a lot, helping Miriam."

Her sigh told him more than he wanted to hear. "I tried not to let on during dinner," she admitted, "but my back's killing me and I can't find a comfortable position to sit in. When I return to the *dawdi haus,* I'll probably rest in my room. The house is really noisy today, and I don't feel like making conversation."

Warning flares went up in Josiah's mind. Did the symptoms she'd mentioned signal the coming of the baby? "Sounds like a *gut* idea," he hastened to assure her. "I bet it's cold in the phone shanty, so I should let you go—but it was really nice of you to call, Lena. Nice of you to think of us."

"I needed to hear your voice, Josiah. I—I love you." *Click.*

Josiah stared at his cell. Not only had Lena declared her love for him, she'd not given him a chance to respond. *What would you have said? After the way you all but told her to hang up, she cut the call short and cut her losses. Who could blame her?*

"What happened?" Savilla asked with a frown. "Did you lose your signal?"

Seems the signal's been strong all along and I've not been picking it up, Josiah thought. But he didn't feel like having that discussion with his sister. "Lena's heading to the house for a nap. They had twenty people there for dinner."

Savilla's rising eyebrows told him she'd seen through his fib, but she didn't quiz him. She looked around at the packing boxes and the cupboards that were hanging open. "The sooner we finish this pizza, the sooner we can clean out more closets, right?"

It was the best exit line he could hope for. Josiah reached for another slice of the pizza, which was getting greasy as it cooled. He had a lot to think about, yet he sensed that cleaning out closets was a lot like clearing away his former assumptions and misconceptions. Maybe by the time he and Savilla had finished with this house, his soul would be free of clutter, too, so he could move forward with a clean slate—and with Lena.

Chapter Fourteen

Friday morning, Lena awoke with a fiery pain gripping her lower back and abdomen. It was still dark, and now that Miriam didn't rise in the wee hours to bake at the café, Lena hated to wake her. She muffled a cry with her pillow when another fierce jolt of pain hit her.

Contractions. Nurse Andy predicted you might be in labor for several hours because this is your first baby.

The next contraction brought tears to Lena's eyes, and as she struggled to sit up, she felt a sticky wetness between her legs. Clutching herself, she went to the bathroom to clean up. The sound of dishes rattling in the kitchen was a welcome sign that Miriam was out of bed, so Lena walked down the short hallway.

But it was Ben, putting the coffee percolator on the stove by the glow of a lamp. It was too embarrassing to tell a man what was happening, so Lena started back to her room—until she cried out with the most brutal contraction yet.

Ben turned to gaze at her. "Lena! Are ya—Miriam'll

want to know your time's comin'," he said quietly. "Can I help ya back to your room? Shall we call—"

"Just tell Miriam, okay?" Lena rasped. "I'll go on back to bed."

"*Jah*, we'll let her take care of it," Ben agreed with a nervous laugh. "It's best if we men just stay out of Mother Nature's way."

Rather than lying down, Lena padded the seat of the rocking chair with a towel and sat down to wait for Miriam. Making the rocker move back and forth gave her something to do, and it felt better to move as she rode out her contractions. She wished Josiah and Savilla were here, even as she sensed Josiah would be as jittery as Ben was.

Or would he? *Maybe he hung up so quickly yesterday because he has no intention of claiming his baby. Maybe he wasn't cleaning out his grandmother's house—maybe that was his cover for getting out of Willow Ridge and out of your life.* Lena rocked faster, caught up in these what ifs and why nots until the door of her room swung open.

"Lena, it's gonna be a day you'll never forget, honey-bug," Miriam said in a soothing voice. "And look who's here to check on ya. We've got ya covered."

Lena's worrisome thoughts fled as both Miriam and Andy Leitner gazed at her. Why had she allowed doubts about Josiah's commitment to sidetrack her from the most important event of her life? "*Denki* so much for coming, Andy. Sorry I got you out of bed so early."

"That happens a lot in my line of work." He smiled as he opened his medical bag. "But what other occupation would allow me to help with the most blessed event on God's earth? Deep breaths now—sorry my stethoscope's cold."

After Andy checked her vital signs, her dilation, and timed a few contractions, he squeezed her shoulder. "I'll make my hospital rounds in New Haven and come back in a couple of hours," he said. "Meanwhile, I want you walking and moving around as much as you can tolerate. If you can eat some nutrient-dense foods now, they"ll sustain you while you're in labor."

"I've got just the thing," Miriam remarked. "I made a batch of muffins with lots of grains and fruits and ground nuts. I'll brew a pot of tea and be ready for your company when ya come out to the kitchen."

Once again, Lena felt blessed by Miriam's kindness, and grateful for her experience in these important matters. When she arrived in the kitchen, wrapped in a thick robe Miriam had loaned her, the aromas of spices and molasses made her realize how hungry she was.

"My Rachel shared this recipe with me," Miriam said as she set out a basket of fragrant muffins. "I've got some beef broth and other *gut* liquids for ya, too. Eat now, Lena, while ya feel up to it. You'll do a lot better when the serious pushin'll have to get done."

"I'm so glad you know all this stuff, Miriam," Lena murmured as she buttered one of the warm muffins. She wasn't so sure her own mother could've taken such fine care of her, but she didn't say that out loud. Thinking about her family only made her miss them more.

While Lena ate, she focused on talking to Miriam. Then, for the umpteenth time, she took out the tiny baby clothes, diapers, and other supplies she'd received at the shower Nora had held. She walked. She rocked. She told herself each painful contraction took her closer to holding her baby in her arms. And as Lena imagined Josiah, he was smiling at her as though he was totally delighted—as though he intended to take good care of her and their baby forever.

The mental image of Josiah's rugged, handsome face helped her endure the hours of nerve-racking contractions, some of them so sharp Lena thought she might pass out. Finally, Nurse Andy told her to get into the bed Miriam had prepared for her. Through a haze of pain she kept breathing, pushing when she had no more strength to push, believing that someday Josiah would realize how much he meant to her. Lena needed him, yes, but she loved him more.

"Don't give up, Lena. You're almost there!" Andy encouraged her from the end of the bed. "Here comes a head with dark, wavy hair."

Josiah, I'm doing this for you! Lord, give me one more gut, strong—

When Lena bore down, she felt a surge of momentum—a sudden relief—and then a tiny cry became loud enough to fill the room.

"You've got a fine little boy here, Lena," Andy announced.

"Just like ya thought," Miriam chimed in happily. "He's wigglin' and fussin' just right, too. We'll clean him up so ya can hold him. Oh, but he's a honey-bug, this boy is."

Lena smiled weakly. She glanced at the red-faced, blanketed baby Miriam showed her a few minutes later and then drifted off into exhausted oblivion.

Once Rachel and Rhoda were sitting with Lena, who held her newborn son in the crook of her arm, Miriam joined Andy in the kitchen. "I'm gonna pay your birthin' fee right now, so don't quibble with me," she insisted as she reached into a coffee can she kept in the pantry. "It's anybody's guess when Lena—or Josiah— might think to settle up with ya."

Andy eyed her over the top of a muffin he'd taken from the basket on the kitchen counter. "I feel a lot better about Lena's situation because she's here with you. Where'd Josiah take off to, anyway?"

Miriam counted out Andy's cash before she answered. "He and Savilla are cleanin' out their farmhouse so the new owner can take it over. He'll be back, though," she said, hoping she'd assessed Josiah correctly. "His sister's committed herself to working at the Sweet Seasons, and he's smart enough to stick with her because she's got a head for running a business."

"Glad to hear it." Andy groaned appreciatively as he looked at the muffin he was eating. "This is *fabulous*. I'm guessing it's got lots of whole grain and down-to-earth real food in it."

"*Jah*, when Rachel swore it got her through Amelia's birth, I added the recipe to my collection," Miriam said. "I used whole wheat flour from Luke's mill, along with ground apple and carrot, some pumpkin puree, and honey."

"Carbs that won't spike your blood sugar and then bottom out—not that you have to be a woman in labor to love them," Andy added as he snatched another one. The beard he'd started when he got married rippled as he grinned at her. "Between you, me, and this muffin basket, I think Rhoda might be pregnant—but it's too early to tell anybody else."

Miriam let out a squeal and hugged him. "I was wonderin' about that as I watched her at dinner yesterday. And right now, while she and Rachel are keepin' an eye on Lena, I've got a couple of calls to make. Stay as long as ya want, Andy."

"I'll walk with you. Annie Mae Wagler's on my list of appointments today, so I'll stop by her house before I head back to the clinic."

It was a pleasure to talk with her new son-in-law about his flourishing medical practice, and a blessing that his love for Rhoda had brought him to Willow Ridge and led him to joining the Old Order, as well. They parted ways at the county blacktop, and Miriam continued to the phone shanty behind the Sweet Seasons, which was still closed for the Thanksgiving holiday.

Miriam sat down in the shanty and closed the door against the wintry wind. As she thumbed through the list of numbers she kept in the drawer of the telephone table, she pondered what she'd say to Lena's parents. They hadn't called back when she'd phoned them about Lena being in Willow Ridge, but maybe news of their new grandson would open their hearts.

Miriam dialed and then waited for the beep of the Eshs' message machine. "*Jah*, it's Miriam Hooley. You've got a fine, healthy grandson, born just a couple of hours ago," she said cheerfully. "Lena's doin' fine. Just my opinion, but at a time like this, there's nobody a girl needs more than her *mamm*. I—I hope ya can look beyond what's happened in the past and focus on the future of your family," she insisted. "Come and see her and the wee one any time. We'd be pleased to have ya here."

She hung up, wondering if she'd spoken out of turn. *Ya told the truth. And ya spoke up for Lena when she can't speak for herself.*

Satisfied with that idea, Miriam ran her finger down the list of phone numbers again. She dialed and waited through four rings, disappointed that Josiah didn't answer—but the Witmers had a lot of family business to take care of. "Josiah, it's Miriam," she said when his phone prompted her. "You've got a sweet, healthy little son now—and he looks just like ya," she added with a chuckle. "Lena's restin'. She's a strong young woman who deserves a committed man every bit as much as your boy needs a *dat* he can rely on. Just sayin'."

Pausing, Miriam once again decided she had spoken the truth, whether or not Josiah wanted to hear it. Deep down, however, she sensed that he would listen now. "Hope you and Savilla are makin' *gut* progress on the house," she went on. "We're glad you're settlin' in Willow Ridge, and we're lookin' forward to havin' ya as partners at the Sweet Seasons. Take care and God bless."

As she replaced the receiver, Miriam prayed that Josiah and Savilla would have safe travels on their way back through Missouri. December was a couple of days away, so snow and icy roads would become more of a possibility.

Miriam rocked from side to side for a few blissful moments, hugging her unborn child. Watching the miracle of birth had made her more keenly eager to hold her new baby, and to share the wee one with Ben. When her triplets had been born twenty-two years ago, her husband Jesse had remained a traditional Amish male—no diaper changing or spoiling the girls by holding them when they cried. He had loved them dearly, and had eventually gotten over his wish for a boy, but an invisible fence had been in place: Jesse Lantz had remained in control of his household, his children, and his emotions. His emotional fence had become a more obvious boundary between him and

Miriam after Rebecca had washed away in the flood. He'd agreed with their bishop at the time that outside help shouldn't be called in to search for their toddler, so Miriam had mourned her lost daughter without being able to bury her little body and find closure.

Ben would be different, though. He wouldn't feel that his manhood—or his position as head of the family—would be compromised if he gave himself over to cooing and cuddling.

What a blessing he'll be! Miriam left the phone shanty with a grin on her face. In about a month, this dream would come true, just as every other wish and prayer had been granted her since Ben had come into her life. As tiny snowflakes tingled on her cheeks, Miriam thanked God for the life and the love He'd bestowed upon her.

She made her way up the lane to the house again. As she chatted with Rhoda and Rachel, Miriam was struck by a wonderful idea. When her girls left, she went upstairs to the room beside the one she shared with Ben, which was set up as the nursery. The beautiful cradle Ben had made sat beside her rocking chair, and she picked it up to admire the flawless woodworking and the hummingbird her husband had created in pewter.

Every time she touched this cradle, she felt the love of Ben's hands as he'd crafted it for her—a priceless gift, that love was. Miriam had made a little mattress and a cover for it, as well as a crocheted blanket in shades of sunshine yellow, so the cradle was ready to welcome their child.

Downstairs she went, to find Lena nursing her new son. Lena didn't look completely comfortable with feeding him yet, but she was doing her best. The baby's eyes were closed contentedly in his puckered pink face.

"I want ya to have this cradle," Miriam murmured. "I want it back, understand, but until ya find a bassinet or something else for your boy to sleep in, he can use this."

Lena's mouth fell open. "But Ben made that for *you*," she protested. "He'll be upset if I—"

Miriam held up her hand to silence the girl. "Ben often quotes the verse in the Bible where Jesus says that foxes have dens and birds have nests, but He had no place to lay his head," she explained gently. "There's no reason your wee boy should suffer that same lack— not if *I* have anything to say about it."

Miriam gently set the cradle on the floor. She leaned over the bed to smile at Lena's son, smoothing his dark hair. "Have ya picked a name for him?"

"This is Isaiah Daniel," Lena replied softly. "That was Josiah's *dat*'s name."

"Well, ya couldn't have chosen two finer fellas from the Bible to name him for, and you're honorin' the boy's *dawdi*, too," Miriam said. "What with Isaiah bein' the prophet who foretold the comin' of our Savior, and Daniel havin' such faith as to remain unharmed in a den of hungry lions, this young man has a lot to live up to."

As though Isaiah knew they were talking about him, he looked up at Miriam with his deep blue eyes. Such sweetness filled her that she was speechless for a moment.

Miriam sighed wistfully. "I'll leave you two to get better acquainted," she murmured. "It's been a big day for all of us."

Chapter Fifteen

Ben sipped a mug of cocoa, grateful that the kitchen was warm and that Miriam had spent the morning baking cookies. About four inches of snow had fallen during the night, so he—and most of the other men around Willow Ridge—had been out on their horse-drawn plows clearing the roads and lanes. He bit into a cookie with colorful gumdrop chunks.

"I've not seen a cookie like this one before, and it's real tasty," he said. "But then, I've never met a cookie of yours I didn't like."

Miriam chuckled and took a similar cookie from the plate. "Slice-and-bake recipes are handy because after ya roll up the dough, it waits in the fridge until you've got time to bake. Taylor and Brett will gobble these up."

"*Jah*, they will. You're a fine, fun *mammi* for those kids—and a shinin' example of what bein' Amish is all about."

Ben adored the roses that bloomed in Miriam's cheeks. She was getting rounder by the day, even more beautiful than when they'd married.

"Maybe I am a *gut* example," she murmured as she poured them more cocoa. "This morning Lena said it was time she joined the church, now that Isaiah's been born."

"Glad to hear that. Maybe Josiah will follow her lead." Ben glanced out the window as another plow drawn by a pair of Belgians cleared the road shoulder. "Any idea when he and Savilla will be back?"

"All I know is what he said about the new owner gettin' possession of their place sometime this week. I hope they've waited for the roads to be cleared before they start—"

Lena's loud cry of alarm startled Ben enough that his cocoa sloshed onto the table. He and Miriam both hurried down the back hall toward the *dawdi haus* just as Lena came rushing out of her room, clutching her son.

"What happened?" Miriam asked as she wrapped her arm around Lena. "You're shakin' like a scared rabbit."

"I *am* scared!" she rasped. "I saw a face at the window and it was—it was that Hiram guy, I just know it!"

Ben's insides tightened as his gaze met Miriam's, but he wanted to be sure Lena's impression was accurate. "Are ya sure? You've only seen him once, at Nora's wedding."

"Nobody else has a black pointy beard," Lena replied in a shaky voice. "I'd been feeding Isaiah in the rocking chair, and—and—"

Miriam was frowning but trying to remain calm. "Were ya havin' a dream, maybe? When I get startled out of a nap, my mind's not always workin' real logical."

"I can't think why Hiram would be trompin' around behind the house, either," Ben murmured.

"But I saw him!" Lena declared. "He was looking in the window, staring at Isaiah and me—like maybe he was going to come in the back door."

Ben left the two women in the hallway and entered the *dawdi haus*. This apartment, built for when he and Miriam became unable to climb stairs, was on the ground level, so it was possible that a person outside could peer in—although nobody ever worried about that sort of thing in Willow Ridge. As Ben thought about the scene Lena had described, he realized that Hiram, a fairly tall fellow, would be able to peer in through the open bedroom curtains—and the rocking chair wasn't far from the window, so Lena would certainly have been startled if a face had appeared on the other side of the glass.

If *is the operative word*, Ben reminded himself. Lena was young and vulnerable, and if she'd been dozing, her imagination might've raced like a spooked horse. There was an easy way to find out.

Ben went into the sitting room and opened the door. If the fresh snow was smooth and undisturbed—

His mouth clapped shut. Both of the back windows had several footprints under them, big enough to be made by a man's boot. The footprints were right outside the door, too, so if their intruder had wanted to, he could've let himself in. Ben knew he and Miriam wouldn't have heard the door from the kitchen, and a napping Lena wouldn't have known about an uninvited guest until he'd entered her bedroom.

Goose bumps rushed up Ben's spine. What if this had happened while he'd been working in his shop and Miriam and Lena were here by themselves? He shut the door hard and twisted the knob lock. It might be time to install deadbolts, the way Nora had at her place. Ben inhaled deeply, trying to corral his runaway thoughts before he reported to Miriam.

The two women and the baby were in the kitchen. Miriam looked up at him, her mouth in a tight line. "What'd ya see?"

"Footprints. At both back windows," he said as he took his coat from its peg. "I locked the *dawdi haus* door, and I want ya to lock this one and the front door, too, while I'm out lookin' around. I can't imagine why anybody would be snoopin' behind the house, but considerin' what we heard about Hiram when Officer McClatchey led him away, we can't take any chances."

Miriam's face puckered with concern. "Guess I've got to remember where I put the keys," she murmured. "Be careful out there, Bennie."

Ben buttoned his coat and pulled his stocking cap over his ears. "If I see a black Cadillac, we'll know he's in town. Don't fret over it, though. Once Hiram knows I'm lookin' for him, he'll not try anything."

Bracing himself for whatever he might find, Ben stepped outside—and hopped over the fresh footprints outside the kitchen door. Tracks went between the house and the barn as well. Instinct warned him not to burst into the barn, considering that Hiram might get the jump on him, so he placed an ear against the walk-in door instead.

Quiet. No nervous stomping of feet, and no whickering among his horses. The footprints began and ended in the lane, which he'd plowed clean earlier that morning, so there was no telling where Hiram might've gone.

Ben gazed at the homes and buildings he could see from his hilltop vantage point, scowling. He saw no sign of a Cadillac—no tire tracks in the lane, no black car parked near the Sweet Seasons, his smithy, or the clinic. Hiram had never been a man to walk or drive a horse-drawn rig after Aunt Jerusalem had discovered his car last year—and why would he have been tromping through the snow around the house and the barn, anyway?

To see what he could see. And to scare the living daylights out of Lena.

Ben was on his way inside to tell Miriam he was going to Bishop Tom's to discuss their intruder when he spotted a familiar buggy and horse approaching down the lane. Josiah and Savilla needed to be made aware of what had happened this morning, so Ben stepped aside as Dolly pulled the rig up beside the house.

"You two must've left mighty early this morning," Ben remarked as Josiah halted the horse and opened the buggy door. "Guess I figured you'd be hauling a load of furniture. Did everything go all right?"

Josiah smiled tiredly. "*Jah*, but instead of packing Mammi's stuff, we ended up pitching most of it. She'd worn everything out."

"Just kept a few family odds and ends," Savilla added. "It feels strange, knowing we've spent our last night in that house. But it's all cleaned out, and we'll have a fresh start in Willow Ridge now—and we want to see the baby, of course!"

Ben smiled at the young woman's eagerness. Savilla was a wonderful addition to their community, and he predicted she'd soon have fellows hoping to date and court her. "There's something ya should know," he began in a low voice. "Lena got a nasty scare a little while ago. Looked up to see Hiram Knepp peerin' in the window at her."

Josiah's face hardened as Savilla gasped. "Oh, that's just creepy," she muttered. "Lena won't want to sleep in that room anymore, and I can't say I blame her."

"*Jah*, it might be a *gut* idea to move you girls upstairs. We're lockin' the doors from here on out," Ben insisted. "I have no idea where Hiram got off to, but I'm on my way to let Bishop Tom know what's happened."

"But how'd he know Lena would be in that back room?" Josiah demanded. "I can't think anyone in Willow Ridge would tip him off after the scene he made at Luke and Nora's wedding."

"Hiram's probably the smartest man I know—not necessarily in a *gut* way," Ben answered. "Now that he knows Lena saw him and was scared witless, she'll be an easy target. We've got to keep everybody posted about this incident—"

"And it's all my fault," Josiah muttered as he looked away. "If I'd contacted him, like you told me, we wouldn't be dealing with his warped craziness."

Ben was pleased to hear true remorse in Josiah's tone, yet he shook his head. "We can't know that for sure, Josiah. Hiram's sneakier than a snake. He was doin' stuff like this before you Witmers showed up, so I can't let ya take all the blame."

"Even so, I'm going to give Knepp a piece of my mind—after I visit with Lena and see the baby," he added quickly. "She's nervous, I bet. I shouldn't have been gone so long."

Ben nodded, hearing a different attitude than Josiah had displayed before he'd left for Iowa. "Tell Miriam I'll be back in a while. Don't want her thinkin' I met up with Hiram and didn't make it home."

"Be careful," Savilla warned. "For all we know,

Knepp could be watching us right this minute. And that idea turns my stomach."

Ben nodded and started toward the county road. Never had he foreseen the evil mischief their former bishop was capable of. It was a sad commentary on the state of God's world when innocent folks suffered at the hands of religious leaders who'd gone bad.

He prayed for guidance as he walked down the snowy road to Tom's house.

Josiah turned the knob of the Hooleys' back door and then realized why it was locked. "We'll go around front to ring the doorbell," he said to Savilla. "I don't want to knock on a window—and scare Lena again—to get somebody's attention."

His sister's face lit up, and she waved at whomever had caught sight of her through the window. As the door swung open, Miriam welcomed them with a warm smile. "*Gut* to see you kids. I suppose Ben told ya about our little *incident* this morning."

"I'm glad you're locking the doors now," Josiah replied. "I'll tell you the same thing I said to Ben— I'm really, *really* sorry I didn't follow through with a phone call or a note to Knepp. I had no idea—"

"None of us could've guessed he'd take his pranks this far," Miriam interrupted with a shake of her head. She twisted the lock button and gestured toward a plate of cookies on the counter. "You kids're probably hungry after your long ride. If ya need a sandwich to hold ya over until dinner—"

"I want to see the baby." Josiah was surprised at the way those words had popped out of his mouth.

"Glad to hear it," Miriam said with a little smile.

"Lena's in the front room with him. We've decided you girls are gonna move upstairs, away from pryin' eyes. So if ya could help us shift their clothes a little later, Josiah, I'd be grateful."

He chuckled. "Why did I know you'd be way ahead of us?"

"*Denki* for that," Savilla said as she hung up her coat. "Ben's account of your intruder gave me the willies—but a couple of these cookies will help."

Josiah eyed the plate, spotting dark chocolate bars and lemony-looking cut-out cookies that called to him, but he headed for the front room. It felt so good to return to Miriam's sunny kitchen, to the fragrance of her baking—to the gentle wisdom and compassion that filled whichever room she occupied. Silly as it seemed at his age, Josiah suddenly wanted to adopt Miriam as his *mamm*. His grandmother had done her best, but his need for a mother had remained unfulfilled since he'd been bereaved as a toddler. When he spotted Lena on the sofa holding a black-haired baby, however, his wistful thoughts took a back seat.

Josiah swallowed hard. He really, really didn't want to mess up this moment.

Lena's delighted smile made his heart shimmer. "Josiah! I'm glad you're here."

"Me, too."

Somehow he was putting one foot in front of the other, for Josiah had never felt so tongue-tied or unsure of what to do next. He'd not been around many babies—they fell into that broad category of something women took care of—yet he couldn't stop gazing at the tiny creature in the crook of Lena's arm. "Wow," he murmured when he'd reached the end of the sofa. "He's so tiny. So *awesome*."

"He is," Lena agreed with a chuckle. Her blond hair was tucked neatly beneath a crisp white *kapp* and her blue eyes twinkled as she looked up at Josiah. "Want to hold him?"

Josiah blinked. Handling hundred-pound hog carcasses posed no problem at all, yet he was worried about dropping this tiny creature or holding him too tightly. He sensed that a totally different kind of strength was required around babies, and he wasn't sure he possessed it.

Lena was patting a sofa cushion, so Josiah sat down. He scooted all the way back, his eyes never leaving the boy . . . his son. When Lena offered him the baby, he gingerly took him in the bend of his elbow as he'd seen her holding him. The baby immediately knew someone else—a rookie—had taken him, and when his eyes opened, Josiah got sucked into that blue-eyed gaze without resisting it. He felt powerless, mesmerized by the small, puckered pink face and the tiny eyelashes and the way the little guy began to squirm.

"I'm going to make him cry," Josiah moaned. "I didn't mean to."

Lena chuckled. "I think he's filling his diaper."

"Ah. Nice to know I have that effect on him—I guess." It seemed like a totally stupid thing to say, but Josiah had no idea what you discussed while you held your child . . . your firstborn, while you sat beside his mother. When a tiny hand gripped his finger, Josiah thought he might cry—partly from wonder and partly from the fear that he'd lost his sense of direction and would never return to being the man he'd been before he'd entered the room.

"I've named him Isaiah Daniel," Lena said as she held Josiah's gaze. "What name will *you* give him?"

Her question nailed him, begging for the obvious response that he would marry her and make everything right. And although Josiah knew that was the proper answer, he hedged. "That was Dat's name," he whispered. "What a wonderful-*gut*—well, you made all the rational thought fly right out of my head."

"I have that effect on people, it seems," Lena quipped. "Rational thought's been the furthest thing from our minds more than once, but I don't regret a thing, Josiah. I'm grateful to God that Isaiah's a fine, healthy boy—and I'm *really* glad to have his birthing behind me."

Josiah laughed softly. "I can't imagine. I—I'm sorry I wasn't here to—"

"Miriam and Andy were the perfect people to have at my side. Angels, they were," she replied softly. "They've gotten us off to a solid start, so now you're welcome to step in and be the *dat*—but I'm not going to make you do that."

"Why not?" he challenged. "Most folks think it's past time that I assumed responsibility—"

"Not me, Josiah." When Lena riveted him with her blue-eyed gaze, Josiah saw no judgment or disappointment there. "I want you to decide, freely and from the deepest part of your heart, that you *want* to raise this boy with me. I won't accept second best, or a part-time commitment. It's all or nothing."

"I'm in or I'm out," Josiah murmured. He looked at Isaiah again, aware of how fast and hard his heart was pounding—and of how utterly innocent, defenseless, and dependent this baby was. For the next few years, Isaiah would demand care and feeding and constant attention, no matter what else was happening to the adults he'd been entrusted to. The scope of such responsibility made Josiah squeeze his eyes shut.

In his heart, however, he knew it was time to answer Lena's unspoken question. Sometimes being a man required heavy equipment and tools and the money to purchase necessities. At this moment, however, all he needed was the faith to give a simple *yes*. Josiah didn't know how Lena would raise this child if he went his own way, but he suddenly didn't want to find out that she could get along without him.

"I'm going to stand by you, Lena," he said in a firm, quiet voice. "I can't leave you to be a *mamm* without me being the *dat* this boy needs me to be. I—I love you. Really I do, even if I've had a funny way of showing it."

"Oh, Josiah," she whispered as she blinked back tears. "I knew you'd come through. I never really doubted you."

Josiah's eyes widened. During the past nine months, he'd had more than his share of doubts—about Lena and marriage and parenthood, not to mention joining the church. Yet now that he'd opted in, the scariness of his decision was draining away. Yes, he was younger than most guys were when they started families. But he'd always been crazy for Lena—even during their fights—and he couldn't imagine himself with any other woman. Her strength inspired him to rise to her level, to believe he was capable of being a *man*. As he held tiny Isaiah, his heart overflowed with a strange yet wonderful sense that he wanted life to go right for this little guy—and for the girl who'd had the courage to birth him.

He sensed that once he was *in*, the Hooleys and other folks around Willow Ridge would help them find a home and get established. One of the benefits of belonging to the Old Order was the assurance that he and Lena would never be left to flounder and fail. They would have a support system here in Willow Ridge, even if Lena's family refused to accept him and his relationship with their daughter.

When Josiah noticed his sister watching him from the doorway, he smiled. "Somebody wants a turn at holding her new nephew," he said as he carefully gave Isaiah back to Lena. "And that gives me a chance to call Hiram Knepp and inform him that the Witmer family will no longer tolerate his scare tactics."

Lena's blue eyes widened. "Be careful, Josiah. Don't get so riled up that he'll have you saying things you don't mean—or making threats you can't back up."

Josiah rose from the sofa, humbled by her astute observation. It seemed that Lena knew him better than he knew himself. Maybe if he started listening to her—and to Savilla, Miriam, and Ben—instead of believing he knew better than they did, his life would be a lot simpler.

"If Knepp's still on the loose, he won't be answering his phone," Savilla pointed out as she sat down on the couch. "And if you leave a message—"

"He's got a cell phone. When he sees my name on his caller ID, he'll probably pick right up to brag about spying on Lena," Josiah said. "But I'm not the only one who knows what he's done. United we stand here in Willow Ridge."

"I like the sound of that," Miriam remarked from the kitchen. "We've stood by each other through thick and thin in this town. Never imagined we'd be standin' against a former bishop, though. But we're with ya, Josiah."

He gazed at Miriam and then gave in to the urge to

hug her. She barely came to his shoulder, but Josiah knew better than to think of her as Ben's *little woman.* "*Denki* for saying that," he murmured.

"*Denki* for signin' on with Lena and your little boy," she replied as she beamed up at him. "Your blessings are gonna start pilin' up like a little kid's Christmas gifts. That's how it works when ya say *yes* to God's call."

Josiah didn't tell Miriam that the presents hadn't made a very tall pile when he and Savilla had been kids—because it didn't matter. He and his sister had received everything they needed, and they knew they were loved. It was his turn to be the giver rather than the receiver.

"I'll be back after I've talked to Hiram," he said as he slipped into his coat. "I'm hoping the cold air will keep my temper under control."

"One of these days Hiram's gonna be put in his place. I can't think the Lord's gonna tolerate his shenanigans forever," Miriam predicted in a faraway voice. "But it's not for us to know when that judgmen- t'll come, or how. We need to keep mindin' our own business, doin' *gut* for the folks who need it. I'll be prayin' for ya, Josiah."

Listen closely. Miriam is one of the wisest people you know.

He stepped outside, lifting his face to the weak sunshine that was filtered by gray clouds. It looked like snow. The damp breeze pierced his coat and made him shiver. But thoughts of little Isaiah Daniel—Isaiah Daniel Witmer, he would soon be—gave Josiah the fortitude to tap the shunned bishop's number into his phone. As it rang, he paced in the Hooleys' plowed lane.

"Well, well, to what do I owe this honor?" Hiram's voice slithered through the phone, as slick and seamless as a serpent. "Calling to apologize for standing me up, Witmer? Saying you're on your way to Higher Ground to run my supper club?"

Josiah nipped his lip against a retort that would get him into trouble. "No, but I'm going to report your invasion of our privacy to Sheriff—"

"As if I should be concerned about Clyde Banks," Knepp cut in with a laugh. "He's in my pocket, kid. I pay him to arrest me now and again to make you people think he's doing his job. But he works for the highest bidder, believe me."

Josiah's eyebrows rose. Nora Hooley had told him that when Hiram had made a deal with the Realtor who'd hit the Knepp twins' sleigh, he'd gotten the land for Higher Ground. Josiah didn't want to believe that the local law officers had succumbed to his bribery—

"Your life would go a lot smoother if you'd honor your agreement with me, Witmer," Knepp continued. "You'd have a nice home in Higher Ground for that pretty young woman and your new baby—and your sister," he added with a suggestive rise in his voice. "And if you come to work for me, I'll leave Miriam alone, too. And two little babies will stay safe with their mothers."

Josiah sucked in his breath. Surely Knepp wouldn't try to kidnap his son and the Hooley child. Would he?

"But it's up to you, kid. How's it feel to have so many peoples' lives riding on your decision?" Hiram asked in a no-nonsense tone. "Make me happy and everyone's world will keep turning. If you continue to defy me . . . ."

Josiah swallowed hard. He knew better than to accept Knepp's offer, but if he refused, how many more nasty incidents would befall the people he loved? The idea of Knepp doing something to little

Isaiah and the Hooleys' baby—not to mention Lena and Miriam—made him stiffen with anger.

It happened this way when the Devil tempted Christ in the desert, an inner voice reminded him. *Jesus sent Satan packing—called him by name and declared that we are to worship only the Lord. And from there the angels took over.*

Josiah blinked. He'd never followed Sunday sermons very closely, but this tidbit from the Scriptures had come to him at just the right moment, hadn't it? "Get thee behind me, Satan," he muttered. "As for me and my house, we'll serve the Lord."

Hiram's laughter was so raucous and loud that Josiah yanked his cell phone away from his ear. He hung up. In a contest of trading Bible verses he wouldn't last thirty seconds—and the more he talked, the more lies and threats Hiram would inject into the conversation.

Josiah inhaled some cold winter air. He'd spoken his mind. He'd told Hiram that no one in Willow Ridge would give in to his threats. It wasn't the Old Order way to invite the involvement of outsiders, but he left a message on the sheriff's phone about Hiram's peeping activities and his insinuations about harming the babies, because someone official needed to know what was going on.

Then Josiah stared at his cell phone. He'd become accustomed to Googling for information and having technology at his fingertips, and he would have to give that up when he joined the Old Order Church so he could marry Lena.

Folks survived for centuries without the Internet or even phones, he reminded himself. *Miriam's got it right: Knepp will run headlong into a wall one of these days. Your job is to take care of Lena, Isaiah, and your sister, and to let God be in charge of rogue bishops. Knepp will someday answer to a higher power, even if he no longer follows one.*

Josiah wasn't sure where these suggestions were coming from, but he sensed that because Miriam had been praying for him, he'd finally chosen the right road. Following her advice made him feel settled and competent, capable of taking on the challenges of a new life in Willow Ridge with Lena and their son.

He smiled. If he didn't give up—and didn't fly off the handle at every little criticism—he might actually make something of himself. And that was an idea worth hanging on to.

Chapter Sixteen

Miriam glanced across her kitchen and smiled. Lena was frosting cut-out sugar cookies at the table while Isaiah dozed in the wooden cradle on the floor beside her. The first week of December had already slipped past them, and Miriam was in the mood for baking stars, angels, bells, and other Christmas shapes—and then she was taking them to the Sweet Seasons. She craved Naomi's company and wanted to get a feel for how Josiah and Savilla were doing at the café.

Truth be told, even with Lena and little Isaiah around, it got awfully quiet at home. And Bishop Tom couldn't say anything against her baking here and then selling the goodies at the restaurant—especially because she'd decided the money from selling them would go toward the Witmers' new home.

"What do you think of this camel?" Lena asked as she held it up.

"That fancy blanket you've put on his hump is something I'd never have thought of!" Miriam replied. "You have a talent for makin' these cookies look special, Lena. Folks are gonna snap these up."

The girl's face turned a pretty shade of pink. "I've always loved making Christmas cookies," she murmured. "It's so nice of you to let us have the money they'll earn, Miriam."

Miriam cut out more shapes from her dough. "It's a simple thing, makin' cookies, but we might be surprised at how much income they'll generate for ya. Mighty oaks from little acorns grow—and can ya go open the door for Rachel and Amelia?"

As Lena rose from the table and her array of colored frostings and sprinkles, Miriam placed another sheet of cookies in the oven. It felt odd to have the doors locked—to make family members and friends wait outside. But after Josiah had recounted the details of his phone call to Hiram, they were taking the banned bishop's threats very seriously.

"And how're my girls this morning?" Miriam called out as her daughter entered the kitchen. "As ya can see, Lena and I have been busy bees today."

Rachel gazed at the trays of decorated cookies. "You used the same cutters when we were kids, Mamma, but these cookies look really *cute!* Not that you haven't always made the best cookies I ever put in my mouth."

Miriam chuckled as she wiped her floury hands. "I kept the decoratin' simple back then because you girls and your *dat* gobbled them up so quick," she replied. "But we'll be sellin' these. What brings you and the wee one over this morning? Amelia, you're growin' like a weed, honey-bug!" she declared as she lifted her granddaughter from her basket.

"Teacher Alberta has asked if Micah, Amelia, and I would be the holy family for the live Nativity scene this year," Rachel replied. "They still have so few kids in school that puttin' on the usual Christmas Eve program won't work too well."

"It was a wonderful-*gut* pageant last year," Miriam recalled fondly. "Lena, we had hundreds of folks stoppin' by to visit our outdoor manger scene. Ben set everything up in our barn, with one of Bishop Tom's cows and a couple of my brother-in-law's sheep, along with the Kauffman kids' pony. It was Mary Kauffman and Seth Brenneman playin' Mary and Joseph with little Emmanuel, while the other kids were the angels and shepherds and Wise Men."

"And thanks to Rebecca, we had costumes and a star balloon up in the sky," Rachel added.

"That sounds really neat," Lena replied as she spread frosting on a house-shaped cookie. "I can't imagine our bishop back home allowing the school to put on that sort of program."

"We prayed over it a while before Bishop Tom agreed to it." Miriam gazed at her granddaughter as she positioned her against her shoulder. "It all came down to whether Mary felt comfortable havin' her wee one outside on a December night, but with hay bales and a space heater, they got along just fine. What'd ya tell Teacher Alberta?"

Rachel's face lit up. "Micah was tickled that she asked us, and I think Amelia will do just fine, so we said *jah.* I was really touched last year, when so many folks who weren't Plain were singin' the carols with us. It was a really special Christmas Eve."

"I thought so, too," Miriam replied with a fond smile. "There's a place for all of us in the story of Jesus's birth. It never grows old, and we never know whose hearts'll be opened when we invite them to the manger."

"*Jah*, a baby changes everything," Lena murmured. She picked up a cookie in the shape of the star of Bethlehem. "Isaiah's coming doesn't make much difference to most folks, but he's opened up a whole new world to me."

Miriam laughed and handed Amelia to Rachel. "Don't underestimate the effect he's had on Josiah. Your young man's got a whole new attitude. I like it that he and Savilla will be Naomi's helpers for a while rather than just runnin' a supper shift on their own. She's tickled to have them—and I'm glad he's gonna take care of *you*, Lena."

Rachel settled Amelia back in her basket, seeming eager to decorate cookies with Lena. "When do ya figure to join the church?" she asked. "Most new *mamms* allow six weeks before they take their newborns to church, but if ya wait that long, it'll be into next year before ya start takin' your instruction—and weeks longer before ya finish."

Lena sighed wistfully. "That's a long while, but I can't just start back to church without Isaiah coming, too."

Miriam rolled out more cookie dough, admiring Lena's insistence on being with her newborn. More than once she'd offered to watch Isaiah, but mother and son seemed inseparable. "If a little bird told Bishop Tom that you and Josiah wanted to start takin' your instruction right away, maybe he'd come to *you*," she suggested. "With Ben already here and Preacher Henry just across the road, Tom might even meet more often with you so you three can be a family sooner. But that's just me thinkin' out loud."

"I like that idea, Mamma!" Rachel swirled pink frosting over an angel-shaped cookie and then picked up a pastry bag to outline it. "I might just be that little bird. I can walk past Tom's house on the way home, and he can be considerin' your idea while he milks his cows this afternoon."

"I like the way ya think, Rachel," Miriam said with a chuckle. "We couldn't do our farmin' or snow plowin' without big Belgian horses, but it's usually the little birds who get things movin' quicker, ain't so?"

After breakfast the next morning, Lena offered to redd up the kitchen so Miriam could take their big bin of decorated Christmas cookies over to the Sweet Seasons. "Have a nice visit with Naomi," Lena said as she ran hot water into the sink. "And if she thinks a dollar is too much for one of those cookies—"

"Oh, Naomi'll probably say to charge a quarter more apiece," Miriam insisted as she put on her coat. "She knows how much work you've put into them."

"They're big cookies, too," Ben said. He helped Miriam with her coat and then picked up the cookie bin. "Once the fellas who're eatin' breakfast see these in the bakery case—and they know you made them, Lena—I predict every one of them will be gone by lunchtime. Luke and Ira might sell some for ya in the mill shop, too."

Wouldn't that be something? We made more than seven dozen cookies, so at a dollar apiece . . . As Lena did the math, she decided to mix more cookie dough to store in the fridge so she could bake several mornings a week. It was a project she really enjoyed, and an easy way to earn money toward a new home.

When the door had closed behind Ben and Miriam, however, Lena hoped to share some quiet time with

Josiah before he went to work in the café. Savilla had agreed to be an early-morning baker for Naomi, while Josiah was grilling meat for each day's lunch menu. He was also ordering food, keeping the steam table filled, and assisting whenever Rebecca and Rhoda needed a hand—learning the restaurant business from the ground floor up. He and his sister would serve their first supper shift this Saturday evening.

"Ben and Miriam look so happy together," Lena remarked as she washed the glasses. When she glanced over her shoulder, her breath caught. Josiah had lifted Isaiah from the wooden cradle to hold him! "You and your son look *gut* together, too," she said softly.

Josiah grinned at her. "He must be getting used to me. He's stopped squirming so much when I handle him."

"I'm glad you're staying here for a while this morning," she murmured. "With Ben and Miriam gone, it's almost like we're in our own place."

"And speaking of that, Rebecca printed out some listings for nearby rental houses, as well as places that are for sale," he said as he rose from the table. "I wanted us to look at them while nobody else was here. They're upstairs."

Lena's heartbeat sped up. It was such a pleasant change for Josiah to consider her feelings first—not to mention the way he'd cradled Isaiah in the crook of his arm, holding his head in his hand as though he felt totally comfortable with their son now. By the time Josiah returned and spread the pages on the table, Lena was getting excited. It seemed their future might finally be falling into place.

When she spotted the monthly rental rates and the

prices on the homes, however, Lena sighed forlornly. "Oh, my. Can we afford *any* of these, Josiah?"

"Actually, this bungalow's rent isn't that different from what folks were paying in Bloomfield," he replied as he shifted the baby to his shoulder. "The thought of scraping up four hundred fifty dollars a month probably seems like a lot to you—"

"No, it seems downright *impossible*," Lena interrupted with a catch in her voice.

Josiah wrapped his free arm around her, coaxing her closer. "But see, the utilities are included in that, and there's a shed for the horses and rigs. And it's on the county highway, about half a mile beyond the clinic," he pointed out. "To put it in perspective, if you sell those cookies Miriam took to the Sweet Seasons this morning for a buck each, what'll you be making?"

Lena quickly recalculated. "About eighty-five dollars."

"From one morning's baking," Josiah pointed out. "So if you divide four hundred fifty by eighty-five . . . you'd come up with five and some left over—about six mornings' worth of baking at the rate you did yesterday. And if Savilla and I can't make a lot more than that on our dinner shift, we shouldn't be in business."

Once again Lena glanced at the pages that showed homes for sale, but she still doubted they could ever afford to own one. "So if we start small, paying rent for a while, you're thinking we could set aside money toward buying a place."

Josiah kissed her lightly. "Don't forget that Savilla and I just sold a farm, honey-girl," he murmured. "We've used some of that money to buy food for the first week of our dinner shift—and we paid off the expenses from the sale of Mammi's place—but we've got a nice chunk left. It's going toward a home when the right one comes along. *Our* home."

Lena sat absolutely still, absorbing what Josiah had just said. Did she dare believe he was ready to become a homeowner and a church member and a *dat* and a husband and a partner in the Sweet Seasons, all at once?

"It'll be Savilla's home, too, of course," Josiah remarked.

"Of course it will!" Lena blurted out.

Her outburst startled Isaiah from his nap and his face puckered unhappily. When she reached for the baby, Josiah handed him over, but for a brief moment the baby was supported by their four hands, halfway between them.

Their son stopped fussing. He glanced at her and then at Josiah, as though deciding what he thought about his position. When he let out a brief "heh!" and wiggled his arms and legs, Lena took it to mean he felt happy. Secure. *Loved.*

Maybe her imagination was playing up her newborn's sounds and gestures, but it felt like a special, timeless moment when her world seemed to be spinning in the right direction at last. Josiah was gazing at the baby as though he, too, had interpreted Isaiah's actions as something that bound them together as a family. He placed the boy gently against her shoulder.

"What a picture. Mother and child," he murmured. "Prettier than the paintings I've seen of Mary and Jesus on Christmas cards."

Lena swallowed hard. Who could ever have imagined Josiah expressing such a thought? "Well, except for the halos," she pointed out. "Isaiah and I don't have those rings of golden light around our heads because we're not—"

"Not holy? Not angels?" he asked in a voice she could barely hear. "Far as I can see, God sent the two of you to save me from myself. And if that doesn't make you saints already, you'll work your way up to that level if you stick with me." Josiah smiled, yet he maintained the stirring, solemn mood he'd been setting.

Lena wondered what sort of special air they were breathing—what was causing the Josiah Witmer she'd known most of her life to wax so poetic. So perfect.

"Lena, will you marry me?" he breathed. "I—I don't think I can move out of this chair or function for the rest of the day without knowing you'll always be here for me."

Tears sprang to Lena's eyes. "Oh, Josiah, of course I'll marry you," she replied in a tight voice. "It's all I've ever wanted."

Josiah wrapped his arms around her and Isaiah. He kissed her gently on the lips, once, twice. When Isaiah began to wiggle between them, he placed a tender kiss on his son's forehead, as well. "I feel so much better knowing that," he admitted. "I've been trying for the longest time to ask you just the right way. Now that the words have rushed out of me of their own accord—"

"Sometimes it's best to say something when the spirit moves you," Lena whispered. "We'll be fine, Josiah. You and me and Isaiah—and Savilla," she added quickly. "It's meant to be if we believe it is."

"Well, you've made a believer of *me*, Lena. When the baby became real to me, I saw everything in a whole different light." Josiah's lips twitched in a sheepish grin. "I'm glad you've stuck by me. I'll try real hard to be a better man—"

"I love you just the way you are this minute, Josiah. Don't go messing with perfection."

His dark brows rose and his brown eyes widened, suggesting that she'd amazed him as much as he'd astounded her. "Well, then. I guess I won't."

"*Gut.* You're learning to listen and to let me have my say," she teased as she tweaked his nose. "I think that's how Ben and Miriam stay so happy. They both speak their minds and each listens to the other—give and take. That's not how it is between my parents."

"Nor in a lot of families we know, I suspect," Josiah said after he'd thought about it. "I'll keep that in mind, Lena."

"And I'll remind you when you forget."

Josiah's laughter filled the kitchen, and Isaiah began to flap his arms happily. It was a moment Lena knew she would remember forever, the way Mary had pondered so many wondrous things in her heart at the birth of Jesus.

For the twinkling of an eye, a little ring of sunlight from the window glowed above Josiah's head. Lena knew her imagination was playing with her, but it was an image worth remembering—for weren't all of God's children holy? Didn't He love every single one of them, even as He taught them difficult life lessons and led them where He intended for them to go?

Chapter Seventeen

"Bishop Tom, we really appreciate you and Ben being willing to work with us this morning, giving us our church instruction," Josiah said as he extended his hand. "The preachers in Bloomfield wouldn't be so flexible."

As Ben took Tom's wraps, he was pleased with Josiah's attitude of gratitude. He'd never heard of a district's leaders bending the rules about young adults taking their classes, either—they met every other week, before the service on church Sundays. But he agreed with Tom's reasoning and was willing to devote some weekday mornings to this endeavor, as well. Preacher Henry had decided to join them only for the normal prechurch sessions because he made out orders and did the bookwork for Zook's Market at this hour of the morning.

"I've never known a district's leaders to speed up the instruction process, either," Bishop Tom remarked as they all entered the kitchen. "But in the interest of you kids becomin' a family—givin' Isaiah his parents— I want to help ya out," he explained. "And look who we've got here!"

Tom walked toward the cradle Lena had set on the table near her seat, smiling as he studied the baby. "Isaiah's a keeper, I'd say. Got his *dat*'s long lashes and his *mamm*'s sweet face," he remarked as he gently stroked the baby's cheek. "And what a beautiful bed he's got, too."

Lena's cheeks flushed as she set warm syrup on the table. "Ben made that cradle for Miriam, and she was kind enough to loan it to us," she replied. "It's just one more way they've helped us that we can't possibly repay."

The bishop ran a fingertip over the pewter hummingbird on the cradle's headboard. "Never figure anything for bein' impossible," he said. "If ya believe the engineers that've studied how a hummingbird flies, sayin' its body is way too heavy for its wings, then by all logic the species couldn't survive. But God's in charge," Tom continued in a rising voice, "and with Him all things are possible. So if ya look for ways to return the favors these folks have done for ya, you'll find them."

Ben stood with his hands on the back of his chair. How did a simple dairy farmer so effortlessly deliver a sermon in a sentence or two? "We're glad you've come to our home to teach, Tom," he remarked. "You're a busy man, and Miriam and I feel blessed to have ya here."

Bishop Tom chuckled as he sat in the chair Ben had pulled out for him. "It doesn't hurt that eatin' breakfast in Miriam's kitchen is part of the deal."

Laughter filled the room, which glowed in the light of the lamps Miriam had set around. It was still dark outside at six in the morning, but she'd made their pale yellow kitchen shine with love and light. "You've already milked your herd, I take it?" Josiah asked as he and Ben took their seats.

"*Jah*, and Naz has milked the goats and plans to spend her day makin' cheese," Tom replied. "I'm amazed at how many containers of my butter and her cheese get snapped up in Luke and Ira's mill store. Keeps us busier in the winter than we used to be—and I'm thankful for that."

Aromas of sweet cinnamon, coffee, and savory meat wafted around the kitchen. Lena and Miriam carried platters of French toast, large sausage links, and fried eggs to the table, where a bowl of fried apples and a pitcher of milk awaited them. Ben suspected his wife was also pleased about having Tom here because it gave her a chance to catch up on the goings-on around Willow Ridge.

"Are ya still carvin' and paintin' your Nativity sets?" Miriam asked. "This time of year, I can imagine ya have trouble keepin' up with the orders for those."

"I stopped takin' orders a couple of months ago," the bishop replied with a chuckle. "Nora's sellin' those sets in her store faster than I can keep up with them."

As they bowed in silent prayer, Ben thanked God for the prosperity He'd brought to their family and friends, as well as for prompting Josiah and Lena to join the church. When everyone had opened their eyes, he passed the sausage platter to Tom. "What with all the business the mill store and Nora's place is bringin' into town, I'm thinkin' Josiah and Savilla can make a new evening shift profitable even in January."

"*Jah*, Willow Ridge used to fold in on itself during the winter," Bishop Tom remarked. "Miriam and Naomi started a real surge of interest in our little town when they opened their café, though. And the Schrocks' quilt shop is goin' full tilt, and so's the Brennemans' carpentry business and Matthias Wagler's harness shop. Every new business we add boosts everyone else's, it seems."

Josiah smiled at Lena as he stabbed two thick slices of French toast. "I'm glad to hear you fellows say that, because we'd like to find a house as soon as we can. If you know of any place that's for sale or rent, Savilla and I could move in and get out of Ben and Miriam's hair," he added with an appreciative nod in their direction. "Then we'd have the place all set for when Lena and I tie the knot."

"And congratulations to ya on that," Bishop Tom responded. "I'm pleased ya want Willow Ridge to be your new home. A lot of our young people are startin' families now, and that'll keep our community goin' strong."

"It does my heart *gut* to see so many little ones sittin' with their *mamms* during church, too," Miriam chimed in. "What with all that wigglin' and keepin' the kids quiet, there's not much chance for anybody to snooze during your sermons, Tom."

"I need all the help I can get with that, too," the bishop agreed good-naturedly. He smiled at Isaiah, who seemed to be following their chatter from his cradle. "Won't be long before your boy'll be out runnin' and hollerin' with the others. They grow up faster than any of us can keep track of, it seems."

"He's got the lungs for the hollering part," Josiah agreed.

As they all enjoyed their breakfast, Ben felt blessed to be surrounded by folks who were of one mind, and who had the best intentions. When he and Tom took Lena and Josiah into the front room to begin their instruction, Ben was also grateful for Tom's humble leadership, his patient kindness. Had he been serving as a preacher under Hiram Knepp, the relationship would've been difficult indeed, considering the way their former bishop had harassed Miriam about so many different issues. Ben wished he didn't feel so antsy about Hiram's recent behavior—and then reminded himself to focus on Josiah and Lena as they discussed the basic tenets of the Old Order faith.

In the back of his mind, however, Ben still pictured a face with a devilish black beard peering through the window, terrifying Lena. No one had heard anything from Hiram since the incident last week, but Ben sensed their banished bishop wasn't finished toying with them. As long as Hiram felt cheated out of Josiah's cooking—or anything else he wanted—he would find ways to wreak his revenge.

"Do ya have any questions?" Tom asked the young couple seated on the couch. "In a nutshell, we believe the Bible's the word of God, and that He directly inspired all the prophets, apostles, and the other fellas who wrote the individual books in it."

Josiah and Lena glanced at each other, and then she spoke up. She looked alert and lovely, despite tending to Isaiah's needs in the night. "What are your thoughts about having Bible studies and devotional readings at home?" she asked. "Ben often reads to us from the Scriptures in the evening, but my *dat* says that should be left to the preachers and the bishop on Sunday mornings."

"That's an astute question," Tom replied as he smiled at Ben. "A lot of church leaders believe more harm than *gut* comes from members tryin' to interpret passages of Scripture because we have a tendency to twist those ancient words into arguments for provin' our own opinions," he said with a rise of his eyebrows. "And because we folks today don't fully understand how Jesus's actions and parables were shaped by the situations of His time, Bible stories can take on a completely different meaning."

The bishop stroked his gray-shot beard as he glanced at Ben. "I believe that when Ben reads the Bible aloud, and when he preaches on a passage during a sermon, we're gettin' the benefit of a truly devout Christian heart and mind because God speaks through him. You kids are blessed to be stayin' in the home of a fella who—along with Vernon Gingerich, the bishop his Aunt Jerusalem's married to—is one of the godliest men I know. And I don't say that lightly."

Ben's face went hot. "My understanding of the Scriptures isn't anything out of the ordinary—"

"I beg to differ, Preacher Ben," came a voice from the doorway.

Ben turned to see Miriam drying her hands on a kitchen towel. Her sweet smile appeared so sincere that his heart swelled a couple of sizes, but it seemed prideful to accept such praise from his friend and his wife—especially when they were instructing Josiah and Lena in the ways of their faith.

"Bishop Tom's got it right," Miriam continued with a solemn nod. "Every time I listen to your Bible readin' and your sermons in church, I come away with a new perspective on how God wants me to live. You've got a genuine gift, Ben. God knew exactly what He was doin' when He chose ya to be our preacher—and my husband."

Ben sat speechless. If he insisted that Tom and his wife were mistaken, he would appear argumentative, which went against the basic grain of the Amish faith.

Yet their compliments felt overblown to him. He didn't want to puff himself up with their praise because that would be wrong in God's eyes, too. When he noticed how intently Josiah and Lena were watching him, awaiting his response, Ben let out the breath he'd been holding.

"I appreciate those kind words," he replied softly. "But we can't forget that we're all sinners, fallin' short of God's vision for us. Without His grace, I couldn't make it through one single day."

"And on that note, let's close with a prayer and call this a *gut* morning's work," Bishop Tom said.

Ben bowed his head. *Make me aware of things I could be doin' better, Lord—all the ways I don't measure up to what You'd have me be. I ask Your blessing and protection for these two lambs seekin' a home in Your fold . . . even as we know You also created wolves and You love them, too.*

As Josiah tacked one end of his yellow banner inside the big front window of the Sweet Seasons, his fingers trembled. BARBEQUE BUFFET TONIGHT! 5–8 P.M. it said in large red letters. In just a few hours, he and Savilla would be making their dream come true. When he tacked the end his sister had been holding up, she clasped her hands.

"I'm going outside to see how it looks!" she said as she jogged toward the door. "This is so exciting, Josiah. I hope lots of people come to eat all this food we've been making."

"I told Rebecca her meal was free tonight and to bring her *dat* along," he replied, chuckling at Savilla's little-girl eagerness. "The ads she's put up on the Internet will be the reason folks outside of Willow Ridge find us."

"And don't forget the signs she's posted in the local stores, and in New Haven and Morning Star," his sister replied. "Lots of shoppers have seen those this week."

Josiah went to another window to watch his sister's reaction from the roadside. He was amazed at the amount of baked beans, slaw, mac and cheese, fresh rolls, corn bread, and other side dishes she'd been cooking, and he hoped they had a good turnout so a lot of leftovers didn't sit in the fridge. He firmly believed that food should be served fresh—but until they'd been open for several evenings, they would have no idea how much to prepare.

"Are ya ready for your big night?" Naomi asked as she came up beside him. "The whole Brenneman tribe's comin' because after Nora and Luke's wedding, my boys have all been lookin' forward to more of your grillin'. And me," she added with a grin, "I'm lookin' forward to sittin' at one of these tables they built and enjoyin' a meal I didn't cook myself."

Josiah's eyes widened. "You've never eaten here in the dining room?"

"Nope. Couldn't take the time out from cookin' most days—but I'm glad for that," Naomi added pertly. "If Miriam and I had time to lollygag over a sit-down meal, it would mean nobody else was eatin' here."

As Josiah watched his sister flash him a big thumbs-up from the roadside, he thought about what Naomi had said. If the café's two proprietors were too busy to sit down for a meal, maybe he hadn't lined up enough help. "Lena's coming over soon and she'll be in the kitchen this evening—and Rebecca, your Hannah, Nellie Knepp, and Katie Zook will be seating people and pouring drinks tonight," he said. "Do you think that's enough of us to handle a crowd? It's not like we're taking orders from a menu."

Naomi's brown eyes sparkled. "You'll soon find out. But if ya get behind, ask some of our women for help," she suggested. "Tendin' to full tables here won't be any different from takin' care of folks at a common meal after church."

And wasn't *that* another interesting observation? Josiah had never considered how women would look at serving meals from a completely different perspective than he did.

"Rebecca's banner really shows up from the road," his sister said as she hurried in out of the cold. Then she smiled at Naomi. "And thanks for suggesting we close the place between two and five to get everything set up. I'm going to cut cake and pies now."

"And I'm goin' home to put my feet up," Naomi said. "What with that busload of folks that came to eat after shoppin' at Simple Gifts and the mill store, it's been a busy afternoon."

"I'm glad Nora told us ahead of time they were coming," Savilla remarked. "Most of them bought something from the bakery case to take home, too—including all of Lena's cookies," she added as she smiled at Josiah. "We might create a whole new cottage industry with home bakers around town at this rate."

Josiah's heartbeat sped up. Lena would be tickled to hear how well her sugar cookies had sold again today. She was now doing the baking as well as the decorating so Miriam wouldn't be spending so much time on her feet. The Hooley baby was due in a week or two, and Miriam was looking uncomfortable, allowing herself more time to rest—and it was only right that Lena do most of the work because she was getting the money.

"Time to check my cookers," he said as he followed Naomi to the kitchen door. "Some of those ribs and briskets will soon be ready to come off the grill, and the pig's done, too."

"They smell wonderful-*gut*," she said as they slipped into their coats. "You kids have a fine afternoon. I'll see ya later."

"*Denki* for everything, Naomi!" Savilla called out behind them.

"*Jah*, we're really grateful for the help you've given us," Josiah added as he grabbed some tongs and metal steam table pans. "Without you and Miriam, there's no way we could be serving our supper tonight."

Josiah stepped outside with Naomi and then stood in the crisp winter air, inhaling the savory aroma of the meats he'd put into the grills and barrel cookers early that morning. He opened the two grills nearest the back wall of the café, where he'd been cooking large foil-wrapped beef briskets.

He scowled. When he'd checked them a few hours ago, the coals and wood were at the perfect temperature—and now they were out. *And the wood's not just cold, it's wet,* he realized as he poked beneath the grill rack with his tongs.

Josiah quickly went down the row of cookers, opening them in a panic. He was greatly relieved that the smoke was still coming out of the barrel cooker where his whole hog was roasting—and glad as well that the ribs in the gas grills appeared to be done to perfection. The foil around the briskets hadn't been disturbed, and as he calculated the time they'd been cooking, he was confident that spoilage wouldn't be an issue.

But how had this happened? The top vents were open, as they should be—

He spotted a big dent in the snow that had drifted along the windbreak wall. *Somebody scooped up snow and dumped it on these coals.* But who would tamper with his equipment? No one in Willow Ridge would intentionally ruin the main course of the first meal he and Savilla were serving.

Josiah's heart thudded. *Hiram's been here.*

He removed the briskets and ribs from the cookers. Knepp would *not* spoil their first evening shift! Josiah had no time to hunt down the renegade bishop who'd sabotaged his grills, but he could salvage these meats by finishing them in the oven. He'd take his roasted hog inside right away, too, because for all he knew, Knepp was hiding nearby, watching him sweat—or ready to strike again.

"Get the ovens going for me, will you?" he asked Savilla as he began carrying the meat into the kitchen. "We've got a problem—but thank the Lord the pig's done and it's not been messed with."

Savilla frowned as she set down her knife to turn on the ovens. "What on earth are you talking about? Last time you checked—"

"Seems Knepp thought he could rain on our parade by dousing two of my fires," Josiah replied. "We should tell Ben and the other men to keep an eye out—but don't breathe a word of this while we're serving dinner. The meat will be fine. No need to get Lena and Miriam and everybody else stirred up."

Savilla's face had gone as pale as her piecrusts. "Are—are you *sure* he didn't mess with the hog or your other cookers?" she rasped. "If people get sick—"

"I'll check it over real close. If I have the slightest suspicion the meat's not good, we won't serve it."

"Oh, Josiah." His sister's face crumpled and she looked ready to cry. "I didn't trust Hiram from the moment I met him, but I never dreamed he might stoop so low as to . . . taint our food."

"Let's don't assume that before we have to," he replied, hoping he sounded convincing—and praying he would find no evidence of the pork being unfit to eat. "He *wants* us to worry about that, but we won't let him scare us into leaving Willow Ridge. First thing Monday, I'll buy padlocks for the cookers. Meanwhile, I've got some catch-up cooking to do."

Josiah carried the rest of his meat into the kitchen and shut the vents on his grills. Once inside, he began turning each brisket and slab of ribs, looking for signs that Hiram had done more than douse the fires. *Lord, I'm going on instinct and Your guidance here,* he prayed as he worked. *Give me a great big obvious sign if something's wrong, because we can't have folks getting sick.*

He couldn't recall ever asking for God's assistance as he cooked, yet as Savilla worked alongside him, unwrapping the briskets and checking them, Josiah felt his nerves settling. "See anything suspicious?"

"No. Everything smells fabulous, but—" His sister looked up at him with wide, doelike eyes. "But what if we're just saying that because we don't want to throw away all of this meat or explain to everybody why we won't be open tonight?"

Josiah wrapped an arm around Savilla's shoulders and held her close. "Let's stand here for a moment and see if God puts any ideas in our minds."

Savilla seemed surprised at his suggestion, but she bowed her head. They stood in the warm, fragrant kitchen for several moments, breathing together . . . dealing with yet another tough decision after making so many of those while they'd been cleaning out the farmhouse. Josiah wondered if this string of difficulties was God's way of saying they'd made one mistake after another when his sister raised her head.

"Let's ask Miriam. If she says we shouldn't take a chance, we'll adjust the price and we won't serve anything but the side dishes tonight," Savilla said. "Everybody will understand—and they'll appreciate our honesty."

Josiah nodded. "I'll go talk to her while you finish with your desserts. By that time the hog will be cool enough to cut—or we'll figure out how to dispose of it."

As he jogged across the road and up the Hooleys' lane, Josiah thought about what questions to ask and what signs he had seen—or hadn't—of Hiram's tampering. Maybe he was making knee-jerk assumptions. Maybe someone else had monkeyed with his cookers.

When he told Miriam what he'd discovered, however, she immediately came to the same conclusion about who was responsible for dousing his fires. As she sat in a recliner with her feet up and an afghan draped over her, her eyes widened with fear and sadness. "My stars, who would've ever believed he would . . . let me think about this," she said wearily. "You're tellin' me that the big barrel cooker and the gas grills were still burnin' and hot, and that your briskets were still covered with foil the way they were supposed to be?"

"*Jah.* And from what Savilla and I could see and smell, there was no sign of anything having been done to the meat itself," Josiah recounted. "The ribs were totally cooked and ready to come off the fire."

"But what if Hiram did somethin' we have no notion of?" Miriam asked in a faraway voice. "What if he tossed somethin' toxic on that pig—or injected it into the meat with a needle, or—well, who knows what wickedness that man might concoct?"

"If he'd tossed anything on the pig, I'm pretty sure I'd see—or smell—a difference in the meat. And throwing something into the cooker would probably make the fire flare up, too, so the pig would be charred," Josiah reasoned. "But the needle idea bothers me. I inject a mixture of vinegar, salt, and sugar into several places in a hog before I cook it to keep the meat moist. If he found the syringe I threw away this morning—"

"Oh, but that sounds like a disaster waitin' to happen," Miriam interrupted fearfully. "I'm not eatin' a bite of that meat, Josiah, even though I know ya spent a lot of time and money cookin' it up just right."

Josiah sighed bleakly. Miriam's instant reaction told him exactly what he should do. "That settles it, then. The money I spent on the meat is nothing compared to what we'd be dealing with if people got sick."

"I'm so sorry, Josiah. You and Savilla have been workin' real hard."

As Miriam squirmed in the recliner, trying to get comfortable, Josiah knew he'd never forgive himself if she or anyone else got food poisoning—or worse. "We'll do what Savilla suggested and serve only the side dishes," he said ruefully. "I'll put a sign on the buffet table about why there's no meat, and think about how to keep this from happening again."

"Better safe than sorry."

Oh, I'm still sorry, Josiah mused as he returned to the Sweet Seasons. He wanted to catch Hiram and force him to eat some of those beautifully grilled ribs or some pulled pork—to see if he refused. But that scenario wasn't going to happen, so he focused on getting ready for the supper shift he'd promised everyone in Willow Ridge. Savilla's side dishes and desserts would simply have to suffice.

Chapter Eighteen

Miriam held tightly to Ben's arm as they started down their lane. Enough snow had fallen to make walking tricky, and she was feeling so bulky with the baby that she was off balance. She couldn't recall the last time she'd seen her feet, and she didn't need them to go flying out from under her. It was the thirteenth of December. Andy was saying their child would be born before Christmas—and she was more than ready.

"My stars, would ya look at that line," she murmured. "I've never had anybody waitin' outside to eat in my café before!"

Ben held her steady with his strong gloved hands. "It's a cryin' shame, what happened to Josiah's cookers," he said with a disgusted sigh. "Those folks are surely gettin' word about why the buffet table's gonna be limited tonight, yet they're stayin' to eat anyway. I like that about the people around here."

"I'm thinkin' they'll all be on the lookout for Hiram, too," Miriam replied.

Ben stopped to lift her chin. "Right now, let's both

of us set aside all thoughts of Hiram and how he perturbs us," he stated gently. "I'm takin' my honey-girl out for supper, happy she doesn't have to cook tonight. We'll enjoy bein' with our friends and we'll be grateful that Josiah and Savilla are off to such a successful start. *Jah?*"

Miriam smiled up at her husband, loving the way his hazel eyes held hers as powerfully as his arms steadied the rest of her. "You've got the best plan, as always, Bennie-bug. I'm so glad I've got ya takin' care of me and this wee one—who's not seemin' very wee anymore," she said with a chuckle. "I don't recall feelin' this awkward when I was carryin' the three girls. But Andy would've said so if I had more than one in there, don't ya think?"

"Some things remain a mystery until it's time for them to be revealed," he replied. "They say women forget the pain of their previous pregnancies, so maybe ya just don't recall how ya were feelin' twenty-some years ago."

"Back when I was the age my triplets are now," Miriam remarked. Then she laughed. "But if we stand here reviewin' ancient history, we won't get any supper. Let's scoot across the road and—oh, there's Nora and Luke!"

Miriam's spirits lifted immediately when Ben's brother and his new bride waved at them. It appeared that about half the folks waiting in line didn't live in Willow Ridge—and wasn't that something, that so many from other towns had come here tonight?

Nora gestured for them to step in front of her. "You two are going ahead of us, Miriam. But better yet—" The redhead hurried to the front of the line to open the door. "You folks way up toward the buffet table," she called inside. "Miriam's here! Let's get her and Ben some seats!"

"Miriam! You can squeeze in ahead of me!" someone hollered back.

"Come on in here, you Hooleys!" another diner insisted. "We've got seats at our table!"

"And there ya have it," Ben remarked as he steered Miriam toward the doorway, where Nora was waving them inside. "Sometimes it pays to be the best cook in Willow Ridge, and everybody's best friend. You and Luke are on my tab tonight, Nora. We'll talk to ya later."

Miriam's heart danced as folks stepped back to make way for her and Ben to ease between the crowded tables. All along the line folks greeted her, pointing toward the table where Ira Hooley and his fiancée, Millie Glick, were waving wildly, gesturing at two empty chairs between them and Millie's grandparents, Gabe and Wilma. From the looks of the noisy crowd, they were the only two empty seats in the dining room.

"Miriam, you and Ben get yourselves up there to the buffet table," her sister Leah insisted from near the front of the line.

"That's right, Miriam, there'll be no waiting for you two," Savilla said as she hurried over to grab their hands. Then she spoke above the chatter. "Folks, let's give a big hand to Miriam and Ben," she said loudly. "We have them to thank for making this buffet a reality."

Thunderous applause and cheers filled the dining room. Miriam clutched Ben's hand as her face flashed hot with embarrassed excitement. Even people she'd never met were clapping wildly. Then Josiah came out of the kitchen and raised his hand for silence.

"We're also deeply indebted to Bishops Tom Hostetler and Vernon Gingerich for buying out the entire meat supply at Zook's Market this afternoon when they heard someone had tampered with my grills," he announced in a solemn voice. "And we thank Vernon's wife Jerusalem and Tom's wife Nazareth, and Lydia Zook and Naomi Brenneman for jumping in to cook it all at the last minute so we'd have something to serve you besides side dishes tonight. I am just *amazed* by such generosity," he added with a hitch in his voice. "Next time you folks stop by, we'll be serving the Witmer-style barbeque you came for tonight. *Denki* for your patience, and we hope you'll enjoy your meal."

For a moment an awed silence rang in the dining room. Soon, another round of respectful applause filled the café.

"My stars. Isn't *that* something?" Miriam murmured as she stepped ahead of her sister to take a warm plate. Along with Savilla's wonderful baked beans, potatoes, and vegetables, the steam table's pans were brimming over with sliced pork loin, baked chicken, fried pork chops, and hamburger patties—and Josiah was carrying out a fresh supply of meat that included sizzling T-bones and gravied pot roast. "The news must've traveled mighty fast after Josiah decided he'd better not serve what he'd grilled."

Ben surveyed the buffet table with wide eyes. "Must've been a little bird who told them," he murmured. "Sometimes news travels on the wings of the Holy Spirit, and God's helpers step in and take it from there."

Miriam spooned up creamy mac and cheese and chose a crispy baked chicken thigh, wondering who that little bird had been. But it didn't really matter how word had gotten around. It was the instant response to a potential disaster—and Josiah's loss—that warmed her heart. Folks in Willow Ridge wanted the Witmers to raise Isaiah here, and they'd given an undeniable affirmation that Hiram Knepp's insidious tricks would not overcome the goodness—the love and faith and kindness—they all believed in.

Miriam waved at Lena, who was plating pie at the back kitchen counter while Isaiah snoozed in his basket. Lena waved back, appearing pleased to be helping her brother and Savilla serve this big crowd. Meanwhile, Hannah Brenneman and Katie Zook were bustling between the tables to pour water and coffee while Rebecca bussed tables as folks finished eating.

"It's a *gut* thing the kids decided on a buffet meal and serve-yourself desserts," she remarked to Ben as she finished filling her plate. "The helpers are havin' to scurry. Makes me glad I'm not in on this new venture."

Ben chuckled. "Seems ya got out of your café and off your feet just in time, honey-girl. It all works out."

Miriam squeezed between the crowded tables, greeting the Schrocks, who ran the quilt shop next door. She landed heavily in the chair Ira had pulled out for her. "Can't tell ya how glad I am that ya had a couple of empty seats," she said as she smiled at Millie and the Glicks. "Can ya believe this crowd?"

"It's fabulous," Ira agreed before he lowered his voice. "Rumor has it that Hiram was the one messin' with Josiah's cookers. Is that true?"

"Who else would it've been?" Miriam murmured. "We shouldn't go jumpin' to conclusions, but I can't think of another soul who would've even *thought* about such meanness—especially because we caught Hiram peerin' in the window at Lena not long ago," she continued. "The worst part is that he might've just doused two of the fires and left all the meat alone to get back at Josiah. A bunch of nice brisket, ribs, and a whole roasted hog had to be thrown out, just to be sure nobody got sick."

"That kind of waste is shameful," Wilma Glick put in with a scowl. "How do we know what Hiram might do next?"

"And who ever dreamed we'd have to worry about such a thing?" old Gabe said with a shake of his head.

"Josiah has said he'll get padlocks for his grills, but maybe we'd best build another couple of walls around his cookin' area," Ben remarked as he sat down across from Miriam. "We can make the whole area more secure if ya have to go through the kitchen to get to Josiah's cookers."

"Let's get the lumber and *do* it," Ira said as he cut into a thick wedge of cherry pie. "With you and me and Luke workin' at it, we'll have that enclosure up in no time."

"I'll talk to the Brenneman boys tomorrow after church about some wood," Ben replied with a nod. "The sooner we let Hiram see that he's not shuttin' down Josiah's business, the sooner he'll leave us be— or at least we can hope so."

Miriam closed her eyes over a mouthful of cheesy macaroni. It was such a blessing to hear the men in her family working together to help the Witmers after Tom, Vernon, and several of the local women had also come to Josiah's aid today.

Lord, Your spirit's moved amongst us again, and I'm so grateful that we didn't take any chances—and that Josiah didn't have to disappoint all these folks who came here to eat tonight.

Miriam scraped up the last of her baked beans, wondering if she dared venture over to the dessert table. The baby was shifting and kicking so vigorously, she wasn't sure she should eat anything more—yet Savilla's chocolate pie looked too tempting to ignore. She was ready to scoot her chair back when a pair of slender arms wrapped around her shoulders from behind.

"Mamma, I'm so glad ya made it through this crowd without havin' to wait outside in the cold," her daughter Rhoda said. "How're ya feelin'?"

Miriam grasped Rhoda's wrists. "Bigger than a barn," she replied. "And by the way this baby's movin' around at all hours, it'll surely hit the ground runnin' the minute it's born. I'll probably never catch up!"

When Rhoda giggled, Miriam noticed she looked pale—and hoped she hadn't caught a flu bug that might be contagious. "But if the baby's movin' around so much, it's surely healthy, ain't so?" she asked. Then she whispered near Miriam's ear. "I've been busy gettin' to the bathroom or a basin lately, Mamma. How long did you keep throwin' up before ya got past—"

"Rhoda, are ya tellin' me what I think ya are?" Miriam gasped excitedly.

Her daughter hugged her, chuckling. "Andy says I'm probably a couple of months along. Kind of embarrassing that he figured it out before I did."

Miriam laughed out loud and turned in her chair to hug Rhoda close. "Ya just made my day, honey-bug— my whole week, as a matter of fact!" she said as she looked at the other folks around their table. "It's official! Rhoda and Andy are expandin' their family."

Millie and Ira clapped their hands as Ben's face lit up. "Congratulations, Rhoda," he said happily. "A baby's livin' proof that the Lord's workin' amongst us, blessin' us with joy even when other folks try to bring us down. Pretty soon Willow Ridge is gonna need a new population sign on the highway!"

Like a bee to a flower, Rebecca hurried over to grab her sister's hand. "Did I just hear some really good news?"

Rhoda nodded as they slung their arms around each other. "*Jah*, and with Christmas comin', and now a baby, Taylor and Brett are twinklin' like that star ya made us for the live Nativity last year."

"As well they should be," Rebecca said. "And speaking of that, I've washed the costumes. Teacher Alberta thinks tomorrow after church would be a good time for a fitting, and to decide who will play which roles this year."

"I'm so glad Bishop Tom's lettin' us do that again," Millie spoke up. "Lizzie's Ella is hopin' to be an angel. All the younger kids are so excited that they don't have to be scholars to play a part."

"We drew such a crowd last year, I believe we blessed Plain and English folks alike," Ben chimed in. "We'll soon have enough school-age kids to do our Christmas Eve program at the schoolhouse again, but for now, I'm pleased that my barn will be the setting for another live Nativity."

Miriam listened, her hand on her undulating belly. She had a pretty good idea that—for one reason or another—she wouldn't be standing outside singing carols and watching the pageant this year. And that suited her just fine.

Chapter Nineteen

Lena sat taller on the pew bench as the church service wound down. Being seated among the younger women—Annie Mae Wagler, Millie Glick, Rachel, and Rhoda—had made the long morning pass more quickly, and she'd been able to watch Rachel handling baby Amelia, who'd made her first appearance in church today. Isaiah was with Miriam because Nurse Andy had instructed them both to stay home when he'd seen them at the Sweet Seasons the evening before.

"No telling how many viruses and flu germs you might've been exposed to in that crowd," Andy had warned Miriam. "We can't have you getting ill before you deliver your baby. Isaiah's to stay home for at least six weeks, too," he'd added when he'd seen the baby in the kitchen with Lena.

Lena felt odd without her son in her arms, but she'd been able to pay closer attention during her instruction class with Josiah. She'd focused closely on Bishop Vernon's sermon based upon the story of the angel Gabriel appearing to Zacharias, announcing the birth of John the Baptist. What a way with words Vernon had, and what a rolling, mellow voice he spoke with, as though God had been whispering in his ear as he preached.

"As we go out into the world, let's see ourselves as John was destined to be." Bishop Tom gazed around the crowded front room of his home as he gave the benediction. "We're to point other folks toward Christ the Savior, to turn the hearts of fathers to their children, and the hearts of the disobedient toward the wisdom of those who're just and righteous."

"We should also pray for the person who tampered with Josiah's grills yesterday," Bishop Vernon continued earnestly. "Let us allow our Lord to work His justice while we open ourselves to forgiving those who intend us harm. As we do this, however, we're called to take precautions—to protect those who might fall prey to future danger. Let us forgive, forget, and move forward with joyous hearts that will welcome the Christ Child. God bless you, my friends."

As everyone rose, it occurred to Lena that Miriam and Isaiah were home alone while everyone else in Willow Ridge was gathered at the Hostetler place. Surely they were safe behind those locked doors, for how could Hiram possibly know that they were in that big house all by themselves? Even so, Lena suddenly felt compelled to skip the common meal. She squeezed between the clusters of chatting menfolk to grab Josiah's hand.

"Shall we head back to check on Miriam?" she asked. "Isaiah's probably getting hungry, and I feel funny about them being there—"

"While everyone else is here?" Josiah finished with

raised eyebrows. "I see what you're saying. Get our coats while I tell Ben we're leaving."

Lena made her way through the crowd to the back room where the women's black coats and bonnets were piled on a bed. She hoped her doubts about Hiram were unfounded, but the banished bishop had caused more harm than just the potential contamination of Josiah's meat: he'd poisoned every heart in Willow Ridge with fear about what he might do next. Lena felt sorry for Annie Mae, who had to deal with her four youngest siblings and their questions about their father's wrongdoing. What an awful burden to bear.

She found her coat and bonnet, and then pulled Josiah's coat from a similar pile in the adjoining room. On her way to the kitchen door she chatted with the women she met, explaining why she was leaving before they ate.

"Give Miriam our best," said Lizzie Glick as she shifted Ella on her hip. "I'm sure she's ready to deliver her baby—and I'm sure Isaiah's ready to see his *mamm,* as well."

Lena smiled because she was feeling very swollen with milk. Before she could reply, however, Josiah made his way to her side. His face was lit up like the Christmas lights he'd strung around his buggy when he was younger.

"Reuben Riehl—the deacon—just told me about an acreage that's going up for sale soon," he said as he put on his coat. "It's right down the road, so maybe after Ben gets home we can check it out. There's a house, a barn, and a shed—a combination of pastureland and tillable acres—and he thought the owner was pricing it so it would sell quickly."

From the kitchen counter where she was unwrapping food, Savilla waved at them. "Don't go over there without me!"

"And don't leave here until I can wrap up some food," Nazareth Hostetler insisted. "Miriam can't feel much like cooking. I'm glad you kids are there to look after her now. She's not one to ask anybody for help."

"*Jah*, you've got that right," Lena replied with a chuckle.

About ten minutes later, Josiah was carrying a box of sliced ham, deviled eggs, sandwiches, and desserts that Tom's wife had packed for them. As they walked along the edge of the plowed road, Lena held her bonnet to keep the wind from blowing it off. She sensed Josiah was studying the pastures and the spaces between the homes of Willow Ridge—not to mention watching for a black Cadillac on the county highway.

When they unlocked the Hooleys' back door and stepped into the kitchen, Lena sighed with relief. The house welcomed them with its warmth, and Miriam's relaxed smile told them she was totally unconcerned about her safety. Isaiah rested contentedly in his basket on the table.

"By the looks of that box, Christmas is comin' early," she teased as Josiah set it on the table. "Isn't that just like Naz, to send ya home with an armload of food?"

When Lena was ready to mention that they'd not seen any sign of Hiram, the slight shaking of Josiah's head told her to keep that disturbing train of thought to themselves. Their worries had been unfounded, and for that she was grateful. "Everyone sends their best, Miriam," she said as she smiled at her son. "Nobody could recall the last time you weren't in church."

Miriam chuckled. "Isaiah and I napped in the recliner and wrote out a few Christmas cards. Didn't think much about church," she admitted. "But we're grateful to God for this warm home and our lovin' family and friends—and thankful that Andy said it was time for stayin' away from crowds. I didn't think a thing about catchin' a bug until I was already amongst all those folks at dinner last night."

Josiah smiled as Miriam removed the packages from the box. "Reuben gave me the address of a place that's going up for sale soon. He says it's about half a mile on the other side of the clinic, between here and New Haven." He fished a slip of paper from his coat pocket. "The guy's name is Homer Yoder."

Miriam stopped unpacking, her eyes wide. "Now why would Homer be sellin' out? He's a Mennonite fella—eats in the Sweet Seasons every now and again," she said. "Never married. I don't know anything more about him, but if the inside of the house looks anything like he keeps his yard and outbuildings, it's neat as a pin."

Lena's heart beat faster as she lifted Isaiah to quiet his fussing. "That sounds promising," she murmured. "It would be nice to find a place that doesn't need much work before you and Savilla could move in."

"And before *you* move in, Lena," Josiah clarified. "Bishop Tom told me we only have a few more instruction sessions, and he'll marry us any time after that."

"Well, that's the best news I've heard today!" Miriam said. "Congratulations, you two. Ya must be doin' real well in your class. Tom's lenient about things like the live Nativity, but he's a stickler about knowin' our Old Order beliefs."

Lena held the baby close as she gazed at Josiah, basking in the love that glowed on his face. "Your son and I are going back to our room," she murmured. "Seems we've got some happy things to discuss while he eats."

A few hours later, the *clip-clop, clip-clop* of Dolly's hooves made Josiah's heart dance to its cadence as they rolled down the road. He told himself not to get his hopes up, not to figure that the first place they looked at would be the future home of the Witmer family, yet he dared to hope that another piece of their future would be revealed today. The profits from last night's supper shift, even after he'd repaid the two bishops for the meat, had convinced him that he and Savilla could earn a livable wage at the Sweet Seasons.

"Do you suppose this is it?" he asked as a farmstead came into view. "It fits with Reuben's directions."

Savilla and Lena both peered through the windshield of the buggy. "It's either this farm or the one beyond it," his sister remarked.

Josiah slowed the horse. The nearer of the two farmsteads appeared run-down, and the barn clearly needed a new roof. "Nope," he said as he clapped the lines on the horse's back. "The name on the mailbox is Hilty."

"*Gut*," Lena murmured. "I didn't want to think Miriam was wrong, but this house looks pretty rickety."

"*Jah*, the porch roof is sagging," Savilla said. "The whole place seems kind of sad, like the folks who live here have fallen on hard times."

"I've noticed that about several places around the Missouri countryside," Josiah remarked. "I think Willow

Ridge is moving in the right direction, with Bishop Tom allowing Amish and Mennonites to run businesses together and to advertise them online. We saw the benefits of that last night, when so many customers came from as far away as Warrensburg and Boonville."

"Now this place looks better," Savilla said in a perkier voice. "The fencerows are all upright and the house doesn't look like it's been added on to slapdab, like some of them do."

"The barn has fresh red paint—and the shed behind it, too," Lena chimed in. "There's a fellow sweeping snow off the porch. Shall we stop to ask him about it?"

Josiah longed to do that, yet he didn't want to impose on the man when the place wasn't officially up for sale yet. "This has to be it. The mailbox says Yoder, and everything seems to be in good repair. We'll drive on a little farther and turn around—look at the place from the other direction."

Josiah steered the horse in a circle at the next intersection and clucked for Dolly to pick up the pace. He was as eager as the girls to at least meet the man they'd seen—he could give Reuben Riehl's name after all, so it wasn't as if they were just pulling off the road without any reason.

Josiah returned the man's wave as he drove the rig toward the house. "How about if you two stay in here?" he suggested. "He might not be ready for anyone to see the house—and he might not appreciate it that Reuben gave me his name. Could be a tough subject, depending on why he's selling the place."

As Josiah stepped out of the buggy, his heart was beating so hard he wasn't sure he could talk. Lena and

Savilla encouraged him with their smiles, so he figured he'd just come out and ask what he wanted to know. Wouldn't take but a few seconds to assess Yoder's response.

"How are you on this fine winter's day?" the man called out as Josiah approached. "Good to see the sunshine, ain't so?"

"You've got that right," Josiah replied as he stuck out his hand. "I'm Josiah Witmer from Willow Ridge—"

"The fellow who put on that big feed last night," he replied as he gave Josiah's hand a hearty shake. "Well done! Folks there must think a lot of you, to supply you with so much meat after somebody tampered with your grills. I've got a pretty *gut* idea who it was, but it's not my place to judge. I'm Homer Yoder, by the way. Happy to meet you."

Josiah nodded. He liked this guy already.

"I'm real sorry I'll not be around this neck of the woods much longer," Homer continued. "I always enjoy eating at Miriam's place, but my older brother passed away and his family needs a man to keep things together at their farm."

Josiah blinked. He'd just been handed the perfect opening. "I'm very sorry about your brother," he said, "and I hope you won't think I'm out of line, but Reuben Riehl told me you were looking to sell this place, and I—" He gestured toward the buggy, where Lena and Savilla waved from behind the windshield. "Well, my sister and my fiancée and I are hoping to find a home in this area. Miriam gives you high marks for neatness and keeping things in *gut* repair."

Homer let out a laugh that made him look several years younger. "Can't do any better than getting Miriam

Hooley's seal of approval," he remarked. "I'll be honest with you—I haven't thought much about an asking price yet. And I have no idea how long it'll take me to clear out the furniture, or what I'll do with it all. But if you folks want to come inside—"

"The girls were hoping you'd say that." It was all Josiah could do not to wiggle like an excited puppy. He waved at Savilla and Lena, and moments later they were stepping inside a snug home where everything was as tidy as Miriam had predicted.

"Not a very big house," Homer remarked, "because after the love of my life died while we were courting, I swore I'd never marry. It's been a *gut* twenty-three years that I've lived here, and I'll be sorry to go. My brother's place is old and drafty, and I'll have to get used to having three teenagers and four youngsters around— all of them girls," he added with a knowing smile.

"That could be a challenge," Savilla agreed. "We really appreciate your letting us look around without a call beforehand."

"I'd like to think of my home going to a young family," Homer said as he gazed fondly around the front room. "Look upstairs if you like. Three bedrooms and a bath up there. Space enough in the cellar to finish off another bedroom or two."

Josiah held Lena's gaze, sensing she was as eager as he was to live here. "You girls go on up. You've got a better idea of how much closet space we'll need, and how big you want the rooms."

He watched them ascend the staircase, which was crafted of a simple design in oak, matching the rest of the home's woodwork. "Any idea when you might come to a figure?" Josiah asked. "We're bunking at Miriam and Ben's, so we'd even take your furniture—"

Homer's eyes widened.

"—and since we just sold our home place in Iowa, I can pay with cash—or at least give you a hefty down payment," Josiah continued earnestly. It was bad bargaining strategy to lay out all of his cards before Homer named a price, but what did he have to lose? If the place cost more than he could afford, he would have to walk away. "I've got a baby son, and I have to keep enough in reserve to get us through this winter in case our new catering business flounders. But I can offer you a hundred twenty thousand."

Homer stroked his chin. "I've got some prime pastureland, and the tillable acres usually yield pretty well, so I was thinking the place was worth more than that," he mused aloud. "But you'd be saving me a real estate agent's fee—and it would be a huge load off my mind not to have to deal with the furnishings. Can I think on it for a few days?"

"I'll do the same," Josiah replied. He kicked himself for not asking more about the property's size, and for talking about money before he'd even set foot in the barn. But at least he'd set his price limit—and he'd made a bid before anyone else could snap this place up. Very few other houses within easy driving distance of the Sweet Seasons were likely to become available any time soon. And he would have so much more to offer Lena when they married if they already had a home.

As Lena and Savilla's voices echoed in the stairway, Josiah smiled. He could hear their excitement, and he sensed they'd be disappointed—as he would be—if this deal didn't go through.

"Kitchen's that way," Homer said, pointing toward the back of the main floor. "The appliances aren't the newest, but everything works just fine."

Josiah followed his sister and Lena because he would be spending a lot of time in the hub of the house, making the sauces and rubs for his meat. He noticed how all the furniture in the front room was plain but sturdy—no water rings on the tabletops or slipcovers on the upholstered chairs and sofa. The furnace hummed and the windows seemed tight. The gas stove and fridge were quite a bit older than Miriam's, and so were the sink fixtures and cabinets, yet everything was spotless.

"What a lovely home," Savilla remarked as she ran a hand over the countertops. "When Miriam mentioned that you were a bachelor, I—well, I expected more *clutter.*"

Homer laughed out loud, and then a secret twitched at his lips. "I have a gal who cleans for me every week," he confessed. "She lectures me if she finds the place in a mess, so I guess she's got me trained."

As the three of them laughed together, Josiah watched the way Savilla and Lena gazed at the cabinet space and the countertops, in addition to the well-maintained vinyl flooring. After living in their *mammi*'s poor old place, this house would be a huge improvement for his sister—and it was comparable to what Lena had grown up with. "If you girls have seen enough, we should let Homer get on with his day," Josiah said. He shook hands with Homer again. "*Denki* so much for letting us look around. You've got a really homey place here."

Homer gestured for the three of them to precede him to the front door. As Savilla and Lena headed outside to the buggy, he clasped Josiah's shoulder. "What say you and I meet at the bank in New Haven this week and talk with the loan officer?" he murmured. "I'll have an appraisal done to give us a better idea of the land's value so we'll both feel we're getting a fair shake. I'm impressed that a fellow your age can offer me cash, and I like the idea of a young family living here—and I like *you*, Josiah. Glad you stopped by. You've set a whole passel of concerns to rest for me."

Josiah's eyes widened. "Oh, you have no idea how happy we are that I heard about this place at church today," he replied. "Let me know when to meet you at the bank."

As he hurried toward the buggy, Josiah felt like turning cartwheels in the snow. He reminded himself that he still had to jump through a few hoops. He and Homer had only discussed a good-faith agreement, which was no guarantee that the transaction would take place.

But when he climbed into the rig and saw the wide-eyed, questioning expressions on Lena and Savilla's faces, Josiah flashed them a grin. "Homer and I are meeting at the bank this week and I—I think he wants us to have this place as much as we all want to live here!"

"Oh! I was hoping this would work out!" his sister said with a squeal. She hugged Lena excitedly. "See? It wasn't too soon to decide who would sleep in which room!"

"And the kitchen's roomy, too," Lena said as she hugged Josiah in turn. "We can invite the Hooleys over for dinner to repay all the meals they've been feeding us, and it'll be just like having family over."

Josiah caught a flash of sadness in Lena's blue eyes,

probably as she thought about spending Christmas away from her family. She didn't dwell on the absence of letters or a call asking her to return home, but he suspected the separation from her parents weighed on Lena's mind—all because he'd succumbed to his desire for her before it was proper.

"Fine idea, having the Hooleys over," he agreed. As he drove them back to Willow Ridge, Josiah vowed that Lena and Isaiah would want for nothing. Providing well for them was the least he could do—and it was the way he wanted to spend the rest of his life because he loved them. He could finally admit that to himself.

"I think Homer's got a *thing* going with his house-keeper," Savilla said after they'd ridden for a few minutes. She'd been keeping a perfectly straight face until Lena giggled.

"*Jah*—unless he wears that pink bathrobe that's hanging on the bathroom door."

It took Josiah a while to stop laughing at that remark. "He's probably as concerned about what'll happen with her as he is about selling his farm—but I doubt he'll take a girlfriend along to live with his sister-in-law and seven nieces."

"I can't see that happening," Lena agreed.

"Do you suppose Miriam and Ben know who she is?" Savilla asked. "They would be familiar with all the *maidels*—"

"Hey—that's none of our business," Josiah insisted, although he was still chuckling. "If Homer gets wind of such speculation, he'll know who started the grapevine buzzing. Let's not push our luck."

"You're right. My lips are sealed," Savilla said, pulling an imaginary zipper across her lips.

"Mine, too," Lena said as one last smile tickled her lips. "It's still fun to think about, though. And even more fun to think that maybe we'll be living there soon, *jah?*"

"I like the sound of that," Josiah agreed. His heart thrummed as the Willow Ridge Clinic and the Sweet Seasons came into view. "I like it a lot."

Chapter Twenty

Lena focused on her cookie dough, cutting out as many houses and stars as she could before rerolling it. It was Friday afternoon, and Josiah had ridden to the New Haven bank with Homer Yoder a couple of hours earlier—and the air was so thick with snow she couldn't see across the road. Although she was glad the two men were traveling in Homer's black pickup truck instead of the rig, she tried not to imagine the vehicle sliding off the pavement into a snowy ditch. Lena also hoped the Mennonite bachelor wouldn't change his mind about selling his farm to Josiah. All week she'd pictured herself in that house . . . singing to Isaiah in his room, cooking with Savilla in that big kitchen, sitting on the couch with Josiah of an evening . . .

What if Homer's housekeeper doesn't want him to leave? Maybe she's talked him out of living with his sister-in-law and her large family. What if—

"Can ya unlock the door for Rebecca?" Miriam asked with a lift in her voice "She'll be covered with snow if she waits for *me* to waddle over there."

Lena dropped her cookie cutter and hurried to the

door. Miriam had been unusually quiet today, which probably meant she was very uncomfortable. "Come on in before you blow away!" she said as she swung open the door. "Oh, my! We've gotten three or four more inches of snow since lunch."

"*Jah*, Naomi went home early," Rebecca said as she stomped her snowy feet on the throw rug. "Savilla's not sure whether to keep cooking or to call off the dinner shift for the evening—especially because Josiah's not back from New Haven."

"I'm thinkin' he and Homer and Derek Shotwell, the loan officer, are dottin' the I's and crossin' the T's for sellin' that farm," Miriam said. "That sort of business can take a while."

"It can—and Josiah brought all the meat inside before he left, so Savilla can put it in the fridge for tomorrow if she wants." Rebecca slipped out of her coat, smiling. "I can see the newest cottage industry in Willow Ridge is going full force in spite of the snow. Look at these shimmery angels! And the snowman in his striped scarf and hat."

"Miriam and I have baked and decorated nearly ten dozen today, for a lady who goes to Nora's church," Lena said as she returned to her dough. "She must be having quite a Christmas party."

"And you must be making quite a name for yourself, Lena." Rebecca picked up a sleigh cookie her mother had just decorated. "You should name your business. I could make you some labels with a phone number on it so people who pick up cookies at the mill store or the Sweet Seasons can call you with orders."

"Oh, that's a *gut* idea!" Miriam said as she shifted in her chair. "Those labels ya designed for Nazareth's goat cheese and Tom's butter are so cute, I suspect folks buy their stuff just for the pictures of the goat and the cow."

Lena arranged the final cookies on her baking sheet and slipped it into the oven. "Are they sticky on the back? A label might keep the plastic wrap in place— and cover the overdone spots on the backs," she added with a grin.

"Yep, they are. Think up a clever name and I'll come up with a cute design for you." Rebecca sat down and slung her arm around Miriam's shoulders. "And how are you today, Mamma?"

"Ready for this baby to be *out*," Miriam replied. "If I didn't have these cookies to frost and Lena to chat with, I'd be goin' crazy."

"If your back gets cranky in that chair, take a rest in your recliner, Miriam," Lena suggested. "It's so nice of you to help me with these cookies—and with everything else. I hate to think about what might've happened to Isaiah and me if we'd stayed with Aunt Clara, or if Josiah had left Iowa without me."

Lena lifted her son into her arms, amazed at the depth of her love for him. How could anything be more satisfying than the warm weight of his little body and the shine in Isaiah's eyes as he gazed at her? She found herself at the kitchen window again, sending up a prayer for Josiah's safe return. Peering through the thick white snowflakes was a lot like trying to see into the future—the details weren't clear, but Lena felt certain that looking ahead was far better than looking back.

"What a day!" Josiah said as he gazed through the fogged-over window of Homer's truck. "*Denki* for driving me into New Haven. I'm not sure I'd have made it back in a rig."

"You'd have waited for the snow plow to go by, no doubt," Homer replied as he steered carefully along the county highway. "But *jah*, what a day! I figured my farm might sit empty for quite a while in the winter, and now it's a done deal. I owe Reuben Riehl a favor."

"Me too," Josiah replied. "And I appreciate Derek Shotwell's explaining the contract details in a way I could understand. Nice guy."

"I've done a lot of business with him over the years. He has a *gut* feel for how Plain folks want to keep things simple, and he respects our way of living." Homer glanced over at Josiah. "I'll drop you at the Sweet Seasons, but would it be all right if we stop at Nora's gift store first? I have some Christmas shopping to do, and I've heard all manner of *gut* things about her shop."

Josiah's eyes widened. "I guess Christmas *is* next week—and I haven't given a thought to what to get for Lena or my sister," he said. "I could cook dinner for everybody, I suppose, but after an hour it's gone and we've got nothing to show for it except dirty dishes. *Jah*, let's stop at Nora's—if she hasn't closed early because of all this snow."

Josiah saw the large wooden mill building ahead, and Homer turned at the next intersection. "Hang on," he said with a boyish grin. "I'll have to gun it to get us up the hill."

With a whoop, Yoder hit the gas pedal. The back end of the truck fishtailed, but the truck roared up the snowy lane and made both of them laugh out loud. Such shenanigans had been part and parcel of riding in his friends' cars during their *Rumspringa*, but Josiah hadn't expected such a burst of exuberance from the middle-aged Mennonite in the driver's seat.

Homer chuckled. "Better get that wild driving out of my system, I suppose," he said as he stuck his keys in his coat pocket. "Along with moving to my brother's farm, I'm going to be tying the knot soon—with that gal I told you about, who's been cleaning for me. She kicked up a big fuss when I told her I had to move. Seems women are training us men even while we believe we're in control, ain't so?"

Josiah laughed as they got out of the truck. "I know a little bit about that, *jah*,"

He couldn't wait to tell Lena and Savilla that their speculations had been correct—but once he stepped through the door of the Simple Gifts store, he forgot about the weather and his fiancée and his sister. Nora had transformed an enormous horse barn into a shop filled with glossy Amish-made furniture, quilts, toys, leather saddles and tack, and other handmade items that made him stop in his tracks to gawk.

"And how are you fellows on this blustery afternoon?" Nora asked as she stepped away from a little table where her computer was. "I didn't figure anybody would stop in, so I'm catching up on some bookwork. Can I help you find anything, Josiah?"

Josiah smiled at the attractive redhead, who stood before them in a red and green plaid cape dress with a white shawl around her shoulders. "Nora, this is Homer Yoder. He wants to do some shopping—and I just bought his farm down the road!"

Nora's green eyes lit up in her freckled face. "Congratulations to both of you! Do you have anything in mind, Homer? We have a lot of wonderful items, all crafted by Plain folks who live around central Missouri."

"This is quite a place." Homer gazed up to where quilts and colorful three-dimensional banners were hanging along the loft railing. "I've been a bachelor for so long, I don't have any idea how to shop for, well—a special gift for a special lady."

"Ah," Nora replied with a knowing nod. "Christmas is the perfect time for giving gifts of the heart. A lot of gals admire the embroidered kitchen towel sets displayed in the loft," she said, gesturing up the stairway. "These pottery pieces are very popular, as well—and the lady who makes them takes orders for special pieces or full sets of dishes. Actually, all of my crafters take orders, but at this point it'll be next year before they can deliver them."

Josiah ambled between the displays, noting the fabulous furniture built by the Brenneman brothers, the unique Nativity scenes Bishop Tom had crafted, the beautiful, sturdy pottery Nora was pointing out—and then his breath caught. Beside a sleigh-style bed where a quilt and some Amish dolls were displayed, he spotted a cradle fashioned from walnut. The bed was suspended between two pedestals and had spindled sides that were high enough to keep Isaiah from climbing out of it. Its overall height would allow him and Lena to easily tend to their son, and the mattress was large enough that Isaiah wouldn't outgrow it any time soon.

Josiah didn't even check the price tag. "This is perfect!" he exclaimed. "Miriam's been so generous, sharing the cradle Ben made, but now Isaiah can have his own bed—just in time for our move, and for the arrival of Miriam's baby."

"Micah Brenneman brought that in just yesterday,"

Nora said. "You can't go wrong with furniture those brothers have made—"

"And I'll take this sleigh bed and the matching dresser and wardrobe," Homer blurted out. He looked as excited as a little kid as he ran his hand over the lustrous wood. "I want these embroidered sheets and the quilt that's on it, too—and this braided rug that's beside it. When we move into my brother's place, Fannie and I will have our own cozy little nook. She won't have to settle for a saggy old mattress or thread-bare sheets, or for the furniture that's been in that bedroom forever. She said *yes* yesterday, you see."

"Well, congratulations yet again, Homer! Fannie will be a very grateful woman," Nora added. "What a lovely, thoughtful gift for your new bride."

"May I leave everything here until we're ready to move in a couple of weeks?" Homer asked. "No sense in hauling it out to my place and then having to load it up again—and risk scratching this beautiful wood."

"If you ask the Brennemans," Nora said as she handed him a business card from the display, "I'm sure they'll be happy to haul it for you. They deliver furniture all the time."

"Perfect. Absolutely perfect." Homer let out a grati-fied sigh and clapped Josiah on the back. "Now I know why the Bible tells us it's better to give than to receive. I feel so excited—and grateful to God that I'll soon have a wife."

"I'm happy for both of you," Josiah said. He smiled at Nora. "Do you have something to wrap around this cradle so it won't get snowed on in the back of Homer's truck? I'd like to give it to Lena this evening. If anybody deserves an early Christmas gift, she does."

Nora stopped removing the tags from the furniture to gaze at both of them. "You fellows are an inspiration," she said. "Not just because you've purchased so much on a slow afternoon but because you're being generous and kind to your women. They're lucky to have you."

Josiah's eyes widened. Not long ago, Savilla and Miriam had scolded him for being oblivious to Lena's needs—or to anyone's needs except his own—and now Nora Hooley was commending him for his generosity and kindness.

Maybe there's hope for you yet, Witmer. Better see if your sister's still at the café—and help her close up early—and then deliver this gift to Lena while you're on a roll.

Chapter Twenty-One

At the sound of a roaring engine, Miriam looked out the kitchen window to see a black pickup truck top their lane and stop near the house. One look at Josiah's face told her that his afternoon at the bank had gone well. The happiness he exuded as he stepped out into the snow eased some of her aches and pains.

"Ya might wanna come open the door, Lena," she called into the front room. "Josiah's headin' this way and he's carryin' something, well—*interesting*— wrapped in a blanket. Savilla's with him, too."

Lena hurried toward the back door with Isaiah cradled in the crook of her arm and a relieved expression on her face. "Oh, I was imagining all the worst possible accidents," she murmured. "They must've decided not to serve supper this evening."

"A wise decision, nasty as the road looks." Miriam continued scrubbing potatoes and carrots for their supper, curious about Josiah's bulky item. He looked terribly pleased with himself, so she hoped Lena would be receptive to whatever he was bringing in.

"Oh, but it's *gut* to see you, Josiah!" Lena blurted

out as she held the door for him and Savilla. "You've been gone so long, I was beginning to—"

When Josiah set his parcel down and gazed directly into Lena's eyes, she stopped fussing. "We have a home!" he announced jubilantly. "And I brought you—and Isaiah—your Christmas gift a little early. Because I love you both."

Tears welled up in Miriam's eyes, and she couldn't have talked if she'd wanted to. Watching Lena throw her arm around him, and the way Josiah embraced her and his son, was sweet compensation for the times when Miriam had scolded him for being so self-absorbed. When the young couple kissed, Savilla glanced over their heads and gave Miriam a thumbs-up. Ben came in from the front room in time to witness the touching scene, and he lingered in the doorway so he wouldn't interrupt it.

When Josiah eased away, his dark eyes were shining. "Part of the reason we took so long was that Homer wanted to stop at Nora's store," he explained. "You and Savilla had it right! He and the gal who's been cleaning for him are getting hitched. He bought the entire display of the Brennemans' bedroom furniture— plus the sheets and quilt and braided rug that were with it—for her wedding present."

"Oh, my," Miriam remarked. "I never figured Homer for such a spendy fellow. I'm sure Nora was happy he stopped by."

"*Jah*—but before Homer announced he was buying practically everything in sight, I spotted this," Josiah went on. He kept his hands on the blanket for a moment, although the two pedestal legs and rollers were a sure giveaway as to what he'd selected.

Miriam's hand fluttered to her chest as she glanced over at Ben.

"Merry Christmas, Lena," the young man whispered as he slid the blanket aside.

Lena inhaled deeply. "Oh, Josiah, that's the prettiest cradle I've ever seen," she said in a tight voice. She touched the side of the spindled bed, rocking it with her fingertips. "You must've spent a fortune for—"

"Never mind about that," Josiah insisted. "Isaiah can sleep in this bed for a *gut* long while. And—and I wanted the Hooleys to have their beautiful cradle for their own baby before it's born." He focused intently on Miriam and then smiled gratefully at Ben. "We owe you *so much*," he murmured. "I can't thank you enough for the way you've taken us in and put up with our spats."

Ben came over to put his arm around Miriam. "I'm happy the both of ya have come so far," he said. "It was our pleasure to provide Isaiah his first bed, and we hope to be seein' a lot of him—and all of ya—for years to come."

Savilla's smile softened as she ran a hand over the glossy walnut cradle. "I hope you can forgive all the times I've nagged at you, as well, Josiah," she murmured. "This would've been a proud moment for Mammi and Dawdi—and our parents, too. I think they're smiling down at you from Heaven, little brother."

For a long, sweet moment, the kitchen glowed in the light of the lamps. Miriam held her breath, watching as Lena placed her child in the new cradle and then rocked it. It was just the right height for her to lean over, and the mechanism functioned so smoothly and quietly that Isaiah must've felt as though he were floating from side to side on a cloud.

After she gazed adoringly at her son, Lena looked up at Josiah. "So the farm purchase went the way you hoped? Did the money you got from the house in Bloomfield cover the new place?"

Josiah beamed. "I had enough to cover the cost of the farm, but Derek—the loan officer—suggested I keep more back than I'd figured on, to cover expenses until our new café shift makes a reliable income," he replied. "We'll be able to make the small monthly payments with what we earn at the Sweet Seasons this winter, and when the farm's crops come in, we'll have the income from those as well. We can pay the loan off early if we want to, and I'm all for that."

"I don't know what you've planned as far as getting someone to farm your cropland while ya run the café," Ben said, "but Luke and Ira are looking for places to grow the specialty grains and popcorn they process at their mill. Or, if raising cage-free chickens and sellin' the eggs interests ya, they can set ya up with the layin' hens and facilities for that enterprise, too."

"Wow," Josiah murmured. "Now that we've set things into motion, the surprises are piling up. I'll talk to Luke about those ideas real soon."

"For those who love God, all things work together for *gut*," Ben reminded them with a smile. "Nobody's happier for ya than I am, kids. My prayers have been answered."

Miriam smiled and pulled Ben's arms more firmly around her protruding girth. "Amen to that," she murmured. "It's been a blessed day all around."

In the wee hours of Christmas Eve morning, Miriam awoke with a gasp, clutching her belly as a sharp pain

left her too breathless to speak. She'd slept fitfully—
had spent the past few days on the sofa mostly—but she
was determined not to fret and carry on. The last thing
she wanted was for people to hover, or for Andy to put
her in the hospital, so she'd kept wearing a brave face
and forcing a smile whenever someone talked to her.

*Tell Ben you're in labor. If you wait too long, you might not
be able to get out of this bed, it hurts so bad.*

Miriam remained on her side, hugging herself as
her husband snored lightly behind her. *No sense in
waking him and then rousting Andy at this hour. Do your
deep breathing. Focus on the joy of holding your wee one at
long last.*

A few moments later, when another pain made her
cry out, however, Ben stirred. "You all right?" he murmured as he snuggled against her backside.

To her horror, Miriam burst into tears. She was suddenly so overwhelmed with pain she nearly passed out.

Ben sat up so he could peer at her face in the darkness. "Are your labor pains startin'? Shall I fetch
Andy?"

Hearing the apprehension in Ben's dear voice,
Miriam tried her best to say they could wait, but all that
came out was another wail.

"You stay right here where it's warm, honey-girl," he
said as he scrambled out of bed. He fumbled in the
darkness for his clothes, until Miriam managed to flip
the switch of the battery lamp on her nightstand. "I'll
go fetch Andy. And I'll tell Savilla and Lena ya need
some help. Maybe some tea to soothe ya, or—well,
Lena knows about these things."

He tenderly kissed her cheek. "Hang on, honey-girl.
It's gonna be a glorious day, and you're gonna be just

fine. I'll take *gut* care of ya, so don't worry about a thing."

As Ben hurried from the bedroom, Miriam shed fresh tears and clutched the edge of the mattress with another pain. She wanted to believe that her capable, competent husband could ensure that this momentous day would go smoothly, but deep down she sensed something was terribly wrong. Had more than twenty years erased the memory of her difficult labor with the triplets, or was she suffering a *lot* more pain than she'd endured back then?

She was vaguely aware of rapid footsteps in the hall before Lena and Savilla entered the room. Both girls were in their nightgowns and robes, appearing earnestly concerned.

"I'll put the kettle on for tea," Lena murmured as she placed a hand on Miriam's forehead. "Oh, my, you're awfully warm."

"What can I do?" Savilla asked. "Can I bring you some aspirin for the pain?"

"Better wait until Andy looks her over before we give her anything," Lena answered. "I'll go fix that tea."

Nodding, Savilla gazed down at Miriam with a stricken expression. "You're in a bad way, ain't so?"

Miriam nodded emphatically, embarrassed by her uncontrollable crying.

"I'm so glad we've got a clinic just down the street—and here comes Andy's medical wagon now," she remarked. "The moon's so bright on the fresh snow, it's almost like daylight out there."

With what rational thought she could muster, Miriam thanked God that both Ben and Andy must be moving in high gear. *Please, Lord, keep me and this baby safe,* she prayed frantically. *Give me the right words so I can tell Andy what's wrong.*

She drifted on a haze of pain and impending unconsciousness, but she was aware of Andy coming in with his bag. His cold stethoscope and soothing voice helped her to stay mentally afloat, but she couldn't miss the concerned furrow of his brow as he checked her over with his careful hands. The blood pressure cuff squeezed her arm mercilessly and then he removed it.

"I know we were figuring on a home delivery, Miriam, but your blood pressure's dangerously low. I'm calling an ambulance to take you to the hospital in New Haven." He glanced at Ben and the girls as he pulled a cell phone from his pocket. "Pack her an overnight bag. Won't take them long to get here, and they can stabilize her on the way over there."

Miriam swallowed her protest. Andy had been instructed by Bishop Tom to use that cell phone only in *emergencies.* Oh, but she'd counted on a peaceful home delivery, with Ben nearby and Andy in charge, where all would be as calm and bright as the scene from "Silent Night". She trusted his instincts, however, and fought to stay lucid enough to tell the girls where to find her nightgowns and underthings. A siren wailed in the distance.

Miriam clutched Ben's hand as he stood beside the bed, looking scared and helpless. She forced herself to say something helpful, something that would give him a task to occupy his troubled mind. "Tell Rachel I'm countin' on her," she rasped as another pain grabbed her belly like a vise. "I want to picture her and—and Amelia as Mary and Baby Jesus tonight at the pageant. It'll give me . . . somethin' lovely to focus on."

"I'll pass that along to your girls," Savilla assured her. "That way Ben can concentrate on you at the hospital, and Rachel and Rebecca will know you want the live Nativity to go on, just like everyone's been planning."

"*Jah,*" Miriam rasped. "I'll be doin' my work, and they'll be . . . doin' God's work in the world."

As the siren blared in front of the house, Andy hurried downstairs. Soon hushed voices and several sets of footsteps echoed in the stairwell—or was her pain so severe that her head was getting all funny? The paramedics got right to work starting an IV as Andy explained to her and Ben that this would help her relax and relieve her pain. They wrapped her in warm blankets and gently eased her onto a stretcher, and somehow—miraculously—they bore her and the IV apparatus down the stairs without dropping her. She was vaguely aware that Josiah was holding the door open, and that Ben and Andy were climbing into the back of the ambulance with her as the paramedics shifted her onto a solid mattress.

After a brief, wondrous sense of release, Miriam drifted into oblivion.

Chapter Twenty-Two

Ben sat in the hospital waiting room, gripping the arms of his chair so hard his hands throbbed. A wall-mounted TV flashed scenes of well-dressed people who chatted jovially about their plans for tonight and Christmas Day—about the toys that had been so popular this season that stores had run out of them and frantic English parents had searched online and paid outlandish prices to acquire them.

But what did those things matter? In his mind, he still saw Miriam's pale, slack face and a lot of hoses and tubes attached to her as masked hospital attendants wheeled her toward the operating room. Andy had donned his scrubs and a mask, too. Before he'd disappeared behind an ominous pair of stainless-steel doors, he'd reassured Ben that everything would be fine.

But how could that be true? His Miriam knew how to have a baby without any such assistance. She'd been so calm and capable, so mentally ready to endure the long hours of labor—until she'd cried out with a pain that had terrified him even more than it had rendered her helpless. Something horrific surely must be wrong that Andy would check her over and so quickly summon emergency medical help.

What if she never woke up? What if the cord had wrapped around the baby's neck? What if the baby came out fine but his Miriam never recovered? How could he possibly raise a child without her? *No, how can you possibly* live *without her?*

His frantic thoughts taunted him as the hands on the clock refused to move. Ben knew he should pray—should focus on the fact that God was in charge and that everything would go according to His will.

But what if He calls Miriam home, thinking she belongs there now instead of with me?

Ben propelled himself from the chair and began to pace the perimeter of the waiting area. He was grateful that no one else was there to witness his lack of faith, his desperation—even as he yearned for a reassuring word about Miriam's progress, or for an angel to appear and tell him to fear not. That was the way angels talked in the Bible, but he was pretty sure he'd be even more terrified if one of them did show up. He would immediately assume that the angel had come to escort Miriam out of this life and into the next. . . .

"'And there were in the same country shepherds abiding in the field, keeping watch over their flock by night,'" Teacher Alberta Zook read in a clear, ringing voice. "'And lo, the angel of the Lord came upon them and the glory of the Lord shone round about them: and they were sore afraid.'"

As Lena gazed at the young shepherds in their costumes, she felt awestruck and totally caught up in the enchantment of the live Nativity. One little boy clutched a stuffed lamb while the older ones acted out the words, gazing into the sky and then covering their heads with their arms, fearful of that angel described in the Scripture. Dan Kanagy's sheep bleated from their pen in Ben's barn, while Bishop Tom's Holstein cow and Lucy and Sol Brenneman's miniature pony looked on from behind another section of fencing. The Brenneman kids' border collie, Rowdy, was keeping watch over the livestock and the kids with bright, intelligent eyes.

Above the barn, a spotlighted, sparkly star drifted peacefully in the night sky—another of Rebecca's contributions to this simple yet amazing pageant. Lena could not imagine a more perfect evening, or a more enchanting rendition of Jesus's birth as she rocked from side to side with a bundled Isaiah in her arms.

"'And the angel said unto them Fear not: for behold, I bring you good tidings of great joy, which shall be to all people,'" Teacher Alberta continued jubilantly. "'For unto you is born this day in the city of David a Savior, which is Christ the Lord.'"

As the children began to sing "Silent Night," joined by everyone in the growing crowd of onlookers, Lena gazed up at Josiah. "This is nothing like I've ever seen," she murmured beneath the music. "There must be a couple of hundred people here! I wish Miriam and Ben could see how beautiful Rachel and little Amelia are, and how Micah's standing so steadfastly beside them. I—I hope she's all right," she added with a catch in her voice. "I thought we would've heard something by now."

"*Jah*, me too," Savilla said. "Surely the baby's come by now, unless . . . well, I don't want to think about something going seriously wrong."

Josiah slipped an arm around Lena's shoulders and pulled his sister close, as well. "Could be there's a message on the machine in the Sweet Seasons phone shanty. I'll look when I go over to check my cookers."

Lena nodded as she and Savilla eased out of Josiah's embrace. Along with the heartfelt singing and the children's charming performance, the rich aromas of brisket, turkey, and pork loin drifted over the crowd from the café across the road. She'd agreed wholeheartedly when Josiah had offered to grill enough meat for the entire Hooley family's meals for Christmas and Second Christmas as his gift to them. Savilla had prepared everyone's favorite side dishes, as well, and had stored them in the café's refrigerator to be taken home after the pageant tonight, along with packets of the meat. Lena had baked fresh cookies to go with the meals. She was glad everyone would spend Christmas Day in the proper prayerful meditation instead of in the kitchen.

It would be so wonderful if Miriam, Ben, and the baby could be home for Christmas, Lena thought as she gazed at the faces around her. She felt an uplifting kinship with the people of Willow Ridge. As she joined in the singing of "O Little Town of Bethlehem," she spotted Bishop Tom and his wife Nazareth standing alongside Nazareth's sister Jerusalem and Bishop Vernon. Nora and Luke Hooley, Annie Mae and Adam Wagler, Gabe and Wilma Glick, and Naomi Brenneman and her sons were in the crowd, too, wedged among more English visitors than Lena could count. Rhoda and Rebecca beamed at Rachel and the kids from the sidelines.

What an incredible six weeks it's been since Ben insisted that you and Josiah stop squabbling, Lena thought with a satisfied smile. *We've made so many friends who feel like family, and we've found a new home.*

As Teacher Alberta began "O Come, All Ye Faithful," the back of Lena's neck prickled so intensely that she gazed around the crowd again. Although folks were tightly bunched together, no one had touched her or—

Lena's mouth dropped open. At the edge of the crowd, coming up the Hooleys' lane, she thought she saw a dearly familiar face. It was after dark, and Plain women looked a lot alike in their black winter coats and bonnets, but no one else resembled—

"Mamm!" she cried, aware that everyone was staring at her. Josiah's eyes widened as he gazed in the same direction she had, but Lena couldn't stand still. Clutching Isaiah, grabbing Josiah's hand, she squeezed between the people who were singing. Some of them looked mildly irritated that she was passing in front of them, interrupting their song, but Lena was too ecstatic to care. "Mamm, is it really you?" she called out.

Lena's heart was racing as she made her way through the last few rows of people. All she could hear was her thundering pulse as she held her mother's gaze. When she'd reached the outer edge of the crowd, Lena stopped and stared, willing herself not to bawl like a baby. "Mamm, I—I wasn't sure when I'd ever see you again, and here you are in Willow Ridge!"

In the blink of an eye her mother was grabbing her, holding her close, exclaiming over Isaiah—all at once. "When I got Miriam's Christmas card, saying you and Josiah were taking your instruction to join the church," her mother blurted out, "and when she told me about little Isaiah being born such a perfect baby, well—I couldn't stay away! I told your *dat* I'd drive all the way here by myself if he insisted on being a stubborn old stick in the mud!"

Lena blinked back tears and hugged her mother again. Then she looked at her father, who stood behind Mamm, trying to keep a straight, stoic expression on his face. Was it her imagination, or did Dat seem older and more pinched? "I'm glad you came along," she told him. "I know I disobeyed you and disappointed you—"

"Shh!" said the woman behind Lena.

Josiah leaned closer, his voice low. "Shall we go to the house where we can talk?" he suggested. "It's right this way."

Lena was as grateful for Josiah's suggestion as she was for the few minutes it took to skirt the edge of the crowd and cut through to the back door of Ben and Miriam's house. She waved at Officer McClatchey and Sheriff Banks, who were gazing raptly at the costumed Wise Men as they began to sing "We Three Kings." Her parents raised their eyebrows when Josiah pulled a key from his coat pocket.

"We've had some unfortunate incidents lately," he explained as they entered the house, "so folks have been encouraged to lock their doors. Ben and Miriam live here, but they're at the hospital—"

"Miriam's having her baby," Lena jumped in, "and I hope everything's all right. She was in a bad way when the ambulance took her to the hospital early this morning."

Mamm's brow furrowed. "I was hoping to meet Miriam and Ben, to thank them for taking care of you," she murmured. She gazed around the kitchen, where Lena had left a lamp burning. "Standing here, I can feel the *love* in this home. After I read Miriam's card—

and listened to her phone messages again and again," she admitted, "I couldn't ignore her point. Jesus was born to save us from our sins, and we in turn must forgive each other the way God has forgiven us."

Lena held her breath. While her parents faithfully followed Old Order ways, neither of them was inclined toward discussing their Christian beliefs on an everyday basis. Whatever Miriam had written and said to them had moved them deeply. *And isn't it just like Miriam to contact them on my behalf without making a big deal of it?*

Josiah smiled cautiously. "You have a lot to forgive, considering everything I've done these past several months," he said. "I hope you'll accept my apologies for interfering with your family, but I—I really do love your Lena and our boy, and we plan to marry on January first. I've bought us a farm outside of town. Savilla and I are doing well enough with our cooking at the Sweet Seasons Café across the road to support our family, too."

When her mother reached for Isaiah, Lena handed him over. He would be the glue that cemented their new relationship with her parents, just as Miriam had predicted. What a lovely sight it was, watching her mother nuzzle Isaiah's downy hair and hold him close. "I've started up a baking business, too," Lena said. "Miriam's been such a help to us, and Ben is a rock of faith. Wonderful examples they are, of how loving Christian couples should live their lives."

When an uncomfortable expression crossed her father's face, Josiah cleared his throat. "Want to go across the street and help me take the meat off my grills, Emory? I've been roasting turkeys, pork loins, and briskets for the whole Hooley family as my

Christmas gift to them. It's time I took everything out of the cookers."

When her *dat* smiled, Lena's heart thrummed with sweet relief. While the pageant and the carols had filled her with a wondrous renewal of faith and love, it was a sign of her father's forgiveness that he would even consider helping Josiah.

"You fellows run along," Mamm said as she headed for the front room. "Isaiah, his *mamm,* and I have some catching up to do."

Chapter Twenty-Three

Josiah inhaled the brisk night air and sent up thanks to God that this day was ending so much better than it had begun. Lena's *dat* had never been a man inclined toward chitchat, but he seemed genuinely pleased to be here in Willow Ridge with his daughter, and sincerely interested in seeing the grills and hearing about the new restaurant venture and the farm.

"So you found a place near here?" he asked as they made their way around the edge of the crowd. "How're land prices compared to up our way?"

Josiah waved again at Officer McClatchey and Sheriff Banks, who were still caught up in the children's pageant. When he saw Bishop Tom standing near the two lawmen, he decided a detour was in order. "It would've been about an even trade, moneywise until you consider that we'll have a much smaller acreage than my *mammi*'s now, but a much newer house," he replied. "This is Bishop Tom Hostetler, who's to marry Lena and me—and his wife Nazareth, along with her sister Jerusalem and Bishop Vernon Gingerich. Tom, we've had quite a nice surprise!" he exclaimed. "Lena's parents have come, and this is her *dat*, Emory Esh."

Tom's face lit up, and as the crowd began singing "Joy to the World" with loud exuberance, both bishops reached for Emory's hand. "Oh, but it's *gut* that you folks have made it down to see the kids!" Tom said beneath the singing. "They've come a long way in a short time, and we're mighty pleased that they're makin' Willow Ridge their new home."

Emory smiled wryly. "*Jah*, I've noticed a few improvements," he said as he glanced at Josiah. "And you know how it is when the women keep insisting it's time for a change of attitude—and time to meet the grandchild."

Vernon's eyes twinkled as he laughed. "Were it not for Mary and the baby Jesus, where would any of us be?" he reminded them. "The hand that rocks the cradle has ruled the world for centuries, and I don't see that changing."

"Have you heard any word about Miriam?" Josiah asked beneath the voices around them, raised in song.

Tom shook his head. "All we can believe is that she's gettin' the best of care, and that she's in God's hands. I figure to head to the hospital after the crowd's cleared out."

Josiah nodded. "Give her and Ben our best. Emory and I are going over to take Christmas dinner out of the cookers now, so—"

A loud *kaboom* made everyone in the crowd suck in their breath and stop singing. Across the road, a huge fireball flared up behind the Sweet Seasons, so bright that Josiah couldn't look directly at it. Folks in the crowd cried out, and parents grabbed their children.

"What in the—*fire!*" Josiah cried out. "One of the grill's propane tanks must've exploded, or—"

He started to run toward the road, but Bishop Tom and Officer McClatchey both grabbed him. "You don't want to go anywhere near there, son," the lawman insisted as he pulled out his cell phone. "If the gas appliances in the café's kitchen catch fire, you'll be blown to Kingdom Come. Yeah—" he said into his phone. "We've got an explosion and fire in Willow Ridge at the Sweet Seasons Café—natural gas and propane involved," he added urgently. "Send the fire crew and an ambulance and some deputies for backup. Clyde Banks and I are already here."

When Sheriff Banks saw how folks in the crowd were heading toward the cars parked along the side of the road, he hurried in their direction. "Stay right here, folks!" he hollered. "Take cover in the house and the barn!"

Bishop Tom jogged over to where the kids were huddling with Teacher Alberta and their parents. "Let's get in the house," he insisted as he opened the back door. "Nice and calm now, so nobody gets hurt. Might be best if local folks go on upstairs to make room for everybody who's here."

"Walk through the kitchen and into the front room," Vernon reassured the frightened English guests. "We often seat a couple hundred folks here on Sunday, so there's plenty of space for everyone."

Josiah stared in horrified fascination at the blaze but then steered Lena's *dat* ahead of him as folks filed inside. He found Lena and her *mamm* in the front room, huddled with Isaiah between them. Savilla stood nearby, staring out the picture window in disbelief.

"What *happened?*" Lena rasped. "We heard a *boom* and—my first thought was that you and Dat were over there and—oh, but I'm glad you're here with us, Josiah!"

As Lena grabbed him so tightly that he gasped, Josiah held her close and let her cry against his chest. People were crowding into the front room, murmuring fearfully, some of them going upstairs with their wide-eyed costumed children. As he watched the fire raging across the road, a horrible idea occurred to him: Had he and Emory gone right over to check his cookers instead of stopping to talk with Bishop Tom, they would have been blown to bits.

For a moment, Josiah couldn't think or breathe.

But what caused this? I checked the propane tanks and all the grills an hour before the pageant, he fretted as several sirens blared in the distance.

Bishop Tom's voice rose above the others as he called in from the doorway. "The sheriff wants us to get away from the windows," he explained. "We've got almost everybody inside now, so let's stay safe. A prayer for our lawmen and firefighters would be a *gut* idea, too."

Seeing how crowded the front room and the kitchen were, Josiah motioned Savilla and Lena's family down the hall toward the *dawdi haus.* As they entered the rooms where his sister and Lena had once stayed, he heard the kitchen door close on the other side of the wall. Everyone was inside now.

The sirens blared and came to a stop in front of the Hooley house. When another explosion rattled the windows, everyone grimaced and got quiet.

"Sounds like Miriam's gas appliances just went up," Josiah murmured. His throat was so tight and dry he could hardly speak as he slung his arms around Lena and his sister. "I can't think much will be left standing now."

A few moments later, Bishop Tom, Nazareth, Jerusalem, and Bishop Vernon joined them in the *dawdi haus* sitting room. Tom removed his black hat, shaking his head sadly. "This is gonna be a hard piece of news to break to Miriam, when she's already had such a rough day."

"Maybe it would be best to keep this under your hat until you see how she and Ben and the baby are doing," Savilla suggested. "They'll have all kinds of questions about what triggered the explosions, and until we know—"

"Unfortunately, I have an idea who might be behind it," Tom muttered. "And I hate jumpin' to that conclusion as much as I detest the devastation we've all witnessed on this holiest of nights. At least nobody at the live Nativity was hurt."

"It's another blessing that the pageant was still in progress so people weren't on the road, getting into their vehicles," Vernon murmured.

After they stood in silence for a few moments, Josiah let out a long sigh. "It's a pretty sure thing that Ben's smithy—and the apartment upstairs, where Rebecca lives—have been destroyed along with the café," he murmured. "Not to mention the Schrocks' quilt shop and all their inventory, and the equipment and furniture in the Sweet Seasons."

"And Christmas dinner," Lena joined in sadly. She eased away from Josiah to take Isaiah from her *mamm.* The baby was getting fussy, as though he, too, sensed something too horrible for words had just happened.

In his mind's eye, Josiah once again saw the ball of

flame billowing up from behind the café, and it didn't take much to imagine a bigger, hotter inferno engulfing the nearby buildings. The other folks in the *dawdi haus* settled into chairs or perched on the beds. Too nervous to sit, Josiah peered down the hallway. Some of the people in the front room were cross-legged on the floor, while others had scooted the chairs away from the glass to sit in them. A few whispered to each other, but most of the crowd waited in apprehensive silence—until someone upstairs cried out, "Who's that on the stretcher? They found somebody over there!"

Unable to endure another moment inside, Josiah slipped out the back door of the *dawdi·haus*. He shook his head as he recalled that Lena had seen a face peering through the nearby window not long ago. Had a propane tank on one of his grills malfunctioned, or had Hiram Knepp tampered with it? Had Knepp somehow gotten over the enclosure's walls—or had he broken into the Sweet Seasons and accessed the cookers through the kitchen? When Josiah stepped around the end of the house, he saw two huge fire engines pumping white foam over the Sweet Seasons building, while safety-suited firefighters aimed other streams of foam at the area behind it.

Josiah nipped his lip. The paramedics loaded a stretcher into one of the ambulances, and then the vehicle took off down the county highway with its lights pulsing and its siren slicing through the night. About ten minutes later, the flames were extinguished. The entire area appeared to be coated with steaming white shaving cream.

Ben's smithy was an empty shell. The building that had housed the quilt shop and the café had burned to the ground. Only the forge and odd remnants of the stoves and fridges stuck up out of the foam-coated ashes.

In a matter of minutes, Ben and Miriam Hooley, Naomi Brenneman, and the three Schrock sisters had lost their places of business—and Josiah's future had gone up in smoke, as well. A sob tore at his throat as he wondered how he would support Lena, his sister, and his son, and how he'd make the monthly loan payment on the farm he'd just bought.

It was conceivable that the Eshes might take Lena and Isaiah back to Bloomfield once they found out that Josiah's own stubborn foolishness had been at the heart of this catastrophe. If only he hadn't agreed to cook for Hiram before he'd visited Higher Ground in person. If only he'd taken Ben's advice and come to terms with Knepp about staying in Willow Ridge.

If only you hadn't spent most of your life believing you were right and everyone else was following stupid rules that didn't apply to you.

With a heavy heart and slumped shoulders, Josiah turned away from the scene across the road. Bishop Tom's black and white cow, the sheep, and the miniature pony were watching him from between the rails of their pens. He noticed that the floodlight from the live Nativity was still pointed upward.

The star balloon drifted on its long ribbon, shimmering serenely in the night sky.

Josiah kicked the hay bale where Rachel had sat with Amelia an hour earlier. The whole Christmas story suddenly seemed as fake and meaningless as these props from the kids' pageant. What did it matter that God's Son had been born centuries ago? Evil and meanness still ran rampant in the world, and from what Josiah could tell, God wasn't doing a thing about it. If He rewarded the righteous and the pure, why had Miriam Hooley suffered such agony this morning? And why had she lost the restaurant she'd poured her heart and soul into? Why had Hiram Knepp been allowed to torment so many people who'd not gone along with his wishes?

Josiah shivered with cold, but he wasn't ready to go inside. He wasn't sure he could face Lena and her family—and when he glanced toward the devastation again, he saw Officer McClatchey and Sheriff Banks coming up the Hooleys' lane. Even in the darkness, their expressions were grim.

Chapter Twenty-Four

"Ben, congratulations! You've got a baby girl!"

Ben stopped staring into the worst cup of coffee he'd ever tried to drink. He'd been so absorbed in his worrisome thoughts about losing Miriam that he'd lost track of the time and the senseless blather playing on the TV. He raised his head and gazed blankly at the man who was approaching him in blue scrubs and odd plastic slippers that matched the puffy shower cap on his head.

Andy Leitner removed his hat, his smile fading. "Are you all right, Ben?" he murmured. "I thought you'd be a little more excited about the birth of your—"

"Is Miriam alive?" Ben rasped. "If she didn't make it through the delivery, I don't know how I can possibly go on—"

"Did you hear me?" Andy insisted in a low voice. He grasped Ben's shoulders and gazed directly into his eyes. "You have a perfect baby girl. Miriam's all sewn up and she'll be fine. After we got her stabilized, she gave the delivery everything she had, but we finally did a C-section. As the hours went by, her blood pressure and sugar weren't cooperating and she was losing her strength." Andy smiled kindly. "I sent nurses out here a couple of times to keep you informed, but I guess you were so preoccupied you didn't grasp what they were saying."

Light began to dawn in Ben's frightened mind. He exhaled, allowing himself to believe that his wife had survived—and that she'd borne him a daughter. "Don't mind me," he said, shaking his head to clear it. "I was all alone out here, and I've never been in a hospital before, and—and I guess I lost my faith for a bit." He glanced at the clock on the wall. "It's only eight o'clock? Seems like I've been goin' through my own little hell for a lot longer than that today."

Andy's eyebrows rose. "You've never been in a hospital?"

"Nope. And I thank God I've had no reason to be." Ben sucked in a long breath as happier thoughts began to dance in his mind. "It's a girl? And she's healthy?"

"She's a beauty," Andy replied with a grin. "Ten pounds, three ounces. Strong set of lungs on her, too."

Ben let out a nervous but ecstatic laugh. "Ten pounds? No wonder Miriam felt bigger than a barn this past month. I—can I see them?"

Andy clapped him on the shoulder and steered him down the hallway. "Now you're sounding like the Ben I know. The first words out of Miriam's mouth when she regained consciousness were 'where's my Benniebug?' She was threatening to get out of bed to find you herself, so I came to fetch you."

Where's my Bennie-bug? Ben's heart thrummed with exhilaration as he strode down the corridor. His Miriam was just fine. It was he who'd been too fearful to notice the pleasant colors of the hospital decor—or even the nice gal who'd brought him that awful cup of coffee. *I hope you'll forgive me, Lord, for forgetting that You've been in charge,* he prayed as Andy paused in front of a wooden door with a rectangular window in it.

Ben's breath caught. Even standing outside the room, he could see that Miriam looked peaceful and composed—enthralled with the bundle she held in the crook of her arm. He raked his fingers through his uncombed hair and fumbled with his half-tucked shirttail. Although she'd been through a major surgery and had given birth, his wife's dark hair was neatly tucked beneath a fresh white *kapp*, and she wore the new robe he'd gotten her a few months ago. Her color had returned, and she looked much better than when he'd gazed so helplessly at her during the ambulance ride in the wee hours.

"Congratulations again," Andy murmured as he opened the door. "She's tired, so don't stay too long."

Nodding, Ben stepped into the room. He could only gape, unsure of the proper thing to do or say—until Miriam's shining eyes set his heart to beating again. "Hey there, honey-girl," he murmured as he approached her bedside. "Who's this you've got hold of?"

"She's the sweetest little miracle you've ever seen in your life, Bennie," Miriam whispered. "This being Christmas Eve—and what with the names your aunts and uncles have—what would ya think of callin' her Bethlehem?"

Ben's mouth dropped open, but no sound came out. The blanketed bundle in Miriam's arms had opened her eyes and was wiggling her arms and legs as her mouth opened and closed. When Miriam offered the baby to him, Ben scooted an upholstered chair to the bedside and sat down so he wouldn't drop her. "How do I—what if I—"

"Support her head with your hand. Other than that, she's a sturdy little thing."

Swallowing hard, Ben carefully did as Miriam had instructed—and then he rested against the back of the chair with a surprisingly solid, warm little body that fit perfectly against his chest. "Bethlehem," he breathed.

He had no idea how long he gazed at the red, wrinkled face and the puckered forehead with such perfectly arched brows . . . the tiny bow-shaped lips and quivering little nostrils. Although he knew the world was still turning, and ordinary folks were performing their jobs as usual, Ben felt the universe hold its breath for a long, lovely moment—a moment that redefined life as he knew it. He'd spent his first thirty-five years wandering like a gypsy, until one look at Miriam Lantz on a stormy morning had grounded him. Now he sensed an entirely different path opening before him—an event every bit as momentous as Moses parting the Red Sea or the angel Gabriel telling Mary she would conceive God's own Son.

"Bethlehem. Bethlehem Hooley," he whispered in awe. Then he glanced at his wife. "What's her middle name?"

Miriam giggled. "With a name like Bethlehem, ya think she needs a middle name to clarify who she is?" she teased. "After all, Jerusalem and Nazareth have no middle names, either."

"*Jah*, you're right. I'm so jumbled up, it's a *gut* thing you've got all this figured out," he replied with a chuckle. Then he gazed at his daughter again, so totally in love with her that he let himself drift in the perfection of this warm, cuddly moment. "It's been quite a day, little girl," he murmured. "A Christmas Eve like no other."

When Josiah came back into the *dawdi haus*, followed by Officer McClatchey and Sheriff Banks, Lena protectively held her little son closer. Although she'd met these lawmen before, she and her family—like most Plain folks—associated policemen with bad news and an unwelcome intrusion into their community. The grim expression on Josiah's face bespoke his own misgivings about the message they were about to share.

Bishop Tom rose from his chair. "What've ya found out? I hope nobody's been hurt," he added in a concerned voice. "Back at this end of the house, we've not been able to see what's happenin', but somebody hollered about a stretcher bein' put into an ambulance."

Sheriff Banks nodded. "The news isn't good—and I'm really sorry all this commotion interrupted your Nativity pageant," he added. "The firefighters found a fellow several feet away from the buildings, badly burned and unconscious. It was Hiram Knepp."

Lena and those around her sucked in their breath. Her heart pounded as she swayed from side to side, cradling Isaiah as though to protect him from the nastiness they were hearing about. "It's wrong to wish Hiram ill, even after all he's done," she murmured, "but—well, is he going to live?"

Officer McClatchey smiled ruefully. "We don't know yet. We found one of those plastic wands you use to light grills nearby, but it's the arson squad's job to determine whether the explosion was caused by a malfunction of a propane tank or if Hiram was to blame."

"We have our theory about that," the portly sheriff added. "And I'm guessing you folks do, too."

Bishop Vernon let out a long sigh. "No matter what our theories are, we must pray for Hiram's healing and his soul—for God's will to be done. And we must find it in our hearts to forgive whatever part he played in tonight's disaster."

"I'm gonna let Annie Mae know about this before we tell the rest of these folks," Tom said as he went toward the hallway door. "Hiram's four youngest kids were in the pageant, and Annie Mae and Adam will have a tough time explainin' to them about what's happened to their *dat* tonight."

Josiah nodded solemnly. "*Jah*. Nellie's with them, too. I think they went upstairs."

"Let's keep everyone here in the house while you talk to them," Sheriff Banks suggested. "McClatchey and I will go back across the road to finish taping off the area so nobody disturbs any evidence before the arson squad investigates."

"Are Miriam and Ben here?" the deputy asked. "I sure hate it that they lost both of their businesses—"

"And Rebecca lost her apartment," Lena added in a small voice.

"They rushed Miriam to the hospital this morning. I'm hopin' the Hooleys have a fine, healthy baby to help offset what's happened in their absence," Bishop Tom replied. "I'm goin' to the hospital as soon as we're finished here."

Officer McClatchey clapped Tom on the shoulder. "I'm sorry you've got such a heavy message to bear to so many tonight, when just an hour ago we were all celebrating the good news of Jesus's birth, Bishop."

"I appreciate your concern—and all of your help

while we've been dealin' with Hiram these past months," Tom replied with a sad smile.

"God be with you both," Vernon added. "What a blessing that you were with us this evening. Men in your line of work see the dark side of human nature all too often."

Lena watched the two officers and the bishops leave, sensing that the moment the *dawdi haus* door closed behind them, her parents would be spouting questions about Hiram and the trouble he'd caused. Before her *dat* could speak, however, Josiah came over to stand behind Lena, wrapping his arms around her and the baby.

"Emory and Dorcas, I want you to know that I nearly hired on with this Hiram fellow we're talking about— because I was foolish enough to believe his pie-in-the-sky promises about a supper club he was opening," Josiah began solemnly. "I'm indebted to Miriam and Ben for warning me about him, and for taking us into their home—not to mention the thanks I owe God for waylaying us in Willow Ridge the night we were heading to Higher Ground," he added. "I'm also grateful to Lena and Savilla for standing by me when I was too hardheaded to listen to the advice I was receiving."

Lena's heart stood still. The expressions on her parents' faces were priceless: They had a hard time believing that the wild, reckless young man who'd split up their family was now acting so penitent—sincerely trying to prove himself worthy of their acceptance.

"Bishop Tom will be marrying us next week," Josiah continued as he hugged Lena closer, "and I hope you'll join us for our big day. It would mean the world to both of us to have your blessing—and your forgiveness for the heartache we've caused you."

Lena thought her mother might melt. Mamm's face softened as she swiped at her eyes. "Ohh," she murmured as she came toward them with open arms. "This is such a fine turn of events, seeing the way you've both grown up since you came here. I'll be the happiest person at your wedding! Wouldn't miss it—would you, Emory?"

Her *dat*'s reaction was predictably less emotional, yet his steady gaze made Lena's heart thrum. "It seems you two are finally on the right path," he said. Then he cleared his throat. "I've got to wonder, though, what with the restaurant burning to the ground, how you expect to make a living—"

When a raised voice in the front room caught their attention, Savilla opened the door into the main part of the house.

"If I could have your attention, please." Bishop Tom was speaking above the chatter. "I'll give ya the update on that ambulance ya saw, and then you folks who've joined us from other towns are free to go out to your vehicles."

Lena and Savilla preceded Josiah into the hallway so they could hear what was being said. As her parents stood beside her, Lena sensed a new hopefulness in them, despite the unfortunate events that had disrupted life in Willow Ridge.

Bishops Tom and Vernon stood near the front window, clasping their hands in front of them as though they were preparing to preach on a Sunday morning. "Sheriff Banks and Officer McClatchey have informed me that the fella in the ambulance was Hiram Knepp, who used to be our bishop here in Willow Ridge," Tom said in a solemn voice. "Whether or not ya know him,

I'd ask ya to bow your head in silent prayer for his soul and his young family."

"We've witnessed an unthinkable disaster this evening," Vernon continued as he gazed around at the silent, stunned crowd. "As horrible as it appears to us now, we're grateful that the words written in the Gospel of John still hold true for us today. John tells us that the light of Christ came into the world and the darkness did not comprehend it—and in a more modern translation, the darkness did not *overcome* the light. Shall we pray on these things together?"

When the bishops bowed their heads, the entire crowd—English and Plain alike—joined them. As Lena closed her eyes, she was in awe that so many folks who didn't live there were willing to pray with them. It felt like a holy moment, standing in silence with more than a hundred other souls who were united in their petitions to God on behalf of the Knepps, and the rest of Willow Ridge as well.

Your will be done, Lord, Lena prayed as she bounced Isaiah to keep him from fussing. *Please keep Annie Mae, Nellie, and the younger Knepp kids in Your care as they deal with another sad example of how their* dat *has strayed from the higher road. Bless Miriam and Ben, too, as they face such an unexpected disaster.*

After a few moments, Bishop Tom spoke again. "We here in Willow Ridge wish all of ya a blessed Christmas, and we thank ya for comin' tonight to honor the Savior we celebrate and depend upon," he said. "Be careful goin' home. Please don't cross the tape boundary Sheriff Banks has set up around the burned-out buildings, so their investigation can go the way it's supposed to."

"Did Knepp set the fire?" someone in the back of the crowd asked.

Bishop Tom smiled patiently. "We don't know that. We're lettin' the police figure it out."

"Will Miriam rebuild the Sweet Seasons?" somebody else called out. "And what about Ben's smithy? He's the only farrier we've got in this area."

Bishop Vernon raised his hands to bring the questions to a close. "I ask your prayers on the Hooleys' behalf, as well," he said. "All of our questions will be answered in God's perfect time—which means we'll need to be patient," he added with a wry smile. "Good evening to all of you. Go home in peace to contemplate the birth of our Lord."

Josiah remained in a back corner of the Hooleys' front room as he watched the crowd disperse. Even though he was now in Lena's parents' good graces, he felt isolated—removed from reality—as he overheard snatches of peoples' speculative conversations. Perhaps if he didn't look across the road again, he would awaken on Christmas Day to see that the Sweet Seasons was still intact, and that the explosions, sirens, and mayhem had all been part of a bad dream. It would be wonderful to sit down to brisket, pork loin, turkey, and Savilla's side dishes, knowing that Bishop Tom's family, Luke and Nora, and Lena's family would also enjoy the meal he and his sister had prepared to thank the folks who'd helped them so much these past weeks.

But it was a fool's game he played, pretending disaster hadn't struck. He'd been wrong to rail at God about why He'd apparently done nothing to curb Hiram Knepp's wickedness; Josiah still felt a void within himself. Although he'd completed his instruction and was to join the church this Sunday, he still had

trouble believing that God was in control of their lives
and wanted them to prosper.

Emory Esh's earlier question pecked at him like a
troublesome hen. How was he supposed to support his
young family now? How was he to pay the monthly
mortgage and bills for the farm he'd bought? True,
he'd kept back money to get through the winter, but
what was he supposed to *do* with himself if he and
Savilla couldn't cook in the Sweet Seasons kitchen?

When Josiah saw Annie Mae and her family coming
downstairs, he made his way through the crowd to
express his condolences. Her husband Adam carried
little Timmy, still wearing his shepherd costume, while
Nellie cradled angel Sarah in her arms and Annie Mae
grasped the hands of Josh and Joey, who had por-
trayed two of the three Wise Men. The children wore
solemn, stunned expressions, as though they were too
shocked to comprehend what had happened to their
father.

"I'm so sorry about your *dat*, Annie Mae," Josiah
murmured when he reached the young woman's side.
"If there's anything I can do—"

Annie Mae's huge blue eyes held his gaze through
her rimless glasses. "I'm sorry all this has happened to
you and Savilla, too," she replied in a halting voice.
"We're taking the kids home, and then Bishop Tom's
giving Nellie and me a ride to the hospital. I—I have
no idea what we'll say to Dat, or if he'll even be able to
hear us. But it seems like the right thing to do."

"Somebody should be with him. And you'll need to
take care of the hospital details," Josiah pointed out. "I
wish you both comfort and strength."

"*Denki*, Josiah. With the help of our family and

friends—and the love of Jesus—we'll come out on the other side of this. We *will*," Annie Mae added emphatically.

Josiah admired her strength in the face of such a daunting task. While he'd always regretted losing his parents as a youngster—not really getting to know them, or to say good-bye to them—at least he'd not seen them burned to a crisp. Once again he wondered what God had been doing when his *mamm* and *dat* had drowned in the flood and why He'd left two little children without their parents—just as the six Knepp kids had lost their mothers years ago and might well lose their *dat*, too.

Josiah caught sight of Rebecca and scolded himself for succumbing to self-pity and such a lack of faith again. Miriam's daughter had lost her home, her clothing—*everything*—yet as she spoke with Derek Shotwell and another English fellow, she appeared animated rather than destitute. Although her smudged eye makeup reminded Josiah of a raccoon's mask, he sensed a hopefulness about Rebecca that made him downright curious, considering her belongings—maybe even her computer—had been destroyed that evening.

"The insurance adjuster has already spoken with the firefighters," the balding man alongside Derek was saying. "No matter what the arson investigation reveals, the building that housed the Sweet Seasons and the Schrocks' quilt shop is covered—and we'll help with replacing Ben's smithy, as well."

Josiah stopped a few feet away from Rebecca and the men who were speaking with her, puzzled. Amish folks never carried insurance—didn't believe in it. So why was this fellow talking about adjusters and promising to replace the burned buildings?

Rebecca nodded as she listened. "I'll help Mamma, Ben, and Mary Schrock list all the appliances and tools and inventory they lost so we can figure out the replacement value for all that stuff," she said. "If their ledgers were lost in the fire, we might not be able to document everything—"

"But we'll be able to put them back in business sooner rather than later," the English fellow beside Derek remarked as he slipped his arm around Rebecca's shoulders. "It looks like you'll be getting a whole new wardrobe and a laptop, too, sweetie."

Unable to corral his curiosity any longer, Josiah approached the little group as the last of the visitors were leaving the front room. "Rebecca, I'm really sorry about your apartment," he began, figuring it wasn't his business to inquire about the insurance issue.

Rebecca grabbed his hands between hers. "Josiah! I'm so glad you weren't checking your grills when they blew up," she exclaimed. "We're really fortunate that everyone was on this side of the road, away from the flying debris, too. This is my dad, Bob Oliveri—the man who raised me after I was washed downriver as a toddler."

Bob reached out to shake Josiah's hand. "It's wonderful to meet you—despite tonight's unfortunate circumstances," he said with a kind smile. "I was at Luke and Nora's wedding party, and one plateful of your cooking convinced me you'd be a fabulous addition to Miriam's staff and menu."

Josiah returned Bob's firm grip. "Well, I appreciate that—even though it was my cooking that blew up two buildings tonight," he added ruefully.

"We all know better than that," Derek insisted. "And at times like these, we can be grateful that Bob owns Miriam's building. It means you'll all be back in business soon."

An English fellow owned the Sweet Seasons building? Why had Miriam never mentioned this to him? As Josiah's thoughts raced, he felt Rebecca squeezing his forearm. Her blue eyes sparkled with fierce determination as she gazed up at him.

"Fear not, Josiah," she said, much as the angel in the Nativity story had spoken. "You might be thinking that Hiram finally got the best of us, but you're about to see what the people of Willow Ridge are made of! We will rise again—believe it!"

Chapter Twenty-Five

Miriam shifted carefully on the hospital bed to make room for Ben to sit beside her. Her incision throbbed and she still felt weary from delivering Bethlehem, but now that the morning's crises were behind her, she welcomed this time of cuddling with her husband as they watched their newborn sleep.

Ben eased over the top of the covers and slipped his arm around Miriam's shoulders. "How sweet is this picture?" he murmured as he gazed at their daughter. "She's been nursin' just fine, and she's perfect—and now we're a family."

Miriam smiled. "Ya know, of course, that had I not been able to have your babies, I would've considered you and me a family anyway," she said. "But then, I already have three girls. It's a wonderful-*gut* thing that you've got a child of your own now, Bennie-bug."

"She's a Christmas gift like no other," he agreed as he kissed Miriam's temple. "And soon we'll be home again, livin' in our own little slice of paradise. God's been mighty *gut* to us, honey-girl."

"Ya said a mouthful there," Miriam replied. She rested

her head against Ben's sturdy shoulder and allowed his warmth to seep into her. Could there possibly be any cozier place on earth than her husband's embrace? It would be so easy to drift off to sleep. . . .

"What a blessing it is to see this peaceful scene," a familiar voice said from the doorway.

Miriam's eyes flew open. "Tom! It's *gut* to see ya— and I'm guessin' the Nativity pageant must be over. How'd it go?"

Tom paused before he answered. "Well, it's hard to beat watchin' the kids act out the birth of Jesus, and leadin' folks in our favorite carols," he replied. "I think our crowd might've been bigger than we had last year, too."

Miriam sensed something wasn't quite right about his response. Long before he'd become the bishop of Willow Ridge, Tom had been a good friend—had gone through his share of trials and tribulations—and she'd usually been able to tell when he was keeping things to himself.

"I'm glad to see ya lookin' so chipper, Miriam," the bishop went on, rolling the band of his felt hat in his hands. "Everybody sends their best. Naz and I were mighty concerned when the ambulance shot down the road so early this mornin'."

Ben squeezed her shoulders. "Andy was worried about her blood pressure droppin'—and about all the pain she was in," he added. "I'm glad we didn't dig in our heels and insist on a home birth. A lot of things could've gone wrong."

Once again Miriam noticed a telltale flicker of emotion passing over the bishop's face, but she didn't press him for details. "Come over and meet our wee girl, Tom," she said. "On account of it bein' Christmas

Eve—and what with the way Hooley names run—we're callin' her Bethlehem."

Tom's face softened. As he approached the bed, he gazed eagerly at the baby. "Oh, would ya look at that dimpled chin and those long eyelashes," he murmured. "I think she favors the both of ya. It's the best part of my day, bein' here to witness God's love come down at Christmas to fine parents like you."

Miriam gazed at the bishop's silver-spangled beard and weathered face. Now that Tom stood at her bedside, she could see he carried a burden—and he was going to rub away one side of his hat if he didn't stop fussing with it.

"What's on your mind, Tom?" she asked softly. "Your words sound cheerful enough, but whenever I see that line between your eyebrows diggin' in so deep, I suspect you're not tellin' me everything ya know."

Tom's eyes widened and his soft laugh sounded like a sigh. "You're too sharp for me," he murmured. "I—I hate to spoil this special moment. Especially because you're not gonna believe what all happened during the pageant."

Ben sat up straighter. "The animals didn't knock down their pens and get out of the barn, I hope. I didn't get to check things over out there as I'd planned to. Was anyone hurt?"

"Not as you're thinkin'," Tom hedged. He looked away for a moment, sighing as though he was perplexed. "There's just no easy way to tell ya—"

"The truth'll set ya free, Tom," Miriam murmured as her heart began to pound faster. How could anything have gone wrong with the pageant? Rebecca and Teacher Alberta had kept to the program they'd presented last year, and Rachel and Micah were confident little Amelia would be fine while they sat in the shelter of the barn. "Just say it out. It's like rippin' off a Band-Aid real fast. Hurts like crazy for a bit, but then ya get over it."

"Oh, this'll take a lot longer to recover from, I'm afraid." Tom straightened to his full height and gazed at her with a desolate sorrow that deepened his crow's-feet. "First, everyone from Willow Ridge, including your girls, is okay, but Josiah's grills caught fire and exploded and—and then your Sweet Seasons appliances blew up, too—"

Miriam's breath stuck in her throat as she gaped at the bishop. Ben's arm tightened around her shoulders.

"—and I'm sorry to have to tell ya this," Tom continued in a wavering voice, "but there's nothin' left standin'. Your smithy's gone, too, Ben. The fire trucks got there in a hurry, but all that's left of either place is burned-up rubble."

Had she not been holding her sleeping infant, Miriam would've cried out in protest. She tried to picture what Tom was describing, but her mind refused to form the images. A sob choked her. "How did *that* happen?" she rasped. "Josiah's usually so *gut* about checkin' his propane tanks and—"

"Maybe we were wrong to put up that wall around the cookers," Ben murmured. "I thought there was plenty of ventilation—"

"Don't go blamin' Josiah or second-guessin' yourself," Tom insisted. "The firefighters found one of those plastic lighter gadgets a little distance from the buildings. And they, uh, found Hiram on the ground, too. Burned real bad and unconscious."

"Sweet Lord Jesus," Miriam murmured, hoping the

Man in question wouldn't think she'd taken His name in vain. "So he was messin' with Josiah's cookers again?"

"That's what we're all thinkin', but we'll see what the arson investigator comes up with," Tom replied glumly. "Hiram's here at the hospital now. I brought Annie Mae and Nellie with me to tend to the administrative details and see how he's doin'."

"Oh, those poor girls. They've had such a time with that man." Tears trickled down Miriam's cheeks and she made no attempt to blot them. "Do they know if Hiram'll survive?"

"Officer McClatchey and Sheriff Banks weren't sure. Said he was in mighty bad shape, though."

Ben let out the breath he'd been holding. "I'm glad they arrived in time to help. They understand our ways better than other lawmen do."

"Oh, they were already there, watchin' the pageant," Tom said as a slight smile curved his lips. "We were all singin' 'Joy to the World,' and then—pardon me for sayin' it this way—all hell broke loose. At least that surely must be what hell looks like. And it's worse than I ever imagined."

Miriam stared ahead of her, visualizing the inferno Tom had described and trying to comprehend its consequences. The bakery she'd nurtured with the love in her heart and the labor of her hands was gone. Ben's shop—which had first belonged to her previous husband, Jesse—was demolished, as well. It hurt too badly to think about it, so she focused on other details. "Was anybody else hurt?"

"Nope. Everyone was still at your place, and we all went inside to stay safe."

"How's Naomi takin' this?" Miriam asked, and then

her brow furrowed. "And what of poor Rebecca, losin' her apartment? What a snug little place that was, too, with those rollin' walls Micah designed."

"They're both doin' well, all things considered."

"We can be grateful that with winter and the snow, I'd parked my farrier wagon behind the barn instead of beside the smithy," Ben said in a faraway voice. "And the animals are safe, and our home's still intact. Could've been a lot worse."

"*Jah*, there's that," Miriam murmured. "Sounds like Hiram's meddlin' backfired on him in a big way this time. I'm glad nobody else got hurt."

Bishop Tom was nodding as they counted their blessings. "*Jah*, had folks been leavin' because the pageant was over, we might've had a lot more injuries. I think some debris shot far enough to hit some of the cars parked along the roadside."

Miriam shook her head sadly as the ramifications of Hiram's misdeed began to sink in. "I feel real bad for Josiah and his sister," she said. "They were cookin' Christmas dinner for half of Willow Ridge or he wouldn't have had his cookers goin' tonight. Don't ya wonder how Hiram always seems to know when he can do the most damage?"

"Ah, but there's a brighter bit of news I almost forgot!" Tom said in a more cheerful voice. "Josiah introduced me to Lena's *dat* right before the explosion. Seems your Christmas card and phone calls convinced her parents to come see their new grandson and mend some fences."

A smile spread over Miriam's face. "Every cloud's got its silver linin'," she stated. "I'm happy to hear the Eshes have reconsidered their feelings about Josiah and Lena. They must be wonderin' what sort of town we've got, though, after all the hubbub this evening."

Tom smiled. "I'm sure a lot of our visitors were appalled," he agreed. "But when they saw the paramedics loadin' Hiram into the ambulance, I think they realized that in this case, one bad apple doesn't spoil the whole barrel. Derek Shotwell and Bob Oliveri were in the crowd tonight, too, so I won't be surprised if they're already puttin' their heads together."

"They've been *gut* friends to us and to Willow Ridge—more than once," Miriam added. "That's another thing to be grateful for."

As the details of Tom's story sank in, Miriam felt the urge to get up and move around—to release some nervous energy. She glanced at Bethlehem, who was sleeping soundly. "How about if we put this wee one in the nursery for the night? Andy told me to take it slow, just to walk around when I felt like it—and we'll take my ride along," she added as she nodded toward the wheelchair in the corner of the room. "I know just where I want to go, too."

A few minutes after she'd pressed the CALL button, a nurse came to take Bethlehem, and Miriam eased out of bed. With Ben at her side, she took a few slow steps. Even though her incision ached badly, she made it to the doorway before she motioned for Tom to help her into the wheelchair.

"Let's check at the nurse's station to see where Hiram is," she said as she carefully settled herself in the seat. "I know a couple of young girls who're hurtin' a lot worse than I am right now."

A short ride down the hall and a trip on the elevator took them to the Intensive Care Unit, which was hushed and almost peaceful—until Miriam spotted familiar figures in Plain dresses standing in front of a room with their *kapped* heads bowed. Annie Mae had her arm around Nellie's shoulders, and the dazed expressions on their dear faces tugged hard at Miriam's heartstrings.

"What's the word on your *dat*, girls?" Ben asked as he walked ahead to stand beside them.

Annie Mae wiped her eyes while her sister turned away from the window. "It's not looking *gut*," she rasped. "He's burned so awfully bad, and he's still not opening his eyes or responding to talk. Has a lot of damage to his lungs, and if he lives . . . well, Andy told us it would take a long time and a lot of surgery to fix his skin. And even then, he'll never look like he did before the fire. His face is nearly . . . gone."

"I'm so glad the little ones didn't see him this way," Nellie blurted out. She hugged herself, choking on a sob. "All those tubes and bandages and machines—it's too scary to watch anymore. I'm glad they didn't let us go in."

"I'm so sorry about this, girls," Miriam murmured. She opened her arms, and the sisters rushed over to embrace her from either side of the wheelchair. Their tears and quiet sobs tore at her. It would take a lot of love and healing and time before Annie Mae and Nellie got past the damage their *dat* had done to their family—let alone dealing with his physical and emotional scarring, if he pulled through.

"When the doctor asked if we wanted to keep Dat on a ventilator—asked if he had a living will—I said I didn't want to prolong his suffering," Annie Mae murmured. "Andy told him we Plain folks don't believe in using machines to keep folks alive, so he's just got an IV now." Her slender body shuddered and she curved her arm around the fullness of her unborn child. "I hope I didn't speak out of turn, as if I want Dat to die, but—"

"Ya did just right, Annie Mae," Bishop Tom confirmed. "God decides whether we live or die, and He alone knows when our time on this earth is finished. Shall we pray on it? God'll give us the strength to see this through if we ask Him."

The Knepp girls bowed their heads with Tom, and so did Miriam—until Ben's sudden intake of breath made her open her eyes. When his hand went to his heart and his eyes widened, Miriam sensed her husband was witnessing Hiram's final moments. His expression brought to mind her memories of Jesse's passing, when she'd been sitting at his bedside, gripping his hand as it went limp and his next breath didn't come. Ben was young enough that he might not have been present previously when a soul left a body. Miriam knew he'd never forget what he'd experienced.

Beside her, the girls and the bishop remained in a state of prayer so Miriam rejoined them. *Bless us all, dear Lord, and hold Hiram's family in Your hand, even as we do our best to help them along. You give us life and You take it away . . . ashes to ashes and dust to dust. Forgive us our debts as we forgive our debtors.*

When she raised her head, Ben was gazing at the four of them. He looked stricken yet somehow settled, as though a moment of truth had shown him a previously unknown reality. When the girls and Bishop Tom opened their eyes, Ben approached and placed his hands on Annie Mae and Nellie's slender shoulders. "I'm real sorry, girls," he murmured. "The nurse checked your *dat*'s breathin' and called in the doctor. They're takin' the tubes from his nose and removin' the IV now. He's gone, God rest his soul."

A low cry escaped Annie Mae as she grabbed Nellie in a fierce hug. Miriam pressed her lips together against a surge of grief and pity as she watched the sisters struggle with the finality of Ben's observation. Although she realized it was for the best—that Hiram wouldn't suffer any longer from his injuries—she still had difficulty believing that the former bishop of Willow Ridge was gone.

Tom walked over and gazed into the room. "Bless us, Father, for we've all sinned and fallen short," he murmured. "Let us not be castin' stones, knowin' that every one of us is guilty and in need of Your forgiveness."

When the nurse stepped out and spoke a few words to Tom, he turned and looked at Annie Mae and Nellie. "Do ya want to go in and say your *gut*-byes? Spend as much time with your *dat* as ya need—"

"No way!" Nellie gasped, while Annie Mae shook her head and blew her nose.

"All right, then. Whenever you're ready, I'll drive ya back to town," the bishop said gently. "We've got a lot of hard talkin' to do, and a lot of little hands to hold."

"God go with ya, Tom," Miriam said as she wiped her eyes.

He smiled tiredly. "Don't worry about a thing. Your job's to get strong enough to bring Bethlehem home."

"I've got the easier task, Bishop."

"Can't argue with that." Tom put on his black hat while the girls fetched their coats from the rack nearby. "Kiss that baby for me. She's God's promise that we've always got a reason to go forward and to believe that the best is yet to be. I know a lot of folks who're waitin' to hear that mother and child are doin' well."

When Tom had accompanied the Knepp girls down the hall, Miriam let out a long sigh. "Well, now. As much as we've disliked Hiram and his threats and lies these past couple of years, it feels odd to think about him bein' . . . gone."

Ben steered her wheelchair down the hall toward the elevator. "I keep thinkin' that Hiram had more sense than to use a lighter around Josiah's gas grills," he murmured as they waited for the steel doors to open. "Unless he *intended* to blow himself up along with the café."

Miriam's eyes widened. "Are ya sayin' he took his own life?"

After they'd entered the elevator, Ben gazed at her with eyes the color of warm pancake syrup. "It's just a hunch. Hiram wasn't a fella to admit how desperate he was, but what with bein' on the wrong side of the law lately, and his kids and Delilah walkin' out on him—well," he said with a shrug. "I guess we'll never know, unless he left a note somewhere."

Miriam suddenly felt too weary to contemplate the circumstances of Hiram Knepp's death. After starting the day in excruciating pain and giving birth to Bethlehem, and then learning her business had been destroyed, she wanted to fall into a deep sleep for several hours—even though she realized a night's rest probably wouldn't be so easy to come by.

"It's a mystery," she murmured. "Some things are best left for God to figure out."

Chapter Twenty-Six

Breakfast on Christmas morning felt odd without Miriam bustling around the kitchen, but Lena enjoyed having her mother and Savilla helping her. "I'm glad we'd already made our Three Kings banana bread and the egg casserole," she said as they sat down to eat. "I guess we'll scratch up something to have for dinner, and be thankful we're all unharmed."

"*Jah*, I was looking forward to some smoked turkey and pork loin," Savilla said ruefully. "And I'd made pans of stuffing with pecans and raisins, and scalloped potatoes—but we'll not dwell on what we've lost. It's Christmas Day and I'm glad you Eshes have joined us."

As Lena settled Isaiah into a basket on the end of the table, an idea occurred to her. "You know, the cookies I made to go with our meals for the Hooleys are still here—in those tins," she said as she gestured toward the counter. "What if we took some to the Waglers' for the little Knepp kids? And delivered the ones we intended for Bishop Tom and Luke and Nora? It'll be a way to thank them for their help, even if we don't have their meats and side dishes."

"Those little kids would be happy to see your cute cookies," Lena's mother agreed as she passed the platter of breads and rolls. "And what a *gut* business that makes for you now that you're staying home with Isaiah."

Josiah took a big spoonful of the egg casserole. "It's even better because Nora and Luke have offered to sell Lena's cookies in their stores, and Lena's been offered some shelf space in the market, too," he said. "What with Miriam not baking pies for them anymore, I think Lydia Zook's tickled to have a new bakery item to sell."

Lena smiled. It was nice to hear Josiah speaking so positively to her parents about her baking business, considering he'd lost the café's facilities. When they'd finished eating, he and her father loaded the cookie tins into a buggy and took off. Dat seemed eager to look around Willow Ridge, and Lena was pleased he was warming up to Josiah. She waved at them, closed the kitchen door—and then smiled at Savilla.

"I'm leaving the door unlocked," she announced. "I'm not glad that Hiram died, but I won't miss looking over my shoulder, wondering what he might do next to get back at Josiah."

"That's the spirit," Savilla agreed. "I'll unlock the front door, too. I'm glad we won't have to keep track of the keys anymore when we come and go."

Lena's mother raised her eyebrows as she ran hot water into the sink. "What kind of orneriness are we talking about? Had that man been pestering Josiah ever since you got here?"

"Oh, the way Miriam tells it, Hiram was a pest long before we arrived. He was once determined to marry her—before Ben came to town," Lena replied with a shake of her head. "And he tried to come between

Nora and Luke by playing one against the other with his lies, and he cut off Annie Mae's hair last spring—"

When her mother sucked in her breath, Lena stopped talking. With a glance at Isaiah, who was watching them happily from his basket, she lowered her voice. Her heartbeat had accelerated and her body had tightened, and the rise in her stress level felt totally inappropriate.

"I'm not going to speak of Hiram's wrongdoings anymore," she murmured. "Christmas Day is when we celebrate Jesus's birth, and digging around in someone's dirt only leads to negative thoughts. Who needs that? I'm so glad you're here with us, Mamm."

A smile overtook her mother's face. "You're exactly right, daughter, and we'll steer the conversation in a different direction. It's not proper to speak ill of the dead, especially on Christmas. Even if it's the truth."

When the three of them had redded up the kitchen, they settled in the front room to visit and play with Isaiah. Not long after that, Lena heard the back door open. "Come and see, girls!" Josiah called out. "You won't believe what Emory and I brought home with us."

Lena led the way into the kitchen and stopped before she got to the table—which was covered with casserole pans and wrapped bundles. "What's all this?"

Josiah shook his head in disbelief. "When I stopped at Nora and Luke's with the cookies, they said I'd saved them a trip over with this spiral-sliced ham and a pan of hash brown casserole," he began. "It was the same at Bishop Tom's. Nazareth and Jerusalem had cooked up some yams with marshmallows and a big bowl of green beans with bacon and onion—"

"And a cherry cobbler," her father added happily. "These Willow Ridge folks must be the nicest people

I've ever met, all of them real sorry about the way Josiah lost his cookers and Miriam lost her café. It was like they couldn't do enough for you kids—and that tells me you've made quite an impression in a short time."

Lena couldn't help smiling. Coming from her father, those words were the ultimate compliment. Some of the food on the table was still warm, filling the air with aromas that made the house smell as though Miriam were here cooking. "You're right about these people," she replied softly. "They've been nothing but nice to us, helping us every way they—"

A roaring outside made them look out the kitchen window as a big black pickup truck topped the hill of the lane.

"That's Homer Yoder, the fellow we bought the farm from," Josiah explained as he went to the door. Then he chuckled. "Sure hope his bride-to-be hasn't changed her mind about getting hitched."

When Homer stepped inside with a big box, how-ever, it was immediately apparent that only good news was on his mind. "Say, I thought you kids might be interested in some of this commercial kitchen equip-ment one of my buddies is getting rid of," he said as he set the box on the floor. "He's retiring from the restau-rant business over near Warrensburg and when I men-tioned your predicament after the fire, he refused to take any money for it. There's more where this came from, if you're interested."

Josiah looked into the box, speechless. "My word, here's a bunch of ladles and butcher knives and bread pans and—" He stopped to gaze at Homer. "Now tell the truth: Did that fellow really give this stuff away or did you pay him for it?"

Homer's lips flickered. "Does it matter, really?" he asked slyly. "If this equipment means you'll be able to cook again sooner, I know a bunch of families who'd contribute to that cause because they *love* your food—and they want you and your sister to succeed, Josiah."

As Savilla gazed into the box, Lena noticed her eyes shining with grateful tears. "This is incredible," she murmured. "*Denki* so much, Homer."

Homer shrugged modestly. Then he looked at Lena's parents. "When I noticed you folks meeting Lena on the edge of the crowd last night, I was tickled that you're making peace amongst yourselves. Would you like to see where the kids are going to live?" he asked. "I bet you're curious."

"Oh, *jah,* I'd love to go!" Lena's *mamm* exclaimed. Then her hand fluttered to her chest and she looked to Dat for his reaction. "But Emory, if you don't think that's an appropriate thing to do on Christmas Day, we'll take a rain check."

Lena held her breath. It was common for Amish wives to defer to their husbands, and she'd witnessed this family dynamic all her life, even as she'd watched Miriam and Ben behave as equals.

Dat, however, was stroking his beard. "Well, it's not like we'd be *working* on a holy day," he reasoned aloud. "And Homer's helping the kids along, so it would be no different from visiting family and friends—which is what Christmas is all about. Let's get our coats and go!"

Lena's heart danced as she grinned at Josiah. This was certainly a better Christmas morning than she'd anticipated after last night's fire.

"You go on with your folks," Josiah said as he slipped an arm around his sister's shoulders. "Not all of us will fit in Homer's truck—and by the time you get back, Savilla and I will have Christmas dinner under control."

"There's an offer I won't refuse!" Lena's *mamm* teased. "Off we go."

Lena couldn't stop smiling as she slipped into her coat and bonnet. Yes, they were going down the road to their future home, but it felt more like she and her parents were heading toward a whole new relationship. The smiles on their faces were proof that their forgiveness was the finest gift she could ever hope to receive.

As Nora's black van approached Willow Ridge, Miriam shifted in the backseat and gazed at the baby in her arms. Because it was Second Christmas—the day after Christmas, when Plain families had their fun— Andy had allowed her to come home if she promised to let everyone else wait on her hand and foot. It was an uncomfortable homecoming, however. Her incision still hurt like the dickens every time she moved—and she didn't want to see the charred remains of the Sweet Seasons and Ben's smithy.

"I'm gonna take my time about lookin' at the fire site," she murmured as she turned her back to the window. They were passing Bishop Tom's pasture, and when Nora turned onto the county blacktop, there would be no ignoring the damage that had been done in her absence. "Look all you want to, Ben, but don't tell me about it, all right? I'm just not ready to face it yet."

Concern furrowed Ben's brow. "Are ya sure you're ready to come home, honey-girl? Are your pain pills not workin'?" he asked gently. "Usually ya face such things head-on."

"*Jah*, that's true," she said with a sigh. "But I'm gonna

spend what's left of Christmas settlin' in with this girl you've given me, thinkin' happier thoughts and eatin' something better than hospital food. Just bein' with folks I love."

"That's a fine idea," Nora said from the driver's seat. "I saw Rebecca walking around there this morning with Bob Oliveri. Now that we're sure Hiram caused the fire, they were probably seeing if they could find anything worth salvaging."

"And that's a *gut* job for them, too, because it was Bob's building." For a moment Miriam couldn't find words for the great sadness that had hit her like a slap in the face. "I'm in no shape to be bendin' over and pickin' up whatever might be in the ashes, anyway," she rasped. "And it's not like I'm plannin' to cook there anymore."

While she'd spoken the truth, the words burned her throat. Miriam didn't want to burst into tears—didn't want to cause an uproar—because folks at the house were waiting to welcome her and Bethlehem home. Andy had warned her that her emotions might be riding a roller coaster for a while, so why make her face blotchy and red while she cried her eyes out over her café? She would do her grieving in private.

Ben, however, was staring out the van window. His face paled. Although his mouth opened, no sound came out as he stared fixedly at the damage. He didn't say anything until the van had turned and topped the hill of their lane. Nora pulled up behind the kitchen door so Miriam didn't have far to walk in the snow.

"You're a wise woman, honey-girl," he murmured in a thin voice. "It looks worse than I figured."

Miriam didn't ask for details. She handed the baby to Ben while Nora slid the van door aside and helped her to the ground. When the kitchen door flew open and Josiah, Lena, and Savilla rushed out, she focused on their fresh young faces and their bright smiles.

"We were hoping you'd get to come home this afternoon!" Lena exclaimed as she wrapped her arms around Miriam's shoulders. "My parents can't wait to meet you—but when you need to rest, don't you dare pretend you can sit there talking to them all evening. They're going home tomorrow and then coming back for our wedding."

Miriam chuckled. "Listen to you, girlie, tellin' me what to do," she teased. Then she bussed Lena's temple. "I'm so happy your folks showed up. I can tell by your faces that they're behavin' themselves—openin' their hearts to you and Josiah and that wee boy of yours. That's just as it should be at Christmas, too."

Lena hugged her hard. "You've done me such a favor, telling them about Isaiah and inviting them here," she murmured. "I'm going to find a way to pay you back, again and again."

Miriam gazed at Lena's pretty blue eyes and neatly tucked blond hair, recalling how frazzled this young woman had been when she and Josiah had arrived in Willow Ridge. So much had changed since then, in ways none of them could've predicted. Even though some of these changes weighed heavily on her heart, Miriam reminded herself that God was working out His purpose even if she couldn't yet understand the whys and wherefores of His plan.

"Miriam! Welcome home," Savilla said as she opened her arms.

As Miriam returned her hug, she inhaled delectable aromas . . . beef and vegetables simmering on the stove. "Supper smells wonderful," she remarked. "Can't say

that the food was the best part of bein' in the hospital—
but I did bring home a sweet little Christmas package.
Gut luck pryin' her out of Ben's arms, though."

As Lena introduced Miriam and Ben to her parents,
Ben remained near the end of the kitchen table, sway-
ing side to side with his baby daughter. The warmth
had rekindled in his eyes as he gazed at Bethlehem, and
he seemed to be recovering from his first encounter
with the scorched remains of his shop.

As he gently laid the baby in the cradle he'd made
for her, Miriam held her breath. It was a wondrous
sight, watching his large, sturdy hand support Bethlehem's little head, and the way she snuggled into the
soft mattress with the pewter hummingbird keeping
watch above her. Tears prickled at Miriam's eyes when
Ben tucked the little yellow blanket she'd crocheted
around Bethlehem and then gently kissed her. Although
her husband Jesse had loved Rachel, Rhoda, and Rebecca, he'd not been one to show a lot of emotion or
to dote on them the way Ben had already taken to his
daughter.

*And isn't that reason enough to be joyful and grateful to
God? What've ya got to cry about, really?*

Chapter Twenty-Seven

Saturday morning dawned foggy and overcast, and as Ben gazed out the window of the front room, gloom and resentment filled his heart. His Aunt Jerusalem and Bishop Vernon had returned to Cedar Creek, and Preacher Henry Zook had succumbed to the flu, so that left Ben and Tom to preach Hiram Knepp's funeral service. As he sighed once again at the destruction across the road, Ben prayed for a major attitude adjustment. How could he preach about God's love and hope and light to the Knepp children—and to the town of Willow Ridge—when he was struggling with the personal devastation Hiram had caused him and Miriam? Horse-drawn rigs were pulling into the lane over at the Wagler place, so he didn't have any more time to brood.

Ben smoothed the front of his black vest and buttoned the cuffs of his best white shirt. He turned to savor the sight of Miriam sitting in the recliner with baby Bethlehem in her arms. "Are ya sure you'll be all right here by yourself? It's time for me to go."

"Ah, but I'm not alone," Miriam reminded him.

"I've got this baby of yours—and God'll be here with us, as well."

Ben smiled at her answer. He suspected Miriam was relieved that Andy had stopped by yesterday with strict instructions: she wasn't to strain herself or expose the baby to crowds yet. A part of him envied her excuse for staying home.

"I'm hopin' that by the time I have to stand up in front of that houseful of people, God'll give me something appropriate to say," he admitted. "I've always known that funerals would be tough services to preach for somebody I knew and liked, but it's not gonna be any easier to speak about Hiram. How do ya commit somebody's soul over to God when you're not sure that's the direction he went—or intended to go?"

"There are folks thinkin' it was no mistake that he died in a fiery blast," Miriam remarked. When Bethlehem coughed, she turned the baby onto the towel draped over her shoulder. "Maybe it's best to focus on helpin' Annie Mae, Nellie, and the four younger ones. If *we* have angry, mixed thoughts about Hiram, think about the guilt and pain his kids will be dealin' with for a long, long time yet."

"*Jah*, it's *gut* that they've got a home with Adam and Matthias—fine men who can stand in for a *dat* who was hard to understand. You're right, honey-girl," Ben said as he bent to kiss her. "I should focus on the rainbow rather than the rain."

"Of course I'm right," Miriam teased. "Ya knew that when ya married me, Bennie-bug."

"I'll be back as soon as I can. There's still plenty of nice leftovers for your dinner and—"

"Are ya sayin' I forgot how to look after myself when I birthed this wee one?" she countered with a chuckle.

"Better skedaddle. You're stallin'—and ya don't want to be the last one to show up."

As Ben began the short walk to the Wagler place, he was grateful for his wife's sense of humor and perspective. Funerals weren't so much for the soul who'd passed away as they were for the folks left behind—in this case, not just the Knepp children but also the members of a church district who had once followed their faith with Hiram as their bishop. Once again Ben asked God to fill his heart with compassion and his mind with pertinent words. This would be the first funeral he'd preached, and he was feeling jittery and inadequate.

As he entered the crowded house, shaking hands with everyone eased his nerves. When he'd come to Willow Ridge a little more than a year earlier, these folks had immediately welcomed him—and had embraced him this past spring as their new preacher, when Tom had become the bishop in the wake of Hiram's banishment. At times his head spun with how many major life events had befallen him since he'd met Miriam—yet the solemn smiles of these neighbors affirmed their belief that Ben Hooley had been chosen by God to lead them.

And with Your help, God, I will. He glanced into the main room of the house, which had been expanded by taking down some of the house's interior walls. After yesterday's visitation, the Waglers had moved their furniture and arranged the pew benches in the usual pattern, so the men would sit on one side facing the women on the other. A simple wooden coffin rested on a bench behind where the preachers would sit. Ben was relieved it would remain closed.

A short time before the service was to start, Ben and

Tom and their deacon, Reuben Riehl, slipped upstairs. Funeral services had followed the same order for decades, so the only decision they had to make was who would preach the shorter sermon and who would preach the main one. Ben and Tom each chose a passage of Scripture for Reuben to read, and then the redheaded deacon cleared his throat. "Esther and I'll be taking off right after the service," he murmured. "My cousin in Roseville called, saying my *dat*'s in a bad way and might not make it through the day."

"I'm real sorry to hear that," Ben replied.

"Travel safely. We'll send our prayers along with ya," Bishop Tom added as he clasped Reuben's shoulder. "Let us know what all we can do while ya need to be gone."

Tom looked at Ben with an odd expression on his face, then pulled a quarter from his pocket. "Unless you're sayin' straight out that ya want to preach the main sermon today—"

"Nope, ya didn't hear that from me," Ben insisted.

"—maybe we should flip for it," the bishop continued. "We can say that God determines how the coin'll land, just as He selected us to be preachers by the fallin' of the lot. Or is my theology too far outside the lines?"

Ben chuckled. It was a relief to see that even after years of experience, Tom was no more eager to preach Hiram's funeral sermon than he was. "Heads."

The coin spun in the air between them. When Tom caught it and slapped it onto the back of his hand, George Washington was looking away from them, as though he wanted no part of the proceedings, either.

"There ya have it," the bishop murmured, tapping the coin with his finger. "'In God we trust,' it says. Can't go wrong believin' that—but if ya don't have the heart to preach the longer sermon about a fella who caused ya so much trouble, it's my job to assume that responsibility. Your call."

A smile found its way to Ben's face. "In for a dime, in for a dollar," he quipped. "I'd better take the talent my Master's entrusted to me and make it pay, *jah?*"

"You're a *gut* man, Hooley. I'll keep the first sermon short, followin' the Twenty-Third Psalm, and leave ya plenty to say about Paul's passage from Romans." Tom marked a few hymns in his copy of the *Ausbund* and then looked at Ben and Reuben. "Let's go. Folks need to hear what God tells us to say today."

From there, Ben allowed ritual to carry him. He and Tom and Reuben reentered the main downstairs room to walk down the aisle between the folks who'd taken their seats and sat in solemn silence. After the bishop said a few opening words, everyone bowed in prayer and then—because singing had no part in a Plain funeral—Tom read the words of one of the hymns he'd chosen. After Reuben read the Twenty-Third Psalm and the passages Ben had chosen from the Book of Romans, the bishop began the shorter of the morning's two sermons.

Ben listened, yet he drifted . . . not planning out what he would say exactly, but allowing the familiar cadence of Tom Hostetler's homespun speech pattern to soothe him. It was a balm to his soul to recognize every solemn face in the congregation, friends who were trying to make sense of a disaster such as they'd not experienced before. Although each family had its own concerns, they'd set aside their individual cares to give the Knepp kids their support.

In the back row, Ben spotted Derek Shotwell from the bank sitting beside Bob Oliveri. While it was unusual for

English folks to attend Amish funerals, these two men felt a close kinship with the people of Willow Ridge— and they'd been directly affected by Hiram's wrong-doings, too. They were listening attentively to Tom's message, words of comfort and assurance from a psalm that had served as the basis for many a funeral, Plain and English.

After Tom read the words of another hymn and led a prayer, Ben stood up. He had no notes, and his only instruction for becoming a preacher had come from studying the Bible with Tom and Vernon's guidance. He gazed around the crowded room. *From Your lips to my ears, Lord,* he prayed as he clasped his hands. *Help me to be a blessing and to make a positive difference in the lives of Your people.*

"We're familiar with the first chapter of Genesis, where God created the world and called it *gut,*" he began quietly. "But right now we're caught up in a dilemma, in which a church leader we've known and trusted has caused trouble like we've not had to fathom before. And even if we're not sayin' them out loud, we're probably askin' some mighty tough questions. If God made the world to be *gut,* how can He allow such evil as we've seen this week to exist? Or does God sometimes turn a blind eye when we need Him most?"

Ben swallowed so hard his parched throat clicked. Within a few short sentences he'd strayed from the comforting tone Bishop Tom had set and had painted himself into a very tight theological corner. Had he been wrong to speak of evil when the Knepp kids needed peace that would allow them to forgive their errant father?

He glanced at Annie Mae and Nellie, whose heads

remained bowed as they sat with little Sarah between them. Then he saw that Adam and Matthias Wagler, with Timmy between them and Joey and Josh on their laps, were focusing very intently on him. Josiah, too, was sitting tall on the backless bench, appearing hungry for whatever words of wisdom he could impart. Judging from the intense expressions on several faces, folks had indeed questioned God's presence when part of their town had gone up in smoke.

Ben took a deep breath and went on, for there was no going back. "I don't know the answers to those questions," he admitted. "But when I hear Paul's letter to the Roman church, which Reuben read for us, a few important points help me to keep believin' in a God who loves us even when it seems His creation has gone astray. 'If God be for us, who can be against us?'"

Ben paused to recall the verses he wanted to lift up. The house was filled with an expectant silence as nearly three hundred people watched and waited for what he would say next. "'Who shall separate us from the love of Christ?'" he went on in a stronger voice. "'Shall tribulation, or distress, or persecution, or famine, or nakedness, or peril, or sword?' If we say we believe in a God who loves us despite our sins, then we must also believe that *nothing* comes between us and our Lord, even in times of deepest doubt and grief. When it seems He's turned His back on us and our troubles, maybe . . ."

Ben closed his eyes, hoping something brilliant and uplifting would come to him. *What would Miriam say?* He opened his mouth, hoping that some of her innate faith and goodness would see him through to the end of this difficult sermon.

"When it seems God has turned His back," he

repeated—and then he reached toward home in his mind, visualizing his dear wife and their newborn child. "Maybe that's when He's leadin' us toward a better life, a future that He alone can see—but we have to *follow* Him. We must have faith that He knows best, and that He knows what lies ahead for us, even when we're standin' in the ashes, shakin' our heads and thinkin' all is lost."

Ben wasn't entirely sure what came out of his mouth for the rest of his sermon, but when he saw Josiah's expression of awe—noticed that Gabe Glick, who'd preached hundreds of sermons before he'd retired, was nodding in agreement—he continued in a voice that rang with confidence. "'For I am persuaded that neither death nor life, nor angels'—nor any of the other things Paul listed," he paraphrased, "'shall be able to separate us from the love of God, which is in Christ Jesus our Lord.'"

Ben looked out over the congregation, smiling solemnly. He knew now how it would end—his sermon, as well as his personal grudge against Hiram Knepp. While he'd been exhorting everyone else to believe, he'd talked himself out of his own faltering faith. "In this season when we celebrate the birth of our Jesus, let us not dwell upon death or destruction," he said. "Let us renew our faith, believing that God will show us the way we're to go."

"Amen," Bishop Tom murmured behind him.

Moments later, when folks were expressing condolences to Annie Mae and her siblings, Tom sidled up to Ben with a wry smile. "See there? God knew you'd do a better job preachin' over Hiram than I would," he murmured. "I wish Miriam could've heard the conviction and inspiration that rang in your words this morning, Ben. You've blessed us all on a difficult day."

Oh, but Miriam was here in spirit, guiding every word, Ben realized with a smile. *Denki for the fine woman You've blessed me with, Lord. With Your help we'll figure out what comes next, as far as how we'll rebuild our lives and livelihood.*

A few minutes after Ben left for the funeral, Miriam gently laid Bethlehem in the cradle he'd made for her. She gazed at their dozing daughter with such love in her heart and such hope in her soul, knowing she would need all the love and hope she could muster for what she must do this morning. While everyone else in Willow Ridge gathered at the Wagler home, she would come to terms with the destruction of the Sweet Seasons Bakery Café.

With her eyes closed, Miriam went to the big picture window. She stood for several moments with her head bowed, praying for strength. When she at last opened her eyes, it took a moment for the devastation to register. Where once had stood a sturdy frame building with signs for the SWEET SEASONS BAKERY CAFÉ on one side and SCHROCK'S QUILTS on the other—and where the white farrier shop had stood behind them—only charred pieces of the smithy's forge remained recognizable in the rubble. The restaurant where she'd fed so many friends and baked away her troubles alongside Naomi, where she'd reunited with her lost daughter Rebecca and first met Ben on a stormy morning, was gone. In its place, a large, dark scar ravaged the snowy face of Willow Ridge.

"Sweet Jesus, hold me in Your ever-lovin' arms," she rasped.

Miriam pressed her palms against the cold glass, staring in desperate disbelief. A sob escaped her, and she allowed all her pent-up emotions to boil over. Surely it was acceptable in God's sight to weep, to grieve over the place He'd led her to in her time of need after Jesse had passed. While she'd recently accepted that her place was now at home with Ben and their baby, pain stabbed her like a meat fork.

A landmark of her life was gone forever. Not since she'd watched her toddler Rebecca get swept away in the flood-swollen river had Miriam felt such anguish.

And didn't I bring Rebecca back to you?

Miriam sniffled and looked around the front room. She and Bethlehem were the only ones at home, yet she could've sworn she'd heard a deep, resonant voice much like Vernon Gingerich's. And the voice was speaking directly to her. "*Jah*, Rebecca's back—and she's been such a blessing to me, and to everyone else in our little town, too," Miriam whispered.

She held her breath, waiting. Were her imagination and her postpartum hormones playing tricks on her?

And didn't I lead Ben to Willow Ridge, as well—just in time to keep Hiram at bay?

Miriam sucked in her breath. Had it happened this way when angels came to visit Mary and Joseph? She wiped her wet cheeks on her sleeve and checked to be sure the baby was all right.

Bethlehem slept sweetly in the cradle Ben had crafted. Just gazing at her made Miriam feel better.

"*Jah*, my Ben's been a mighty fine blessing, too," she admitted. "And he's at the Wagler place right now, talkin' to folks about havin' faith and trust—in You, God."

There—she'd said it. She'd declared aloud that God was speaking to her, and she was answering back. It was a good thing no one else was home, or they might think she was losing her marbles.

Fear not, Miriam, your marbles are rolling in the right direction. Forward rather than backward.

Swallowing hard, Miriam gazed around the front room again. Nothing had changed. She was still standing at the window and Bethlehem was now smiling in her sleep, as though she felt as safe and comfortable as she did when her father held her in his strong, steady arms.

Miriam relaxed. A sense of serenity filled her as she envisioned herself being held in her Father's strong, steady arms . . . allowed herself to believe that she and God were conversing, just as Mary had listened to Him and responded long ago. Her gaze shifted to the house where the Knepp kids were at their father's funeral. They had lost so much more than she had.

Father, hold those lambs in Your arms—and give Ben Your best guidance. He was scared when he left here, thinkin' he wouldn't be gut *enough to preach such a tough service. He's stronger than he knows.*

From Your lips to Ben's ears.

Miriam smiled. In her mind, she kissed Ben and held him close. Even so, as she focused on the soot and ashes and destruction across the road, there was no getting around the fact that two of the most vital businesses in Willow Ridge had burned to the ground, and that Hiram Knepp had destroyed them.

She sighed as recollections of the past year filled

her mind . . . Hiram ordering her to marry him, and expecting Rhoda to repent for loving Englishman Andy Leitner . . . leveraging his twins' sleigh accident to procure the land for Higher Ground . . . boldly displaying his picture on his Web site . . . hiding a black Cadillac in his horse barn. And no one could forget the Sunday mornings when he'd stormed out of church rather than confessing these sins—and when he'd barged in on her and Ben's wedding ceremony and interrupted another service to snatch his young children away from Annie Mae. Hiram had tried to come between Nora and Luke, too—and had repeatedly threatened Josiah and peered into Lena's window.

"What am I missin', Lord?" Miriam murmured. "I believe You want the best for me—for all of Your children. And yet again and again Hiram tormented us." She pressed her lips together, hoping she hadn't sounded petty or ungrateful for the wonderful life God had granted her.

Again and again Hiram was given opportunities to change his ways and make better choices. I didn't give up on him.

Miriam sucked in her breath. While she'd agreed with everyone's remarks about Hiram's wicked intentions and unthinkable sins, no one had ever considered the possibility that God was showing Hiram the patience of a Father's love . . . the same great patience He displayed to each and every one of them despite the many ways they displeased and disobeyed Him every single day.

"Oh, my," she whispered. "Please Father, don't ever give up on me. I'm doin' the best I can, and—"

When folks in black coats, hats, and bonnets began to

stream out of the Wagler place, Miriam watched the six men who bore Hiram's plain wooden coffin to the horse-drawn hearse that waited near the house. Everyone would walk down the hill to the small cemetery, where her Jesse, her stillborn child, and others had been laid to rest over the years. After Bishop Tom said the final words over Hiram's grave, everyone would eat lunch at Nora and Luke's large home—a meal that Josiah, Savilla, and Lena had prepared.

Miriam watched respectfully, praying that God would look after Hiram's soul in the hereafter even as He nurtured the souls of His living children. Then she stood up straighter. Three identical young women, one of them carrying a baby basket, began walking toward town rather than following the funeral procession. Two other women joined them, along with a couple of hatless fellows who wore English-cut topcoats.

Miriam watched these people, who talked and nodded their heads as they passed Nora's big white house and reached the county highway. When they turned, approaching her house, Miriam carried Bethlehem's cradle to the kitchen to splash cool water on her face. She had a feeling she was about to have company—and that this group who were skipping the graveside service and the lunch had a very important reason to be visiting her instead.

Chapter Twenty-Eight

"Mamma, how're ya feelin' today? We missed ya!" Rhoda said as she burst through the back kitchen door.

"Everyone says hello and sends their congratulations about Bethlehem, too," Rebecca joined in.

"And oh, but ya should've heard Ben's preachin'!" Rachel exclaimed as she set baby Amelia's basket on the table near Bethlehem's cradle. "He closed his eyes and then it was like God was whisperin' in his ear. We were all sittin' on the edge of the benches, wonderin' what he'd say next."

Miriam smiled to herself as she lit the stove burner under a percolator of fresh water and coffee. She was tickled to see Rebecca wearing a Plain black dress—probably one of Rachel's, because she'd been staying with Rachel and Micah since she'd lost her apartment. "And what did he say about Hiram?" she asked. "He was nervous when he left home."

"I stand in awe, Miriam," Bob Oliveri remarked as he and Derek Shotwell came inside, along with Mary Schrock and Naomi. "Here was a fellow who'd just had his business—and his wife's—burned down by the man he was preaching over, yet Ben talked of forgiving those who do us harm and following God to a new life. You Amish amaze me."

As Miriam shared a hug with her triplets, she looked between their black bonnets to meet Bob's gaze. "Well, now. I'm sorry I missed that."

"Oh, it was something," Naomi agreed as she removed her wraps. "He started out by talkin' about how it sometimes seems that God turns His back and looks the other way while people get away with all manner of evil—"

"But that's when God's already leadin' us toward something new and better, and we're supposed to *follow* Him," Rhoda murmured. "It was awesome. Even Bishop Tom was wipin' his eyes."

Miriam thanked the Lord for providing Ben with such an uplifting message. "To God be the glory," she murmured as she gave her girls a final squeeze. She was pleased that her guests were hanging up their coats, as though they felt right at home and planned to visit for a while. "When I saw ya comin', I was glad Lena left some of her cookies. It seems you're skippin' the funeral lunch and I'm sure it'll be tasty, what with Josiah and Savilla fixin' the food."

Bob and Derek shared a glance and then took seats at the table, while Naomi grabbed the cookie tins. "We thought this would be a good opportunity to discuss your options, while Josiah's busy cooking," Bob began in a matter-of-fact tone.

"Not that we want to exclude him," Derek assured her. He chose a frosted star cookie covered with sprinkles. "But the Sweet Seasons and the quilt shop belonged to you three women, and we want you to know where things stand so you can make some informed decisions."

Miriam sat down beside Naomi, clasping her hand as she reached for Mary's, as well. Both women appeared as curious as she was about what Bob Oliveri and the banker were hinting at. As the man who'd bought the Sweet Seasons building to prevent Hiram from taking control of the café, Bob had saved them from a lot of heartache. "What kind of decisions are ya talkin' about? I finally got up the nerve to look at what's left—or *not* left—of the two buildings this morning. It seems pretty clear to me. They're *gone*."

"And we lost a dozen or more handmade quilts, not to mention all those bolts of fabric and sewing supplies," Mary said sadly. "It'll take months to replace those quilts. And the ladies who made them didn't get paid."

"Same goes for the food and equipment in the Sweet Seasons," Naomi said. "Miriam and I scraped together a lot of start-up money to buy our appliances and to pay my boys for the chairs and tables they built. Now that Miriam's stayin' home with her baby, I can't expect her to invest that much money again—and I can't come up with that kind of cash," she continued earnestly. "Ezra wants me to quit cookin' there, but he'll feel the pinch when I'm not bringin' home my share of the café's income."

Bob nodded, listening carefully to their concerns. He smiled as he chose a green cookie in the shape of a wreath, with red candies for holly berries. "The bright side of this situation is that you sold me the building and I've carried insurance on it. Now that the police have determined it was arson—which means Hiram started the blaze—we can collect on the policy."

Miriam saw that Mary and Naomi were as puzzled by these words as she was. "So what're ya sayin', Bob? We Plain ladies don't understand the details about insurance," she pointed out. "We Amish don't believe in makin' payments for years and years based on a piece of paper. We pay for what we need as we go along."

Bob looked at Miriam, Mary, and Naomi, and then smiled at Rebecca—the daughter he'd raised English—as though they shared a delightful secret. "Because I've carried insurance that will pay for what you've lost, plus whatever it costs to replace it—inflation and inventory included—we can rebuild the Sweet Seasons and the quilt shop," he explained. "You ladies can be back in business as soon as the new structure goes up. That's how insurance works."

Mary's mouth dropped open. "You'd *do* that for us?"

"In a heartbeat," Bob replied. "Your businesses have been an enjoyable investment for me because I love being part of Willow Ridge's growth and prosperity— and I'd be foolish not to accept the money I have coming to me. I've paid the premiums and now the insurance company will honor the policy by covering what you've lost."

Naomi and Mary gripped Miriam's hands and stared at each other in disbelief. "My stars—and Merry Christmas!" Naomi blurted out. "That's a fine gift you've given us, Bob. *Denki* ever so much."

Bob flushed. "I also believe that if you rebuild your businesses, it's a sign to all the world that Hiram didn't get the best of you—that your goodness has won out over his evil."

A hush settled over the kitchen. Miriam liked the

sound of that, and she was pleased that the man who'd raised her Rebecca was speaking so eloquently on their behalf. "Ya said a mouthful there, Bob."

"And I stand with him a hundred percent." Derek smiled kindly at all of them as he reached for another cookie. "We'll need a list of the quilts you lost, Mary, along with the approximate value of each one. You all need to write out the equipment and furnishings and shelving you lost, plus the appliances and inventory—everything it would take to replace what was in your shops when they burned down."

Miriam had been following the conversation closely, yet a little red flag waved in the back of her mind. "We should be talkin' to Josiah about what he wants. Now that I've got baby Bethlehem, I'm out of the bakin' business."

Odd expressions came over Bob and Derek's clean-shaven faces. "Are you *sure*, Miriam?" the banker asked. "You've been the backbone of the Sweet Seasons—"

Miriam raised both of her hands. "I know why you're thinkin' that way because for a long while I did, too," she said. "But that wee baby in the cradle Ben made is my new mission, fellas. I'm livin' the life of a happy Amish wife and mother now. No ifs, ands, or buts about it."

"Nevertheless, that land belongs to *you*, Miriam," Bob pointed out. "Legally, when I bought the Sweet Seasons, you and I entered into a leasing situation, with the stipulation that if something happened to me, the entire property would revert to you. So while the money to rebuild your businesses will come to me, it's your call as to whether another structure will be built on your property."

Miriam blinked. The detail about land ownership had slipped her mind—and it hadn't mattered while she and her two closest friends had worked together these past couple of years. Did it matter now that she was staying home? *Is it proper for an Amish wife and mother to invest in a business she'll no longer participate in?*

The percolator's last gasp announced that the coffee was ready, so Miriam rose to remove the basket and fill the mugs Rhoda and Rebecca were taking from the cupboard. She couldn't miss the intense expressions Naomi and Mary wore, and she realized that Josiah, Savilla, and Lena had a stake in her decision, as well. Even so, she'd recently vowed to follow Plain ways and God's plan for her life rather than just forging ahead with what she *wanted* to do. If she gave in to her first impulse and agreed to a new building, would He think she'd already gone back on her promise? That she wasn't really dedicated to living her life His way?

Everyone in the kitchen sat in silence, awaiting what Miriam would say . . . how she would determine the fate of her friends and the future of Willow Ridge.

I could use a sign from You, Lord, Miriam prayed as she concentrated on the full mugs of coffee she carried to the table. When she sat down again after everyone had been served, she looked apologetically at Naomi and Mary. "If it was only up to me, I'd tell ya—"

Outside, a loud stomping announced that someone was knocking snow off his boots. When Ben entered the kitchen, Miriam smiled at him despite the tension she'd created. "I hear ya preached a mighty fine sermon today, and I'm wishin' I could've heard it."

"With God's help we've buried our dead, and we can move on now," Ben replied. He wore an expression of humility, yet there was fresh energy in his voice. "And ya know, after starin' again at the rubble that used to be my smithy, I've decided to rebuild on this side of the road, where folks'll have easier access to my shop."

Miriam smiled wryly as she fetched him a cup of coffee. Ben wasn't saying so, but she sensed he wanted his new smithy on his own property, rather than on hers. "It just so happens we've been talkin' about that very subject," she remarked. Then she looked at Bob. "I don't suppose that insurance money covers Ben's business, does it?"

"No," he replied, "but I'd be happy to contribute to the rebuilding of—"

"*Denki*, Bob, but you're too late!" Ben interrupted in a jovial tone. "Before we went over to Nora's for the lunch, the Brenneman boys showed me their drawing for a new smithy—said they were figurin' to build my new shop and Miriam's before the ashes of the old ones had even gone cold! Then Homer Yoder said he was bringin' in some Mennonite fellas with heavy equipment to dig and pour a foundation for my new place tomorrow, while the ground's still warm enough."

Ben grabbed a frosted angel cookie from the plate, waving it at them in his excitement. "Homer's friends plan to clear away the mess across the road, too, so you gals can rebuild as soon as you've worked up a floor plan with Naomi's boys," he went on in a rush. "Bishop Tom was in on the conversation, too, and he said our district's Amish Aid fund would pay for replacin' both buildings. All the church members have been payin' into the fund for years to cover this sort of emergency. I came straight home instead of goin' to the lunch because I just had to tell ya the *gut* news, honey-girl."

"So there ya have it!" Miriam giggled as she grabbed

Mary and Naomi's hands again. God had already foreseen her difficult decision about rebuilding the Sweet Seasons on her land and He'd given His answer. "Who am I to argue with Bishop Tom? If he sees a problem with me ownin' the land the new café's on, we'll settle it later. Onward and upward!"

"That's the spirit, Mamma," Rhoda exclaimed.

"Can't argue with that kind of support, Ben," Derek agreed with an astonished smile. "If more towns operated on the same principles we've seen here in Willow Ridge, the world would be a different place."

Ben nodded, smiling at their two English friends. "Here in Willow Ridge, we take care of each other," he explained. "Micah, Seth, and Aaron Brenneman have already rearranged their schedule so they can start our buildings when the foundations are set. We're *gut* to go."

Bob was shaking his head, chuckling. "Once again, you Amish amaze and inspire me," he said. When he smiled at Miriam, his respect for her shone on his face. "My offer for assistance with replacement costs and supplies still stands. The insurance money will be available for—"

"However this all gets paid for," Miriam interrupted, "I still want your name on the papers, Bob. Bishop Tom's probably not thought of this, but in order for us to have electricity, as the health department requires, somebody who's not Amish has to own the building."

"*Jah*, I want that, too," Mary insisted. "We Mennonites would be allowed to install the electricity, but I can't expect the Amish Aid fund to cover the costs of those quilts and the inventory we lost—and Eva, Priscilla, and I surely can't afford to replace them. If you're willing to help us with that, Bob, you should have the building as one of your assets. Something to show for what you're investing in us."

Bob and Derek exchanged a glance. "Seems clear to me that however we divvy up the replacement costs, everybody's covered," the banker remarked.

"I'm confident we'll work it all out and that everyone'll be back in business as though the fire had never happened," Bob said with an emphatic nod.

Miriam smiled, relieved that these friends were so willing to move forward without asking her to be directly involved anymore. As she watched Rebecca choose a dark chocolate sleigh cookie, however, it occurred to her that they weren't finished with this discussion. "Ya know what we haven't talked about? Our Rebecca's lost her home. I'm tickled that since she's come back she's been willin' to bunk here and there, dependin' on where we've had space for her—"

"Because I want to be near you, Mamma," Rebecca said with a sparkle in her blue eyes. "And because I love it here in Willow Ridge."

Miriam's heart swelled and she blinked back tears. It was such a blessing that her English-raised daughter wanted to live near her Amish family, even though they all understood that Rebecca had no intention of joining the Old Order.

"Matter of fact, Rebecca has mentioned that she'd like to build a home here," Bob replied, "so it's just a matter of finding a plot of ground—"

"You could live on Lantz Lane, just down from our house—right, Mamma?" Rachel blurted out.

"She could build here on our land," Ben insisted.

"Or we've got room at our place, behind the clinic!" Rhoda chimed in. "Andy would be *gut* with that because you'd be close by for runnin' the reception desk."

"So there you have it!" Bob quipped as he grinned at Rebecca. "Pick your plot, honey. We'll start your house when you've decided on your floor plan."

As the kitchen rang with clapping and congratulations, Rebecca wiped her eyes. Miriam went to stand behind Rebecca's chair, putting her arms around her shoulders. "We've come a long way since ya showed up in the Sweet Seasons with your spiky black hair and metal jewelry," she murmured. "I'm grateful to God that all the details have worked out this way. It's everything a mother could want, havin' all her girls here together *fer gut* and forever."

"*Fer gut* and forever!" Rhoda echoed, grabbing her sisters' hands.

"*Jah*, that's how it is in our family," Rachel agreed. "We're tied pretty tight."

Derek smiled at everyone as he rose from his chair. "Can't argue with that—and I'm glad we've settled so many important matters during this discussion. We should let you folks get on with your day."

"Does my heart good to know you can all move forward now, without any more threats or intimidation," Bob added as he, too, stood up.

"We can't thank ya enough for all you fellas do for us," Miriam said as the men put on their coats. "I have a real *gut* feelin' about the future of Willow Ridge."

Everyone watched out the window until Derek and Bob had gone down the lane to the road. Then they all grabbed one another, laughing and hugging and talking all at once. As their chatter filled the kitchen, even the two babies began to squeal and squawk.

Ben chuckled at their ruckus and gently scooped Bethlehem from her cradle while Miriam eased Amelia from her basket. When he walked into the front room,

Miriam and the rest of them followed him to the picture window.

It didn't hurt so badly now, seeing the burned-out remains of their buildings. Miriam was buzzing like an excited bee even though she would no longer be involved in the day-to-day business of the Sweet Seasons. "There's the Witmers and Lena, lookin' at the ashes," she murmured. "Josiah's got to be wonderin' about a lot of things—most especially about whether he can support his family now. I say we bring them in here and tell them what's what."

Rebecca bussed Miriam's cheek. "I'll be right back, Mamma. I don't want to miss the looks on their faces when you break the news."

Chapter Twenty-Nine

Josiah sighed glumly. He wanted to believe Ben's sermon about how, when it seemed God had turned His back, it was time to follow Him, but this devastation sucked all positive thoughts from his mind. Hiram Knepp had wiped him out with a wave of that fire-starting wand. Everyone at the lunch had asked if he and Savilla would be cooking again soon, but he hadn't had an answer to give them.

"I wish I could believe that we'll be using those boxes of utensils Homer brought us," he said to his sister. "But the money I've kept back from selling Mammi's house won't touch the replacement cost of the cookers and other stuff we lost in the fire because we'll need to live on it until Miriam and Naomi get a new building built. *If* they do."

"Why would Miriam invest so much money in a café where she won't be working anymore?" Savilla asked sadly. "She's ready to stay home with Bethlehem."

"Even if you two catered from the new house and I kept baking cookies," Lena joined in, "it would take us months and months to save up enough money for a café."

"It would take *years*," Josiah insisted. "And I refuse to rely on the Hooleys' goodwill for that long. Maybe we should sell the new farm—except we need a roof over our heads, too. I don't know. I just don't know."

When he couldn't bear to look at the sooty ruins of the Sweet Seasons any longer, Josiah turned away. He saw one of Miriam's triplets approaching them and wondered why she would be waving so cheerfully.

"Hello there, you three!" she called out. "We've got a fresh pot of coffee and some of Lena's cookies over home—not to mention some tasty morsels of conversation to share with you."

"We ate while Nora and the other gals were cleaning up," Josiah replied. "But I appreciate—"

"No, you don't understand. We *need* you to come talk to us."

Josiah realized then that it was Rebecca standing before them with an impetuous grin on her face—when dressed alike, the triplets were impossible to tell apart, except now Rachel had a baby and Rhoda was expecting one. He'd never been around an English woman who sometimes wore Plain clothing—but then, Miriam and her girls defied a lot of Amish ways. And Rebecca wasn't one to mince words when it came to doing business in Willow Ridge.

"All right," he said. "We need to get Isaiah in out of the cold anyway."

Josiah grabbed the handle of the baby's basket and started across the county highway with the three young women. He could feel people watching them from the Hooleys' window, but he didn't have the heart to wave at them.

When he entered the kitchen and saw the expectant faces around the table, however, Josiah paused. Not only were Miriam, Ben, and Rebecca's sisters smiling at him, but Naomi and Mary Schrock were as well. Even little Amelia grinned at him from her mother's arms. How was it possible that everyone except Miriam had spent the morning at Hiram's funeral yet they radiated a sense of hope?

That's joy on their faces, and they're struggling to keep it under control. What did that mean?

Josiah set Isaiah's basket on the table. "Coffee smells *gut*," he remarked as he and the girls removed their wraps.

Naomi, Mary, and Miriam grinned at one another. "Not as *gut* as your grilled meats are gonna smell," Miriam hinted as she filled three more mugs. "*If ya want to keep cookin'* here, that is."

Josiah's heartbeat sped up. "What do you mean? I'd like nothing better than to be serving meals like we were doing before Hiram—"

"We can leave him out of the picture now," Ben reminded him.

"If ya had your way about it, how would ya set up a new café?" Naomi asked as her smile came out to shine like the sun. "Homer's got fellas comin' to clear away the rubble and my boys are gonna put up a new building—and Ben's relocatin' his smithy to this side of the road, which'll give us space for a bigger dinin' room and more parkin'. If that's what we want."

Josiah dropped into a chair, afraid to believe what he was hearing. He held Naomi's gaze over the top of his mug as he fortified himself with hot coffee. He'd worked alongside Naomi long enough to recognize the mischievous sparkle in her brown eyes—and to know she wouldn't lead him astray with promises she couldn't keep. "What do you mean, *if that's what we want?*" he whispered.

Naomi giggled, grabbing Miriam's hand. "This gal says we're gonna rebuild—but she's out of the bakin' business. I sure can't manage a restaurant all by myself. Without you and Savilla cookin', there's no point in goin' forward with a new building."

Glancing at Lena and his wide-eyed sister, Josiah asked the question that burned in his mind. "How's this going to happen? We don't believe in Santa Claus—"

"No, but English folks sometimes deliver gifts, and in this case it's Bob Oliveri's insurance money," Miriam clarified. Her smile rivaled the way snow glistened in sunshine. "Rebecca's *dat* owned the Sweet Seasons building—bought it back when Hiram was tryin' to finagle it away from me."

"But we can leave him out of the picture now," Ben repeated with a smile. "Bishop Tom's also promised us help from our district's Amish Aid fund. Here's your chance to have whatever sort of appliances ya want, and whatever size café will work for ya. After the way folks had to wait in line last time, I think ya should expand, Josiah."

Grabbing Lena's hand, Josiah gaped at the others around the table. "So we could serve our suppers every night?"

Naomi's eyebrows rose. "I don't think we can muster up enough help to serve three meals every day—but it wouldn't hurt my feelings if we didn't get up in the middle of the night to cook breakfast. Miriam's the early bird, not me."

"Most of the single fellas who've been eatin' breakfast are married now—or gettin' that way—so they could eat their eggs at home," Miriam pointed out. "Why not go with lunch and supper?"

"I think you'd draw a good crowd even on week-nights," Rebecca said earnestly. "The only other option around here is carryout pizza. When word gets out that you're serving supper, folks will make the drive to eat your great food—and I'll help you get the word out, of course."

Josiah's pulse was pounding so hard, he could barely think. "So we could be more like a grill—without a bar, of course," he added quickly. "To save on serving help, maybe we should only have buffet tables. We could give the place a little different look—"

"Anything ya want," Naomi said with a nod. "As long as we've got dependable gas stoves and plenty of storage and counter space, I'll be happy. You can give the place a new name, even," she added gleefully. "We want you and Savilla and Lena to be so tickled and busy that you'll never leave us."

Josiah stared at the cookie crumbs on the tabletop. Not long ago Ben had insisted on a written business agreement and now Naomi was giving them complete control of the dining room. Lena returned his dumb-founded gaze. "Ten minutes ago we didn't think we could support our family with our cooking again and now you're telling me—"

"With God—and Miriam and Naomi helpin' Him—all things are possible," Ben said happily. "That's how it works in our town, Josiah. And if ya say *jah*, Willow Ridge will be your town, too."

When Lena and Savilla grabbed his hands, Josiah got caught up in their merriment. "*Jah!*" he exclaimed. "We'll do it! If Miriam and Naomi are for us, who can be against us?"

"I like what I'm hearin'." Ben reached across the table to shake their hands. "Congratulations, you three. This is just the beginning—a fresh start for our families and for Willow Ridge, too."

On New Year's Eve, the night sky was a velvet canopy accented with diamond stars. As Ben gazed around the peaceful panorama of snowy hillsides gleaming in the moonlight, dotted with lamplit windows in the homes of folks he knew and loved, he gave thanks to God. Yesterday all evidence of the fire had been cleared away and the foundation for his new smithy had been poured. The Brennemans had finalized the floor plan for Willow Ridge Quilts and the Grill N Skillet Café, nearly doubling the Schrocks' display area and the restaurant's dining space. Everyone in town was ecstatic to hear that these places would soon be back in business—and they all planned to attend Josiah and Lena's wedding tomorrow.

Ben set aside his thoughts of other folks, however, as he flipped a switch outside his barn door. Tomorrow was also his and Miriam's first anniversary, and he didn't want other festivities to overshadow his commemoration of the most important day of his life. He stepped inside the house, smiling at the sight that greeted him. Miriam wore her coat and bonnet, as he'd asked her to. She was rocking a bundled-up Bethlehem in the cradle he'd made as she sang "O Little Town of Bethlehem" in her clear, sweet voice. She smiled at him, her face alight with love.

"Sorry I interrupted your singin', honey-girl," Ben murmured.

"Oh, there's more where that came from," she

replied pertly. "Your daughter and I are wonderin' about this surprise you've got for us. We love your *dat*'s surprises, don't we, honey-bug?" she said as she kissed the baby's face.

When Bethlehem patted her mother's cheeks with her tiny hands, Ben's heart overflowed. What a blessing it was to behold mother and child, a dream come true since he'd dared to pray for it last year at this time. "Come on out," he said in a voice tight with emotion. "It's a beautiful evening. I—I hope ya won't be disappointed by this anniversary gift I—"

"And when have ya ever disappointed me, Ben?" Miriam insisted. Lifting the bundled baby to her shoulder, she preceded him out the back door, humming the carol she'd been singing.

Her voice soothed him, healing the emotional wounds of the past week as nothing else could. Ben steered Miriam toward the barn and then stopped about ten feet from the door. "Look up," he whispered.

Miriam sucked in her breath. "Oh—it's the star from the pageant! Shinin' just for us." She continued gazing upward, sighing happily. "Isn't that just the prettiest sight? Doesn't matter that it's a balloon with gold glitter, it's the true meaning that counts."

Ben heard joy in her voice and felt grateful that his wife could be so pleased with such a small gift. "We missed out on the pageant last week so I asked Rebecca to leave us the spotlight and the star—" He paused, hoping his words came out right. "I wanted to tell ya that your love makes me feel all peaceful and sparkly, like that star, Miriam. You're the bright spot in my life and I love ya, honey-girl. Happy anniversary tomorrow."

"Aw, Bennie, and what would I do without *you*?"

she whispered with a hitch in her voice. "I love ya right back. *Fer gut* and forever."

When she tipped her head, Ben kissed her for a glorious long while. With Josiah and Lena living with them, he'd missed some opportunities to show his affection as freely as he'd liked to. He would truly be celebrating the kids' wedding day—and their move to their own home—tomorrow.

He stood gazing upward with his wife, basking in the glow of this special moment. They had so many reasons to be happy and hopeful in the New Year. Ben felt as though they were standing on the threshold of a new dream, and for that, too, he was grateful to God.

"It's like Vernon said in his sermon when he and Tom baptized Josiah and Lena on Sunday," he murmured. "Wise men still follow His star."

Miriam leaned into him, her arm around his waist. "I'll be followin' you, too, Bennie-bug," she said with a contented sigh. "We can't always see very far down the road ahead, but as long as you're by my side, we'll be where we're meant to be—children in God's big, blessed family. And that's all I need to know."

What's Cookin' at the Sweet Seasons Bakery Café?

I love to cook as much as Miriam does, and I love to share recipes for the food that's served in my stories! The cold, snowy holidays inspire us to make special treats and dishes, and I've included some favorite quick breads and cookies Lena bakes in THE CHRISTMAS CRADLE. Some of these recipes come from Amish and Mennonite sources, and some have been long-time favorites in my family.

I've also posted these recipes on my website, www.CharlotteHubbard.com. If you don't see the recipe you want, please email me via my website to request it—you can ask for bookmarks, too, and you can sign up for my newsletter at the bottom of my home page.

Want more how-to about roasting whole hogs and the type of grilling Josiah does in this story? You'll find great tips at www.porkbeinspired.com or in other books dedicated to grilling. The details of preparing the cookers, rubs, etc. take up more room than I can spare here!

~Charlotte

Fruit and Nut Angel Biscuits

I recall seeing these high, rounded yeast biscuits called "angel buns" years ago, and I took the liberty of adding some sunflower seeds and golden raisins just for fun. If you prefer a fluffy light biscuit without the chewies and crunchies, simply omit them. These are great for any meal of the day, with anything you're serving—and they freeze well, too.

1 T. yeast
¼ cup warm water
½ cup butter, softened
3 T. sugar
1 cup buttermilk
½ tsp. baking soda
2¾ cups flour
1 tsp. salt
1½ tsp. baking powder
⅓ cup sunflower seed kernels
⅓ cup golden raisins or dried cranberries

Preheat the oven to 400° and spray a large cookie sheet or jelly roll pan with nonstick coating.

Dissolve the yeast in water that feels warm but not hot. Cream the butter and sugar, and mix in the buttermilk, baking soda, and the yeast mixture. Stir in the flour, salt, and baking powder until the dry ingredients are incorporated, to make a sticky, elastic dough. Stir in the sunflower seeds and fruit. On a lightly floured surface, roll the dough about 1 inch thick and cut with a biscuit cutter or a drinking glass. No rising time is required. Bake 12–15 minutes until the tops start to brown (don't overbake!) Transfer to a rack or serve immediately. Makes 12–20 biscuits, depending on the size of your cutter.

Kitchen Hint: Instead of buttermilk, I've used ¾ cup of milk with ¼ cup of plain yogurt stirred in. Works great.

Chocolate Apple Bread

Here's a quick bread that satisfies your craving for chocolate and features the extra chewiness of apple and walnut pieces. It makes a great breakfast bread, and you can warm it in the microwave—or spread it with cream cheese and your favorite jam to make a sandwich!

½ cup butter, softened
1 cup sugar
2 eggs
1 tsp. vanilla extract
2 T. plain yogurt
2 cups flour
¼ cup cocoa powder
½ tsp. each of salt, baking powder, and baking soda
½ tsp. nutmeg
1 cup coarsely chopped apples
½ cup chopped walnuts, divided
1 cup chocolate chips

Topping

>   2 tsp. sugar
>   1 tsp. cinnamon
>   ¼ cup finely chopped walnuts

Preheat the oven to 350°. Spray or grease a 9" x 5" bread pan.

In a large mixing bowl, cream the butter and sugar, then add the eggs, vanilla extract, and the yogurt and mix well. Gradually mix in the flour, cocoa powder, and remaining dry ingredients. Stir in the apples, the ½ cup of walnuts, and chocolate chips. Spread the batter in the prepared pan. Mix the topping ingredients and sprinkle over the batter. Bake for 50–60 minutes, or until a toothpick stuck in the center comes out clean. Cool in the pan for 15 minutes and finish cooling the bread on a rack. Best if wrapped and served the following day. Freezes well.

Kitchen Hint: *For a festive touch, make a frosting of 1 cup powdered sugar, ½ tsp. almond extract, and 2 T. milk (or enough to make a thin drizzle). Drizzle over top of cooled bread.*

Apricot Banana Bread

Here's a moist twist on banana bread, with chunks of sweet dried apricot and the added nutrition of bran (but no one will accuse you of serving health food!) Like a lot of quick breads, this one tastes richer after it's been wrapped and stored for a day. I like to make breads like this ahead of the holidays and freeze them so I have special treats to serve visiting family and friends.

⅓ cup softened butter or margarine
⅔ cup sugar
2 eggs
1 cup mashed ripe bananas (2–3 medium)
¼ cup buttermilk or plain yogurt
1¼ cups flour
1 tsp. baking powder
½ tsp. each baking soda and salt
1 cup 100% bran cereal (buds, not flakes)
¾ cup chopped dried apricots
½ cup chopped walnuts

Preheat oven to 350°. Spray or grease a 9" x 5" bread pan.

In a large mixing bowl, cream the butter or margarine and sugar. Blend in the eggs, and then the mashed bananas and buttermilk or yogurt. Combine the flour, baking powder, baking soda, and salt and gradually mix into the batter. Stir in the bran, apricots, and walnuts. Pour into the prepared pan and bake for 55–60 minutes or until a toothpick stuck in the center comes out clean. Cool 10 minutes before removing from the pan to a wire rack. Freezes well.

Kitchen Hint: You can make this (or any quick bread recipe) as muffins! Simply spoon the dough into a sprayed muffin pan, each cup about ⅔ full, and bake for about 15 minutes or until muffins spring back when touched in the center.

Tutti Frutti Banana Bread

Here's a special quick bread loaded with colorful fruits, nuts, and chips. It's great for giving to friends or for enjoying on Christmas morning.

½ cup butter or margarine, softened
1 cup sugar
2 eggs
1 tsp. vanilla extract
2 cups flour
1 tsp. baking soda
1 cup mashed ripe bananas (2–3 medium)
1 11-oz. can mandarin oranges, drained
1 cup flaked coconut
1 cup mini chocolate chips
⅔ cup coarsely chopped pecans
½ cup chopped maraschino cherries
½ cup chopped dates

Preheat oven to 350°. Grease/spray two 8" x 4" loaf pans. Cream the butter and sugar, then beat in the eggs and vanilla. Combine the flour and baking soda and mix into the creamed mixture alternately with the bananas. Stir in the remaining ingredients.

Pour into the prepared pans and bake for 45–50 minutes, or until a toothpick inserted in the center comes out clean. Cool 10 minutes before removing from the pans to a wire rack to cool completely. Freezes well.

Kitchen Hint: I often bake this batter in mini bread loaves or muffin tins (adjust the baking time: about 12–15 minutes for muffins, about 20–25 minutes for mini loaves)—and I usually double the recipe so I can use the entire box of dates and jar of cherries.

Stained Glass Cookies

This slice-and-bake cookie is so easy and so colorful, it's a must-add to your Christmas cookie trays!

2 cups butter, softened
2 cups powdered sugar
2 eggs
2 tsp. vanilla
4 cups flour
½ tsp. baking powder
½ tsp. salt
3 cups gumdrops, cut into small pieces
½ cup colored decorating sugars (or more,
  as needed)

In a large mixing bowl, combine the butter and powdered sugar until creamy. Beat in the eggs and vanilla, then add the flour, baking powder, and salt and mix until blended. Stir in the gumdrops. Divide the dough into quarters. On a lightly floured surface, roll each quarter into an 8-inch log.

Sprinkle 2 T. of the colored sugar on a sheet of waxed paper. Roll one of the logs in the sugar until the outside is coated, and then wrap the log in the waxed paper. Repeat with the remaining dough logs and chill until firm (at least 8 hours, or up to 3 days).

Heat the oven to 350°. Cover cookie sheets with parchment paper. Carefully cut each log into ¼-inch slices with a sharp knife. Place slices 1 inch apart on the baking sheets (put most colorful side up!) and bake until set but not browned, about 8–10 minutes. Cool cookies for a minute before moving them to a rack. Makes about 6½ dozen. Freezes well.

Kitchen Hint: Gumdrops are easier to cut if you spray your knife or scissors with cooking spray. I like to use "fruit slice" gumdrops *because of their intense flavor. You can roll each dough log in a different color of decorating sugar to add variety.*

Dark Chocolate Fruitcake Bars

Not a fan of fruitcake? These bars are so chewy and chocolaty, you'll forget all those jokes about using fruitcake as a doorstop—and because you frost and decorate them right out of the oven, you can make classy-looking cookies without much fuss.

1½ cups each whole red and green candied
    cherries, divided
64 pecan halves
2 dark chocolate pudding-in-the-mix cake mixes
4 eggs
1 cup oil
1 cup golden raisins
1 cup coconut
1 bag mini chocolate chips
1 cup coarsely chopped pecans
2 12-oz. bags of real chocolate chips

Preheat oven to 350°. Fit foil into two 9" x 13" baking pans to allow a "handle" on each end, and spray the foil with cooking spray. Cut 16 red cherries and 16 green cherries in half, and set these out on wax paper with the pecan halves, either before you mix the dough or while the bars are baking.

In a large mixing bowl, combine the cake mixes, eggs, and oil until well blended. Add the remaining whole cherries, raisins, coconut, mini chips, and chopped pecans, blending until everything's mixed in—batter will be thick. Press half of the batter into each prepared pan (a spatula makes this easier) and bake for 20 minutes or until a toothpick comes out clean from the center.

Immediately spread a bag of chocolate chips on top of each pan of bars. Allow a minute or so for the chips to soften, and then spread the melted chips on the hot bars to make the topping. With a toothpick, score each pan into 4 columns and 8 rows of bars. Press a pecan half sideways into each bar, and then press a cherry half next to it. Cool bars in the pans until the frosting is set and not sticky—several hours. Remove from pan by lifting the foil, peel away the foil, and cut along the score marks with a sharp knife. Makes 64. Store/freeze between layers of wax paper.

Lemon Cream Cheese Cut-Outs

These have become one of my favorite holiday cookies! They remain soft and chewy, and the lemon glaze gives them a pop of tart flavor.

   1 cup butter, softened
   1 cup sugar
   3 oz. cream cheese, softened
   1 egg yolk
   2 T. lemon juice concentrate
   1 tsp. vanilla extract
   2¼ cups flour

Cream all the ingredients except the flour until well blended, and then add the flour. Roll dough into a ball, cover with plastic wrap or wax paper, and chill at least an hour (or overnight).

Preheat oven to 350°. On a floured surface, roll out half the dough at a time and cut into shapes. Place an inch apart on a cookie sheet covered with parchment paper and bake about 8 minutes until firm but not brown. Cool on wire racks. For glaze, mix 1 cup of powdered sugar with 2 T. lemon juice concentrate (or enough to make a thin mixture). Brush on cooled cookies with a pastry brush and allow to dry. Leave plain, or decorate with buttercream (recipe below) or your favorite frosting. About 4 dozen.

Buttercream Frosting

I put this recipe in AN AMISH COUNTRY CHRISTMAS and WINTER OF WISHES but it bears repeating! I love it because it doesn't taste like shortening, and it dries firm when you decorate cookies or cake. It also freezes well in a covered container if you have any left over.

½ cup milk
½ cup softened butter (no substitutes)
½ cup shortening
½ tsp. salt
1 tsp. vanilla
1 tsp. lemon flavoring
6–8 cups (about a pound) powdered sugar

In a mixing bowl, blend the milk, butter, shortening, and flavorings. Blend in the sugar a cup or two at a time, scraping the bowl, until the frosting is thick and forms peaks.

For colored frosting, use paste coloring to maintain a thickness that will hold its shape during decorating. Makes enough to decorate/frost 6 batches of sugar cookies, or a cake.

<u>Kitchen Hint</u>: *I divide my frosting into 4 or 5 plastic containers and color one batch with deep pink, one batch with yellow, one with green, one with sky blue, and I leave some white. Use paste colors to keep the frosting firm. Let the decorated cookies dry/set up for several hours before you store or freeze them.*

Chocolate Shortbread

If you love dark chocolate, this cookie's for you—and the cinnamon adds a spicy little kick. These look pretty on a plate because they're a dark contrast to other cut-outs.

1 cup butter, softened
1 cup powdered sugar
1 tsp. vanilla extract
1¾ cups flour
⅓ cup unsweetened cocoa
½ tsp. ground cinnamon

Preheat oven to 350°. Cream butter, powdered sugar, and vanilla. At a lower speed, beat in the flour, cocoa and cinnamon until well mixed. On a lightly floured surface, roll out half the dough at a time, ¼" thick, and cut into desired shapes. Place 1 inch apart on cookie sheets covered with parchment paper. Bake 8–10 minutes, or until set but not browned. Cool on wire racks. Decorate with buttercream or your favorite frosting.

Kitchen Hint: For a different decoration, you can melt 1½ cups of white baking chips with 2 T. shortening. Spoon this into a plastic food bag and snip off a tiny corner—or into a pastry bag with a tip—and pipe icing over cooled cookies. Let stand until set.

Kitchen Hint: You can make this dough ahead and chill it, but you'll have to bring it to room temperature before rolling it out.

Baby Cake

I stumbled across this recipe recommended for women in labor, and was so fascinated by the healthful ingredients and the unusual blend of flavorings I had to try it. Wow, is this moist and tasty! You get the best of both cake and bread—lots of nutrition without refined sugars. Great for breakfast or dessert!

3 cups whole wheat flour
2 tsp. baking powder
1 tsp. baking soda
1 T. cinnamon
½ tsp. ground cloves
4 eggs
1 15-oz. can pumpkin puree
¾ cup coconut oil, melted and cooled but still liquid
zest from 2 large oranges
¼ cup molasses
1 tsp. almond extract
¾ cup honey and/or maple syrup
1½ cups peeled, grated apple (about 1 very large apple)
½ cup very finely chopped walnuts or pecans
1 large carrot, finely grated
¼ cup finely chopped dates or raisins

Preheat oven to 350° and grease a Bundt pan, 24 muffin tins, or two 9" x 5" loaf pans.

Sift the dry ingredients together in a large bowl. In a separate bowl, lightly beat the eggs, then blend in the pumpkin, coconut oil, orange zest, molasses, almond extract, and honey and/or maple syrup until smooth, using a whisk or a mixer.

Pour the wet ingredients into the dry ingredients and mix well. Add in the grated apple, nuts, carrots and raisins. Smooth batter into prepared pan and bake until a skewer inserted in the middle comes out clean. For a Bundt pan, allow 50–70 minutes, about 10–12 minutes for muffins, and about 30 minutes for loaf pans—or until the cracks in the top are no longer wet and doughy. Don't overbake!

Kitchen Hint: *I placed the apple, walnuts, carrot, and raisins in the food processor with the blade and processed them all at once. Quick and easy! This recipe freezes well.*

Kitchen Hint: *In a pinch, you can use canola oil instead of the coconut oil, and you can mix/match honey and maple syrup, as long as your total is ¾ cup.*

If you love the Seasons of the Heart,
you won't want to miss Charlotte Hubbard's
new Promise Lodge series,
launching next March!

Rosetta Bender stepped out of the stable with a bucket of fresh goat milk in each hand, gazing toward the pink and peach horizon. Sunrises felt special here at her new home. She was grateful to God for helping her and her two sisters jump through all the necessary hoops to acquire this abandoned church camp. Its name alone—Promise Lodge—made Rosetta feel hopeful, made her dare to dream of a better life for her family and for the other Plain folks they hoped to attract to their new settlement. Even so, she let out a long sigh.

"You sound all tuckered out and we've not even had breakfast yet."

Rosetta turned to smile at her eldest sister, Mattie Schwartz, who'd just come from the chicken house with a wire basket of fresh eggs. The sun's first rays made a few silvery strands sparkle in her dark hair, which was tucked up beneath a blue kerchief.

"There's no denying that we set ourselves up for a lot of work when we bought this property," Rosetta replied wistfully. "I wouldn't move back to Coldstream for love nor money, but I wish I could join the gals who'll be cleaning at the King place this week, helping Anna get their house ready for Sunday's service. And I'd like to be at the common meal with everyone after church, too."

Mattie looked away. "So I'm not the only one who's been missing our *gut* friends?" she asked. "In all the hustle and bustle of selling our farms and shifting our households to Promise, I hadn't thought about leaving everyone we've known all our lives. Takes some getting used to, how *quiet* it is out here in the middle of no-where, ain't so?"

"Is this a meeting of the Promise Lodge Lonely Hearts Club?" their sister Christine demanded playfully. As she stopped beside them, she shifted a bouquet of colorful iris so she could shield her eyes from the sun with her hand. "That gorgeous sunrise comes with the reminder that the heavens declare the glory of God and that we should, too—and I for one will *not* miss plenty of things about Coldstream. Every time I saw that new barn out of my kitchen window, it reminded me of how my Willis died because someone set the old barn on fire," she declared. "I—I'm glad to be leaving old ghosts behind. Focusing forward."

Rosetta nodded, because she'd sold the house where Mamm and Dat had died, too—but Christine's tragedy was far worse than the passing of their elderly parents. The Hershberger family had returned home last fall to discover their barn in flames. When Willis had rushed in to shoo out the spooked horses, one of them had kicked him against a burning support beam—and then part of the barn had collapsed on him.

"And I won't miss the way Bishop Obadiah refused to allow an investigation into that fire at your place, Christine," Mattie continued in a stronger voice. "God might've chosen him to lead our church district—and I understand about Old Order folks not wanting English policemen interfering in their lives. But Obadiah turns a blind eye whenever his son's name is connected to trouble."

"Isaac Chupp and his *dat* know more about that barn fire than they're telling," Rosetta agreed. "And while I miss the company of our women friends, I do *not* want to endure another of Obadiah's lectures about how you two should get married again and how *I* need to get hitched now that Mamm and Dat have passed on."

Christine chuckled. "*Jah,* he's not one for tolerating women off the leash—"

"Or women who don't submit to husbands anymore, and who don't keep their opinions to themselves," Mattie added with a sparkle in her eyes. "If I live to be a hundred, I'll never forget the look on his face when he heard we'd sold our farms so we could buy this tract of land."

"I thought Obadiah's eyes would pop out of his head when Preacher Amos declared he was coming to Promise Lodge with us, too!" Rosetta chimed in. Just thinking about their last chat with Coldstream's bishop made her laugh out loud. "We broke a few rules, leaving our old colony to start a new one, but I believe the pieces wouldn't have fallen into place had the Lord not been urging us to break away and start fresh."

Mattie glanced toward the barn, where Preacher Amos and her two sons were milking Christine's dairy cows. "Don't expect Roman and Noah to agree with that," she said. "My boys don't like it that I sold the farm where they'd figured on living out their lives and starting families. But I figure they'll have a whole world of new opportunities here—"

"And chances to meet a bunch of girls as well, when other families join us," Christine pointed out. "That's how my Phoebe and Laura see it. They're both relieved that Isaac Chupp's not pestering them to go out on dates anymore. And so am I."

"It should be easier on Noah, too, now that he won't be seeing Deborah Peterscheim wherever he goes," Rosetta remarked. "I was sad to hear that they broke their engagement. They'd been sweet on each other for most of their lives."

"Oh, there's more to that story than anybody's telling." As though she sensed her sons might finish their milking and come out of the barn at any moment, Mattie started walking toward the lodge. "Noah would never admit it, but I have a feeling he did something stupid and Deborah decided she'd had enough. But don't quote me on that."

"And we all know that Preacher Amos really came along to look after Mattie," Christine murmured, smiling slyly at Rosetta. "She's pretending he doesn't make eyes at her when he thinks we're not looking."

As the three of them laughed and strode toward the timbered lodge, Rosetta's heart felt lighter. Was there anything deeper than the love she and her two sisters shared? The surface of Rainbow Lake reflected the glorious sunrise, and as they passed the tilled plots that would soon supply produce for Mattie's roadside stand,

Rosetta gazed at the rows of newly sprouted lettuce, peas, and green beans that glistened with dew.

That's how it is with us, too, Jesus, she thought. *You planted us here in Promise, in fresh soil and sunshine, so we can grow again.*

"What'll we cook for breakfast?" Rosetta asked. Her old tennis shoes were saturated with the grass's wetness, so she toed them off. Could anything feel better than walking barefoot in the cool green grass? "We could make French toast with the rest of that white bread in the pantry."

"And fry up the ham left from last night's supper," Christine added as she grabbed Rosetta's wet shoes.

"And nothing's fresher than these eggs," Mattie declared. "Your hens are laying as though they like their new home—even if it needs a few new boards and some paint."

Rosetta gazed at the lodge building ahead of them, thinking a double coat of stain and a new roof would be welcome improvements. "Did we bite off more than we can chew?" she asked softly. "It's going to take a lot of money and elbow grease to convert this lodge into apartments. Every time I turn around, I see something that needs fixing. I didn't notice so many problems before we decided to buy the place."

"Are you saying we got a little too excited before we plunked down our money?" Christine replied as she slung an arm around Rosetta's shoulders. "Don't you dare admit that to the men."

"Are you forgetting that once the Bender sisters decide to make something work, nothing and nobody can stand in their way?" Mattie challenged, slipping her arm around Rosetta's waist. "I'm the big sister, and I say we'll handle everything that comes along."

"You'll feel better after you eat a *gut* breakfast," Christine assured her. Then one of her eyebrows arched. "Have you had any coffee yet, Rosetta?"

Chuckling, Rosetta shook her head. "I filled the percolator, but I didn't want to wait for it to finish perking—and didn't want to leave that old stove burning while I milked the goats."

"There's your answer!" Mattie crowed as the three of them climbed the steps to the lodge's porch. "Everything'll look perkier after you've had a shot of coffee."

"And if the caffeine doesn't kick you into gear, I will," Christine teased. "You were born the youngest so Mattie and I would have somebody to boss around, after all."

"*Jah*, Mamm and Dat knew what they were doing when they made you last, Rosetta," Mattie agreed. She held Rosetta's gaze, her expression softening. "And they couldn't have had a better caretaker in their later years, either. They'd be so tickled to know that the three of us are starting up a place for all kinds of folks to call home—folks like us, who need a fresh start and something to *hope* for."

Rosetta smiled as goose bumps rushed up her spine. Mattie had always been good at seeing the rainbow behind life's storm clouds—and good at pointing out what others did best, as well.

"It's my fondest hope," Christine murmured, "that amongst the new families we'll meet is a fellow who's just right for *you*, Rosetta. A fellow who's been waiting for the best cook and the sweetest soul and the prettiest smile he could ever find."

"Amen, sister." Mattie squeezed Rosetta before opening the screen door for them. "How about if Christine and I cook breakfast so you can freeze your milk? I think our new families—and the guests at your B and B—are going to feel mighty special when they use the soap you make from it, Rosetta."

"*Jah,* I love your rosemary and mint bars," Christine remarked as she led the way inside the lodge. "And the boys really like the cornmeal soap you make for scrubbing up. It cleans their grimy hands without making them smell girly."

Rosetta smiled. It was part of her dream, when the Promise Lodge Apartments were established, to welcome new tenants with her handcrafted soap and to sell it in her gift shop, too. As she imagined the smiles and appreciative comments the colony's new residents would make about her lovely, simple rooms and her special soaps, she once again believed she could accomplish all the necessary preparations to make her inn a reality.

"You girls are the best, you know that?" she asked softly. "And you're right. With the three of us helping one another, our dreams will all come true—because we won't quit until they do."

"We'll make it happen," Christine agreed.

Mattie's laughter echoed in the high-ceilinged lobby in which they stood. Hours of scrubbing had cleaned the soot from the stone fireplace and their intense efforts with polish and rags had made the majestic double wooden staircase glimmer again. "We can't fail," she reminded them playfully. "Too many men are waiting for that to happen, and we can't let them say *I told you so.*"

"*Jah*, you've got it right—and you'll not hear another peep of wishful thinking from me," Rosetta stated. "We'll make do, and we'll make it all work out, and we'll make new friends. Right after we've had our breakfast and a pot of coffee."

Books by Bestselling Author
Fern Michaels

___**The Jury**	0-8217-7878-1	$6.99US/$9.99CAN
___**Sweet Revenge**	0-8217-7879-X	$6.99US/$9.99CAN
___**Lethal Justice**	0-8217-7880-3	$6.99US/$9.99CAN
___**Free Fall**	0-8217-7881-1	$6.99US/$9.99CAN
___**Fool Me Once**	0-8217-8071-9	$7.99US/$10.99CAN
___**Vegas Rich**	0-8217-8112-X	$7.99US/$10.99CAN
___**Hide and Seek**	1-4201-0184-6	$6.99US/$9.99CAN
___**Hokus Pokus**	1-4201-0185-4	$6.99US/$9.99CAN
___**Fast Track**	1-4201-0186-2	$6.99US/$9.99CAN
___**Collateral Damage**	1-4201-0187-0	$6.99US/$9.99CAN
___**Final Justice**	1-4201-0188-9	$6.99US/$9.99CAN
___**Up Close and Personal**	0-8217-7956-7	$7.99US/$9.99CAN
___**Under the Radar**	1-4201-0683-X	$6.99US/$9.99CAN
___**Razor Sharp**	1-4201-0684-8	$7.99US/$10.99CAN
___**Yesterday**	1-4201-1494-8	$5.99US/$6.99CAN
___**Vanishing Act**	1-4201-0685-6	$7.99US/$10.99CAN
___**Sara's Song**	1-4201-1493-X	$5.99US/$6.99CAN
___**Deadly Deals**	1-4201-0686-4	$7.99US/$10.99CAN
___**Game Over**	1-4201-0687-2	$7.99US/$10.99CAN
___**Sins of Omission**	1-4201-1153-1	$7.99US/$10.99CAN
___**Sins of the Flesh**	1-4201-1154-X	$7.99US/$10.99CAN
___**Cross Roads**	1-4201-1192-2	$7.99US/$10.99CAN

Available Wherever Books Are Sold!
Check out our website at www.kensingtonbooks.com

More by Bestselling Author
Hannah Howell

__Highland Angel	978-1-4201-0864-4	$6.99US/$8.99CAN
__If He's Sinful	978-1-4201-0461-5	$6.99US/$8.99CAN
__Wild Conquest	978-1-4201-0464-6	$6.99US/$8.99CAN
__If He's Wicked	978-1-4201-0460-8	$6.99US/$8.49CAN
__My Lady Captor	978-0-8217-7430-4	$6.99US/$8.49CAN
__Highland Sinner	978-0-8217-8001-5	$6.99US/$8.49CAN
__Highland Captive	978-0-8217-8003-9	$6.99US/$8.49CAN
__Nature of the Beast	978-1-4201-0435-6	$6.99US/$8.49CAN
__Highland Fire	978-0-8217-7429-8	$6.99US/$8.49CAN
__Silver Flame	978-1-4201-0107-2	$6.99US/$8.49CAN
__Highland Wolf	978-0-8217-8000-8	$6.99US/$9.99CAN
__Highland Wedding	978-0-8217-8002-2	$4.99US/$6.99CAN
__Highland Destiny	978-1-4201-0259-8	$4.99US/$6.99CAN
__Only for You	978-0-8217-8151-7	$6.99US/$8.99CAN
__Highland Promise	978-1-4201-0261-1	$4.99US/$6.99CAN
__Highland Vow	978-1-4201-0260-4	$4.99US/$6.99CAN
__Highland Savage	978-0-8217-7999-6	$6.99US/$9.99CAN
__Beauty and the Beast	978-0-8217-8004-6	$4.99US/$6.99CAN
__Unconquered	978-0-8217-8088-6	$4.99US/$6.99CAN
__Highland Barbarian	978-0-8217-7998-9	$6.99US/$9.99CAN
__Highland Conqueror	978-0-8217-8148-7	$6.99US/$9.99CAN
__Conqueror's Kiss	978-0-8217-8005-3	$4.99US/$6.99CAN
__A Stockingful of Joy	978-1-4201-0018-1	$4.99US/$6.99CAN
__Highland Bride	978-0-8217-7995-8	$4.99US/$6.99CAN
__Highland Lover	978-0-8217-7759-6	$6.99US/$9.99CAN

Available Wherever Books Are Sold!

Check out our website at
http://www.kensingtonbooks.com